MW00592259

Restraint

Erica Chilson

A Mistress & Master of Restraint Novel

Wicked Reads
PO Box 29
Nelson, PA 16940

www.ericachilson.com/wicked-reads

Printed in the United States of America

First Printing, 2015

ISBN-13: 978-0692371763
ISBN-10: 0692371761

Dedication

My parents. Unconditionally.

M– for warping naïve Erica's sense of self to the point that the Wicked Writer was born from her ashes.

Titles by Erica Chilson

𝔐istress & 𝔐aster of 𝔯estraint
-series order-

Restraint
Unleashed
Dexter
Dalton
Queen Omnibus*
Jaded*
Queened*
Checkmate*
King
Faithless
The Hunter
Integrated

-Coming Soon-
Hero
Empowered

Blended
-Series order-

Good Girl
Wildly Wedded Wife (Blended #1.5)
Widow
Wanton (Blended #2.5)

-Coming Soon-
Warped

I am Katya Waters.
A survivor of violence.
I fought death and won.
So why do I feel so dead inside?

Katya Waters is a small-town girl, mentally unprepared to deal with her deep, dark past. While walking in her sanctuary, her innocence was torn from her in the most brutal fashion– run to the ground as if she were an animal by a pack of vicious Hunters. After they wounded her spirit, they left her for dead.

How does one overcome a debilitating, tragic event? By strength, perseverance, and an unrelenting will to survive.

Out of desire, Katya no longer wanted to be the hunted. She hungered to be the hunter. Finally taking her life into her own hands, Katya reached for what she'd earned, for the respect every human being so rightfully deserves.

By moving to a new city for the job of her dreams, Katya unwittingly brought her past nightmares to life, slowly drawing the repressed, dark memories into the light. With a deep desire to explore her true nature, Katya entered the BDSM Club, Restraint; never realizing there would be no escape from her secrets within the club's walls. Katya's entire existence turned into a living, breathing, never-ending therapy session from Hell.

The Boss pulled Katya into a thrilling game of Kat & Mouse as a way to force Katya to accept the truth of her past. Follow Katya's heartbreaking journey as she connected the mystery of her past with her thrilling present.

... As long as I have a tomorrow, I can endure today.

Prologue

My feet pound the ground with such force it reverberates up my legs and trails up my spine. The sharp snap of twigs breaking under the impact echoes in my ears, along with the deafening tattoo of my panicked heart. My terror-filled breath saws out my lips, exhale clouding the air across my face as I run—

Run for my life.

A looming pine tree is a taunting, solid barrier, directly in my path of escape. Precious life-saving seconds are lost as I veer around the tree, or else risk smacking headlong into it. Upheaved from the ground, gnarled roots catch my toes and upend my balance. I catch my fall with outstretched palms upon the pine-needle-laden ground, bruising and tearing my flesh. With a forceful lunge, I propel myself forward to gain momentum.

Droplets of blood nourish the soil from deep cuts welling on my hands. Branches slash my cheeks and thorny vines snag my skin and clothing, almost as if they are offering aid to my hunters. My mind is clear of all thought, except for the inborn flight reflex of someone desperate to survive.

Self-preservation forces my muscles to maintain their wild run, even as my body protests the movement with bloody and bruised, burning limbs. My hands instinctively rise and fall, protecting me from the brutal violence of nature.

Four hunters stalk me as if I were a wounded animal— their prey. They gain on me steadily, even if their visages are blurry to my tear-stung eyes. With rapid movements too quick for me to register, they converge, charging me from different directions— herding me, running me to ground as a pack.

Territorial rage explodes through the simmering fear in my blood. As their target, not only am I being assaulted, my sanctuary is being violated right alongside me. I've hiked this wooded lakeside trail since I was a child. When I was small, I'd venture out farther, creating a larger boundary of my own backyard. As an adult, the lake and the wooded trail surrounding it, are my home. We're being invaded, and I'm powerless to stop it.

I know every dip, curve, and incline of the landscape. Up until just moments ago, this was where I went to clear my mind and seek solitude. Childlike dreams of the future were forged here, right alongside the adult decision of what my college major would be. My bubble of safety, the trust I have in my land to protect me, and the courage I have to protect it in return, bursts on the whims of ruthless men.

Now, I run for my life, hoping my lifelong knowledge of the landscape will pull me through to the other side– safety.

In tune, somehow connected as pack animals, they hunt in perfect synchronization: breathing in harmony, legs moving with the same graceful fluidity, intuitively knowing where to head me off to push me towards their partners and propel me to their destination.

If it weren't me versus them, I may have found their symmetry breathtakingly beautiful.

I speed up on the descent down a steep ravine, drawing me closer to the lake and its imminent comfort. My sneakers skid on soft dirt, pebbles rolling me, making it nearly impossible to stay upright. I catch my fall several times by sightlessly grabbing for roots and branches. Thorns jab into my flesh with my hold, only to tear my skin as I pull away. I acknowledge no pain from my wounded palms as they rapidly beat with the pounding of my heart. Falling backwards, head hitting a rock with a great, jarring force, I fear I'll be rendered unconscious, unable to protect myself. Inertia has other plans for me, causing me to slide down the embankment on my rear while I regain my senses. By the time I reach the bottom, my shorts are shredded by the earth and damp from the blood seeping from the resulting wounds.

Rolling to a stop, I crawl to all fours. In shock, I barely wince as the jagged edges of river rock and the grit of ballast from the long-ago railroad bed embed into my knees and palms. I try to right myself on stable ground, but my energy is waning. Agile footfalls catch my notice, driving fear and adrenaline to flood my system, fortifying my survival instincts.

With a deep, pain-filled keen, I propel myself to my feet, and take off towards safety.

They allow me no rest as they close in from all sides, like the shadow of darkness creeping across the land every sunset—sure and swift, and unavoidable. They try to pull me off course by rerouting me with their movements. Driving me like an animal, they prove their adept hunting skills by forcing me off the hiking trail. Separating me from any other hikers we may encounter, from the safety of the known, I'm now parallel to the path, going away from it at an abrupt angle. The one in charge is wordlessly maneuvering me to his destination, and I am powerless to stop it.

The primal, animalistic side of my brain already recognizes its capture. I can see it playing out in my mind's eye: the four hunters felling my body, tearing into me like lions on a fresh kill, stripping my dignity away along with the last vestiges of my cherished innocence. My system floods with adrenaline. A vicious quaking rocks my entire body, slowing my pace. I shiver in the cold of impending doom, even as my body erupts with a feverish sweat.

My logical brain, the part of me that holds self-preservation above all else, overpowers my fears. From my depths, I scream, "I will not give up! Never surrender!" I will fight to my very death just so I can wear my pride as a badge of honor in the afterlife. Furiously, my mind spins escape routes and defense plans as I am led, pushed, and driven by the unit.

My only salvation is the lake. If I can get to the water, I can swim to safety. Like the trail, I know everything about the lake: the inlets, the currents, and the boat-tied docks. As a balm to my soul, I can feel the caress of its chilled water welcoming me into its promise of safety and comfort. The tree canopy overhead casts rays of light for my path. The crystalline waters glisten invitingly, beckoning me towards its secure embrace.

Half in the now, half inside my fantasy of escape, I'm taken aback when the leader comes into sharp focus just off to my right. I stumble when I see the fierce expression on his face,

the look of triumph as he gains on his prize.

"It won't be long, boys," his smug voice projects, filling the woods with his victory. The shrill cadence of his voice sounds like broken glass to my sensitive ears.

In a futile dance of survival, I go left, and then right. Left, and then right, panting wildly as I look for a hole in their defenses. My injured foot slips on a patch of moss, situating the leader within easy reach of my bleeding arms. In a pitiful, last ditch effort, I veer to the left, away from his grasp, only to miscalculate the trajectory of the other hunters.

Arms enclose me from the side. Startled, yet not surprised by the inevitable, I close my eyes in defeat. "I'm so sorry," a young, somber voice whispers softly against my hair.

Chapter One

I'm stone-cold.
A stone-cold bitch.

I wasn't born this way. Circumstances outside of my control created the emotionless creature I've become. Dr. Jeannine, my therapist, stresses home the point that I'm letting my assailants win by allowing a moment from my past to irreparably change me.

There is comfort and safety in being in control, of being the guide to your own destiny. Just as there is true freedom in letting go.

I walk a precarious balance of doing one thing while secretly desiring another.

I have no close friends, and only a handful of relatives, none of which who live near me as of a month ago. I'm alone. I have no coworkers to commiserate with because I am their boss. I have a boss who I've yet to meet face-to-face since I was hired online because of my impeccable credentials. There are no shopping trips or lunches out with the girls. There are no crying sessions while eating vast quantities of ice cream from the carton while blubbering about a douchebag who broke my stupid heart. There are no heart-breaking douchebags, because I don't date. There are no shoulders to cry upon, because I don't cry. If I did, I'd do so in private because I wouldn't trust anyone to shoulder my burdens.

I have no idea if that is what real life entails, as I've never lived that way, or had a girlfriend who showed me the way. Everything I know about that kind of life, I've learned from contemporary romance novels, which hold a sick fascination for me. Romance and friendship: an unfathomable concept I've yet to experience, have an insane desire to feel, and it never fails to leave a sour taste in my mouth at the thought.

There is safety in responsibility. You are the master of your own destiny, by calling all the shots and doing what you wish when you wish to do it. There is no fear of getting hurt, because you never let anyone in. There is no risk of failure, because you do everything yourself, you do it with the heart you fail to give to humankind, and you do it right, the first time.

My way of life is lonely and cold, yet safe.

There are people who have a protective bubble, or those with a fortified wall around their hearts. I have a veritable fortress of protection, one which is impenetrable by anyone I don't allow to enter, and I never let anyone in.

Herein lies my conundrum, I don't like this person I've become to survive, because I dream of the freedom and the heady rush that only recklessness offers. With true fear comes the sensation of feeling alive, heart beating out of your chest, throat closing as suffocation overcomes you, muscles quivering with a potent mix of anticipation and trepidation, while a feverish sweat flashes over your body as an intoxicating cocktail of chemicals invade your system. Fear is a high unlike any other. When the moment passes, you're left with a great sense of accomplishment, because not only did you look your fears in the face, you met them head-on and conquered them.

I am in control of my life because I must be, even though I long for someone to walk beside me, to carry me when I fall, to pick up the pieces I might drop, and to allow me to do the same in return.

Only I know safety is a fairytale we tell our daughters to help them sleep soundly at night, while reality's shadowy tendrils of misery are slowly creeping into their beds. I know how peace and tranquility are merely an illusion, one that quickly fades when someone presses their will upon you, forcing you to do things you never in your wildest imaginings thought you'd ever endure.

I am Katya Waters.

A survivor of violence.

I fought death and won.

So why do I feel so dead inside?

So why is this cold-hearted bitch sitting in a meeting, being ignored by her minions? For the past hour, we've gone 'round and 'round in a circular argument over the worst manuscript that has ever crossed my desk.

"Mr. Abernathy's newest manuscript should be completely scrapped. Nothing is salvageable," I say ruthlessly, tossing the draft onto the table with a loud thud. It skids across the surface, almost taking out our coffee mugs. Even the manuscript understands it's an imminent disaster.

"Ms. Waters, that's completely inappropriate." Monica's haughty voice grates on my nerves as she chastises me– *her* boss.

If I didn't have someone who depended on me, I'd hit the bitch and be done with it. I'm trying to build a stable career– family, friends, and a social life be damned… and this snooty, always in my shit, bitch is driving me to madness. I love my job at Edge Publishing, and I'm great at it. I won't allow Monica to push me out, which is exactly what she's trying to do. Instead, I push her back without breaking any laws.

"Did you suddenly forget why we are here?" I ask, an edge of incredulity creeping into my tone.

I joined Edge Publishing a month ago, and I've yet to get Monica to do her job. She's always trying to do mine. I usually remind her half a dozen times throughout the day that I am *her* boss, not the other way around. She never listens.

Conversing with Monica is like butting heads with a brick wall. When she does do her job, I'm impressed. The rest of the time she's up in everyone else's business, telling them how to perform their duties while neglecting her own. Why do I even bother?

"Words have power," passion flows from my voice. There is no denying I was meant to be the executive editor– the job Monica thought she was a shoe-in to get, only for me to step on her toes when I took the top spot. "Words should be used with caution. They should be used with purpose. They should be used in a manner which makes them matter, or else why do we even read them?"

Monica scoffs. "What are you waxing poetic about?"

I flick a fingertip at the manuscript in question. "Abernathy's newest '*bestseller*,'" I state sarcastically, "Is meaningless. Nothing happens from the first page to the last, with everything in between utter fluff. Where's the growth in the story? Words should educate me or make me feel emotions, not piss me off. He didn't even bother to self-edit."

"That's your job," Monica says pointedly.

"Abernathy's work reads like a high school student in remedial English wrote it. He didn't put one single comma in the entire body of the manuscript. He even spelled his own name wrong."

"Again. Your job," my flippant underling reminds me.

"It's rude and lazy arrogance," I sputter. Knowing Monica won't agree with me, even if she knows I'm right, I try another tactic. "What about you, Alec?" I ask the more reasonable of my minions.

Sheepishly, Alec looks at the table and shakes his head. He's torn between Monica and me. Monica was here first, but I'm his boss, and both of us are ball-busting bitches. If I was Alec, I'd hide underneath the table.

"I'm sorry. I have to go with Katya on this one. Abernathy's just phoning it in. I don't get it. All of his previous books were fabulous. He seems preoccupied," Alec says kindly– ever the office mediator.

"Why am I even asking your opinions?" I grit out between clenched teeth in response to Monica's narrowed glare at Alec for stating his honest opinion. "I'm the boss," I remind them as much as I remind myself.

Until a month ago, I was a small-town girl living with her parents. Now I hold the top spot at Edge, with the exception of the owner I've never met. It's daunting, and sometimes I forget I have just as much power as the words I wield.

"I want to be there when you tell Mr. Abernathy," Monica threatens gleefully. Her brown eyes twinkle with evil anticipation as the corners of her lips tilt up into a devious smirk.

I've never met the elusive Mr. Abernathy, either. But I've heard the infamous stories. His book *Nocturnal Silence* was terrifying. It was also written almost ten years ago, which means he's regressing instead of growing in his craft, judging by his most recent work.

Huffing a soft laugh, my assistant, Kayla, makes herself

known. I push the manuscript across the table to Kayla when I'd rather feed it to the shredder. The shredder would probably spit it back out. Kayla just worries her pouty bottom lip and stares at the three-inch-thick monstrosity, like it's going to bite her fingertips.

"I don't want to be there when you tell him," my assistant's voice warbles in fear. "No." As Kayla shakes her pretty head, her blonde tresses rub along her ample cleavage, and I imagine it's my cheek instead. I close my eyes to the beauty of it, and release a heavy sigh.

Kayla is my biggest temptation.

Tracking the path of my gaze, Monica snorts at me in disgust. She seems to think I'm a lesbian, and is offended by my presence. I'd tell her otherwise, but what's the fun in that? I like yanking her chain. It's the only recourse I have since she won't follow my orders. I also don't flirt with Monica as I do my assistant, which really annoys her for some reason. I think it's because I'm purposely making Kayla feel good about herself, and since Kayla is Monica's complete opposite, I must find Monica lacking.

While Monica has low self-esteem, which she hides behind a bitchy exterior, Kayla is soft and fleshy, and happy to be in her own skin. I'd love to tell Monica that the difference isn't the outside packages, but how you feel when you're around them. Kayla is pleasant and follows direction, and Monica tests my patience. Who would you rather have on your team?

It doesn't hurt that I hunger to bite Kayla's luscious breasts, to see if they are as warm and juicy as a peach. Monica? Eh, not so much. She is emaciated from her quest of perfection, a quest that is unobtainable and is leaving her miserable. Someday, I will tell Monica that there is no such thing as perfection. It's just what your body chooses for you. Accept who you are and be happy in your own skin.

Monica is the type of woman who looks well-put-together in her designer blouses and pencil skirts. There is never a hair out of place on her head. But she is completely miserable and down on herself, while lashing out by being aggressive and bitchy. She doesn't realize that from the moment I met her, I could see through to her soul. She's dying for approval. I'm not mean to her, but I don't kiss her ass, either. I try to keep a professional distance from Monica because she is fighting tooth and nail for my job.

"I'm the boss," I remind us all again. "I'll tell him. I'm sure Abernathy is a nice guy," I say, sounding hopeful yet disillusioned. Authors are a fickle bunch, especially when you have to inform them how you won't be publishing their book without some major changes, like by killing it with fire and starting a new manuscript from word one.

Kayla giggles into her hand and Monica snorts. I don't know what's so amusing, and Alec joins me in our mutual confusion.

"I have to be there," Monica mutters excitedly, anticipation thick in her voice. "Please, God, let me be there."

Waving a file folder, "Ms. Waters, I have a few contracts you need to sign," Kayla says bashfully. Her skin pinks deliciously and my mouth waters. My assistant spends most of her time blushing around me, and I have no idea why.

"Kayla's inappropriate." Monica points at my assistant, whose blouse is losing the good fight against the strain of her breasts. Lately, Kayla's clothing has been skimpier than usual. "How you ogle her is inappropriate."

"I won't lie. Kayla is gorgeous to look at, so I do. If art were hanging on these walls, I'd be staring at that as well. But I wouldn't be *interacting* with it," I stress, to both Monica and Kayla, hammering home my '*I might look, but I'll never touch*' stance. "Monica, if you have a problem with that, then don't watch me watch her." I say smugly. "You're just jealous that you're not her," I taunt.

I can't outwardly fire Monica, but I can push her to quit. She's not a team player, and she disrupts our daily lives. This isn't the first time I've tried to goad Monica into quitting. It's beneath me, juvenile, and it's not working.

"I. Am. Not!" Monica yells in frustration. "Kayla's fat!" Her fist pounds my table. "You're... You're a lesbian," she spits out the word lesbian like it's synonymous with the Devil, and she manages to insult everyone in the room with her shit-fit.

Alec's head whips back from the verbal bitch-slap. Thoroughly offended, the gay man gets up from the table and leaves my office without a word.

Leaning across the table, I get into Monica's face. I punctuate my commands by slapping my palm on the tabletop with every statement. "First of all, I'm not a lesbian. Secondly, that was a bigoted statement. Thirdly, it is inappropriate to judge someone's physical appearance, especially their weight. Lastly, I'm sending your ass to HR for some sensitivity training. You're the one who is being inappropriate by bringing up catty bullshit. It's none of your business where my eyes are. You're more preoccupied with my sex life, or lack thereof, than I am."

"Am not," Monica mumbles like disobedient child, not like the professional, classy woman who I know she is.

There are people in this world who you hate from the moment you lay eyes upon them. It's irrational and unexplainable. I just so happen to be this person for Monica. There is a part of the hated person that reminds you of the parts you loathe about yourself, either wishing you could change those parts of yourself or remove them entirely. But then this person enters your life and makes you acknowledge your issues' existence. Nothing will ever get Monica to like me or respect me, so I'll have to resort to making her fear me instead.

With one last thwack, my palm lands heavily on the tabletop, causing both Monica and Kayla to flinch. "Get out of my office, do your job, forget about my sexuality, and apologize to Alec and Kayla. I know you're not sorry, and Hell will freeze over before you apologize to me. But somebody has to be willing to work around here, and that won't happen if you're resenting one another. You can all just team up and hate me instead. Get. To. Work. Call Abernathy, and tell him to either get his lazy self to the next meeting, or he can forget about having Edge publish his work."

Monica's skinny behind storms from my office in a huff, and all I can do is breathe a deep sigh of relief. There are people in this world whose sole purpose is to challenge you, annoy you, and make you pray for a reprieve from them. Monica is that person for me.

"Ms. Waters," Kayla says bashfully, trying to regain my undivided attention. The girl blushes if I'm in the room with her, when she talks to me, and when I look at her. It's as unnerving as it is sweet.

Pointing at myself, "Kat," I tell Kayla for the billionth time. She smiles indulgently at me, but I know I'll never get her to say my first name. Kayla Cummings is a '*Yes, Ma'am. Yes, Sir,*' kind of girl.

Why can't people just do as I ask? It would make life so much easier. But we can't have that, now can we? I wait patiently for my assistant to speak, when what I really want to do is sigh and rest my head on the table.

"Don't mind Monica. She and Mr. Abernathy *date.*" '*Date*' suspiciously sounds like the word '*cheat*', since he is a married man. Maybe Abernathy's book sucks because he's preoccupied with Monica.

"Huh?" I huff out. I want to ask why, but that would be rude.

Kayla leans over me to reach for a pen, and lightly brushes her chest over my arms. As the pillowy softness of her breasts envelopes my hand, I fly out of my chair as if electrocuted. I'm a hairsbreadth away from bending Kayla over my desk and seeing if her ass will turn a lovely shade of pink when I smack it. She blushes for me again, the pink creeping up her cheeks, and I know damn well it was on purpose.

"I've got somewhere I need to be," I mutter hastily, voice quivering with nervousness. "Tell HR about Monica, and you and Alec can take the rest of the day off."

In a frozen state of panic, I breathe through the intense need that overpowers me. Leery, I watch as Kayla piles up her paperwork, and then I release a deep sigh of relief when she leaves my office.

Every day has been an uphill battle to maintain control. Every day Kayla's seduction tactics strengthen. Instead of making me feel wanted and warm and fuzzy, it makes me feel sick to my stomach. I'd love to touch Kayla because she's soft and safe, and smells sweet, and her moans of ecstasy would sound like heaven. But the main reason I'm drawn to Kayla is because she elicits no real desire in me to be touched in return, which makes me feel secure. I can't touch Kayla because I'm her boss, and I won't allow her to touch me because I'm irreparably damaged.

Contrary to Monica's belief that I'm a lesbian, I am not. My past has rendered me broken, with my sexuality unexplored, leaving me with a question I can't honestly answer: straight, lesbian, bisexual. I'm bent more towards women because they can't harm me, and they can't manipulate me into falling in love with them– they can't destroy me like a man could.

I hurry around my office like a mini-tornado: heart pounding in my ears, deafening me, muscles shaking, a cold sweat popping goose bumps on my flesh. I'm losing it– Kayla wanting me, and I recognize that she truly does, draws the past into the present. I can't survive the memories once they resurface. I quickly grab my purse, briefcase, and laptop, and make a break for it. I'm cutting out two hours early, which I never do. Usually I'm the first to arrive and the last one here at the end of the day, never leaving until well after dark. It's not like I have a life to run home to anyway.

Restraint 14

Chapter Two

In my haste to evacuate my circumstances, I charge headlong into a solid, strong chest. The impact forces my breath out in a ghastly wheeze. A wash of panic overcomes me, but I dampen it down. This is Edge; I'm safe here.

All of my belongings fall to the floor with a hollow thud, forgotten before they land. The man's hands are warm yet foreign; they shouldn't be on my upper arms, stabilizing me. As I stare at the pale hands, with perfect crescent-shaped nails, wrapped around my arms, I wait for the sensation of death to creep along my spine and lick terror on the edges of my psyche, but it never comes.

In the past twelve years, I've been so careful with men. More often than not, I avoid them at all costs. Other than the males in my family, I've had little to no contact with the opposite sex since that fateful afternoon on the hiking trail. I was relieved to learn Alec, the only male under my command, was gay.

I look up slowly from the man's hands, scared to witness the fury written across his features because I stepped in his way. My eyes roll up, searching his expression, while I formulate an apology for impeding his path of travel. With a flash of surprise, I calm instantly, and in the place of the terror is mortification.

The man, whose chest received the battering ram of my skull, isn't angry. He's mildly amused, as if I was an adorable child whose ball rolled into his path and he helped me pick it up. He's also Mr. Zeitler, the owner of Edge Publishing.

My boss.

After a month, I finally meet my boss in the world's clumsiest introduction. A flush creeps up my face, burning and prickling at my skin. I'm pale, but I do not turn that gorgeous color Kayla does as she blushes. I turn a grotesque, ruddy color, just like the rest of my red-haired, green-eyed brethren. I flush harder from embarrassment.

Intimidating. Imposing. Powerful. Commanding. Dark,

gunmetal-gray eyes captivate me. They hold me in check as a predator holds its prey, but I feel no fear from their capture.

All I feel is a spark of life, as if one gaze into my boss's eyes restarted my long-ago disconnected circuitry.

My breath seizes and turns to little pants of shock. Adrenaline floods my veins, a sensation that is coveted by my kind: the thrill-seeker, the danger-eater, the edge-walker. I survived a violent, tragic event that changed me at a cellular level. Now, in order to feel anything but numb, I need the extreme. This is the first time I've felt it since that life-altering afternoon. The sensation of feeling something, anything other than pure terror, leaves me breathless.

"Katya Waters, I presume," a deep voice whispers across my flesh. Big, gray eyes blink, finally breaking my capture.

The weight of my bags settling into place on my shoulder draws me back from the brink. I hadn't even seen my boss move to pick up my dropped bags. Enchanted by the sensations swirling inside me, I have to shake my head to clear my foggy mind. I'm losing time, and looking like a complete and total dolt in the process.

Suddenly shy, unintentionally appearing coy, "Thank you, Sir," I whisper in a small voice to Mr. Zeitler.

A dimple appears in my boss's cheek as a sly smile spreads across his full lips. It's as if he's secretly pleased with my visceral reaction towards him. Tall and handsome, with short, cropped, white-blond hair, my boss is delectable. His masculine jawline and Romanesque nose entice me. It's been a long time since I've found a man attractive, because I've always been blinded by fear. But one look in Mr. Zeitler's eyes, and it's like a switch was flipped inside my brain.

Not a switch of love, or lust, or even like. A switch to turn off the terror and turn on the ability to live.

Not all men are inherently evil. I've lived the past twelve years with no trust in mankind because it was safer, but I've lost a lot of my life in the process. I've been closed off. There is a difference between suffering and enduring, and surviving and thriving.

It's the unimportant moments in life that have the biggest

impact. In this instance, I decide to live. It has nothing to do with Zeitler's stormy gaze, the way he looks at me like he holds all the secrets to the universe, or the way he makes my flesh weep.

It's simply time I take my power back.

"Thank you," I breathe, meaning it for the war raging in my psyche, not for stopping me from upending in the hallway or for helping me with my bags.

The glint in Zeitler's eye flashes understanding, as if he somehow read my private thoughts. "I'll be at your service at any time," he murmurs in invitation, lips curling up at the corners, looking like a man whose mind has flooded with naughty thoughts of carnality.

"Umm…" maybe not. I thought we had a moment of silent understanding, but like every other male of his species, Zeitler is entering innuendo territory. I don't allow it to bog me down, to change my mind of living versus hiding, though. This isn't about my boss; it's about me.

"Ms. Waters, you need to get your frustrations out before you explode. We can't have you lusting after your assistant, now can we? Are you going to take care of that, or do I need to help you out?" Zeitler tilts his head to the side, issuing a look filled with potent examination. Then he grins, baring his pearly white teeth, and it knocks me stupid.

I blink repeatedly and shake my head to and fro, trying to grasp what my boss meant by *helping me out*. I hear a deep masculine chuckle fading, and glance up to see Zeitler's back moving away from me as he strides down the hallway to parts unknown.

Mr. Zeitler was toying with me for his own amusement.

I stand in the hallway with my bags slung over my shoulder for a long while as I try to get my mind to function properly. I have little doubt as to how stupid I must look, including the expression of awe-filled lunacy stretched across my face.

I've only seen Zeitler from a distance, never having engaged him until today. No one has ever held me in check as he did. I have looked far and wide for a man to ignite me instead of roil fear in my blood. There is something nefarious yet comforting about the man. A shudder rolls through my entire body as I imagine all of the possibilities.

I'm thirty-two years old and I've never willingly been touched by a man. My sexuality was torn from me, violated and assaulted, rendering me petrified of the act. I've been reduced to touching soft girls because they were safe, where I never allowed them to touch me back in return, just so I could feel a fleeting note of human connection.

What if?

What if I could, not only endure a man's touch, but crave it? What if I could finally feel alive, like the woman I was supposed to be before the wicked bitch of Fate intervened?

What if?

Zeitler's stronger than me, but I'm not afraid. It's more like his power would protect me versus harm me. Sweet Jesus, I want him.

Disappointment courses through my veins as I think about how wrong that statement is. Zeitler is my boss, and I heard through the office grapevine that he's engaged to be married to an heiress.

There are a few things I am not: arrogant, over-confident, faithless, or unethical. Not only can I not compete with an heiress, who's to say I'd even want to? Just because my boss ignited my dormant sexuality, doesn't mean I have the right to infringe upon his life.

Even though I can't have Zeitler, our moment together taught me a valuable lesson. There are men in this world who I would not only tolerate but long for, and I must conquer my fear to find one to call my own.

Chapter Three

I was born in a small town in North Central Pennsylvania, bordering Upstate New York, with its lakes, camping, and hiking trails. Residents call our area '*Vacuum Valley*' for many reasons: those born there never escape, those living there have a narrow world view, and their life choices are limited.

I've always believed your environment is a state-of-mind. The '*vacuum*' in valley is self-imposed. By broadening my mind through knowledge and hard work, I was reaching for the stars. In fact, on the day of my assault, I was taking a few hours to myself after working weeks without a day off.

While my body healed from the trauma, I pulled inward– into myself. I began to read a lot, using imaginary worlds to cope with the injustice I couldn't rationalize. Within books, I found a semblance of a life I could lead. I went into publishing, and I found an escape between the pages.

One such escape came from a little-known author, James Atwater. I was drawn to his writing, solely because of our similar surnames: James Atwater versus Katya Waters. Expecting mindless escapism between the pages of his Roman Numeral books, I found hope.

James Atwater wrote books about domination and submission, and my mind latched onto it like a lifeline. The thought of feeling power again was intoxicating. I didn't know which appealed to me more: the potency of wielding power, or the freedom of submission. All I knew, is that I wanted to explore that world, even if it was only in my imagination.

But sometimes life surprises you by coming full-circle, like the day I arrived in Dominion, New York, and was assigned my first client: none other than James Atwater himself. Just being in the presence of the reclusive, mute philanthropist gained me the strength to make a real change.

After reading about the BDSM culture written across the pages of James Atwater's leather-bound books, I went into research-mode. I didn't want to experiment within the bounds of a *life*style. I just wanted to live life. If entering a culture foreign to everything I was taught was the only way to regain the dignity, respect, sexuality, and the trust I'd had brutally stolen from me, then I would gladly embrace it.

This level of open-mindedness was difficult for someone who grew up in a town without a stoplight or stores, where the people I met in kindergarten graduated high school with me. I didn't date because it felt incestuous. Up and until puberty, we all had formed a familial bond, like siblings. Patient, I knew my life would broaden after I moved away and began college.

I didn't allow my assault to ruin me. It wounded me, irrevocably changed me, but I still went about my dreams. Petrified, life changed in inexplicable ways, I went to college. But until recently, I stayed in my area with my family and my safe '*siblings*'.

I wasn't a victim. I was a survivor. I used the strength of my intelligence and my will to survive to propel me forward. But that didn't mean I wasn't frightened of the unknowns. It took me until I was thirty-two years old to gather the courage to leave Vacuum Valley and reach for those long-lost dreams.

Excited, scared, in anticipation of moving to a strange, large city for my new job, I looked up places of interest. No, I've never been attracted to the touristy places where everyone visits when on vacation. I've been to them numerous times with my family when we did day trips to Dominion. I wanted unique places that fascinated me, that weren't the norm. Off the beaten path and away from the mainstream was what I craved. Being a researcher, I created a binder full of restaurants, used bookstores, thrift shops, parks, and one particular type of club that trilled excitement in my blood.

Out of everything, I was the most excited about the club. I'm a complete novice when it comes to the BDSM culture, but it has intrigued me since my eyes lit on Atwater's pages. It was the author himself who gave me the courage to no longer see the club as a name written within a binder, but as a real possibility.

Out of desire, I no longer wanted to be the hunted. I hungered to be the hunter.

I wanted to seek out the club immediately when I hit

Dominion. Instead I got settled into my apartment, my work, and the rhythm of my new life. It's been just over a month, and the need is choking me. I can't keep on a mental path without it infringing upon my thoughts, and it's interfering with my everyday life. This craving has overpowered my survival instincts. I promised my family I wouldn't go anywhere without a friend, but I've yet to forge any alliances in my short time in Dominion.

The need is too strong; I can't wait to visit the club until I make nice with the locals. Like a drug, the possibilities lure me in, beckoning me to savor the intoxicating taste, hoping to addict me.

The club I seek is the only one of its kind in a three hundred mile radius, and it's conveniently four blocks from the Edge building– the building that has become my home, not only housing my apartment but Edge Publishing as well.

The club is so close, I can taste it. I've suffered through its siren call for the past month. It's too close. I can feel the aching throb calling me– summoning me towards its hedonistic delights.

A block from my destination, the line of clubbers looms ahead, proving whoever owns this club is a genius by creating a commodity that can't be rivaled. Insecurity slams into my gut. With a block of people patiently waiting for entrance, why am I arrogant enough to think I should enter out of all them? I'm not any more special than the next person. I may not even get into the club tonight. What if when I get up to the door I'm turned away?

I smother my self-doubt and shield myself with confidence. I might be a stew of insecurity, but no one else needs to know that. Since the day I stepped foot into this city, I've played pretend. Pretend I'm not a petrified fish out of water. Pretend I know what the hell I'm doing. If you project confidence, those around you usually believe it.

Kat, you're getting into the club tonight! You need it! You've earned it by blood and by violence and by survival.

I scan the crowd that flows like a cliché. The majority of the clubbers are dressed in Goth fetish-wear. Black studded-leather from head-to-toe. Their hair is oddly cut and colored, and their bodies are adorned with collars and cuffs. Tattoos, piercings, and sneers, their desire to look criminal is almost amusing. They wear their disguises as well as I wear my false confidence– pretty damn well, but I can see through the guise.

I can easily pick out the tourists from the enthusiasts. The tourists gaze out of large, glassy eyes as they take everything in for the first or tenth time. Their clothing runs the gamut from Mary Sue to Manson– Marilyn, not Chuck.

The tourists are easy to distinguish because they remind me of children playing dress-up in their momma's clothes. There is no aura of power or submission radiating off them, but there is plenty of excitement.

It is an intoxicating mix– the jaded innocence mixed with the exhilaration of anticipation.

The thrum of the club calls me, fills me with the same excitement that every single person in the line is experiencing. Danger. Fear. Lust. Power. Hunger. It flavors the air, luring you into its lair. The beckoning is so tangible that I expect to be able to taste it on back my tongue. Bitter and sweet, and it tastes like power and sex. Greedily, I swallow.

The enthusiasts all wear similar bored expression, as if they don't *need* to be here intermingled with the poseurs. Unlike the wannabes, the dominants wear understated clothing. The submissives stand calmly by their dominants' side, knowing they are safe and secure.

I don't dress like the tourists. I have never been here before, or any club for that matter. But a poseur, I am not. The cliché would demand that I wear leather and a scary facial expression. Unlike the tourists, I do exhibit an aura of power. A power wrought and honed from the miseries of my past. I could wear a feed sack and people would stumble from my path, not from disgust but power. I walk around in a protective bubble of my own creation, warning all those who get too close to *back the fuck off* with my narrowed bitch-glare. It's as natural as any other survival instinct I possess.

No black leather pants, crimson bustier with my tits overflowing, or black Elvira hair for me. This kink is about trust, and I come as myself. Charcoal-gray, tailored pants encase my curvy legs. A turquoise bra flashes color beneath my snug-fitting black vest; and yes, the vest creates ample overflow of my assets. An auburn curly mass is piled high on my head, revealing the curve of my neck and beneath the nape is a tattoo symbolizing my evolution– *Chrysalis*. A set of caps are clicked into place on my teeth, creating dainty fangs. The only hint that if you get too close, I may bite.

As I wait in line, I concentrate on the other occupants as they fidget, with their eyes darting around with anxiety. I am surprisingly calm on the outside. I've waited a long time for this moment. I know I have a right to be here, one I earned. I patiently wait, all the while an inner-conflict rages inside my mind: the past and the present colliding. I refuse to be suffocated by my fears ever again. Hundreds of people are lining the street, filtering into the club, and none of them fear rape and death with every breath they take. At some point, you have to let it go, and realize you've invented a pathology that infects everything you do.

The club is unassuming. Without the sidewinding line as a dead giveaway, you'd assume it was just a four-story brick walkup in the center of town, perhaps housing innocuous office spaces. Without a lighted sign, I would have never found the club during the light of day. The only indication is the line of impatient patrons and the bouncers at the door.

At the head of the line, a male in an expensive business suit waits calmly, as if he doesn't have a care in the world. The tall, tanned-skinned man is at odds with the rest of the line. His gray eyes meet mine over the heads of the crowd, as if he was seeking me out and finally found what he was looking for. I smile faintly at him, confused at the snap of connection when our eyes meet. A sense of déjà vu settles over me. It's as if we are comrades, holding the deep-seated knowledge of self-recognition among all those here who still don't know their true path in life. I've had a lot of years to find my way, as has this man, judging by the level of intensity he is focusing on me.

Standing in line, in front of a club I've never entered before, I feel content, at home, as if I've finally arrived at the destination I've been traveling towards for thirty years. I was meant to be here, as if everything that has happened to me up and until this point in my life was leading me *right* to this very spot.

The handsome gentleman in the suit nods his head in recognition, as if we are of one mind. He glances around at all the poseurs and shakes his head in amusement. He has a smile that weakens knees and drops panties, and I'm surprised it has a mild effect on me. A wicked mouth with lush, full lips that tilt up at the corners. Once your eyes are drawn into their trap, the lips split into a Cheshire Cat grin. It's the smile the Devil uses when he seduces you into selling your soul– a little bit evil and a whole helluva lot naughty.

Expensive suit guy is dirty sexy, and I wonder what drug I've consumed that is making me susceptible to men tonight. First, my boss, and now, this man. Why do they intrigue me out of the hundreds of physically attractive men surrounding me?

When his hypnotic gunmetal gray eyes settle back on me, he huffs an infectious laugh that startles those nearest to him, and then he abruptly turns his back and disappears into the club, completely bypassing the bouncer like he owns the world.

Long minutes pass as I slowly move forward in the sea of clubbers, never pushing the devilish suit man from my mind. I can't help but smile– since my attack, I've never felt the flutter of hunger when I looked at a man. The terrifying and debilitating fear always overrode the craving. Today, of all days, two men captured my interests, made me feel alive, and the moments were all too fleeting: my boss and dirty sexy.

It doesn't matter that I will never see that man again or that my boss is off limits. It just feels freeing to realize I'm no longer numb– dead inside. It's a relief to know I do hunger for something that I thought was stolen from me. It infuses my spirit and makes me feel sure of myself.

Eventually, only the low-rent couple in front of me is keeping me from being at the front of the line. They are the only thing between me and the bouncer barring entrance to the club.

The bouncer is a beefy six-foot-tall mountain of a man. He has skull-cut hair and is wearing jeans and a t-shirt. He calmly and quietly reasons with a smarmy male who is fronting as a dominant. His browbeaten girlfriend is bitching at the bouncer and trying to scratch his thick forearm.

The couple is the epitome of the downside of this lifestyle. They don't actually have the mindset or the need to be here. He simply uses it as an excuse to rough up his girlfriend. He is weak, and he sickens me. My true nature rises to the fore and wants to play, wants to humiliate the little dick who needs to find another sandbox to play in. The bouncer's eyes meet mine above the man's head, and they widen in surprise.

"Mistress, please step forward," a voice filled with gravel announces. He doesn't raise his voice, yet it carries over the din of the crowd. The couple doesn't leave, continuing to argue with the club's security. The bouncer just pushes them to the side, and then motions for me to move forward.

"Is this your first time here, ma'am?" the beefcake cheerily asks. I look around, wondering why he's so happy all of the sudden. I mean, how could you be happy with a couple still shrieking at you while you tolerantly ignore them? But here is this huge mofo of a guy, happily smiling from ear-to-ear. He reminds me of a rowdy puppy.

"Yes, it is." My voice doesn't waver, even though I'm nervous that he'll say I can't enter the club. I can't hide the confusion in my tone, though. Nothing could cover that.

"If you can answer this question, you may enter." His blue eyes glow with amusement and his mouth slides into a grin. "What's your position?"

I cock my head to the side and squint up at him through narrowed eyes. Surely he doesn't mean what I think he means. But I doubt we're talking about baseball.

My mouth blurts out automatically, "Switch," before I can stop it.

It's not that I can't make up my mind on whether or not I'm a domme versus a sub. The thought of taking my power back as a dominant is enticing. But the ability to let go, to put my trust in another human being, to surrender myself to the art of submission, is as inebriating as it is petrifying. For a person like me, being a switch equates the freedom of choice, something I failed to have in the past.

A choice.

Happy chuckles erupt from the burly man, as if what I said was unexpected. His infectious laughter shakes his muscular body. The movement draws my attention to the shirt straining across his pecs. The name of the club spans the front of his tight t-shirt.

Restraint.

My face heats up in a combination of embarrassment and mortification. I worry that I gave the wrong answer to the question as he laughs outright at me. My lips pull down into a frown from the sudden influx of disappointment.

"I want to meet your dom sometime, then, eh?" He continues to chuckle to himself as he raises his hand to his ear to tap his Bluetooth. He nods his head as if rocking out to a bass only he can hear.

"Umm… What's your name, ma'am?" He hesitates as if scared I will reprimand him.

Well, I can understand the bouncer's confusion. He probably thinks I'm 100% domme. If the bouncer is a rowdy puppy, then I'm that bitchy teacup-sized dog elderly rich ladies tote around, the kind that will bite your hand off because it's afraid.

Before I can answer, he is replying to the unknown caller. "Yeah, she has curly red hair. Short little gal. Says she's a switch, but by the look she just gave this guy out here," he hitches a finger in the direction of the pissed off couple. "I wouldn't mess with her. I think she was imagining shoving his balls down his own throat." He finally pauses in his conversation so I can offer my name.

"Katya Waters. Kat," I answer on cue. His body jolts, as if he recognizes my name. If I wasn't already confused by his never-ending jovialness, that would do it.

He doesn't relay what I said, so I can only assume that the person listening on the other end overheard. His baby blues pinch together, creasing his forehead, and then they widen as he listens to the person on the other end of his Bluetooth.

"Yes, Sir! Absolutely!" he says excitedly. Being around this guy would either pep me up or exhaust me. "I'll let the others know." He taps his ear to end the one-sided conversation I was privy to. He smiles brilliantly, almost giddily, causing alarm to ring in my mind.

"Boss says next time just bypass the line, come right up here, and we'll let ya right in." He says this in a way as if he's asking me for my permission on the subject.

"Thank you. Um... what's your name?" I imagine it's something like Harley or Rex. Wouldn't it be hilarious if it was actually Rowdy, like a puppy? His face is adorable. His demeanor is gentle. He's a rough and tumble, happy bastard, that's for sure. But his body makes him look like he eats small children for breakfast. He reminds me of me–don't judge a book by its cover. His body doesn't match his personality, and my needs don't match my demeanor.

"It's Aaron, ma'am," he says while hesitantly motioning for my wrist.

I gently place my hand into his big paw, and I'm surprised to note no fear flows into me. I feel safe around Aaron, like he wouldn't physically maim me. But I'm unsure if I can trust my haywire intuition this evening.

I lean in, trying to be heard over the complaining crowd at my back, who are angry over the holdup at the bottleneck to the club. "Why did your boss want my name? There's no way he'd know who I am. I just moved to Dominion last month."

Aaron's strange behavior is off-putting. No one is this good-natured. I didn't like the alarms that blared in my mind when he asked for my name. I haven't survived this long by letting my guard down. I listen to my instincts, and right now, they are on red alert.

"We were told to call him when someone fitting your description arrived," Aaron answers readily. "Somehow The Boss knows who you are." He stamps my hand, leaving an inked mark on the front: a circle created out of the letters forming *Restraint*, inside the circle is an object that resembles a piece of cane.

The stamp on my hand distracts me from the omnipotent boss. "Let me guess, a switch?" I mutter with great amusement. "Like, go cut a switch off the willow tree and meet Daddy behind the woodshed for your spanking?" I pop an eyebrow at Aaron as I pull my hand from his.

Grinning with delight, "You've been a naughty girl if your daddy made you get your own instruments of punishment."

"That was part of the anticipation of the beating. My hands shook so badly I could barely snap off a twig."

"Somehow, I seriously doubt that," Aaron mumbles as he pulls two more stamps from his apron to show me. "The dominants have a paddle, and the submissives have a gag."

Whispering conspiratorially, "For the tourists?" I ask, knowing when I step foot into Restraint, I won't find what I am looking for. There are too many people out here, with no way to police them if they were here for BDSM activities. I would bet my last dollar, Restraint is a nightclub, hiding a secret membership in its depths. "Is this like Disney World for deviants? Do you sell trinkets and swag, too? Can I get one of these t-shirts?" I tug on the tight material pulling across Aaron's pecs, surprised to find myself flirting with him.

I've never flirted a moment in my life, yet this hulking man makes me feel safe. While tall and broad, Aaron is not only young, but he tastes innocent inside my head. I'm not necessarily attracted to Aaron in a '*I want to sexually corrupt you*' sort of way. It's more like I feel the easiness of my younger, innocent self I lost trying to spring forth, and it's a refreshing change to be playful again.

Aaron's face lights up like it's Christmas, and I realize he's genuinely a happy bastard. "You," he points at me, laughing cheerfully. "I like you." He leans down to whisper like it's a secret, "Restraint's dungeon members have a bracelet. They don't get hand stamps, and they don't bother waiting in line, either."

"Lucky fucks," spills from my lips before I can stop it. "Restraint's VIPs."

"Don't worry about it," Aaron reaches over to pat my

shoulder, but much to my dismay, he decides against it. I miss what I've never had– simple affection. Must be my past is written across my face and Aaron is an avid reader. "Boss will find ya later and give ya one."

Momentarily blinded by Aaron's gleaming smile, I'm slow on the uptake. "Wait? What? Why is this *Boss* giving me a bracelet? How do you become a member, anyway? I haven't even been inside yet to know if I want to join or not. What's going on?" I demand, folding my arms over my chest as I glare Aaron down. He's hiding something. Not only do I know it, I can sense it.

More deep chuckles rumble up from his chest. "Yeah, I'm sure ya won't like Restraint," Aaron says flippantly, and adds an eye roll at my ridiculousness. "You have to apply, get approved, take a course, and pay a fee. But Boss has already taken care of all of that for you. Boss knows you will love it in there, and he's never wrong."

Who the fuck is this *Boss?* My eyes squint as I try to flesh that out. I rub my temples from the strain. Forget it; one thing at a time. I'll figure it out later. But first, I have to actually get inside to locate this infamous Boss.

Katya Waters always pays her own way, and I refuse to allow the *Boss* to pay my membership fee, no matter how much it is. "How much is the cover to get into Restraint?" I ask Aaron of the happy persuasion as I dig my wallet out of my pocket.

Aaron pushes my hand away when I extend a couple of big bills towards him with my fingertips. "As I said, everything has already been taken care of by The Boss. So, go on in." Aaron steps to the side and motions me towards the steel door. "Welcome to Restraint, Katya. Your future awaits you inside," he sings ominously.

Aaron's words bring on a kaleidoscope of responses: the confusion of déjà vu, the zing of intuition, the suffocation of panic, and the rightness of Fate. Deep down, I'm petrified. But for once, all I feel is alive.

Restraint 30

Chapter Four

Sensations engulf me as I open the large, heavy door. Like a blast furnace to the face, all my senses get hit at once. The suffocating pressure of the music drowns out everything, as if it's slowly suppressing my heartbeat. With a forced gasp, the thrill of the adrenaline coursing through my veins jumpstarts me, making my pulse race while rendering me breathless.

The door clanks shut loudly at my back, reverberating with the force of gunshot. Embarrassingly, a girly meep exits my mouth when the sound ricochets. Thank God, it's so loud in here with the booming music that no one could've possibly heard my song of cowardice.

My eyes lock on the bouncer, and I know he heard me, judging by the curve of his lips. Restraint must use an agency that delivers burly men who are quick to smile until you overstep your boundaries, in which case, they will annihilate you.

Meaty arms folded over his chest, the bouncer surveys the inside of the club with one eye, while looking at me with interest with the other. He's wearing the club's standard t-shirt, but he has an added addition above his well-developed pectoral muscle: two name tags are stating his malfunction.

NOT Aaron Frost!
Roarke Walden.

I'm sure there is a pissing contest behind that, but I'm unsure if this was self-imposed because Roarke kept getting mistaken for Aaron, or if Aaron didn't like the other man being mistaken for him.

Not Aaron Frost, Roarke Walden greets me with a stiff nod and a barely suppressed grin as I do my damnedest not to blush. I shuffle past him into the club, while taking a few gulps of air, trying to acclimate to my surroundings.

I pull up my big girl panties and walk forward into Restraint.

Awe– shock and awe are the only ways to explain the emotions that settle over me as I experience Restraint for the very first time.

Shock.

Awe.

… And Holy Shit!

The Hand That Feeds pours from the speaker system at eardrum-rattling-levels. Its pounding bass is keeping time with my heartbeat, or maybe my heart is speeding to match its pace. It's a discombobulating sensation, not being able to control your own body's reactions.

I close my eyes, shuttering out the intense, visual stimuli that inundates me. I allow the music to wash over me and seep into my skin, to bury itself into my soul. My flesh prickles with awareness, my muscles coil for action. I gain courage from the music to move farther into Restraint.

Without the sense of sight, it magnifies all my other senses. I breathe deeply to slow my ragged breath, because as the music accelerated, I began to pant in time with the drumbeats. This causes me to draw more air into my lungs, tasting it on the back of my tongue as it flows into my nostrils.

Scents: some not-so pleasant, mingle with the beyond pleasurable smells, creating an intoxicating combination that thrums inside my veins. Sweat, sex, and perfume are a given in any packed club. But I can almost smell pain, arousal, excitement, lust, and need blending in the air. All of this and I've yet to open my eyes.

I was tested in the most inhumane way imaginable. I found solace and escape in James Atwater's Roman Numeral, leather-bound books. Between my lack of choice, and the drive to take control of my own destiny, BDSM became a fixation I focused on. In the back of my mind, there always a nagging fear that the reality would never live up to the expectations I'd created as a method to survive.

Only one way to find out…

My eyes fly open at the thought, and widen immediately.

Yeah, definitely Holy Shit!

I stand just inside the main door on a platform. Three steps beneath me is a dance floor crowded with several hundred undulating bodies. They blend into a wave of soul pumping rhythms, a group orgy of a mating dance. I'm sure this is exactly what natives considered dancing. In no way could anyone get away with what is being exhibited in front of me in a regular club, short of on stage in a strip bar– no, not even there. I'm not positive, but it would be naïve of me to assume some of the revelers weren't writhing mid-coitus versus actually dancing.

The music changes rhythm from the palpitating thud of rock to the teeth-rattling thump of R&B. Nine Inch Nails to Beyoncé– odd. Normally, I'm annoyed as soon as I hear her voice, but this isn't about the artist. It's the beat and bass, and the effect of their stimuli on your nervous system. I feel my own heart rate and respiration change, along with everyone else in the club. We are of one heartbeat, a single organism controlled by the DJ pumping music through the speakers.

A giant smile breaches my face– a shit-eating grin. Yeah, Boss was right. I love it here already and I've yet to step foot from the entrance.

I walk down the short, wide stairs to the floor, and then flow around the outside of the revelers spilling out the edges of the dance floor. Eyes widening in unexpected delight, my suspicions are rendered as fact. A chick is rubbing her voluptuous booty into some dude's groin, which isn't all that unusual for this type of music. A flash of flesh draws my attention to the fact that her micro-mini is yanked up, his cock is peeking out the zipper of his cargos, and his fingertip is hooked into the ass-string of her thong. All around them, a wall of dancers presses in, offering the fornicators privacy as much as the thrill of exhibitionism. I see no more skin than a brief glimpse, so fast you're sure you're imagining it, thanks to strategically placed hands and the draping of clothing.

Still shaking my head in utter disbelief, I belly up to the crowded bar that was hidden behind the solid wall of hedonists on the dance floor. Luck is with me; I spy a vacated stool, and I slide into it before another ass can inhabit the cushioned seat. I need a drink. Liquid courage– the stronger the better. I sit patiently, eyes flicking all around me, taking everything in as I wait for the bartender who's busting her ass waiting on a swarm of demanding patrons. I try to acclimate to my surroundings so I don't look so awestruck, but I'm sure I fail miserably because of the grin stretched across my face.

A female couple is sitting next to me, and as I watch, they lean into one another and passionately kiss. My mind immediately brings a memory to the fore: my first kiss with another girl when I was only thirteen. Best friends experimenting, and it set the precedent that contact with girls was safe, comforting. Seven years later, four men set the precedent that boys were not safe, and instead of comforting, they were deadly.

I push the memory from my mind, because no matter what, I can make every thought lead me back to the hiking trail. I've allowed the living memory of my assault to turn into my own version of an inescapable addiction.

My neighbors open their lips on a heady moan, their tongues visible as they weave in and out of each other's mouths. The flashes of moist pink are an arousing enticement to witness. The sight brings a montage of pleasant memories: soft, supple lips yielding underneath mine, the sweet kiss of panting breath, how my last conquest sang the cheesy *I kissed a girl* song after I went down on her. I sit on my stool, smiling to myself over happy times. I feel apart from my surroundings yet included. I simply enjoy the environment inside Restraint as if I belong.

"Hey," a husky voice whispers in my ear, startling me.

I glance up, not afraid because it was a female who invaded my personal space. What I behold renders me speechless. A true Dominatrix stands before me in her impressive glory. Her six-foot-tall body is encased in poured-on black leather. A bullwhip coils around her arm, and it doesn't look decorative on her masculine forearm. A leash is wrapped several times around her loose fist.

My gaze follows the length of the black leather leash, adorned with countless rhinestones. At the end of the lead is a soft beauty kneeling at her master's feet. A tiny blonde woman with bottomless blue eyes stares back up at me, before dropping her gaze the moment we forge a connection. I hardly ever use the term *tiny* as I am barely five-foot-two myself. But the submissive can't weigh more than ninety pounds at the most.

I should be creeped out by the sight of a woman who is a foot taller and double the weight of the woman sitting at her feet, but it feels natural and right for some disbelieving reason. I try not to examine why I find it comforting instead of demoralizing. If I analyze it too long, I'll end up changing my mind instead of going with my intuition.

"Hey, yourself." I curl a friendly grin while extending my hand in greeting to the domme. She's sticking out in the club, even with the mating groin-grinders and the tongue-fucking girlfriends. Restraint is a regular club to the casual observers, but then the real members of Restraint filter through the crowd, proving there is more than meets the eye.

The domme's hand encloses my wrist, fingers overlapping, and I suppress a shudder of déjà vu. Suppression or not, she feels it and flashes a large, toothy grin. With a gentle touch, she flips my hand over to check out my stamp. Her eyes widen in disbelief.

Seeming surprised, a strange expression rolls across her features– one I'm not fluent to interpret. "Switch?" Her pale brow arches in silent question, undoubtedly wondering who I'd submit to or who'd submit to me. Or perhaps her eyebrow is a silent invitation. I will assume nothing from this domme. She could beat me senseless with her pinky finger. The same wave of trepidation I encounter with men pings in my fight-or-flight natural instinct, but it's mild by comparison.

Uncomfortable, smile straining my lips, I mutter, "Don't judge a book by its cover, or by its blurb. You have to read me until '*the end*' before you get heads or tails on how I tick… and I'm far from over." It's a subtle warning– one the domme hears loud and clear.

Gazing at me with pleased surprised and a hint of grudging respect, "May I buy you a drink?" she asks softly.

Hesitant to answer, I'm overtaken by the sense there is something inherently familiar about her. Like we have a bond, yet we've just met moments ago.

"Yes, please. Thanks," I murmur, expression tightening when the note of shyness in my voice makes itself known.

The domme snaps her fingers like she owns the place, expecting everyone to cease what they are doing and come to her aid immediately, like the submissive beauty leaning into her tree trunk of a thigh.

Maybe this woman runs the show. She certainly puts off waves and waves of power, as if she expects you to fall to her feet and do her bidding because she owns the world.

Maybe this woman is the *Boss*. Real life is always stranger than fiction. This sense of connection could be because she somehow knows me. Aaron said the Boss knew me enough to alert the staff to prepare for my arrival. A shiver runs up my spine, and it tastes like fear and anticipation.

What could she possibly want from me when I have nothing to offer?

Mid-pour of a draft beer, the tattooed bartender immediately stops to answer the domme's finger snappage. The dude waiting on his Yuengling makes a sharp sound of disappointment. The wiry Latina ignores all of her customers and hurries over to us. She smiles in adoration and asks, "What can I get for ya, Queen?"

Queen?

"Thanks, Kristal. Fate and I'll have the usual." She smiles down at the bartender and winks. "What can I get you?" Queen's intense green eyes flick over to me as she asks the question, acting as if my answer is a missing puzzle piece.

"I'll have a seven-and-seven. Thanks, Kristal," I answer, trying to keep my eyes from narrowing, feeling ill-at-ease.

Suspicious, I look between the three ladies, who are obviously from different walks of life: enigmatic domme, angelic submissive, and bad-assed bartender. Between the three of them and the rowdy Aaron, my intuition is screaming. These ladies keep giving each other '*the look*'. You know the one. The look you deal with from kindergarten until death. It's the '*I'm making fun of you to your face but you're too stupid to realize it*' look. I feel like I'm a part of a game they play, and it makes me ornery.

"Queen?" I ask out of curiosity.

"I don't fancy the term mistress. My ex had one, and not the kind who frequents dungeons," she says cryptically, wincing quite a bit. Instantly, I feel bad for bringing it up. That small pain-filled reaction makes me see her as a human being instead of someone pinging my intuition. "I find it offensive," Queen mutters offhandedly, like it doesn't matter, but you can tell it does.

"Yeah, I could see how that would be the case," I rasp out, unsure how else to respond.

"My name really is Queen. But they don't know that," she admits conspiratorially, leaning into me to whisper. She gazes over the roaring crowd with a look of disgust twisting her lips. "They think it's a term I made up. A few idiots mimic it in their playacting, never once stepping foot into Restraint's dungeon."

Kristal appears with our drinks: a seven-and-seven is handed to me first, and then a shot of what smells like blackberry brandy is passed to the submissive who I assume is named Fate, and to my absolute shock, a bright blue drink with an umbrella in it is fisted in Queen's hand. A giggle sneaks up on me at the sight of a six-foot-tall domme holding a frou-frou drink.

"Book. Cover. No judging, remember?" Queen reminds me, causing a blush to flash over my face in mortification. "I'm sure Fate appreciates me not drinking beer." Queen answers my giggle. Her eyes narrow as if I've insulted her. "Who wants to lock lips when their mouth tastes like stale beer?"

"Huh? I never thought of it that way. I'm guessing you love the taste of brandy." That comment earns me another wink.

"My name's Kat, by the way," I say casually as I sip my drink, realizing I never introduced myself. I nearly choke when the liquor burns the back of my throat. My drink is wicked strong, like high-octane jet fuel. I feel the burn all the way to my stomach before the warmth radiates throughout my body and settles into my toes.

Mmm... nice.

"Oh, so you prefer Kat over Katya?" Queen winces as soon as she asks.

I tilt my head to the side and eye Queen. "How did you know my name is Katya?" I slowly and succinctly ask. "It's not exactly a common name." Confusion is evident in my voice. I want to demand that they all explain what the fuck is going on.

"Boss told us," Queen uses to cover her lie. She doesn't even wince as the words roll off her tongue. Her expression is masked by the blue umbrella crowding her glass. She's good, but I don't buy it for a nanosecond.

Instead of debating me, Queen goes in for the kill with evidence of how she knows the boss personally. She holds out her hand as example, and a platinum chain dangles from it. I lean forward, eyeing it speculatively. It's not as if it was a big leap to assume Queen was a member, or the beautiful submissive for that matter, especially with how their friendly bartender jumped at a simple finger snap.

The bracelet is exquisitely flawless. The Restraint logo is a replica of the membership bracelet's chain. The charm on the bracelet is a Unicode crown like those on a digital chessboard, no doubt symbolizing Queen.

Jesus, membership fees must be astronomical if the tokens are made out of platinum. What happened to a simple keycard, or back in the day, a secret knock or handshake– those were free.

My eyes swivel over to Fate, knowing what I'll find adorning her wrist. Hanging from the chain is a platinum lock embossed with the same crown, with a Q marking Queen as Fate's master.

Kristal is pouring another draft behind the bar, and the bracelet freely swings from her wrist. Its charm is another crown, but that of a King, not a Queen, with **II** boldly overlapping the crown. II must be Kristal's master.

Fire races through my veins upon hearing Queen mention the Boss and seeing her membership bracelet. I will tolerate nothing short of absolute trust after my past. I didn't survive

Hell by being an idiot. But it's not so much wondering if they are in on a secret conspiracy dealing with me, because I know I'm a nobody, so my delusional thinking they are fascinated with me would be pure arrogance on my part, and I am not that. I'm more hurt than suspicious. Knowing that the Boss sent Queen and Fate to occupy my time feels like a tiny betrayal. At first I thought they wanted to enjoy my company, maybe get to know me when gaining friends in Dominion has been next to impossible. But now I'm not so sure, and that's what stings like a bitch-slap to the face.

A true dominant is nothing if not observant. Noticing my narrowed eyes and my tightly controlled emotions, Queen says in a warm yet commanding voice, "There will be none of that! I see your distrust. It's not what you think."

"And what exactly do you think I'm thinking?" hisses from between my clenched teeth. "We're strangers who just met, yet you're telling me what I'm thinking?"

I'm on the edge of losing my temper. My face boils red as an obvious sign of my anger. I silently count to three in my head. When that doesn't work, I close my eyes and count until I reach twenty.

I feel shortchanged. After more than a month of longing, and years before that of trying to gather the courage to grasp what I felt would be healing, I came to Restraint for escapism.

Not to *feel* free.

To *be* free.

These strangers just singled me out of the crowd to toy with. I've been toyed with for far too long, and I promised myself never again. I slide from the barstool, placing my seven-and-seven on the bar, with only one sip taken from the glass. I turn to leave, but Queen's words stop me cold in my tracks.

"The Boss just told us to watch out for you, keep you comfortable and safe– make your first visit to Restraint one that would make you want to come back again. I swear Fate and I came over to meet you because we were curious, not because we were ordered. I know you think it's feigned friendship. It isn't, honest."

Queen tries to placate me, and I do hear genuine concern and curiosity in her voice. I thaw towards her and the quiet woman at her side. But my anger doesn't dissipate. I'm being fucked with, and I don't like it.

"Who the fuck is this Boss, and why does he think he can do anything he wants with me?" I realize how vehement that sounds when Fate cringes into her master's thigh, gripping it like a child seeking protection. She gazes at me with scared blue eyes.

Queen looks shocked. After a second, she tilts her head back and roars laughter at the ceiling.

"I'd hate to be you if he heard that. And I bet he did. He is everywhere... watching.... everything..." Her eyes flit around to specific spots on the ceiling, no doubt security cameras, as she continues to laugh at me.

What the fuck, man?

Only thing I know for sure now is that Queen, Fate, and Aaron are not the Boss, and that he is in fact a *he*.

"Finish up your drink, and then we'll walk around for a bit. I know you didn't come here to sit at the bar and chat, or to dance until your feet hurt. But I can't show you what you want to see."

"Oh, yeah? What's that?" I challenge.

Queen reaches out, placing her fingertip beneath my chin, and slowly lifts until I'm staring her dead-to-rights, our gazes clashing as if in silent battle. Her lips twist into a smirk, looking confused as to why she finds me amusing.

I've always been able to sense the emotions other people project. Right now, Queen is thrown because I'm not as she expected. She doesn't want to respect me, but she does. She doesn't want to like me, but she does. She resents me, and I have no idea why.

I wait Queen out, not flinching. Never blinking. She's bigger, badder, stronger, and probably smarter, too. But once you've looked death in the eye and won, a pair of pale green eyes gazing at you from a dominatrix means jack-shit.

"What do I believe you want to see?" Queen whispers, breath fluttering against my lips. "You want to see the dungeon," she says with little doubt. Her words raise my anticipation, but what she says next stops my heart. Pulling away from me, she states unequivocally with a tinge of irony tainting her tone, "But what you *need* is something else entirely. The Boss *needs* to see you."

"Fuck it," I growl, knowing damned well the only way I will learn a goddamned thing is if I let this play out. I can feel no malice from the woman, more like morbid curiosity and disbelief. I suck back my drink, leaving the ice dry. The alcohol hits like a freight train, flowing in my veins, making me dizzy and buzzed. Lightweight.

The smirk Kristal flashes me screams my seven-and-seven was missing a vital seven– the *7Up*.

Queen strides through the crowd, and the people part like the Red Sea did for Moses. She doesn't look back, secure in the knowledge that curiosity always kills the Kat. Rolling my eyes, I follow just as Queen knew I would. Fate fluidly flows behind me, following us like an eager puppy– obedient and responsive. Perfectly submissive.

Turning, walking backwards, knowing no one will get in her way, Queen chats with Fate and me in a show of great dexterity. I'd trip over my own feet.

"So what's your bag? I would have thought just the ladies until I saw the depths of the Boss's interest. Which made me think you'd be a submissive. But you're a switch, who will need both a master and a submissive to feel fulfilled. Boss won't like not being your be-all, end-all. So what's your deal?" Queen sounds extremely curious, and it loosens my tongue– or maybe that's the alcohol.

I feel like I'm playing mental chess with the domme. One moment she's testing me, and the next she seems genuinely engaged in a friendly conversation. I decide to play along in hopes the truth will come to light. I have no friends in this town, and I'd love to make an acquaintance. Even if it means a lunch out every blue moon with someone who gets me at least a tiny bit. Plus, maybe Queen will get chatty and accidentally spill something about the mysterious Boss.

"I want to top soft, pliant girls. I touch them, but they

aren't allowed to touch me back." I say without shame.

"They can't touch you at all?" Her green eyes scrutinize my expression. I feel like she can pull the answer directly from my mind.

"Nah, I mean sexually." I cringe inside from embarrassment. While I find women beautiful and tempting because my past formed me into who I am today, I know to my core that I would have been happy as a straight woman if I hadn't been assaulted by the gender I was meant to desire.

"All right, we all have our hang-ups." Queen scowls for some unknown reason. "Okay, so who tops you?"

"No one, I guess," I admit bashfully, hating how lonely and hopeless I sound. "It would take a lot for me to trust someone enough to let go."

I don't want to admit that I've never found anyone to dominate me, and that I've never bothered to look. I don't want Queen to know I have issues I'll never resolve. I can't admit out loud that tonight is the first time I've ever went out of my comfort zone and actively pursued a different kind of life, one with the freedom of choice.

Queen is intimidating, and I don't want her to think I'm a naïve fool. Pride will most likely get me killed one of these days.

"You're in the right place if you want to be dominated. You'd be surprised what a session can do for you. Do you want a man or a woman to top you?" She absentmindedly caresses her submissive's hair as she talks, but it's the touch of a mother to her child, not that of a lover.

I look at Fate. The blonde, blue-eyed submissive is silently following our conversation. She looks borderline freaked out. Her tiny hand is clasped in her master's protective grip.

"A man," I murmur, preoccupied with Fate's terror. "Is she all right?"

"Fate doesn't like the main club. This may look like a normal club. But the clientele tends to be vicious, especially the ones who are ignorant of the rules, and then there are those who just blatantly disregard them."

Queen looks around, eyes lighting on strategic spots,

checking to see if everyone is behaving and making sure the staff is in place. She may not be *the* Boss, but she is someone's boss.

"Fate has had some close calls because she's beautiful, innocent looking, and submissive in the extreme. The newbies don't even notice her bracelet."

"Fucking freaks," the petite, demure girl hisses, sounding a surly as a sailor. It's so shocking that I laugh. "I usually stay in the dungeon where it's safe."

"The dungeon is safer?" I ask in disbelief.

"It's filled with my friends, and they all know the rules." Her eyes roam the club, seeking someone, and land on a girl who makes my hair stand on end. She's also tiny, but her expression of pure malice is scary as all hell. The moment Fate and the vicious woman's eyes lock together, Fate relaxes.

"Friend?" I ask, and she nods in assent.

"Syn," Fate's voice is filled with a depth of love that you only reserve for family. Syn is the perfect name for the scary, pale, pierced girl. If I replace Syn's black hair with blonde, I see the resemblance.

Queen points two fingers at her eyes and repeats the gesture at the furious, raven-haired woman across the club, who then nods in return. The raven-haired woman, Syn, does the same thing to a small man across from us, and he returns the gesture to Queen.

"Sorry, we're having more problems now that the club has risen in popularity. It sounds odd that we don't want the publicity, but it's hard to police those who come here as a rite of passage."

I huff a soft laugh, remembering how I'd asked Aaron if Restraint was like Disney World for deviants. I guess I was right.

"The Boss is frantic. All of the members have rotating shifts to compensate for our lack of staff and the increase in clientele. I'm supposed to be in the dungeon right now, that's why I brought Fate tonight, but your arrival trumps that."

"Why?" I ask, but Queen shakes her head, dismissing my question.

"Let's continue our tour," she sounds pleasant, but her eyes take everything in like we're in the middle of a combat zone.

Queen tries to explain the inner-workings of the club, but the din of the crowd eclipses everything. When we reach the middle of the dance floor, I'm overpowered with the need to dance. The thrum is working its way through my body. I need an outlet or I will explode.

I take Queen's hand and sway to the music, drawing her and Fate into our own little world. I glance around at the others on the dance floor and grin. We all have a similar movement. The music causes us to wave our bodies from toes to neck in a churning motion. I draw the girls to me and let my body speak words my mouth will never utter. I lock stares with Queen as my small body flows down her taller frame like water.

Songs later, I'm panting and my body glistens with sweat. I feel more satisfied and relaxed than I did after the three hours I spent brutalizing the treadmill in the gym this afternoon.

"Ladies, I need to rehydrate," I gasp.

"Let's go to my booth. I'll flag us down a server," Queen says breathlessly.

Fate smirks, taunting at her master, blue eyes glittering with mischief. "You dance so much better than the first time we came here." She giggles into her palm demurely.

"It's my new partner," Queen burns Fate.

"Yeah, that's what it is," Fate purrs wryly. '*Yeah, right*' is said underneath her breath.

As we weave through the crowd, I think through the preconceived notions I had about what a BDSM club would be like. I was wrong. Even standing out front in line to get into Restraint, I knew I wouldn't find what I'd imagined. Then Aaron just as much admitted it. Followed by Queen informing me I wouldn't be touring the dungeon this evening. Even with all that knowledge, I'm still shocked that my visions were not brought to light. There are no scenes occurring around the room, no screams and moans echoing from the walls. I pictured blood red décor, instruments of torture, and countless bodies involved in hedonistic rituals.

Reality is encumbering music, a dance floor packed with undulating bodies, but the surrounding areas are mostly vacant for those who want more of a one-on-one experience. The décor is darkly subdued, not industrial BDSM.

Lost in thought, as I usually am, I don't notice an arm reach around me and grab my breast. I react on instinct instead of fear, and jab an elbow back and up. I hit my interloper solid in the chest just as his grip strengthens to the point of pain– pain I hadn't asked for or invited. I peel the hand from my chest, noting the crescent-shaped marks on my breast are filling with my spilled blood.

Anger fills me faster than the adrenaline entering my system, and I thank the heavens above that it overpowers the terror and panic that threatened to leak through. I turn, looking positively feral, baring my caps as if they are real fangs. I glare into the face of an asshole, the dick who stood in line in front of me, arguing with the bouncer. He shies away and immediately drops to the ground.

"I'm sorry, Mistress. I thought you were a sub." His voice shakes like he's on a fault line, and all I feel in that moment is pity. Pity for the man. Pity, that still to this day, the fear almost debilitated me.

I use bravado to hide the quiver in my voice. I will my anger to redden my face to replace the death pallor that had momentarily flashed over me. "Oh, so it was okay to grope me if I were a sub?" Even to me I sound snotty, which is exactly what I need in this moment.

A man touched me.

A man took my choice away.

Again.

I use fury to displace all other emotion. It's a safety mechanism that deploys automatically without thought. No one knows about my past– my family doesn't even know the minute details. It could be one single word uttered, a fleeting thought, an action, a scent on the breeze, and it all comes crashing down on me. Violent waves of horrific memories will inundate me until I'm pulled down into their dark depths.

The man's hand on my skin, touching my private flesh,

brings that last horrific walk on the wooded trail near my childhood home into sharp focus. I shove it down with all of my might. I bury it deep inside my mind and lock it away, as I must. It's the only way to survive and stay sane. I will not freak out in the middle of a club filled with strangers. I will not sit on the floor and rock back and forth while spouting gibberish. Mortification and self-preservation are the only things that keep the panic at bay.

My mind whirls out of control while I wait for his answer to my question. My violator gives me a look of complete astonishment. He knows there is no answer that will get him out of trouble. Yes, you cowardly bastard, I'm smarter than you.

"No, it's not okay. You are just so short. I didn't think you'd be a domme," he stammers.

"Listen clearly, you sniveling idiot." I hold his eyes and grip his chin with my fingertips to gain his total attention. Too late, I notice his greasy complexion. I want to bleach my hand, douse it in hand sanitizer, and maybe boil it. Disgusting.

"First you touch without permission, and then you insult my size. Are you a total moron? Or are you that desperate for punishment, baby dom? I saw you outside with your browbeaten chick; where'd you leave her?"

"I… punish me, mistress. I need it," he begs, sounding breathy and desperate. His blue eyes are glassed over– high from potent drugs. I worry for his girlfriend. His desperate personality combined with narcotics is a recipe for disaster.

I can feel his dirty seeking fingers imprinted on my breast. No one has touched me there in years– not since. In twelve years I've only given pleasure, never receiving. The only people to ever touch me were my rapists. I've never had hands on me willingly.

I'm so angry that I could spit nails. A drug-addled shit thinks he can take whatever he wants, whenever he wants, all because he wants it, with absolutely no thought to the person he is essentially stealing from. He needs to learn a lesson the hard way.

"Open your fly, now!" I growl at him.

Slowly, his fumbling hands unfasten his stained and torn pants. He reveals his flaccid cock, unimpressive– sickly looking from whatever drug he has injected into his system.

"Is that a dick?" I turn to my companions. Queen is wincing and Fate is hiding behind her master, as if scared of that shriveled up piece of man. "Queen, does that look like a dick to you?"

"It's small, but I'm pretty sure it's a cock." She stares at me, wondering where I am headed with this.

The weak man is kneeling before me with his child-size junk on display. I'm angry with him for violating me, and I feel pity for him. I don't like the confusing mix of emotions.

"Pathetic. Yes, that's a dick, and it wants me to top it. Do I look like I would top a weak-assed man who thinks himself a dom? You need to be punished, but I wouldn't give you a second of pleasure. Queen, do you have a sadist who likes to punish naughty boys?" I smile evilly as inspiration strikes.

Sensations zing through my body– enlivening me, making every sense sharper, clearer. The knowledge that someone who violated me will finally be punished for their crimes, gives me a potent high. Vindication. This man didn't do to me what the others did, but they aren't kneeling before me, begging for redemption.

"I will call him over. Are you sure about this?" Queen's confusion is apparent. She didn't see him out front of the club with his poor, abused girlfriend, so she can't possibly know the inner monologue that's pushing my reactions.

After being stalked, taken to the ground, and abased like an animal, I live, breath, and think on instinct.

"Yes, I'm positive," I reply, showing absolutely no doubts while masking my inner torment. "He fondled me without permission. If I were a sub, he would still need a master's permission, which he didn't get. He bloodied me and insulted me. He needs to be punished. Obviously he likes females, so any punishment mete out must be through a male. I desire him no pleasure. He must be bloodied, insulted, and fondled without his permission. It sounds fair."

I must have convinced Queen, because she gives an

unspoken signal to Fate. The submissive woman takes off through the crowd to fetch Restraint's sadist.

A filthy hand touches my arm, beseeching me, begging me to be the one to deal the punishment. My glare is so powerful it should've burst into flame.

"Mistress, please punish me," he desperately begs. I want to close my eyes to the pitiful sight of this young, broken man. His weakness in all things is obvious. He doesn't take care of himself, and I can smell the sour stench of addiction flowing from his pores. If he has the courage to beg me, then who am I to look away?

"Oh, you'll get punished, just not by me." I shudder at the thought. I couldn't touch him like that. I wouldn't be able to get through it.

He moves his hand in slow motion, trying to provoke me. Nothing annoys me more than slowness. If I tell you to do something, you better do it fast. I barely hold my temper. I back up several feet to rest my hip on the side of a booth. I appear relaxed, but inside I am a pit of lava ready to erupt. I also want to wash his filth from my body, and I wish I could remove the feeling of his hand on my breast. If I could erase the sensation, then maybe the memories would stop battering the inside of my mind, demanding to be released from their cage.

Two minutes later, a man walks up with Fate following dutifully behind. Fate holds his hand like he's her lifeline. Yet again, it seems more of a protective gesture than one of a sexual, or even a dominating, nature. The sadist was the small man Syn pointed at earlier.

The sadist isn't much taller than I am. But height will never be an issue for this man. His inky black ringlets are just as tightly coiled as his taut muscles. His tan flesh is glistening with sweat... and I see a lot of it, since he's only wearing a pair of skin-tight leather pants. He doesn't even wear shoes on his perfectly proportionate feet. He radiates suffocating power from his amber-colored eyes. One pass of his gaze over my body and I want to kneel on the ground and grovel.

I can't help the satisfied smirk that spreads across my lips.

This sadist could dominate me with ease. Need tightens in my core. My mind relaxes in relief. Years of worry fades. I've finally arrived at a place where my needs will be met. If he can't help me, someone here will.

"Queen," he nods at the tall blonde. "And you must be Katya." He stares intently at my face, and then softly smiles in welcome.

"Ladies, I see you're having an issue. Neither of you wish to play with this man?" Amusement colors his voice and transforms his face from ruthless bad-ass to gentlemanly handsome. His flushed skin is a beautiful shade of bronze, denoting a Middle Eastern ancestry, and his onyx curls are begging for fingertips to grasp during the height of ecstasy.

"Um, no… and Kat refuses to touch that," Queen says as she points to the grub poking out of a pair of dirty jeans.

"Come," the sadist's deep voice resonates as he holds out his hand to the man on the floor. "I shall punish you, and I will enjoy every second." His eyebrows raise as the younger man clasps his hand. He gently tugs until the man is on his feet. "However, you won't enjoy it. Trust me," he purrs ominously, showing off his sadistic edge. "At first, but then you will eventually grow to become dependent on the pain."

"Ladies, thanks for the toy. Enjoy the rest of your evening." He abruptly turns, and his gaze rakes my body from boots to barrettes. "Welcome, Kat. I look forward to getting to know you better," he says without a trace of innuendo. The sadist takes off towards the back of the club with his new pain slut in tow, holding hands as a father would with his toddler-aged son.

Queen exhales a loud sigh. "That was Dexter, and you just made his night." Her entire body shivers as she imagines Dexter's pleasurable evening.

Queen slides into the booth closest to us and leans into her sub. "Go get us a round of drinks, Angel. I think we need to relax for a while." She doesn't demand. She doesn't even ask. Queen just expects Fate to do whatever she says without a hint of complaint, and that's what she receives as Fate dutifully makes a beeline towards Kris manning the bar.

I move to join Queen in the booth when I feel the stickiness coating my hand. "Where's the restroom?" I ask with a grimace. I have to get this filth off me.

"The hallway at the back. Left-hand corner. Do you need me to go with you?" She slides down the bench to exit the booth, seeming more protective than put-out over having to escort me. Her miss-nothing eyes latch onto the malicious Syn, who's holding up the wall a few paces from us, glaring at me with bitter hatred. No doubt Queen is communicating with Syn that either Fate or I beg watching, depending on who she has to babysit.

I hesitate, a cross between introversion and fear. I need some alone time, but is it safe to venture out alone?

As if reading my mind, but more likely my facial expression, Queen reassures me. "You're safe here at Restraint, even in the darkest nooks and crannies. Everyone just saw what you did, so no one will mess with you again. But more so, the Boss notified all of the members to your presence."

Yeah, I don't want to mull over who the Boss is, or why he is notifying the membership, or why he even bothered. I just want to wash the filth from my skin as a way to cleanse my brain in the process. Winding through the crowd, I head to the bathroom escort-free.

I also need time to push the memories back down where I can firmly bury them until they dig their way out again. Instead, I concentrate on the feeling of euphoria that coursed through my veins when Dexter gave me that potent look.

Mr. Zeitler showed me I could find men attractive without being petrified. Suit guy hammered that same lesson home, along with Aaron's innocent playfulness. Queen, Fate, and Kris proved I can be around others without freaking out, maybe build a budding acquaintance with other women. Dexter showed me there are men who will dominate you because it's what you both need, not because they want to destroy all you are.

I came to Restraint for a reason, and I think I may have found what I was looking for, and then some.

Katya, you're at Restraint to let go of the past, heal, and to finally feel…
Alive.

Restraint 52

Chapter Five

I stared into the bathroom mirror for long minutes as I scrubbed my hands until the hot water made them sting. I disinfected my breast with soap, allowing it to soak in a bit before dabbing it back off with a paper towel. All the while, the woman in the mirror gazing back at me didn't look like my reflection from this morning.

The stone-cold, emotionless expression has vanished. Now my face is flushed, eyes bright, lips parted slightly. I look enlivened, high, and ready for anything.

Scum freshly washed from my flesh, with my past firmly held in check, I wander down the brightly lit hallway from the ladies restroom. Instead of dwelling on the past, I'm in awe of my surroundings. The bathroom was floor to ceiling granite and slate, with the music piped in just as loudly as the rest of the club. The clean freak in me loved that it was spotless. The hallway is slate tile with gray walls. The owner of Restraint must love the smoky color of gray since everything is the same hue.

I push the negative thoughts from my mind and just try to live in the moment, which is something I'm crappy at doing. I don't know what's going on with the Boss and his Restraint membership minions. There is a small part of me that is thrumming over the mystery, and I know all I can do is go with the flow or else I won't solve it. When I leave here tonight, I'll leave the confusion behind as well. I might as well enjoy some companionship with people who are just as freaky as me, because tomorrow I have to go back to work and continue to pretend to be a normal person with a normal life, one who isn't scared of every shadow.

Closing the world out, I let the music drift over me and fill me with anticipation. As I rock down the hall, I'm flung from my path– snatched and grabbed. Before I can even utter a word of protest, a large palm is covering my mouth. I have no time to struggle or scream, or for my heart to register my capture. My survival instincts didn't even get a chance kick in– it was that fast.

In less than five seconds, I'm thrust inside a pitch-black room, and then pushed face-first into a cold metal door with surprising, gentle efficiency. It's the ominous finality of the lock clicking into place that freezes me, pushing fear into the adrenaline flowing in my veins.

A heavy weight presses at my back, blocking off all paths of escape, and I instinctively know it's a man.

The Boss.

This was a well-timed and well-planned attack that offered me no opportunity to panic, much less time to call for help. Now that I am securely in my abductor's clutches, my mind flashes to another time and place, another hand on my mouth, another body pressing into me.

I breathe though the panic that tries to overpower me, refusing to be reduced to the animal I used to be. I whimper as nightmarish flashes of memory assault me: a heavy body on top of mine, the forceful grunt reverberating in my ear as they rut, the desolation of being powerless and scared, and the only option left was to submit or die fighting.

Millions of women always condemn the victim for not fighting back, as if that somehow makes you a survivor versus a victim. A smart woman knows when to fight back and when to surrender to the torture, because it all depends on the assailant. You are powerless, just as they want you to be. Women can condemn all they want, because until they are in a similar position, they are just talking out their asses. Deep down, it's just human nature to judge someone because you're thankful you aren't them.

I had four assailants, and one of them wanted me to fight back so he could break me, and I took his pleasure away by relenting when I knew I couldn't win. With my ability to choose whether or not someone touched me removed, I held on to the fact that at least I had a choice between fight or submit.

I survived because I knew if I fought, he would've beaten me to death. There is no pride in bruises if you don't live to brandish them. You can't think straight with a fist squeezing your throat, choking the very life out of you. But you can still breathe, and your heart still beats, even while a man violates you– stealing your innocence and your humanity with the piercing thrust of his manhood.

I was a victim of an assault. I didn't fight back. The only thing that made me a survivor is the fact that I didn't die. It's not a badge of honor. It's not something to be proud of or ashamed. It just means my assailant didn't kill me.

The difference is what you do from that moment on. It will irreversibly change you. The point is to fight yourself to move forward, especially when you couldn't fight your attackers.

I *was* a victim.

I *am* a survivor.

Which means I'm smart enough to know lightning can strike more than once, and that I don't have any power to stop it. But I'm not stupid enough to put myself in a situation where I'm at risk…

Until tonight.

I don't go looking for it, it just seems I'm a magnet for the tide of darkness that flows through broken men. I might get raped tonight. I might even die when he's done. But if I don't, I'll continue to survive. Regardless, I refuse to hide out in my home. The difference is what you do from that moment on, and I've been allowing them to win by hiding like prey.

It's not my fault.

I've done nothing wrong.

There is no such thing as the wrong place at the right time, or dressing too sexy, or saying yes until you finally say no.

There are monsters on earth who will stalk you, and you are powerless to stop them. It's never about you. You're just the conduit for their issues. They don't see you. They don't know you. They don't want to see you or know you, or treat you like a human being. The way to fight back is to not let them win by breaking you, no matter how fragile you may be.

Pushing the past away, I refuse to allow it to act as a hazy film covering my present. I freeze, using the lack of sight to home in on my surroundings, to taste the emotions of the man at my back.

All I hear is my rapidly beating heart, deafeningly filling

my ears. A feverish sweat breaks out on my flesh, dampening between my breasts and sliding down my spine. I stare sightlessly into the darkness, knowing inches from my face is my only method of escape– the cold, metal door leading to the hallway of Restraint. I begin to hyperventilate as I register I am trapped like prey in a spider's web.

My abductor does nothing, says nothing. The man simply holds me in place against the door while I freak out. Not only does he not harm me, his hands are gentle, almost protective, as if keeping me from harming myself. He's outwaiting my blind panic, like he knows of my past.

I allow my senses to put me at ease. This is the present, and normal people do not abduct and rape people who are walking down hallways. Besides, one man can't do the damage of four.

This is just a game to him, no different than the bouncer, the domme, the submissive, and the bartender. This man is the player known as the Boss.

Frozen just as I am, he's simply breathing softly near my ear, exhibiting tremendous patience. The puffs of air fleeing his lips flutter the small hairs framing my face, causing them to tickle my cheek. His firm, warm body is relaxed yet thrumming with barely suppressed energy. The way he holds me feels more playful than threatening. My instincts calm me. If this man wanted to harm me, he would have done so already.

This isn't like last time. Not all men are monsters; statistically, only a small percentage are. There aren't rapists and murderers on every street corner, waiting for me to let my guard down so they can assault me. I dampen the urge to allow my imagination to run wild with violent, insanity-fueled scenarios.

In a breathy gust of air from my lungs, "Let me guess… the Boss," I say to the heavy weight at my back. My tone is a mix of amused annoyance, and beneath that… terror.

He chuckles softly near my ear, sounding relieved that I've calmed myself down enough to reason out his intentions. It's obvious he wants to play a game with me– whether I'm the game or merely a pawn remains to be seen. He moves slowly, as if not to frighten me further, his fingertips smoothing against my restrained wrists.

Involuntarily, because I can't *not* do it, I test my capture, trying to loosen his hold. The movement starts in my fingertips to radiate down my arm, until my body is jerking roughly against the door. My teeth bite into my bottom lip, denting in and almost blooding me in my effort to keep the building scream from spilling into the air. My muscles become taut, twisting with painful spasms. Panic begins to overtake me again, but the Boss holding me immobile with his solid, larger body is an odd comfort.

Patience tested, something cold and metallic clicks into place on my right wrist. An animalistic hiss slithers out between my clenched teeth. The restraining object causes me to lose any footing I'd gained. My calm dissipates, and on the heels of that is distress. My heart beats so forcefully that I can feel it in every part of my body– throbbing, screaming for release.

The Boss purrs soothingly into my ear, trying to calm me. "Don't take that off… ever." His voice is smoky, deep, and slightly husky from abducting me. It's a threat edged with anticipation. He's practically begging me to try to take the metal off my wrist, and he's looking forward to the aftermath.

The Boss is getting off on this game. Knowing that I have to be alive and well to play with him, I relax. He won't kill me, but I know there are worse fates than death. Things that make you pray for the sweet release from life.

I try to wiggle out of his arms to no avail. Releasing my wrists, finding me no threat to his person, the Boss wraps his arm around my waist and lifts. He picks me up, sliding me up the door, using his chest as a fulcrum point, until we are even in height. My feet dangle a good foot from the ground, putting the boss at over six-foot-tall.

No man has touched me… not since… and the Boss is now curled around my back, his arm wrapped around my waist, with his cheek pressed to mine. It's a stolen intimacy.

Survival instincts finally kicking in, my mind screams, '*use your calf to make that bastard eat his nuts*!' I prepare to thrust my leg backwards, but somehow he knows the direction of my thoughts. Two thick thighs invade my private space, and widen to part my legs, virtually rendering me motionless.

Fucking great!

My head thrusts backwards on its own accord, seeking the satisfying crunch of a broken nose. I swear underneath my breath when it doesn't connect with his face. The Boss laughs playfully in my ear– a sharp taunting edge to the sound. Teasing me, he blows his breath against my earlobe.

With that action, my panic turns to rage. I've lived through the unthinkable, and to have some asshole play with me in a mock version of abduction…

"Let me go!" I demand defiantly. My voice dips to the depths of Hell. "I'm not fucking around. Let. Go."

"Not happening, KitKat. I like it when *my* Kitten fights back," he purrs in an amused tone, trilling a confusing sensation down my spine.

Something about hearing the Boss say *my Kitten,* lights my fire when it should infuriate me. He feels familiar, as if my body recognizes his. But I doubt I've ever met him before. It's more like my nature sees him as my perfect counterpart: the Boss's unrelenting dominance versus my hunger to trust enough to submit.

"I'm the Boss, and I can do anything I wish with you." He's entirely too pleased with himself as he uses my previous words against me. Words I spoke that caused Queen to laugh at the ceiling while staring at the ever-watching security cameras.

More insane chuckling vibrates against my back and tickles the hairs at the nape of my neck. I fall lax in his grip, not giving up, just waiting him out. He takes it as an invitation to get closer. Pressing into me more firmly yet still gentle, his cheek and the tip of his nose nuzzles at my cheek. A deep sigh rumbles up his throat, relieved that I'm behaving and no longer trying to de-man him.

Since the Boss isn't going to kill me, just toy with me until he turns bored, I decide to play along. I could be a victim, or I could take the decision out of his hands, and meet him head-on. One choice is powerless, and one gives me my life back.

I've been mind-bendingly numb, and this is the first day in over a decade that I've felt anything but the suffocating dark void of my soul. The Boss excites me, infuriates me, and ignites a fire in my veins that's the closest thing to lust I've ever felt.

He's dangerous, and when you feel dead inside, only danger makes you feel alive.

"I take it ya heard that, did ya?" I tease him, pretending I'm going with the flow, and not at all fighting panic.

If this is the boss of Restraint, then he's a stickler for rules– the very rules which drew me to the BDSM culture. Instinctively, I know he won't harm me. We're playing a game, and I'm intrigued. Emotions fill my thoughts– long dead emotions that I've tucked safely away for my own protection.

My body warms at every point we connect: the fronts of his legs against my inner thighs, his groin pressing into my ass, his chest tucked against my back, his arm wrapped around my waist, hand rubbing my hip, with the other curling around my wrists, and his face caressing mine. His flesh sears through my clothing, scorching me. I sigh in relief because I've felt nothing but cold for so very long.

Is the Boss offering me what I crave?

"Just remember, Kitten. The Boss is everywhere, hears everything– all-knowing is the Boss." He threatens me, but lessens its sting with his entertained voice.

"The Boss also talks in third person, and apparently has a sick obsession with Bruce Springsteen," I say sarcastically, pleased my voice doesn't show anything other than amusement. "And I will *never* call him the Boss," I growl in defiance.

Knowing I'm in no real danger, knowing he wants me to be feisty, I want to test his patience along with his boundaries. I want him to let me go, yet I want him to hold me forever. But mostly, I just want to see what he'll do next.

"You aren't any boss of mine," I state petulantly, goading him.

I receive a piercing nip of teeth to the back of my neck, right over my tattoo. His teeth press in sharply. His moist breath sears my skin in a warning to behave. I'm shocked senseless at the jolt of lust that hits my core, all because his teeth came close to breaking my skin in a form of punishment. Overcome, I grunt while my fingertips flex against the metal door. I claw my nails down its slick surface as my senses heighten and moisture pools between my thighs.

I liked that.

I can admit that much.

I motherfucking loved that.

His teeth. My neck. Punishment.

What the hell is wrong with me?

"Bad Kitty, I should punish you," he says in a pouty, flirty voice that quickly warps into a sadistic laugh. The intense rumble of laughter is strong enough to seep through me to vibrate the door. The Boss finds himself humorous. Apparently I do, too, since his infectious laughter has a reluctant smirk quirking my lips when I should be otherwise terrified.

"Ahhh…" is torn from my throat when he licks a long, hot line across my tattoo, as if he can see it in the dark. He laps at my skin, tasting me, soothing where he'd punished me with his fierce bite. Shuddering, I try not to moan as the most sexual moment of my life takes me by surprise.

The Boss's wet, flat tongue does strange, carnal things to me, spinning my thoughts out of control. Instead of trying to fuse myself to the door and clawing my way to safety, I find myself pushing off the door to get closer to my abductor.

I'm seriously fucked in the head.

"You will call me Master Ez," he orders in a no-nonsense voice. "And Kitty Kat, I will forever be your boss, whether you like it or not. You must accept this," he breathes the words into my ear, sounding wicked ominous.

Master Ez fists my wrists above my head in one of his large paws, as his other hand ventures upwards from my hip to where the sleaze had bloodied me earlier.

I allow him to touch me– to explore. I don't even attempt to say no. I don't even *think* no. I don't fight him off because I hear **YES** echoing loudly in my head. I realize I *do* have a choice, but it's a conscious decision on my part to say nothing.

Master Ez is the first man to fondle my breasts when I wanted it. Ever.

My reaction thrills Master Ez, as if he understands the gift I'm offering. His breath puffs rapidly against my neck as his body completely envelopes mine. I close my eyes and revel in the warm sensation of intimate connection. I wonder if he's reveling in it, too.

"Maybe you better call my actual boss and tell him the position's been filled," I mutter slyly, trying to distract myself from the feeling of this man holding my breast gently in the palm of his hand like it's a fragile baby bird. My eyes roll up into my skull when he rubs a spine-tingling circle across my budding nipple with his palm. I shiver, and in reaction to my reaction, he moans deep in his throat. The husky sound of his pleasure increases my arousal, causing my body to weep and my thighs to quiver.

It's been so long...

It's been **NEVER**.

"Ah, Kitty," Master Ez purrs, as if he's been waiting a lifetime to tease me with the nickname. "Trust me. Your boss already knows." More irritating snickers rumble up at his private joke. His elation is infectious, and borderlines on insanity.

"You seem to be having tons of fun, Master Ez." He's having way too much fun for the both of us. I am scared shitless and aroused. It's a deadly combination.

The Boss is patient enough to gain my trust, yet strong enough to master me. The power radiating off of him rivals the intensity of a Nuclear Reactor. God help me, I want him to dominate me. I want it so badly that I can taste it on the back of my tongue... and it tastes like sex and power. It tastes like submission.

It tastes of freedom.

"I've waited years for this moment," he growls. "I've planned, schemed, and controlled so many factors to finally have what's mine delivered to my doorstep." Forcefully, he pushes his wide hips between my legs, impressing me with just how *excited* he is to have '*that which is his*' delivered into his arms.

Master Ez repeats the motion as he suckles at my neck, slowly circling and rocking his erection against my ass, then dipping farther south to press into my pussy. A moan spills from my lips at the first welcome contact, causing my sex to clench violently. Unrelenting, he grinds his bulge against me, coaxing an intense, visceral reaction out of me, shocking the pair of us. High on arousal, we lose ourselves in the moment as he tongue-bathes my neck, surely leaving behind a suck-mark of ownership.

I'm taken completely aback by the fact that I'm not panicking. Anxiety doesn't bring forth the nightmarish memories. The only thing that erupts is lust, and it erupts with dizzying ferocity.

"Could you explain that in greater detail, please?" I beg breathlessly, trying to break the moment– to stop the thrill running through my veins. I don't even care that he just admitted to stalking me, and I really should. I'm blinded by lust, proving just how dangerous a place like Restraint is to a woman like me. Worse, how dangerously addictive a man like Master Ez is to a survivor like me.

All I feel is the pleasure grinding into my lonely, weeping flesh. "Aww... that feels so damn good," spills from my lips, unbidden, as my back arches on its own, offering Master Ez greater access. If I'm not careful, I'll be pleading with him to fuck me soon, and then regretting it seconds later when men usually ignore a no.

"Katya. Katya," Master Ez's voice caresses my name, his cadence edged with an unnamed emotion. "You will figure it out. You're one of the smartest women I've ever known," he admits, confusing me further. "Besides, it's more fun watching you struggle with the truth as we play our little game."

No surprise. I'm prey to Master Ez's predator, and I'm playing a long-term game with someone who has the ability to fuck me, especially cerebrally.

"Who says I'll play with you?" Defiant, I test the limits of his boundaries.

"How can you not? You feel more alive right now than

you ever have. Admit it," Master Ez challenges me, and then thrusts up sharply, proving his point.

We both grunt from the force of his thrust. Panting in my ear as wildly as I pant against the door, Master Ez performs a sexual act that can never be described as dry humping. This dominant man is fucking me, standing up against the door, with our clothes still on– that takes pure talent.

Master Ez's hand moves to flick one of the caps on my teeth as he bites my neck hard, drawing a squeak of surprise from my throat. Another flick to the other cap. Another sharp bite, marking the shit out of my neck. Movements jerky, manic, he places his hand back on my injured breast. His thumb rubs over the fingernail indents, reminding me of being accosted earlier.

Instantly, I learn a lesson: this is what it means to be truly dominated by a master. There will be no telling Master Ez no. He does what he wants, when he wants, only because he wants to, and you will like it because he does. I doubt this man uses a safe-word, because he's not in the lifestyle. Dominance *is* his life.

The realization is as terrifying as it is life-altering. It leaves me stripped raw, bared to the man grinding into me. I can't overanalyze it because my mind is fogged with all things Master Ez. I hunger to know what he can do to me, but more so, what I can do for him. I long to feel the sensations he will rent from my body, instinctively knowing he will either be my salvation or my ruination. I can't even make the decision while he clouds my judgment with his very presence.

This is what it means to be at the mercy of a master.

Fingertip tracing the edges of my wound, Master Ez brings up a painful encounter while dry '*fucking*' me. "I gave Dexter special instructions for our mutual friend. I thought I would have to intervene earlier, but you handled yourself very well."

Master Ez's praise warms me in unexpected ways, causing me to gasp in shock, reshaping me into a creature who would do anything to gain his attention. That thought alone has me swimming through the thick fog of lust, trying to clear my mind for rational thinking.

Forcing me beneath the surface again, "I'm not surprised, and I'm very proud of you, Kitty Kat." His voice caresses the nickname he gave me. I've been called Kitty Kat before, but that doesn't matter. It never meant anything until Master Ez murmured it into my ear while praising me.

If Master Ez was a cat, he'd be purring with contentment this very moment. His cheeks, lips, and forehead nuzzle any bared skin of mine that he can access– scent marking me. All the while, his teeth and lips leave behind a lasting mark of ownership.

God, this feels fantastic.

I loosen all my muscles and melt into Master Ez. He smells fantastic, too, like spicy musk. I feel branded by him, and I never want to wash it off.

Master Ez isn't just physically fucking me– he's cerebrally fucking me.

A sharp knock at the door jars us both, drawing an actual growl from Master Ez's chest, while I sigh in relief for the reprieve.

"Go away, for fuck's sake!" he shouts.

Master Ez's demeanor changes from calm and in control, to furious and unhinged, in less than a second. When his control fled, my ease did as well. As he vibrates barely leashed violence, I start to shake as panic sinks its teeth back into me.

"Somebody better be dead, or else I will kill you with my bare hands." His voice isn't loud, but it would scare the Devil himself. I shiver from the menace, and I have no doubt that he's being serious. Whoever is on the other side of this door, they better run for their lives while I chase them down with a thank you.

"I apologize for our interruption," Master Ez murmurs formally as an explanation for his abrupt mood shift. "The club has been most difficult as of late, and it always happens at the most inopportune times."

Master Ez presses a gentle kiss to my neck, and then slowly lowers me to the floor to stand on shaking legs. As if hesitant to allow me from his captive embrace, he hugs me from behind, taking a few moments to regain his composure.

"Katya, please close your eyes," he orders. "Don't open them until you hear the door shut. I mean it. I will punish you beyond belief if you so much as crack a lid." He roughly shakes me in emphasis. "Don't doubt me on this; I know where to find you."

I obey by closing my eyes since the tone in Master Ez's voice screams he's being deadly serious. I stifle a shudder as his fingertip flutters over my eyelids– testing me, seeing if I am trustworthy.

Master Ez grips my upper arms and pulls me back from the door. I hear the snick of the lock, and then a creak as the door opens. Someone brave yet silent enters the room, stirring the air around me.

Master Ez picks me up by the shoulders, moving me several strides before setting me gently on my feet. He taps on my shoulder with a fingertip, and then his warmth dissipates from my back as he moves away.

Just as I was commanded, I open my eyes when I hear the door click shut. I blink repeatedly in the bright light of the hallway. My mind is as muddled as my vision. I'm scared shitless as the insane effect Master Ez had on me clears with his absence.

There is only one thing I'm not confused about; I've never felt as alive as I do in this very moment.

Restraint 66

Chapter Six

Lost, standing in the center of the hallway at Restraint, I'm inundated with every named emotion, and some that defy description. All. At. Once.

Insane laughter bubbles up my throat, and continues to flow until it blends into the music wafting from the speaker system overhead.

I just had what constituted as sex, with a man I don't know, with a man I couldn't see, with a man I've never held a conversation with… he basically took what he wanted until we were interrupted, swatted my ass, and then told me to call him Master Ez.

The only explanation I have for why I enjoyed it, is that I'm clinically insane.

That's all I've got. An insanity plea.

Lost.

It's a wonder I'm not curled up in a ball in the center of the floor, rocking back and forth with hysteria.

In a daze, I make my way back to the main room of the club, sightlessly walking on quivering legs. I fall into the booth with a huge sigh, joining the waiting ladies. It feels like it's been an eternity since I last saw Queen and Fate, but it's probably only been fifteen minutes at the most.

It wasn't time that flowed at a disjointed rate, it was that I underwent a dramatic transformation so quickly. Mentally, emotionally, and physically exhausted, I melt into the booth's bench, feeling like I took a hit of the most potent drug imaginable, and it's called Master Ez.

My eyes are glazed over and heavily lidded, blurry from the shock of lust. I'm so content, lax and boneless, that you'd think I'd been drugged. I can only imagine what my face must look like to others, judging by the awestruck expressions on Master Ez's minions' faces. Fate is rendered speechless, her pretty face vacant as she stares gape-mouthed at me from across the booth. Queen's expression is a mixed bag of chaos, like she's unsure how she feels in this moment. I wonder if my expression mirrors hers.

"Looks like someone met the Boss," Queen states the obvious. She finally manages to choose what she should emote, settling on looking pleased by allowing a satisfied smirk to stretch across her face.

Not able to decipher Queen's moods, or why she's 'acting' a part, I choose to ignore it until I'm capable of solving it. Hell, I may never see any of these fools again after I leave here tonight. I might as well make the most of it. It will be a great story to tell my future grandkids. A cautionary tale.

"Yeah, I guess I did meet the Boss," slips past my numb lips. Sanity returning, I'm too cautious to say more, not fully trusting them.

I run a hand over my face, trying to sober up. When my fingers snare into my hair, I'm shocked because I meet resistance. Usually my hair is free-flowing, not pulled up since it gives me a headache. I yank my barrettes out, tossing them to the tabletop, and let my hair flow in a curly wave to my ass. I shake my head to settle my hair, and finally enjoy the feeling of my fingers gliding through it. Mid-finger-comb, something cold and metallic taps against my nose– a bracelet.

I pull my hand from my hair and openly stare at the platinum circling my wrist, trying to figure out what the hell it means. I know it's a membership to Restraint, but why?

Why me?

Why him?

Before I can thoroughly examine the bracelet, Queen's pulling my arm across the table, lightly cupping her larger hands around my forearm so I can't flinch away.

"Holy fuck, girl… What did you do?" Queen draws out, and all I can do is gape up at her like a startled colt.

Queen looks at me expectantly, but it's Fate who holds my attention. Her eyes are glazed over with a queer little smile flirting along her lips, as if she's reliving the moment her master gave her the bracelet on her wrist.

I've read a lot about the lifestyle in preparation of joining their culture. In most cases, it's collaring your submissive, not giving them a bracelet. I'm positive it's a big deal. Its symbolism is stronger than a wedding band between a married couple.

This bracelet doesn't signify anything more than passage into Restraint– nothing more. Master Ez didn't claim me. He didn't ask me to be his. Out of courtesy and for the ease of the game he's playing, Master Ez was simply giving me a membership bracelet to Restraint so I can enter his playground unimpeded. But I can't tell these women that, even though I'm sure they already know and they're just fucking with me.

"It's nothing," I mutter flippantly, when on the inside I'm a stew of emotions I cannot name. "The Boss just gave me the membership bracelet. It's not like it's a big deal or anything," denial is so thick in my voice that Fate actually rolls her eyes at Queen.

It's nothing. It can't mean any more than it appears, because I cannot fathom why Master Ez would pick me as a submissive, someone he doesn't even know. I'm not even a submissive person. I'm a switch, meaning I like to dominate as much as I like to be dominated. We wouldn't fit, even if Master Ez makes me lose my fucking mind.

For some reason, words start spilling unbiddenly from my lips. "I'm a switch, and I know you guys understand the underlying meaning of that." I quickly gaze up at them, only to lose my nerve and glance away. "No master would allow their submissive to hold dominion over another person when your sole purpose is to be under their total command. A man as dominant as the Boss needs a submissive, not a woman walking a knife's edge between needing control and longing to submit."

My past has taken the playfulness and innocence from my personality, leaving behind someone who is too afraid to let go. It's hardened my heart. I'm not pretty or sexy, but I'm comfortable in my skin and I like who I am. But that doesn't mean a man ever will, though, and I've come to terms with that.

With one glance around this club, you know Master Ez could have the pick of the litter, and I'm sure he picks from it often. I will go a lifetime without, because I refuse to be someone's second or third or fourth choice.

I'm not arrogant enough to assume a man could look past my appearance and find me attractive. The outside package is what draws them in, to keep them preoccupied while they get to know the real you. Your personality is what ultimately hooks them, because beauty fades while intriguing someone is forever.

No one approaches me to get past the exterior, not that I'd let them. I'm satisfactory while clothed, but it all goes to shit when I'm nude. My thighs are almost as pudgy as my belly. I don't have a spankable ass. I do have large tits that sag when the bra comes off, which also isn't an incentive. Mix my disproportionateness with my short height and I look ridiculous. My hair is flaming red and curly. It's not the perfectly straight blonde of Fate's. But it's not looks, or my lack of submissiveness that is my greatest shortcoming.

I'm cold and dead inside.

I use bitchiness as a shield to protect my injured soul.

I'm broken and irreparable.

The only reason Master Ez would ever want me is to trap me in whatever game he's playing, only to toss me away when he becomes bored.

I'm not cynical. I'm realistic.

"Good God, you're naïve," Queen breathes so quietly I'm unsure if I heard her properly. *Naïve? Me?* "You're not the only switch on the planet, ya know? The Boss is your master, Katya, whether you like it or not." She sounds weary, as if she not sure that's a good thing.

"Kat," Fate's eyes cut towards Queen, silently asking for permission to continue. She must receive it, because she keeps talking anyway. "We all have different needs. I'm submissive, but I don't need this kind of stuff," she gestures around the club. "I just need a guide through life, without any kink."

"So true," Queen's voice is filled with affection. "A true master will anticipate your needs and make sure they are fed properly. He'll make sure your dominant nature is nurtured, allowing you to take charge of someone more submissive."

Biting back a laugh, Fate tries to stop herself from blurting out the truth, but fails. "Perceived control. He will make you feel as if you're in control of whomever he chooses for you, but ultimately he will be controlling the both of you, and getting off on it."

"Fate," Queen snarls, admonishment thick in her voice.

"What?" the beautiful woman mouths, looking as innocent as a newborn babe. "It's the truth. He's—"

Cutting Fate off, Queen spits out, "Shut your trap, or else I'll make you bunk with Kris."

Must be Kris is a messy roommate, judging by the grimace Fate pulls. I stop an impending fight between whatever the fuck these ladies are to one another. "I'm not sure why we are even discussing this. The Boss is *not* my master," I stress, trying to yank my arm out of Queen's tight grasp.

"Lookie, lookie…" Queen taps my wrist with a fingertip.

I pull back and stare blankly. I know what's there, but it takes looking at it for it to fully sink into my psyche. A platinum bracelet encircles my wrist. It looks the same as Queen's, except for its additional feature: a lock— a fucking padlock.

You've got to be shitting me!

"Don't take that off…ever," I imitate Master Ez's voice and accent, nastily twisting the words. "No, shit! I guess he meant that. I wasn't even given an option. He hijacked me in the hallway, pulled me into a dark room, and then clicked the bitch in place. You've got to be fucking kidding me," I hiss at the ceiling.

I gently thump my forehead into the booth's tabletop. I'm such a fool. One taste of lust-fueled excitement, and I lose my ever-loving mind.

"I'm stupid…" Thumps my head. "Stupid… I'm a stupid, stupid girl…" Thumps my head. "I let him distract me." I chastise myself for allowing arousal to overpower my survival instincts.

Queen's burst of laughter nearly breaks my concentration as a new option filters into my mind. I didn't seek Master Ez out. We know nothing of one another. I have no idea what this bracelet truly signifies, and until I do, it will only be a removable piece of jewelry.

Padlock.

Another choice taken from me, which infuriates me further. Scowling down at the bracelet, I envisioned the freedom of taking it off. The satisfaction of removing the bracelet will be orgasmic. I smirk to myself, knowing exactly how I will be spending the rest of my evening.

Master Ez, you tricky shit, don't underestimate me. You don't have to give me a choice, because I will create my own.

Master Ez is going to learn what it means to play with a switch. I'm no more or less dominant than him. I will not bend unless I want to, and not a moment sooner. To have me submit is a privilege, an honor– something that cannot be stolen. I am not submissive. I do not listen and follow instruction. I do not obey. Master Ez is going to rue the day he decided to play with me.

Keen eyes noting the resolve in me, Queen draws my attention. "That's not all; look at the lock."

I raise my arm to examine the padlock in the light. It looks pick-proof, and I don't have a key: a challenge wrought is a challenge accepted. The impression on the face of the lock is an unbreakable circle of the word *Restraint.* Unlike the other bracelets, the letters hook together as a chain, a real raised chain. Inside the circle are the letters **E Z**, created out of perfectly cut black diamonds.

"Jesus, I'm wearing thousands upon thousands of dollars' worth of bracelet on my wrist. No wonder there's a lock on it." I shake my head in wonder, reevaluating the evening. I thought I was a stupid girl for my reaction to Master Ez. Now I wonder about his mental state for giving me such a… *gift?* "Either he put the lock on it so no one would steal it from me, or he's worried I'll pawn the sucker."

"That's not why there's a lock, Katya." Queen's look of pity shakes me. Why the pity?

A flash of insight strikes my mind like lightning. I was worried about the lock and the worth of the bracelet, completely missing the symbolism. The finality of the letters finally sinks in.

"I've been pwnt by the Boss." I glance around Restraint, trying to sight my new master, because that is exactly what Master Ez is to me now. Not only did he slap a membership bracelet on my wrist, he placed a stamp of ownership on my ass.

I'm not sure how I feel about that. The larger, more dominant side of me is screaming like a banshee, hating the trapped sensation of being given no choice. While the smaller, submissive part of me is preening like a stupid girl.

I know he's watching. He wouldn't miss this for the world. Master Ez is the Boss, ever-knowing. I pick up the gauntlet he threw down, knowing he can probably read my lips. "Game on, bastard."

Restraint 74

Chapter Seven

My body is running on fumes and black coffee after staying up way too late last night. I didn't remove the bracelet because I was too busy planning a method of attack. Then, this morning, I had to spend a good hour camouflaging the suck and bite marks chained around my neck. I added more foundation to the long list of items I need for bracelet extraction.

Making matters worse than the fact that I look like I've been attacked by a randy vampire hell-bent on marking his territory, is the fact that I'm arguing with Monica... again. Always.

"He's the author. It's his vision," Monica's whiny voice irritates the hell out of me on a good day, and today isn't one of those.

Annoyance #435,532, we're waiting on a very late and irresponsible Mr. Abernathy. Monica is allowing her emotions to cloud her judgment. She's been championing for Abernathy's book all morning long, and I'm at my wit's end. It's a piece of shit, and I wouldn't want to put our publishing house's name on it. Monica is more worried about soothing her lover's wounded ego, while I worry about publishing a book readers want to read, and that is the difference between being a leader and a minion.

I'm just about ready to torch the bitch to get her to shut up. The book. Not Monica. All right, maybe Monica could hold the book while I pour gasoline on it and light a match. Yeah, that's the kind of day I've had.

"My job is to make sure everyone beneath me does their job, and that includes Abernathy, since a novel is the foundation of publishing. If makeup manufacturers gave us Pink Eye, they would go bankrupt. I will not bankrupt Edge because Abernathy is lazy and unimaginative."

Monica is gathering steam, ready to blow up, so I cut her off before she starts her shit. "Your job is to make sure whatever Edge Publishing's authors write is written properly. Your opinion on the content doesn't count. Mine does." I slam the draft on my desk to drive home my point. "And neither of our jobs is to blow smoke up Abernathy's ass. If it sucks, I'm saying it sucks."

Already defeated, Monica starts pouting, and for some reason it makes her more attractive. I like it when she's conquered. "You can't tell an author what to write, Katya. They are inspiration-driven."

"I'd love to know what the inspiration for..." I glance down at the manuscript like I didn't already have the ridiculous title imprinted in my mind for all eternity. **A Romantic Run Through the Forest**. You're shittin' me, right?"

"Yeah, that's a very misfortunate title. I'll agree with that." Monica relents, and that sets off warning alarms. She never gives up. "Your job is to give advice to the authors, and clearly you're dropping the ball with Abernathy."

"He. Won't. Come. To. The. Goddamned. Meetings." Squinting at my editor like she's a lunatic, I blurt out, "Are you purposely fucking with me, Monica?" I move around my desk to lean my ass on its edge, trying to invade Monica's personal space.

Looking me dead-to-rights, "Maybe I could do your job better. Did you ever think about that?" She isn't daunted by my closeness, and it unnerves me. Most people are intimidated by me, but not Monica.

A haughty smile spreads my lips as I cross my arms over my chest. "Nope, that thought has never entered my mind, because I'm confident in my abilities. Do we need to add a psyche evaluation along with your visit to Human Resources?"

"Ladies," an amused, deep voice says from my open door. I could have sworn I shut it. In fact, I know I did.

I look up and my eyes enlarge, my snide response quickly dies on my parted lips. Mr. Zeitler smiles pleasantly as he enters my office to flow across the floor to sit next to Monica in my other guest chair. His knee brushes mine accidentally, causing me to freeze up. His proximity intimidates me as I'd hoped mine would intimidate Monica. Odder still, Monica isn't intimidated by Zeitler, either. She sits here comfortably, with an anticipatory smirk twisting her lips.

I move to the other side of my desk to sit in my office chair, using the movement to distract me from the unexpected presence of the owner of Edge sitting in my office. "Um... Welcome, Mr. Zeitler." For some reason my greeting ends with an upward inflection like it's a question. "I was expecting our elusive Mr. Abernathy this afternoon."

"Ms. Waters," he says warmly, a slight purr in his tone, all the while trying not to smile broadly. "Ms. James," he murmurs with affection, and I realize that I'm at a disadvantage. Monica and Mr. Zeitler know each other well, so he'll probably take her side in the battle over Abernathy's disaster.

"When will Mr. Abernathy be joining us?" I ask to fill the awkward silence. It's awkward for me, not them. Monica looks vindicated now that our boss is here. Mr. Zeitler just smiles like he has nowhere else he'd rather be, and it brightens his stormy-gray eyes to nearly blue.

"I'm sorry, Ms. Waters. Mr. Abernathy had pressing business to attend elsewhere," he explains away the author's continual absence.

Yeah, I'm sure Abernathy has something better to do today— anything better than doing his job. Zeitler smirks at me knowingly, as if the handsome bastard somehow knows the direction of my private thoughts.

"Were we discussing Mr. Abernathy?" surprise is thick in Zeitler's voice, but I'd bet the entirety of my bank account that Zeitler was listening at my door before he entered. His timing was way too perfect. Leaning forward, elegant hands resting on his knees, he stresses, "Abernathy is a special case for us. I need an update on his progress."

"Uh..." I fumble, staring down at the manuscript with the blood-red script– **A Romantic Run Through the Forest** – glaring up at me from my desk.

No doubt deciding I'm inept, Zeitler turns to the side to ask, "Monica what's your opinion?" and she preens under his attention.

As I watch Zeitler's side-profile, the corner of his full lips lifts. I observe him as he looks at Monica, but I can feel one of those piercing gray eyes trained on me.

"Personally, I think we should let Abernathy write the novel as he envisioned it. But, of course, Katya has a different opinion, don't you?" She sets me up to take the fall.

If Monica thinks I will lie to anyone about anything, she has another think coming. Go ahead, throw me under the bus, Bitch. I've been there often. It's my home base.

"Truthfully, it sucks." I meet Zeitler's gaze straight-on. "The timeline is a disaster. The narrator said she was raised by her grandmother, and a paragraph later she was whining about how she lost her grandmother when she was four. It was Monday, and a page later, during the same scene, it changed to Saturday. I won't even go into the fact that Abernathy went out of his way to butcher the English language."

"It's not *that* bad." Monica shakes her head and rolls her eyes as if trying to discredit me.

"Sir, it's worse than that." I shore up my nerves of steel. "I think I'm being punked. This has to be a joke. Abernathy will not answer my calls, my messages, or show up to my meetings, and he sends me **A Romantic Run Through the Forest**. Either it's a parody, or someone is trying to test my integrity," I say pointedly at Monica.

"Do you hear this? This is what it's like with her day in and day out. Ms. Waters is so paranoid, just this morning she asked Kayla if Mr. Abernathy even existed."

That's it! I've had enough of Monica's shit. Normally, I would've ignored her jabs, but not in front of Zeitler. It makes me look like I can't control my own staff. Which is worse, throwing down with your underling, or letting them run wild?

"I don't give a fuck what you think, Monica," I twist her name with that same annoying tone she uses on me. "As I've said countless times, you do your job and I'll do mine. You're the editor because you're as imaginative as a white crayon."

A masculine bark of laughter brings my head up. Last I remembered I was talking to Zeitler, now I am leaning over Monica, seething. I hadn't realized I'd moved. I'm losing it. I shake my head to clear it, and sit back down at my desk. I hide my shaking hands in my lap.

"Ms. Waters, if I were to tell you to leave it as is, what would you do?" Zeitler tries to suppress his laughter: pale face pinking, chest rising and falling rapidly. He gazes at me like I'm the most amusing thing he's ever seen.

I think about his question for a moment. I see things as black and white most of the time. The only time my world enters shades of gray is when I'm in my imagination. I lean my elbows on the desk and rest my chin in my open palms.

"Ultimately, that is your decision to make, sir. It's your money, and your company's name that will look foolish. If you want it kept as is, then don't add my name to the work. Personally, I think Abernathy's just phoning it in. Before I take on a new client, I read their backlist, and his previous works were flawless. I will agree with Alec; it's like Abernathy's distracted. You can feel it page after page."

"Yes, Abernathy has been extremely distracted for a long while now," Zeitler muses as he gazes at me. "He won't admit it, but I think he's been blocked," Zeitler confesses, shocking both Monica and me. "So be it. I will tell him to scrap the manuscript and start again." Mr. Zeitler slaps his palms on his thighs, signaling the finality of his statement.

Abruptly, Monica jumps up from her chair and bolts for the door. Well, I will pay for this later. She may have no imagination, but she is highly aggressive when it comes to retaliation.

"Don't blame Monica too harshly." Did he just roll his eyes? "Mr. Abernathy is the one who brought Monica into Edge Publishing. They were an item," he whispers conspiratorially.

Huh?

Mr. Zeitler likes to gossip.

"That explains why Monica has made my life a living hell for the past eight hours." I lean back in my chair and wonder why Zeitler's still here. What does he want?

"Monica's nose is a bit bent out of shape since I bypassed her promotion by giving you the position instead. That tends to bring the venom out. The best advice I can give is, never let her get away with anything. Nip it in the bud the instant it erupts by forcing her to obey you." Zeitler leans forward, placing his palms on my desktop. "Or else."

"Um…" I reach up, running my fingers through my hair in a gesture of discomfort. "I'd call Monica's and my tentative relationship a work-in-progress."

"Monica is actually rather sweet, and takes direction without complaint."

I want to ask if he's bragging. "With everyone except me," I nearly whine, frustrated.

"That goes without saying," a sly grin pulls at his devastating lips. "That's an interesting bracelet," Zeitler croons. "May I?" He reaches over to take my wrist before I can answer his request.

Drat! I tried hiding the damn bracelet inside the cuff of my shirt. I hadn't realized it escaped when I was combing at my hair– sneaky platinum bastard.

Mr. Zeitler's warm hand engulfs mine, and then he begins running his thumb over my wrist in soothing circles. The sensation feels vaguely perverse, like Master Ez's hand cupping my breast– salacious and seductive. It looks innocent to the outside observer, but inside me, it ignites my libido. I suck in a large breath and hold it. I have to close my eyes to regain my composure.

What is wrong with me?

When my eyelids finally lift, they reveal Mr. Zeitler staring at me, studying my response to his expert touch. The way my body sways towards his, and the '*obey*' comment he made earlier, assures me he at least dabbles in the lifestyle. I don't doubt my intuition for a second. I feel Mr. Zeitler's need mirroring my own.

I tilt my head to the side and study him as well. I want to analyze his reaction to my bracelet. Zeitler's lips lift in a devastating smile, enjoying my eyes on him. He's an arrogant bastard, I'll give him that. His fiancée is a lucky woman.

"Someone has excellent taste," he says softly, almost sounding drowsy, as he lovingly caresses the lock like a lover's flesh.

No two men get the same reaction out of me, not after my

past. Not born yesterday, I bait him purposely. "It's an exquisite dog tag, or maybe an expensive leash," I say snidely, testing to see if my boss is *the* Boss.

As if on cue, Kayla enters my office, leaving me to wonder what response I would've received. My eyes glue to her. Earlier in the day, she'd had on a tight sweater buttoned up to her neck, leaving little to the imagination as it snugly caressed her curves. Now her buttons have lost the fight of restraining her tits. Her shirt is gaping just enough to catch sight of her bra. I can't stop my eyes from feasting on the flashes of flesh as she approaches.

Kayla's lacy pink bra is sheer enough that I can see her nipples peeking at me. I close my eyes against the sight of her bouncing towards me.

It's ridiculous. I feel as if I've stepped on-stage in the middle of a play. A play where I wasn't given a script but forced to perform, and all those around me are consummate actors.

I look at Zeitler, examining the smug expression of supremacy on his face. He's extremely satisfied with something, most likely himself. I'm sure it has nothing to do with me. I doubt anyone would feel proud of their female employee ogling her female assistant's assets.

Maybe Mr. Zeitler is just enjoying the view. It is a splendid sight, after all.

"Ms. Waters, this came for you earlier." Kayla leans around me and places a wrapped box on my desk. As she rises, her breasts '*accidentally*' brush my forearm, begging for my attention. I'm starting to think Kayla is a little tease. I'm sure her buttons magically unhooked themselves and there was a reason to brush herself against me. Again, just like yesterday.

Naughty Kayla, you better hope you don't meet me in a dark alley sometime.

I quirk an eyebrow at Mr. Zeitler's intrigued expression. It's as if he can read the wicked thoughts scrolling through my mind.

"Thank you, Kayla." I dismiss her with an, "Excuse us, please." I don't look away from my boss as Kayla slides the large box in front of me, and then sashays from the room, closing the door behind her.

Since Zeitler isn't leaving, I examine my package while being scrutinized by him. I try to block out the fact that the perfectly square package is wrapped in paper with little logos printed all over it. I don't react, because if I did, I'd end up running from the room as if were on fire... and the package contained explosives.

I have no need to remove the paper since someone, with a lot of time on their hands I might add, wrapped the box perfectly so it hinges open. I slowly lift the flap, waiting for Jack to jump from the box, or maybe a knife-wielding psychopath.

I sigh in relief, slumping farther into my seat.

A chessboard.

I can deal with an innocuous chessboard. I chance a glance at Zeitler, only to find him staring at me and the package, as if curious to see what it is. I lift the board to present it to him, only to startle like a Jack-in-the-box popped out and knifed me.

Awed, "Shit," slips past my lips in barely a breath of a whisper. "Master: two. Katya: zero."

How the fuck can I show Zeitler this? I lick my lips as my mouth suddenly dries up. Shell-shocked, I stare at the black and white chess pieces in utter disbelief.

A chessboard with thirty-six pieces sounds harmless, right?

No fucking way.

How sweet of Master Ez to provide me with my very own BDSM chess set. The Kings are doms, the Queens are dommes, the Pawns are kneeling submissives, and I don't even want to contemplate the pony play going on with the Knights.

I grab the card from the box like the pieces have venomous fangs and if I move too slowly I'll get bitten. I drop the board back into the box, effectively hiding the hedonistic pieces. I tuck the lid shut, and then stow the box under my desk... and put my foot on it.

"Something wrong?" Mr. Zeitler asks, managing to sound inquisitive yet innocent.

"Oh, no. What could possibly be wrong? It's just a beautiful, standard chess set," I lie poorly. Zeitler looks at me crosswise, and I swear he whispers *'fibber'* underneath his breath.

My face flames in embarrassment, skin blazing bright red. I clasp my hands around the note in a death grip, and rest my forearms on my blotter. Nope, I'm just a very good girl. I don't have chess pieces engaged in hedonistic positions beneath my boot. I wouldn't dream of it.

"Aren't you going to read the note?" Zeitler tips his head, motioning to the note crinkled in my fist. "I love chess. Maybe you and I could play sometime." His voice is calming and his expression is ever-so hopeful.

"Ah, I really don't know how to play," I lie for the second time. It's funny how when I'm embarrassed the lies flow from my tongue like water.

"It'd be a pleasure to teach you." His stormy eyes twinkle with mischief. I think the bastard knows I'm lying, and I'm pretty sure I'm not the only fibber in this room.

Fuck.

I open the envelope, yet again, ignoring the logos. I pull out a single sheet of expensive, gray paper with words glowing from it.

My Kitty Kat,
I know how much you love games after hearing, "game on,
bastard," from those supple lips of yours. Let us add a new
game to our repertoire. Place this chess set in your office.
Don't worry, Kitten, no need for rules– anything goes.
Meet me at Restraint tonight.
I look forward to your obedience.
-Forever your boss-
Master EZ

I slowly fold up the sheet of expensive paper and return it to its envelope. I hope my outside demeanor doesn't show the chaos brewing within. Sweat trickles down my spine as I slide the note into my briefcase. I give Mr. Zeitler innocent eyes when I look up.

"Secret admirer?" His stormy gaze tries to capture mine

with no success. The part of me that feels as if I've been thrust into an episode of The Twilight Zone is firmly in control.

"Admirer." I spread my hands out on my desk. "Stalker. Same difference," I mutter while giving a shrug. "Master," I breathe. I twist a smirk and give a light laugh as if I'm joking.

Zeitler joins in with me, as if he's in on the joke, too... or maybe I'm the brunt of the joke. I should feel insulted that he's toying with me and sitting here so he can witness it firsthand, but I'm enveloped by Zeitler's incredible laugh: smoky and masculine. Addictive. You could almost roll the sound around on your tongue and taste its intoxicating carnality.

Mr. Zeitler sounds like naked bodies writhing on silk sheets, and I'm powerless to stop the effect the sound has on my senses.

"It's been a pleasure, Ms. Waters." Zeitler rises smoothly from the chair, flowing like water. As he moves towards the door, his parting words are polite, yet are an issued warning. "Enjoy your weekend, Katya."

As soon as Zeitler exits my office, I grab all of my stuff and start shoving it into its bags. I have to get the hell out of here so I can think. I'm losing my freaking mind– insanity.

My boss is *the* Boss, without a shadow of a doubt. I cannot believe I kept my shit together for the past few minutes while the bite marks on my neck throbbed just as violently as the need between my thighs. I can still feel the press of his cock against my ass from last night.

What the hell is Zeitler doing with me?

Hauling my laptop and briefcase, I flee my office like a bat out of Hell, ignoring the fact that I have a hedonistic chess set beneath my desk that the nighttime janitorial staff will undoubtedly find during their snoop-cleaning.

Halfway to the elevator, my feet stop on their own accord. Before me is the man who was just taunting me. Zeitler's hugging a stick-thin, angular female wearing designer rags. His big palm rubs her back through her straight blonde hair. Her head rests on his shoulder, making her around six-feet tall with thousand dollar heels.

As I approach, I *'accidentally'* overhear their

conversation. Voice no longer warm and smoky, barely maintaining an edge of civility, Zeitler stiffly bites out, "This is such a surprise, Adelaide. What brings you by? I thought we weren't meeting until Monday."

Hmm… Adelaide– how very blueblood.

"Oh, Ezra. You didn't forget, did you?" she admonishes him in a girly voice. "Mother reserved our plates for dinner this evening. The Daniels will be joining us, and you know how they enjoy your company."

Zeitler scowls down at the woman who must be his fiancée. He looks vaguely disappointed, but I think *thrown* is a more accurate description. Adelaide surprised him somehow. Judging by the taut set of his shoulders and the way his eyes are narrowed, it wasn't a happy surprise.

"I have plans this evening, Ade," Zeitler says firmly. "Please give my regards to Priscilla and Daniel and the boys."

"You did forget," Adelaide whines. "Our mothers are co-hosting the charity function for Transcend. How could you forget that?"

"You're as astute as ever. How could I have possibly forgotten that, Ade?" My boss is a mixed bag of tricks, and this time he pulls off sarcasm effortlessly.

With Zeitler's back to me, Adelaide is facing me, her cheek resting on his shoulder. Rolling her vivid blue eyes up to connect with mine, she smirks at me, as if this is somehow a show put on just for me.

I don't know anyone in Dominion. I don't know either of them. I've never seen this woman in my entire life. Plus, I've only spoken to my boss twice, and very briefly I might add. Even if Zeitler is Master Ez, his fiancée wouldn't know what happened between us last night, which makes me feel sick with shame.

Maybe Monica is right, and I'm entering paranoia territory. My intuition is going haywire, causing me to sense something that isn't there. Hell, Mr. Zeitler most likely isn't even Master Ez, which means I just made a complete ass out of myself back in my office.

Letting it go, I enter the elevator and turn to press the floor where my apartment resides. A worldly woman such as myself works and sleeps in the same building, so obviously I'm going mad if I believe all these people are fucking with me.

Pressing floor seven, I sigh deeply, and somehow the sound catches my boss's notice. Zeitler's furious gaze flicks up to connect with mine. He looks beyond wicked-pissed: body frozen, face set in angry lines, nostrils flaring. I imagine steam billowing from his ears. The elevator doors can't close fast enough.

Zeitler doesn't look like the man who was comfortably sitting in my office mere moments ago. Now he's almost unrecognizable with fury.

A word his fiancée said flashes in my mind, causing me to suck in a sharp gasp. "Ezra Zeitler," breathes past my lips as my eyes widen in amazement. The doors shut just as my boss charges towards me like an enraged bull.

Chapter Eight

After Adelaide's revelation of how my boss's given name is Ezra Zeitler, I've been determined to remove Restraint's membership bracelet from my wrist… or as I like to call it, *Master Ez's bitch stamp*. The diamond *EZ* keeps glaring up at me from my wrist.

I don't know if Master Ez and my actual boss are one in the same, but I won't allow anyone to own me without earning the privilege. I should have a choice in the matter. When choosing who you will hand your trust to, you wouldn't pick a man who is cheating on his fiancée. You wouldn't pick a man who gives you no choice, because how can you trust him to stop when you need him to stop. I haven't spent the last decade of my life schooling my emotions and distancing myself, only to be victimized again by someone with a god complex.

My idea was to remove the bracelet, and when Master Ez earned his right to be my master, I'd allow him to put it back on me with a few codicils about maintaining a non-sexual relationship. I will not ruin my integrity to get my rocks off, no matter how hot Master Ez may make me. No matter if that intoxicating level of lust delivers me into madness, I have to sleep at night and look my family in the eye. I will not be the other woman.

I know nothing of this man, but I am highly observant. Other than the fact that he seems to be a faithless, egotistical, domineering bastard, he has a string of loyal followers, as well as how driven he must be to own both Edge Publishing and Restraint. Ezra Zeitler is a well-respected pillar of the community.

What I can't wrap my mind around is why. Why me? All I can come up with, is when Ezra Zeitler hired me, he did a background check from hell, ferreting out all of my secrets. He must sense the broken part of me and it intrigues him. A man such as himself would find me a challenge. Imagine the ego-boost, the inches on your manhood you'd receive for controlling the assault victim whose heart had hardened, how invincible you would feel when you got the woman into your bed.

It has nothing to do with me and everything to do with him, and that is *not* flattering.

I have too much to risk to allow him to toy with me, sleep with me, and then remove me from his life. Not only would I set myself up for being hurt, I'd also lose my job and the life I've been trying to build in Dominion.

Which only makes the disappointment that much stronger, because I'm not resilient enough to overpower the emotions I'm trying to bury. The very real, epically intoxicating emotions that I cannot escape. I don't want to feel a spark of thrill because Master Ez chose me to play with him. I don't want to feel the rush of lust when I hear his voice, or the overwhelming sense of pride I get when I do as I was told.

At the same time, I feel gypped how Master Ez hooked the bracelet on my wrist, and that was it. No ceremonial words– nothing. Just *'don't ever take this off'*. Gypped! Isn't it supposed to be special? Shouldn't I have had a choice in the matter? I was under the impression that choosing your master was a big fucking deal. I feel like instead of having a romantic honeymoon where you connect to your partner on a deeper level, I had grungy sex in a bathroom stall in a dive bar– in the ass –and didn't even get off.

If this is the only effort he makes, which was no real effort at all, then I'm disposable. It's not so much keeping his interest after the game reaches its foregone conclusion. It's about garnering enough respect to maintain my job when it's all said and done. If I allow Master Ez to disrespect me like this, then he'll never respect me in the future. Then I will be back in Vacuum Valley, moving backwards instead of forwards.

Stuck.

I will not give this man that kind of power over me, but I am powerless to stop the game because he might fire me if I refuse to play. Emotional, physical, mental, and monetary extortion.

Ezra Zeitler has effectively trapped me in his inescapable game of dominance.

Why would I want a master I don't know? One who plays as underhanded as this?

I don't.

Master Ez is playing cat and mouse with me. Isn't this supposed to be a bond built on mutual trust? But Master Ez doesn't want a bond, he just wants to get his jollies off while tormenting me, and then he'll leave me like discarded trash alongside the road.

My only solution: meet him head-on, prove I am his equal, prove that I can do my job better than anyone before me or behind me, make myself indispensable.

I'm a switch, but that doesn't mean I am weak, that only means I give my power away to someone I trust. My need to be in control is just as fierce as Master Ez's; I'm just versatile enough to feel power in letting go as well as wielding control over others.

My emotions are all over the place: anger, awe, fury, terror, elation, lust, determination, all mixed with a need to challenge Master Ez. Inundated with so many potent feelings, now I'm just exhausted. Knowing that a man has the right to do whatever he wants with me just because this damned bracelet is on my wrist, makes me feel as powerless as I did while lying on the forest floor. Yet, at the thought of being owned, there is a sense of exhilaration that is ever-present and throbbing for release, and I'm just now grasping why.

As a switch, I love the thought of being owned, of belonging to someone, being cherished, being needed, and having someone be all those things for me in return. But at the same time, I feel utter terror over the prospect of having no control over my life. **Switch: someone who wants their cake, and wants to eat it, too.** While playing around, dominating and being dominated sounds enticing. But it is *not* how I wish to spend my everyday life.

If I remove the bracelet, I gain my control back. By being able to put it on and take it off at will, to be able to use it solely as a way to gain passage into Restraint, I am the master of my own destiny. When I put it back on, it is a choice I am making to obey Master Ez, at which point I can take it back off and tell him *No* with a big, *'Go to Hell!'*. At least that was my idea, until I actually tried to remove the bracelet.

Master Ez earned his right to be my master by sheer genius. I can't get the albatross off my wrist. No matter what I try.

I stare in defeat at the mutilation that used to be the pink, healthy skin of my wrist. I planned all last night and times throughout the day. Then I went to several stores to get the supplies I needed, where I spent a small fortune. All of which took hours upon hours of my time, only to be thwarted by Master Ez.

You would be amazed at how your skin will dry out from things that are extremely slippery. Lined up on my kitchen counter is an assortment of lubricants, listed alphabetically from aloe to *Wet* personal lubricant. I thought to slide the bracelet off my wrist, and then that thought warped into using the slippery stuff as a barrier as I cut the chain from my arm.

Nothing has worked.

It's proof positive that somehow Master Ez managed to get the measurement of my wrist. I'm sure if questioned, he would say it was for my comfort, but the diabolical bastard would secretly preen over the fact that it meant it couldn't slide off.

A shriek of frustration bubbles up, and the need to stomp on my kitchen floor overpowers me. I pitch a fit like a small child, all the while the damned bracelet slops up and down my arm, taunting me as if the inanimate object is Master Ez himself.

Look how loose I am, bitch! Ha-ha! You can't take me off. Nah... Na... Nah... Na.

Calming down, I gaze at my implements of extraction, deciding against it because I've already wounded myself enough to scar. On the counter, opposite from my lineup of lube, is the sharp, cutting objects: wire snips to gardener shears, and several fine-toothed saws, one of which has a diamond blade.

The chain isn't very thick, just the usual for a charm bracelet. Now I doubt my guess at platinum, maybe some titanium mixed in for strength. I'd have to get out the periodic table to venture another guess. I've played Bob Vila at the hardware store, Paula Deen at the grocery store, and Jenna Jameson at the sex-shop. I am beyond playing Bill Nye.

I reach over to **U** in the lineup, and slather Udder Cream onto my sore and tender arm. It looks rather pitiful, all red and blistered. I have four butterfly closures on my wrist from the slip of the snips and blades. When I came close to hitting a major artery I gave up. I leave my instruments of escape on the counter.

Tomorrow is another day.

I'll try again and again until I'm finally free.

Restraint 92

Chapter Nine

With the dark, oppressive fog of sleep upon me, I'm roused awake by a palm covering my mouth. I have no idea how long it's been resting on my face, with the fingertips caressing my hair.

Frozen, I do my damnedest to regulate my breathing to appear asleep while I take note of the situation. Sight removed from the darkness, I try to use the rest of my senses. But my heart is beating so loudly in my ears, it removes any chance of me hearing anything else. I can sense a large body looming over me, and that is it.

I dampen the paranoia that always surrounds me. A few days ago, I would have panicked like a cornered animal. But tonight, I don't struggle as rational thought wins out.

There is only one person who could bypass the four deadbolts on my apartment door, as well as the security throughout the building. The owner of the Edge Building would have complete and total access. On the heels of that realization, I recognize his familiar presence, the way he manages to calm me yet revitalize me.

It's only been thirty-some hours since the last abduction.

The Boss is back.

"Good Kitty, relax and promise not to scream," a velvet voice purrs.

There is a hand on my mouth, how am I to answer? I reach up to tap him on the shoulder, signaling my agreement.

I try to look at Master Ez as he takes his hand away, but it's too dark in my room with my blackout drapes. Instead, I run my hand up his back, imprinting his lean build into memory. He pushes back into my hand, almost nuzzling, as if he's luxuriating in the intimacy while seeking more of my attention.

I realize I should be terrified by the fact that a man is in my bedroom, even if he may or may not be my boss. But with my violent past, it would take a group of gangbanging sadists to frighten me. When you've lived through the worst, the only thing left to fear is your memories. Anything else that could possibly happen will be a pale shadow by comparison. If, by some act of a vicious fate, it is worse, than that would just mean you are dead, and death is painless with no memories haunting your waking hours.

I calm, because this is not four men hunting me in the Pennsylvania wilderness. This is one man in Upstate New York, and if he is my boss, technically he's not even breaking and entering. I learn something else: it's impossible for me to panic, to be overcome with fear, when in the calming presence of Master Ez.

"We're going to put this on and be a good girl, aren't we?" Master Ez says in a coaxing tone, as if he expects me to disobey. Maybe he does know me.

I have to moisten my lips with my tongue before I can speak. "Yyyes?" It comes out sounding like as question.

"Good girl," he praises, and something irreversible happens. I realize all interaction with Master Ez will be based on a reward and punishment system, and I oddly crave it.

A sleep mask snaps onto my face, blanking out any available light. The Boss wants me blind to hide his identity, I'm sure. I swallow down the panic that threatens to overtake me at having one of my senses cut off.

Most survivors have an issue with darkness. It reminds them of what they survived, drawing painful memories into the present to remind them of how they were lowered to the level of a helpless, defenseless animal. But for me, my violation was on a gorgeous, sunny day, making it that much more sickening.

The darkness feels safer somehow. It's not a pretty lie hiding beneath the guise of innocent happiness. You expect bad things to happen in the dark.

"Katya, if you take that off, your punishment will be severe," Master Ez threatens in a cold and calculated voice that seems to calm me further.

Rules are absolute. Do A, receive B. Fail to do A, receive C. Black and white with no room for interpretation.

"Obey me because you trust that I know what I'm doing and why I'm doing it. If not, you will be punished. I won't enjoy punishing you, but I will if you force my hand." Master Ez caresses my face, smoothing my hair off my forehead.

"Katya, it will always be your decision. Let go and trust me, and we will both get what we need. Disobey, and we will both be disappointed in you and hurting from the resulting punishment. Do you understand?"

I'm rendered speechless as I mull over the possibilities. I'm so new to what is happening– the power exchange –that I can't trust the emotions I'm feeling, let alone trust another human being whom I just met. I'm not there yet.

Master Ez takes my non-response as affirmation and leaves the bedside. I can't see but my hearing increases. The brush of fabric as his legs move, the tap of his designer loafers on the floor, and finally the click of the lamp on my nightstand. I can almost envision the way my bedroom becomes illuminated, and I imagine Ezra Zeitler standing at my bedside, looking like a fallen angel with his pale skin and blond hair, yet glowing with dark power.

Suddenly nervous, because I *have* to know for sure who he is, "How did you get in, Master Ez?" flows breathlessly from my parted lips. "I have a lot of locks. How?" I ask, even though I'm in no position to make demands.

Instead of answering me verbally, a deep, long-suffering sigh erupts from Master Ez's chest, as if I'm testing his patience. I'm sure if I could see, he would be wearing an exasperated expression on his face, like the one he wore this afternoon in my office.

"Ah, I forgot," I murmur, attempting to needle him until he spills the truth. "The Boss is omnipotent: he can do anything and is everywhere." It's hard to be mocking with a mask on and a stalker in my room, but I'm pretty sure I manage to pull it off.

Instead of taking the bait, Master Ez retaliates by ignoring me, leaving me to suffer in dark silence, stewing as I try to anticipate his next move. The man must not be human, because his reactions never fit how a rational person would respond.

After what feels like decades, "Katya, I have another *gift* for you." Master Ez twists the word gift, causing my heart to beat into hyper-drive.

He gingerly touches my wrist with a fingertip, yet I still flinch back in pain. Blind with alarm, pain, and the mask, I try to scramble off the bed to get away. I must look like a fool as I pinball off furniture, trying to locate my bedroom door. In my panicked state, it doesn't even dawn on me to take off the mask. So much for a flawless escape.

If this was my room at my parents' house, I could traverse it in the dark from memory alone. Thirty years of knowing your surroundings will do that for you. But I'm at a severe disadvantage. I just moved here a few weeks ago, so I end up running into my dresser, banging my knee on a drawer pull. I hiss sharply as my perfume bottles rattle together. Their tinkle and my hiss is the soundtrack for my assault on the innocent, unsuspecting furniture that means me no harm.

Rationally, I know I'm not in any danger, that Master Ez is *not* here to harm me. But when his fingertip made contact with my abused wrist, it broke something in me– broke the unnatural calm I surround myself with to survive. In that moment, I became an animal trying to flee towards safety, even when safety was where they already were.

A harsh yank to my hair stops me in my tracks, jerking me backwards nearly a foot. Pain radiates around my skull, firing misery down my nerve pathways. Master Ez's hand tightens in my hair, wrapping and wrapping the two feet of red curls around his fist. I halt, suspended from his hand, toes barely finding purchase on my carpeting. The only sound I hear is my tortured gasps.

"Bad Kat!" A large hand swats my ass. Hard. The force rocks me back and forth, swinging from my hair. "Are you done? Can you think straight again?"

I'm stunned stupid for only a moment, and then an animal-like noise builds and rises from my throat just as the sting makes its presence known. Pain spreads across my ass to radiate up my back and down my thighs. Master Ez dwarfs me, with his hand the size of my entire ass. I should scream, cry, fight back, or run. Instead, I'm filled with shame and confusion as moisture runs down my inner thighs, and it's not the kind from fright. Mortified by my arousal, I quiver as Master Ez uses the length of my hair to control me– to dominate me.

"That was for trying to run, but more so to get you to calm down," Master Ez enunciates each word, making sure I can understand as I try to think with a foggy mind. "You will obey me, or you will be punished." His voice is stiff with barely leashed fury. "I do not enjoy punishing you, Katya. I am not a sadist. Your punishment is not for my sick entertainment. It is my way of educating you. That smack was to learn to control yourself, or else I will do it for you."

Master Ez hauls me to the bed by my hair, dropping me roughly because I pissed him off. I learn another lesson. Master Ez takes his moods out on whoever he's dominating. Obeying nets a calm master who will be affectionate, almost playful. Disobeying and freaking out nets you a manic master who will be rough and unkind.

In shock, mind spinning with emotions I don't trust, thoughts forming a puzzle from pieces that make no sense, I turn completely pliant. I'm Master Ez's to render in any fashion. He arranges me on the bed as he sees fit: flat on my back, legs stretched out comfortably, with my arms pulled taut but not restrained towards the headboard.

Bewildered by the influx of emotions I want to shut down, I lay completely taken over by the ache and sting in my body: a handprint is branded into my ass, the tops of my thighs, and my lower back, with my skull aching from my yanked hair. It hurts so badly tears threaten to spill from my eyes, but I'm a tougher bitch than that. I've lived through worse. Much worse.

"You wound me. I bear gifts and you try to run. That is unacceptable, Katya." His voice sounds hurt, and the tears are no longer a threat. I don't know this man at all, but some sick connection makes his dissatisfaction with me feel like a shot to the heart. Somehow Master Ez has entered my mind and warped my thought processes. The tears fall rapidly, dampening the sleep mask, as Master Ez's bitter displeasure rolls me over and takes me under.

Something soft and fuzzy is placed around my wrists– my gifts? Feather-light touches skid across my tender, inflamed skin. The soft mixed with the pain is a surprising sensation of pleasure, causing a ripple to flow up my spine.

Sounding beyond wry, "I see how tenacious you've been about removing my last gift. Katya, are you so desperate to be rid of me that you injure yourself in the process?" Hot breath touches my wrist. The blindness has my nerves on edge, causing every touch to feel ten times more potent. Soft lips flutter on my blistered flesh, and I whimper from the intense shudder that waves through me.

"I don't know," I breathe, answering his rhetorical question. "I don't think I'm ready to be owned by anyone, especially you."

Master Ez ignores my admission, opting to continue to manipulate me in the most effective way possible. "I'll kiss it and make it better," he purrs sweetly, voice holding a childlike edge, as if he is the one needing his pain kissed away.

The mattress dips as Master Ez crawls up onto the bed next to me. His warm body cuddles against my shoulder and hip, cradling me to his wide chest. A heavy thigh slides up and over my waist, pinning me, effectively trapping me in his embrace. A seeking hand slowly draws my injured wrist to his mouth. Slowly and seductively, he kisses my abused flesh as if it hurts him more than it's hurting me. I squeeze my eyes shut even though I wear a mask, trying to block the intense sensations wracking me. Each kiss breathes more life back into me, causing more long-dead emotions to erupt, making their presence known with brutal force. The cacophony roils and melds into mass confusion.

It's been too long.

It's been never.

When Master Ez opens up his mouth, a hot wash of breath sears my flesh, followed by a wet tongue tasting me.

I lose it.

A spontaneous moan rumbles up my throat and I arch up at the feel of Master Ez's soft tongue lapping at my sore skin. It's a pleasurable pain I've never experienced, and its sweet, first kiss is something I will never forget.

Evidently pleased with himself and me again, "Mmm,

responsive little kitty." His teeth pinch my raw skin and I yelp in pain. Pleasurable punishments. In a swift, effortless movement, he straddles my waist and sits on my hips.

"Katya, you and I need to have a talk." His voice is no longer smooth and calming. It holds an edge. He will not be denied. "You may not realize it, but you and I want the same thing."

"The truth?" spills defiantly out of my lips before I can stop it. I flinch, expecting to be '*educated*' for speaking my mind. Instead, Master Ez caresses my cheek with two fingertips, ending their path at the edge of my lips. He pulls away, releasing a long-suffering sigh, and I realize this is a habit of his.

"Yes," he agrees in a breath of a sound. "The truth. *Your* truth. We also want to get to know one another, but we cannot do that if we don't see each other."

Pressing my luck, "You just want to toy with me."

"Katya, that is not entirely true, nor is it fair. Yes, you and I play a game, and we both know what's the game and what is real life. I hope I'm not overestimating your intelligence," he manages to insult me while complimenting me. That is a rare talent.

"With that being said, when I tell you to do something, I expect you to damn well do it." Master Ez grips my wrist in his hand and squeezes until I whimper in pain. "What did I tell you to do, Katya?" He asks calmly, belying the vicious hold on my injury.

My mind races with thoughts. I'm ninety-nine percent positive Master Ez is Ezra Zeitler, but there is still the one percent to acknowledge. So the real question is, which one of those identities did I defy? What if they aren't the same person and I choose wrong?

Master Ez's hold on my arm has me on a precipice. The edge of pain is almost to the point of unbearable. A fingernail bites into my deepest cut, the one that occurred when the diamond blade slipped and gashed my wrist. The pain is growing, making it difficult to think. It's Master Ez's version of the Jeopardy theme song as he quickly loses his patience with me.

Thinking on the fly, I come to a decision. Regardless of whether or not Master Ez is Zeitler, he *is* Master Ez right this very moment. So, therefore, I must have defied him.

"I didn't meet you at Restraint this evening as you requested," I blurt out rapidly, hoping that even if I'm wrong, he'll take pity on me for answering quickly by releasing my wrist.

"Very good. Now, why didn't you show up?" Ever so slightly, he loosens his grip on my wrist as a reward for answering, but he keeps enough pressure on it to still cause a sharp edge of pain.

"I think I figured out who you are, and I think you know I know. Maybe I don't want to play this game." It sounds as if I'm mumbling nonsense because I cannot speak the rest of my thoughts.

Maybe I don't want to play this game with a man who has a fiancée, leaving me with the only recourse to either be a faithless whore for touching him, or to keep my ethics and be in a sexless relationship with my master. Maybe I don't want to play this game because I'm not strong enough to keep my head, let alone my ethics, when you're near me.

Leaning down, pressing his body along the length of mine, Master Ez draws my injured wrist to his lips again. "Hmm, are you sure you don't wish to play with me, Katya?"

More kisses soothe my abused wrist, and he chuckles against my skin when I jerk in response. The amused Master Ez is back. It lends to the fact that he is also the amused Mr. Zeitler. Both seem to think I'm entertaining as all hell. Who the fuck are they? And why did they choose me to play with?

Defiant, I make the decision to be respected, to respect his fiancée, even if it leads to an extended '*education*' at the hands of an angry master. "If you're who I think you are, then I would appreciate it if you didn't touch me intimately. I will not encroach on another woman's territory, even if it's through ignorance. If you touch me, and later on I find out you are exactly who I think you are, you will find out how I am not balanced."

Master Ez bellows the loudest laugh I've ever heard, his body shaking mine. "Katya. Katya. Katya. If only you knew how hilarious that sounded."

"It's not a joke, asshole," I growl, struggling to free myself with the intention of yanking the mask from my face and unmasking this motherfucker.

"Easy. Easy," Ez chants, trying to calm me. With a warning clench of his fingertips into my wrist, "I don't want to accidentally open up your wounds while trying to stop your struggles. I know what you meant, Kat. Not balanced: more dominant than submissive." Chuckling to himself again, "But you have to realize it sounded like you were threatening to murder me, as if you were emotionally unbalanced, as in crazy."

"Pretty sure I am," I breathe, but he hears me anyway.

"No matter who I am, my personal relationships with other people are of theirs and my concern, and you are to not spare it another thought. I will touch you any way I please, as long as it does not cause irreparable harm to your psyche."

"Being the other woman would make it so I couldn't look at myself in the mirror, or look my family in the eye," I grumble.

"Trust me, Katya. That isn't the situation we find ourselves in. You will never be my other woman." The amusement is back in his tone, as if I'm the brunt of an epic fail of a joke.

"As for irreparable harm to your psyche..." Master Ez pushes off of me to kneel by my side. "I don't even have to touch you to know you want me. I wish you and I could look one another in the face, so you could see what I see."

"Then let me take the mask off," I try for negotiating, but it comes off more as begging.

Ignoring me, "Your thighs are positively drenched. I can smell your arousal," I cringe in disgust when the words roll off his tongue. Master Ez's hand rests on my knee, slowly tugging up my nightgown, and then it takes a journey to my inner-thigh. It retreats before I can react or flinch.

I'm thankful that Master Ez didn't go *there*. I am not ready for *that*. Ethics are not my only barrier. I fear I'd freak the fuck out the instant I'm touched in a sexual manner.

A wet smacking sound draws my curiosity at the same time Master Ez erupts with a violent shudder, followed by a heavy sigh.

Sweet Jesus!

Master Ez isn't tasting what I think he's tasting, is he?

My body strings tight when I hear him rumble a throaty, "Lovely."

"I knew you wouldn't join me at Restraint this evening, Katya. You aren't one who submits easily, and I can respect that. But regardless, a command given yet ignored, is a command defied. Since you are so tenacious about removing your bracelet, I found a fitting punishment."

A soft hand places my left wrist in my right palm, reminding me of the gifts he brought this evening. I'd forgotten about everything and anything because Master Ez scrambles my brain.

Master Ez holds my finger, helping me '*see*' what he gave me as an '*educational*' tool. "Fitting, isn't? Admit it, Katya?"

My breath hisses out, a mix between awe and terror. "I have never met a more diabolical human being in my entire life, and I've known some really evil bastards."

"Thank you, Katya." Not sounding sarcastic in the least, Master Ez takes my insult as praise. "Two birds... one stone." Ez clutches my hands together in emphasis. "Punishment for not meeting me when I requested it so nicely and insurance that you will mind my next command performance."

On both of my wrists are leather cuffs. Ez keeps running a fingertip across the metal bands embedded into the leather, showing me the preventative measure he created to stop me from cutting them off. I'm sure the metal is the same mystery alloy as the bracelet chain: indestructible– unbreakable.

"I can't go to work like this. I had a hard enough time hiding the bracelet, let alone two leather and metal cuffs." My voice breaks and tears stream down my face– tears of frustration. Even if Master Ez is Zeitler, I can't get away with this. "My coworkers and clients will see the cuffs, and some may actually know what they mean. Don't do this to me, Master Ez. Please. I'll promise to obey you if you'll take them off."

"Sure you will," Ez sounds incredulous, not trusting me for a moment. In this case, he's correct. Nothing will stop me from attempting to remove whatever he locks on me.

"Kat, I will make a deal with you. If you arrive at Restraint tomorrow *and* obey me, I will remove them. Every time I request your presence, I will put them on, and then I will take them off at the end of the evening. Understood?" Master Ez sounds oh-so reasonable, not as if he using extortion tactics on me.

"Yes, but what about the bracelet?" I demand, the most reluctant switch on the face of the planet. I want to submit, when I want to submit, which defeats the purpose, doesn't it?

"No, I told you that will never come off." I recognize that sigh again— he's losing his patience. "I'm warning you, Katya. If you defy me again, I will show up wherever you are and slap these cuffs on your wrists, and then you will appreciate the anonymity of a flawless bracelet versus the obviousness of a submissive's cuffs. Got it?"

"Yes, sir," I meep out, scared shitless now.

"Go ahead and defy me, Katya. Go ahead and try to see what happens when you defile the cuffs like you did the bracelet," he warns. "They will become as permanent as a tattoo on your wrists. I won't give a fuck who sees you in the cuffs, because I want the world to know you're mine." He sounds more than half crazed, voice as sharp as broken glass. "It will be your pride that will get bent when you wear them in public, and it hurts me that you are not proud to be mine."

Uncomfortable with the ferocity of his erupting emotions, I blurt out as comic relief, "Laying the guilt on a bit thick, there, Master Ez."

"I understand there is an imbalance between us because you don't know me as well as I know you. This game is thrilling until it encroaches on reality. The cuffs and bracelet are NOT part of the game; they are your new reality. Have I made myself clear?" His body is thrumming from the force of the authority he is trying to press upon me.

The cuffs and bracelet aren't a part of the game because Master Ez is using them to control me. No one can control every aspect of a game, and he knows it. But if you can control the other player, then you control the game.

"Yes." Even as I say the word, ways to remove my new restraints flash through my head.

A painful hold on my injured arm releases a blood-curdling scream from my mouth. An iron grip surrounds my wounded wrist and painfully squeezes, fingernails biting into the gashes. I don't know what I've done to cause Master Ez to educate me, but it hurts like a sonofabitch. I whimper and writhe through the pain, regretting that I've gotten myself into this situation. I don't know if I can trust this side of Master Ez. In fact, I know I can't, which is a deal breaker.

Disgusted with me, Master Ez spits out, "You, twit!" He twists the word *twit* like it has some underlying meaning of heinousness. "You may be masked, but *I* can still see you. I know you're lying from the expressions that flashed across your face. I demand absolute truth between us, just as you want in return. So far, you've lied to me six times today. Not a very good start to our arrangement, now is it? You'll learn eventually." The tone in his voice screams that he's excited yet annoyed at the prospect of teaching me.

"You speak of truth, yet I know nothing of you: not your name, who you are, how you know me, why you picked me. I don't know what the fuck is going on. I know nothing," I hiss defiantly. "You punish me for things I don't even understand. You pulled me into this without ever explaining a thing to me, and you expect me to automatically trust you. You're full of shit," I rasp out quickly before I lose my nerve.

Losing his cool, Ez lunges from the bed. His voice comes from the distance across my bedroom. "Katya, goddamn you!"

Long moments pass while I stare at the utter blankness of the mask. The only sound I hear is Master Ez's labored breathing mirroring mine, and finally his sigh.

"Right now, you know all you need to know. I will keep you safe from harm: from others, myself, and especially from yourself. You know that you can trust me. Even if you deny it, you instinctively do."

"I don't trust myself right now, Master Ez," I admit. "I don't trust why I feel what I'm feeling. It's all too new, and I think it's safer to assume my instincts and intuition are broken."

"Trust me on this: we know each other very well, and for a lot longer than you think." Master Ez's voice softens. "Don't move. I'll be right back."

My heightened senses pick up the sound of his feet padding across my floor, and then the click of my bedroom door opening. I can even feel the caress of displaced air as a current flows in from my living room.

I comply. Something about witnessing Master Ez's control fracture made him seem more human, more trustworthy. It intrigues me. The naughty part of me wants to find out if I'm capable of breaking him again. The dominant part of me will do anything to see if I can make him submit, even if I have to bide my time by behaving.

Jesus, I'm fucked in the head.

Even quieter than a church mouse, being blinded means Master Ez still can't sneak up on me. All of my attention is on his near soundless steps and his musky scent wafting in my nostrils as he re-enters my bedroom.

"Good girl," Master Ez coos. "You obeyed me." His body invades my personal space again as he crawls onto the bed beside me. There is no such thing as personal or private with Master Ez.

Cool wetness spreads across my wrist, a soothing balm on my tortured flesh. Master Ez rubs the gel into my skin as he speaks. "It's aloe and antibiotic gel. It will soothe your burns and heal the cuts."

"Thank you," I breathe. "It feels better already," I admit, trying to hide the shudder that rolls along my spine. Master Ez's touch does wicked things to me, even when it hurts.

"You should know better than to mix water, petroleum, and chemical-based products together. I thought you were smarter than that, Katya," he chastises me. "But the evidence to the contrary is staring me in the face. I should let you suffer for your stupidity so you will learn."

"Did you go to catholic school, or something? You seem to be real big on corporal punishment," I mumble, not meaning it as a joke, but Master Ez's snicker says he took it that way.

"Good deduction, Katya. I went to private, and the nuns would beat the shit out of us. I converted to Judaism when I was fourteen, but my mother still forced me to go to Hillbrook Prep." Ez allows some of the real him to be revealed, and it warms me.

"That bit of my history was a reward. But now I want to know if you honestly believed I wouldn't put something far worse on your wrist if you manage to remove your bracelet?"

"I didn't think of that," I grumble, feeling like a stupid bitch. "You're right."

"Remember that phrase for the future, because it will always hold true," Master Ez warns, and I hope he's teasing. Voice laced with confusion, "For heaven's sake, Katya, you tried to destroy a custom-made piece of jewelry worth more than a hundred thousand dollars."

"What?" garbles out of my mouth as I digest what he just said.

Most women would hear the hundred thousand dollars' worth of jewelry and forget about everything else. They would go soft, and then submit to anything the man ever wanted, in hopes of catching a rich man to leach off of.

I'm not most women.

I can't be blinded by money and jewels. I sure as fuck would be happy to give this bracelet back now that I know its true value. Now I'm even more uncomfortable wearing it. But Master Ez won't let me return it. I didn't ask for it, and I feel ungrateful for not fawning all over Master Ez because it's on my wrist.

I've been given an unexpected souvenir by a complete and total stranger before, and there is always a lifelong cost to the recipient.

Right now, I can't even contemplate the bracelet that cost as much as my parents' house, because my mind is absorbed with another fact. What I want to know is, where the hell did this ointment came from? It wasn't in my lineup of goop, that's for damn sure.

"You've had a rough day," Master Ez says, thinking my lack of response is from something entirely different. "You can think in the morning. Let me care for you now." His voice is thick with affection.

Strong hands roll me over onto my stomach and lift my nightgown. I want to protest, but I know there is no sense. Master Ez sees me as his– his to do with whatever he pleases. After being shoved around my bedroom by my hair, having my ass slapped, and my wounded wrist aggravated, I decide to be compliant in fear that he will take further liberties I'm not willing to give. I'm a fast learner, and my education thus far has taught me to acquiesce to Master Ez's initial request, because if he has to ask twice, I will most certainly find what comes next more difficult to swallow.

Cold liquid pours onto my backside and shocks a grunt from me, beading my body with gooseflesh. The sweet scent invigorates my senses as it soothes my tender skin. It's an L: *Bath & Body Works* Lemon Vanilla body lotion. My favorite, and easily found in my apartment, unlike the mysterious ointment smeared across my wrist.

"I hope you don't mind, I borrowed this from your supplies on the kitchen counter," Master Ez says, almost as if he can read the spinning hamster wheel inside my mind. "Leave it to you to alphabetize your products. I normally would have warmed the lotion, but I thought your burning ass would appreciate the coolness."

"Fuck," I breathe, mind completely blanking out. I whimper and wiggle about. No man. No woman. No one. Has ever massaged me, especially my ass cheeks and thighs. I'm ashamed to admit that I make a sound that suspiciously sounds like I'm climaxing.

Two hands rub a delicious rhythm into my flesh, kneading and rolling along my backside. My eyes roll up into the back of my skull, my fingers and toes curl. I moan in agonizing pleasure because this is a first for me on so many levels:

intimacy, affection, being cared after. This is what I longed for, why I wanted a master. I have always been my family's rock. Even when I was broken, I had to be strong to care for those who needed me more than I needed them. Not once, until tonight, has someone shouldered my burdens, and I fear I will become addicted to the sensation.

I want to analyze the implications of a man touching me and expecting repayment, but as the pleasure begins to radiate throughout my body, I can't give a shit about anything except for his hands on my flesh.

Mind twisted from the past, I'm not entirely sure if this experience is the most intense pleasure or pain, but there is an erotic flavor to it that is hard to deny.

My throat and mouth are parched from panting and whimpering. Anticipating my needs, Ez tips a cup to my mouth. Mmm… ginger ale. Bliss. I savor the cool liquid as it flows down my throat and moistens my mouth. Yet another of my supplies pilfered from my kitchen. Master Ez sure did make himself at home.

Heavy hands grip my thighs, gently pulling them apart until my legs are separated. "Well, that answers a question for me. I wondered if your body's natural response to me would overpower your mind." He sounds pleased, and it confuses me even more.

Master Ez places his hands on the backs of my thighs, giving me a moment to acclimate to his touch, and then he slowly smooths his palms up to my ass. I have no idea why he's being so cautious, but my room is suddenly filled with the sound of our mingled gasps, as if we're both anticipating his next move.

As if in slow motion, either waiting for me to freak out or attack him, his thumbs slide inward, beneath the swell of my cheeks until they rest near my pussy lips. He flexes his thumbs, opening my private flesh to his sight. I freeze in fear, half-hoping and half-dreading that he will touch me *there*.

"Oh, Katya," Master Ez groans, evidently enjoying the view. "It seems my fear was misplaced. It was obvious you were aroused by me, but I thought your mind would conquer your body."

Master Ez doesn't move. He just holds my nether lips open to his gaze, and I can sense his eyes branding me. I whimper, a hunger flaring in my belly that has nothing to do with food, and it will go unsatisfied. His hands abruptly release my thighs, my legs snapping back together from their absence.

The lip-smacking noise floods my ears, and this time it's unmistakable what Master Ez is lapping up, causing him to shudder. Suddenly in tuned with his wants, my body produces more for him to taste.

Moods changing swifter than the second hand on a clock, Master Ez fists my aching hair, yanking my head backwards so he can easily rest his lips to my ear without bending down. "You will go to Restraint in the evening. The hour will be your choice. Understood?"

"Yes," I cry out in pain– pain from my pulled hair and from submitting to Master Ez's whims.

"Yes, what?" He growls at me, gripping my hair tighter, shaking my head a bit.

"Yes, Master," I reply dutifully, even if I hate myself for doing so. Worse, a part of me warmed to the sound of '*Yes, Master,*' rolling off my tongue.

"Lovely." His smoky voice hums. "I love the sound of that."

Going from punishing demands back to caregiver, a cloth manifests from the supplies he pilfered from around my apartment. With gentle thoroughness, Master Ez cleans my thighs and sweeps between my legs. I whimper from the contact, simultaneously feeling adored yet humiliated by the attention.

"No solo play. I will find out if you do." His voice takes on a new tenor– hunger.

I snort in response to Master Ez thinking I'll rub one out the second he leaves. I'll have no issue with that edict. I've never masturbated in my life. It wasn't from a lack of desire, knowhow, or trying, either.

My mind is so fogged and blissed out that I can't stop the idiotic words from spewing. "Thank you, Master. For the gifts.

For educating me. For taking care of me." After the words are out, I feel as if I've betrayed myself for saying them. I meant them, but they made me feel weak.

Master Ez settles his large body down the back of mine, reminiscent of when I was shoved against the door at Restraint. He suckles on my tattoo. Lips spread wide open, tongue tracing the letters of **Chrysalis**, he sucks at the marks he left behind last time.

Arms wrapped around me from behind in an affectionate embrace, he sounds content. "Anytime, Kitty Kat. Always." As the punctuation on his comment, he tenderly kisses my neck where he'd brutalized it.

"Is **E Z** your initials, a nickname, or something else?" I try to pull the truth from him.

"All of the above," he chuckles in amusement. "Still trying to get information out of me when you know I won't slip up. Impressive, Katya. Impressive." He hooks one finger beneath my chin to pull my face to the side. A soft kiss brushes my lips, musky yet sweet, tasting exactly like me.

"Be a good girl. I'll see you this evening. Sleep well, my Katya." Another innocent kiss, and then the heavy weight vanishes from my back, suddenly leaving me feeling empty and cold and alone.

***

Hours… or maybe ten minutes later, I find myself guzzling ginger ale straight from the bottle with the refrigerator door open for light. My body aches fiercely, and I'm ravenous. Not bothering to turn on a light, I grab a couple of *Advil*, the two liter bottle of *Canada Dry*, the cottage cheese, and a spoon. I sit down at the table, with my mind whirling.

Two things dominate my thoughts.

One: the ointment.

Two: Master Ez.

With our every encounter, he has yet to breach a sexual boundary. Not once have I touched him in return, nor has he expected it. Everything he has done has been to elicit a reaction out of me: he has commanded me, knowing I would not obey, only to educate me on why I should obey him initially, after which, he has taken care of me. Some of our interactions had sexual connotations, yet all were geared towards my desire directed at him, not our mutual attraction.

Ez's earlier words flow into my mind, taking on a whole new meaning. *"Trust me, Katya. That isn't the situation we find ourselves in. You will never be my other woman."*

It never occurred to me that it wasn't a matter of Master Ez controlling himself around me, that perhaps the desire wasn't mutual. I was arrogant in my thinking. Just because someone wants to meet your needs, take care of you, and guide you, doesn't mean you have anything to offer them in return beside your acquiescence.

I don't know if I should feel relieved, disappointed, or insulted over this new revelation.

I glance over at the counter, the light from the window over the sink lighting the area. All of my sharp implements and cutting edges are missing, presumably while Master Ez was shopping around my apartment. My lubrication lineup has an addition, in between **L** for lotion and **P** for petroleum jelly, stands **O** for ointment: the aloe and antibiotic ointment Master Ez had applied to my wrist. It took the sting out of my injured wrist, and the gesture lessens my annoyance at my missing items. But I still want to know where it came from, how he knew I needed it in the first place, and how he got it so fast.

I smirk in the shadowy darkness of my kitchen. I can't believe I let him touch me, and more so that I responded. I can't believe I didn't freak the fuck out. No matter what else happened, or will happen, conquering that fear is a major win for me.

I may be confused, feeling as if more is going on around me than I can explain, but I've never been one to back down from a challenge. I will uncover Master Ez's identity, with solid proof. I may not understand the game we play, why we play it, or why he chose to play it with me, but it doesn't matter.

I ache to win…

Restraint 112

Chapter Ten

Uncertainty coils in my stomach as I ride the elevator down to the lobby. Things look different in the bright of day. Choices you've made seem ridiculous as indecision plagues you. A small part of me wants to tuck tail and run back to Vacuum Valley, leaving all this insanity behind. But the larger part of me senses I'm on the precipice of a major change, and I owe it to myself to see it through.

I've felt extremely antsy since the wee hours of the morning: muscles knotted tightly, not able to concentrate on the simplest tasks, with my hands visibly shaking. I swear the butterflies in my tummy have grown fangs and claws. The anxiety is so wicked that the instrumental version of a Celine Dion classic makes me wish I'd taken seven flights of stairs instead of the elevator.

Gotta love Muzak.

I check my cuffs for the millionth time today, making sure they are hidden by my cloak. Master Ez is a master at something, all right. Manipulation. Extortion. Annoyance.

Taking a shower, hand-washing dishes, or anything involving water, is difficult while wearing leather strapped to your wrists. I learned my lessons well. Obey, or your life will be even more uncomfortable than it already is.

Master Ez has a lesson he needs to learn: I am **NOT** a submissive. My need to submit is a choice. The more he pushes me, the more I will push back. The more education I receive, the smarter I will become at thwarting his teaching techniques.

I tried to remove the cuffs and the bracelet all damned day without harming the priceless gifts, because to do nothing would be admitting defeat. I doubt Master Ez would respect me if I didn't make it a challenge. The padlocks are all the same: jimmy-proof.

As if taunting me, the padlocks, which costs more than my car, jangle against my hands with every step I take. Fiery licks of anger swiftly replace the worry coiled in my stomach.

I thought all day until my head throbbed with confusion. I finally admitted what I wanted, even if it was only to myself. Ez, whoever the hell he is, intrigues me, ignites my mind and body with the fire of lust, anger, admiration, and respect. I am proud that he is giving me attention, even if I don't understand why, and it has nothing to do with the size of his bank account or the chiseled edge of his jawline.

I just want Ez, like I've never wanted anything before.

I have a problem, because I'm not sure what his intentions are, or if I am strong enough to stick to my convictions and my code of ethics with his presence affecting me in devious ways.

I'm angry– angry at myself.

I'm almost positive that Master Ez is Ezra Zeitler, which means he's engaged, and I'm allowing him to touch me in sensual ways. It's still wrong, even if he doesn't allow me to touch him back. Even if he doesn't want me to touch him. It's wrong because I want to touch him– touch someone who isn't mine to possess.

Ezra Zeitler belongs to Adelaide Whittenhower, even if he thinks he owns me.

While blinded in Master Ez's presence, I have other senses to fall back on, by listening to his voice, remembering the feel of his skin and the shape of his body beneath my fingertips. His natural scent will never change, no matter how much fragrance he douses himself with. I'll have to study Zeitler when I get to work on Monday morning.

One phrase keeps playing on repeat within my mind: *why me*? Who cares if Master Ez is Ezra Zeitler? I do, but I think it's more important to wonder *why me*? What the hell does this man want from me? I'm willing to play along just to find that out.

As I exit the elevator, I pull my dark gray cape closed to prevent any of the residents of the building from seeing what I'm wearing. Mustn't have the natives seeing a dominatrix stride across the tile in their lobby. I'd be lying to myself if I denied why I dressed as I did this evening.

I *almost* want Master Ez to want me as badly as I want him. *Almost* because my ethics are rearing their logical heads.

I'm lost in thought, walking across the lobby, going towards the front doors. "Ma'am. Kat." A hand lands on my forearm, startling me, and I glare at its owner out of reflex. I almost lash out like a wounded animal. But thankfully I don't, because the owner's hand belongs to none other than Aaron Frost from Restraint.

Aaron looks guilty for touching me, and his hand disappears instantly, tucked behind his back like he was caught misbehaving. He flashes his dimples, looking like a little boy trapped inside a grown man's body.

"Oh. Hi, Aaron," I mutter, confused as to why he's stopping me in The Edge Building's lobby. "How are you doing tonight?"

"Ma'am," Aaron leans into my ear, but otherwise he doesn't touch me. "Kat, Ez requested that I accompany you to the club this evening." He sounds hesitant, as if anticipating how much it rankles to have Master Ez tell me what to do, especially through another person.

I walk right out the front doors, nodding to the security guard on my way by, and Aaron follows dutifully. When I start heading down the street towards Restraint, Aaron's sneaky hand makes a reappearance.

"Sorry... Sorry. Ez said I wasn't to touch you unless you wanted me to," Aaron explains why he keeps touching me, only to jerk his hand away as if my flesh burned his.

"It's fine, Aaron. Really. My family gives me constant affection when I'm home. It's not so much about being touched, as being touched by a stranger unexpectedly," I mutter dryly, wondering what else Aaron knows about me.

I turn right, squeezing between a group of people headed in the opposite direction as me. It's a bright, clear night, and the atmosphere is delightful for a short walk.

"Kat," Aaron says, reaching for me again, but he doesn't make contact. "I'm to drive you." He flashes me a bashful grin and hides his hands behind his back again, like he can't help himself. He's so dang cute that I try not to laugh.

"Let's walk." I manage not to pout, but just barely, because I can tell Aaron will never disobey Master Ez. "It's only four blocks. It's beautiful out tonight."

"Ez loves being outside, too," Aaron says fondly, affection thick in his voice. "He spends most of his time in the woods surrounding his family's estate. He and…"

I arch a brow, not moving, barely breathing, scared Aaron will realize he's spilling his master's secrets if I make my presence known. Catching himself, Aaron doesn't continue on his train of thought.

"Katya, I have to take you by car, because at the end of the evening you may need assistance to stand, let alone walk four blocks." Aaron's statement and expression frightens me to my core. He looks scared, too. For me.

I reluctantly follow Aaron towards a large, black SUV idling at the curb. I walk on stiff legs, worrying that I'm making a *'too stupid to live'* mistake. The kind of mistake women make that leads them on a path of violation and humiliation, where they end up wounded or dead. My self-preservation finally kicks in when Aaron closes the backseat passenger door after I've settled myself on the buttery leather seat.

The click of the child-safety locks engaging has my heart beating into hyper-drive and sweat beading on my forehead. The panic dissipates as quickly as it flashed over me when Master Ez's scent fills my nostrils.

Aaron may be driving this SUV, but it's Ez's vehicle.

I don't know Aaron from Adam, and he is a huge dude who could easily harm me. But size isn't always an issue, seeing as how I was attacked by boys not much bigger than myself. Knowing Master Ez trusts Aaron puts me slightly at ease. The only real comfort I feel comes from the fact that my instincts are telling me that Aaron is a sweetheart. But I'm sure there must be sweetheart sociopaths lurking in the world somewhere.

Uncomfortable, I wiggle around the seat as Aaron pulls the vehicle away from the curb. "So, tell me, how does Restraint's bouncer end up being my chauffeur for the evening?"

Aaron's bright blue eyes gaze at me in the rearview

mirror. "I'm Ez's personal assistant, driver, bodyguard, and whatever else he may wish me to do." Aaron speaks as he navigates through traffic.

"Are you his assistant day and night?" I prod, eager for anything that could give me a clue.

"Yes, Katya. I am." Aaron rumbles a hardy laugh– a pleasantly warm sound. "Nope, that isn't going to help you figure out who Master Ez is, either. Seeing as I am with him night and day, I know all of his secrets, which means I know yours."

"Well, that's just great," I mutter sarcastically. But curiosity wins out over irritation. "How the hell do you find any time for yourself if you're always wiping his ass?"

"Such a way with words for a book publisher," Aaron teases me, grinning in the rearview mirror. "Truthfully, the only life I have is the one Ez gives me. But I do have time to myself so I can concentrate on Restraint. I don't know if you met him or not, but Roarke Walden, the other big guy milling around the club, we split our time watching Ez's back."

"Ah, I remember '*I'm not Aaron Frost*,'" I breathe, as if Aaron gave me a usable clue, when we both know very well he didn't. "So, Ez must be pretty important to have constant security." Aaron ignores me, so I try a new tactic. I can tell Aaron is highly intelligent, but maybe he'll slip up. "Um, are you Master Ez's sub?" Jealousy stirs in my blood from the thought, and I have no idea why it bubbled up.

"Nope. It's not like that for us. Ez and I are more like family." Aaron says hesitantly, as if he's worried he's saying too much. "I serve Ez faithfully in everyday affairs, but at the end of the day, he's more like a big brother to me. I've been with him for fifteen years."

My eyebrows pinch together as I ponder Aaron's admission. The reverent quality in his tone speaks volumes. No one gains that level of adoration if they are a piece of shit. So far from what I've seen by the loyalty of Aaron, Queen, Fate, and Kris, Master Ez is an incredible human being worthy of respect. If he truly is Ezra Zeitler, then he has Kayla and Monica's fealty as well.

"Does Master Ez have a submissive? Another switch?" I coax.

But what I really want to ask, is how much competition do I have? Not because I worry that I'll have to compare to these other faceless minions. It's more like having more than one wife. The first wife is bound to hate the newest one. I'd like to know if I have to protect my ass from Master Ez's jealous submissives. I guess if you're as bored and rich as Master Ez, you can make your own rules and have as many submissives as you wish.

"That's hard to explain, really. Master Ez sees himself as the boss of all of us. Except for his father, Marcus is the only person who can make Ez do anything. I'm not sure how to answer this, Katya."

"Try," the order is barely a breath, I'm so eager to learn all I can, and Aaron has told me more in a few minutes than I've learned in a month since I arrived in Dominion.

"Master Ez has no traditional submissive. He has people he cares for. If anything, I'd say he has two people he himself would place in that role." Aaron parks the SUV in an underground parking garage. He stares at me in the rearview mirror for a few moments. "Both of whom are stubborn fools."

I scoff. "Are you calling me a fool, Aaron?"

"I'm glad to see you found the courage to admit that," Aaron says, grinning.

"Wait! What?" I stammer out. "Admit I'm a fool, stubborn, or Master Ez's property?"

His wide, toothy grin is the only answer I receive. "Master Ez has a submissive he provides for us," Aaron supplies instead. "But never for himself."

"Us?" I prompt.

I feel more special by the second. Master Ez is a collector, hoarding people as if they are his property, most likely getting off on the power he wields over them. I try to feel bitter about that, but if a man can take dominion over that many individuals, then he earned the respect. I just worry about the soul-crushing sensation when Master Ez trades me in for a new acquisition, and how low I will feel when he keeps me around to chauffeur them about. Yeah, that's the way to make someone feel special, Master Ez.

"Katya," Aaron breaks into my depressing thoughts. "I don't like the emotions flashing across your face right now."

"I can't help how I feel, Aaron," I mutter, no doubt looking crestfallen.

Aaron slides from the driver's seat, exiting the vehicle. He leans back into the SUV and says, "It's not so much how you're feeling, Katya, but why you're feeling that way."

I go to respond just as the passenger door opens opposite me, revealing Aaron's immense body. Illogical panic overcomes me when Aaron crawls inside the SUV. Well over six feet, with the strength to bench-press small cars, my subconscious mind is terrified of him. He's no longer Aaron, he's a man who could harm me.

Aaron joining me in a confined space sets off warning alarms inside my psyche. I reach for the door handle on instinct, only to find it locked. I curse the creator of child safety locks. An animalistic sound erupts from my throat when I recognize my capture.

"What are you doing?" the words come out quivery, breaking. In a panic to bolt from the SUV, I fuse myself to the door. I look out the heavily tinted window, trying to find an escape route. My mind spins, trying to protect me. My heartbeat is in my throat, filling my ears with the da-dum... da-dum... da-dum. A feverish chill washes through me as the nightmarish memories of my attack threaten to overtake me.

It's illogical to think Aaron wants to harm me, but my mind doesn't give a shit. I go into survival-mode, body shutting down as my mind goes on red-alert.

We're in an underground parking garage, with only a few cars scattered about and absolutely no people. No one to hear me scream, and no one would ever see through the tint on this window as Aaron annihilates me. I prepare to defend myself: knees raising to my chest, feet jutting out to deliver a kick, fingers curling into fists, lungs filling to lend me strength.

When flight is no longer a viable option, and you refuse to surrender, fight is what will keep you alive. "No, don't," I plead, raising my forearms to protect my face.

"Katya, no. Please. It's Aaron. I'd never hurt you, Kat. Never." Palms raised to show me he means no harm, Aaron's expression is agonized because I'm terrified of him, and that is a travesty. The thought of making Aaron sad quiets me some. "Kat. It's me. You have to calm down, or else I'll have to go get Ez."

Jolting, the world sharpens, clears, and I realize I'm freaking out for no logical reason. Shame washes over me. "I'm okay, Aaron. Don't get Master Ez," I mumble, on the verge of tears. "I don't want him to see me as weak. Please, don't tell him I freaked out."

Aaron leans forward, the warmth radiating from his body crowding me, yet he makes no move to touch me. "Kat, this is no way to live, for anyone. Believe me, I understand. There are nights I lock myself in my closet to feel safe."

"What?" I mouth, confused.

"I won't go get Ez on one condition, but know I will be informing him of what just went down. He has to know so he can help you."

"No," I whimper, devastated at the thought of Ez being disappointed in me. "Please, Aaron."

"Listen, Kat. The quicker you do what I ask, the quicker we can get you out of this SUV and up to Ez, where you'll have some room to roam."

"Do what?" I mumble, still not thinking clearly as the panic dissipates.

"I have to place a mask on you since I'm taking you directly to Master Ez." Aaron is calm and relaxed, no-nonsense. His body language emanates how he means me no harm.

My anxiety doesn't give a shit about Aaron's calm body language. My anxiety isn't logical. My anxiety was stalked by three boys and their leader, dragged to the ground and gang raped, and then left for dead. My anxiety is irrational because it's protecting me, because I won't survive if it happens again inside this car in a deserted, underground parking garage.

"Why can't I see?" My voice squeaks as my fingers try to

yank open the door handle, but my sweat-slickened palm slips off the metal. My lips quiver and I whimper like a scared animal. I curl up around myself, rocking back and forth.

I want Ez.

I need Ez.

"Katya," Aaron says with surprising strength, answering what I thought was silent. "The sooner you put the mask on, the faster I can get you to Ez."

Mind and body completely acting on instinct, I agree with Aaron. I want out of this car. If I put the mask on, I get out of this car. That sounds fair to me. "Give it to me. I'll put it on myself," I snap.

A leather mask drops into my lap. "Look it over. It's your permanent mask. I'll put it on you when you're ready." Aaron slumps in the seat, prepared for a long wait.

I finger the small, fur-lined, black leather mask. It's shaped to fit over my eyes, rest on my nose, and to meet my hairline. It reminds me of a masquerade mask. The eyes aren't cut out; they are painted with perfect, green replicas of my eyes.

If I wasn't already freaked out, I'd find this situation creepy.

I hand the mask back to Aaron, ready to be blinded. The last thing I see before Aaron gently fits it to my face, is his boyish, shy smile, rewarding me for my compliance.

"I'm sorry for how I behaved," I murmur to Aaron, ashamed. "This is extremely comfortable," I say of my latest gift, causing Aaron to snort. "Ez managed to measure my face, just as he did my wrists. Didn't he?"

"He's Ez, what do you think?" Aaron takes my hand, no longer reluctant to touch me, because from this moment on, he's my eyes for the evening.

Restraint 122

Chapter Eleven

I used the awkward, dark walk from the garage to Master Ez's office to center myself. Aaron is a gentleman, somehow walking me through Restraint without coming into direct contact with other patrons. Of course, he was acting like I was about to self-destruct, chatting with me about inane things: his buddy Roarke is obsessed with Farmville. Kristal is a sex addict. Queen is a workaholic. The majority of Restraint's membership has their hands in finance because they're addicted to green and power, including the sweet, submissive Fate. The heiress his mother works for married a man only a few years older than her own son— he called this woman a vicious cougar. Someone named Cort— who Aaron seemed to be extremely annoyed by, judging by the cadence of his voice when he spoke of him —binge-eats when he thinks no one is watching, because he sees himself as pudgy even though he's thin. Aaron went on and on about this Cort fella, saying it's the highlight of his day to call him *Piggy*.

Aaron is surprisingly open and honest, highly observant, and a little bit evil and jealous. But it's too bad he steers clear of all subject matter pertaining to Master Ez.

Speaking of Master Ez, when we got to his office, he wasn't there. So Aaron left me to my own devices, promising to torture me if I took the mask off my face. Behaving, because I don't have the energy to do otherwise, I've sat in this chair for the past two-hundred-ninety-four seconds, if my calculations are correct.

Distracting myself, refusing to delve into why I freaked out on Aaron, I skim my hands up and down the arms of the chair I'm sitting in. It feels similar to the sofa and guest seating in my office, which is exactly the same as my living room furniture. It's so discombobulating. If I hadn't gotten out of the SUV in a parking garage I'd never been in, I'd swear I was back in The Edge Building. Must be when Master Ez picks out furnishings, he sticks with a theme. I concentrate on the soft microfiber rubbing against my palms as I try to erase my fears, and I don't need the aid of sight to know it's gray.

Sensory deprivation is the shit. My touch and hearing have heightened just by blocking out sight. It uncomfortable to be blind after using my vision as my primary sense for thirty-two years. But after two minutes of getting acclimated to my surroundings, I can hear sounds outside the room, and I can feel the kiss of air against my skin as the door opens.

Master Ez doesn't sneak up on me because I can hear his approach, as well as smell his addictive scent. So I don't flinch or squeak when he finally speaks.

"You look lovely this evening, Katya," Ez's voice is warm and affectionate.

I'm too relieved to hear his voice after my freak-out in the car, and it worries me on how dependent I've become on him already. I have to stay strong to take care of myself and my family. If I grow too dependent on someone and they fail me, or worse, betray or leave me, then I'm starting out at rock bottom again. I fear Master Ez will weaken me, which would create a disaster when he tosses me away in favor of his next challenge.

"Thank you, sir," I mutter bashfully. I'm sure Aaron tattled on me. I blush bright red, mortified.

Something draws my attention, perhaps my intuition. I tilt my head to the side, trying to home in on the movement around me. There are two people in here with me. I can sense it.

"Is Aaron with you, sir?" I ask unsteadily, unsure if I'm allowed to voice questions or if I'm only allowed to speak when spoken to. Master Ez really is on the '*know as you go*' plan– a plan I despise. But I'm too raw right now to battle him.

"No, Kitty Kat. Aaron had to get back to his duties. You're very observant," he praises, and I try not to allow it to affect me. "I brought you another gift." Master Ez's voice twists with wicked amusement. My stomach clenches in frightful anticipation. His gifts scare the shit out of me.

Voice dripping with sarcasm, "Thank you for the mask." I gesture at the leather covering my face, and the movement rattles the padlocks swinging from my wrists. "I cannot *wait* for another one of your gifts."

A soft snort fills the air. But, otherwise, Ez doesn't comment on my obvious lack of respect for his *kind* gestures. "Pet, please go sit at my desk," Master Ez gently commands the unknown person in the room. "I'll introduce you later."

My mind spins furiously, working out who's in the room with us. At first, I thought Aaron was speaking of inane things, having absolutely nothing to do with Master Ez. But one of my favorite pastimes flashed in my mind only a moment ago.

When I was in high school, my math teacher would pass out logic puzzle to sharpen our comprehension. It was something I did poorly at, so I practiced and practiced until I could solve the puzzles that even stumped my teacher. When I first started, I'd go right for the list of clues, filling in the grid with the information, and then I'd give up when I couldn't connect it all. As I became more proficient, I realized the introduction was much more valuable, hiding the relevant information within the extraneous.

Aaron was doing the exact same thing during our car ride and the walk inside Restraint. I realize he was offering me clues like in a logic puzzle, leaving me to sort out the information. No doubt he was talking around whatever Master Ez ordered him to keep quiet.

That leaves only one of two possibilities: the person sitting at Master Ez's desk is either the stubborn fool who is my counterpart, or the submissive who Aaron said was for *us*. Whoever *us* is.

Startling me from my thoughts, "Stand, Katya." Master Ez's hands grasp my upper arms to pull me from the chair before I can even register his request.

"I'm so glad you obeyed. I was worried that I'd have to educate you." I want to inform Master Ez that I didn't obey because he did it for me. "Thank you," flutters softly against my mouth.

Supple lips meet mine, a tender press of a kiss, jolting me as if shocked. When I don't immediately respond to Master Ez's attentions, a sharp tug pulls on my bottom lip– his teeth, not coaxing me but demanding me to kiss him back. I should clench my lips and deny him, but I cannot. My mouth gives beneath his, and shamefully responds to his every request.

Master Ez greets me with a kiss. It's soft, hesitant– untried. I expected passion and ferocity from him, punishing brutality, not the gentle brushes of affection I receive. There's almost a sense that the touch is platonic, familial, as if I'm something he takes care of, like a pet or child. But it's edged with a deeper, darker emotion I cannot fathom.

"Let us see how you're dressed, shall we?" he murmurs quietly to himself as his fingertips deftly untie my cape. I hear the fabric snap and feel the flush of air as the cape moves from my shoulders.

I dressed for myself this evening, for my protection as usual. My version of armor, I'm wearing a bodysuit beneath my bustier and trousers. It's something I began doing long ago. Even if someone manages to get beneath my clothing, they'd have to go through another layer before finding my flesh. In preparation for Restraint, knowing enticement is part of the game we play, my bodysuit is sleeveless with thin straps, showing however much cleavage I want my pushup bra to showcase.

For Master Ez's benefit, or perhaps because I'm curious to know whether or not the attraction is mutual, I'm dressed more salaciously than usual, but still more conservatively than most. I paired my bodysuit with skin-tight, black pants and a gray bustier that pushes my tits up so high I fear they will hit my chin.

Standing as still as a statue, I endure my master's touches. Touch is a foreign concept for me, even when it's my family members getting inside my personal space while we stand side-by-side at the kitchen stove while cooking. A hug is fleeting, easily endured because it's only a second of contact. Otherwise, I'm always the one in control, the one choosing who and how I touch, never allowing the affection or intimacy to be returned.

It's an unnerving sensation to stand here while being caressed by Master Ez, and knowing the tables have turned and I will not be invited to touch him back. My mind forms words like pawed, groped, violated, and molested. But that is just my fears speaking. He touches me with calming caresses meant to connect us, not divide us.

I'm way out of my comfort zone, heartbeat lodged firmly in my throat. Sensing my discomfort, Master Ez cups my neck in his warm palms and strokes soothing circles on my skin. As I relax and respond to his caresses, my lips part on a breathy moan and my eyelids flutter beneath the mask from the disturbing pleasure of his touch.

"Ah, Kitten. Never fear. I will never harm you." His breath cascades over my face, tickling my nose. I catalogue minty on Master Ez's list of attributes to compare to Ezra Zeitler on Monday morning.

Hands disappearing from my body, a moment later Master Ez is efficiently placing something in my hair. Hardness slides down the sides of my head to rest just behind my ears. Automatically, I lift my hand to feel it out.

Shaking my head in utter disbelief, "Seriously?" Even though I can't see, I scowl up at him while my mouth twists into a frown.

"So unappreciative. Will you always insult your gifts?" His voice is laced with amusement, not offense. Amused goes onto the Master Ez is Ezra Zeitler list. Gift-giving diabolical bastard from Hell goes onto Master Ez's list.

"Your gifts scare me," I grumble. "They're never for my benefit." That earns me a chuckle.

"What fun are your toys if you can't trick them out?" He reaches over to straighten my '*gift*'.

Master Ez's newest acquisition is tricked-out with a pair of kitten ears attached to a headband. The Boss has me thinking in third person already. Not a good sign.

"Beware: your toys may play back," I threaten him, followed by a mock-hiss to bare my fangs.

"Oh, of that I have very little doubt, Kitty Kat." His voice drops deep, and I know he's dreaming of me fighting back, followed by the level of education he will provide.

Hands clasping my shoulders, Master Ez pushes me back down until my ass hits the chair cushion. He stands behind me with his hands still on my shoulders, his fingers inching towards my breasts. Under no conscious command of mine, my breathing picks up, causing my chest to rapidly rise and fall. You'd think my breasts were trying to meet his hands halfway or something.

"Pet, come meet your mistress." Master Ez commands the unknown person in the room as his hands tighten on my shoulders, rendering me completely immobile.

Ez leans down to whisper in my ear, his hair tickling my cheek. "Our pet was the first gift I ever gave you. Your restraint is remarkable to resist such constant temptation."

"What?" I garble.

A loud sigh flutters the hair on the top of my head as he pulls away. I know what that habit signifies, he's about to turn mercurial on my ass because I've disappointed him somehow, or thwarted him, or confused him.

"I thought you'd appreciate the fact that I'm making sure all of your needs are met. Not many dominants would allow their subordinates access to a highly trained submissive. Being a switch, I'm trying to provide for all of your needs."

Behind me, his fingers tighten on my shoulders, fingertips just this side of bruising, as if he's getting angrier by the second.

Voice warping as he mocks me, "*What? What, she asks.* Katya, I'm introducing you to our submissive. Really, even you can't be that daft," he snaps.

Master Ez's impatience and the attitude he is radiating, have the opposite effect on me from what he thought to achieve. I'm sure I was to swoon from the care he was giving me, from the thought he put into taking care of me, but it angers me instead.

Sounding ungrateful, even to my own ears, I spew, "Shouldn't I get to choose? Wait. Forget that I even asked, since you didn't let me choose my own master, either."

Controlling, ego-maniacal man with a god complex also goes onto the Master Ez list.

"Hmm…" Ez hums, but it comes out sounding more like a low growl. "You act so grateful when trapped. If *we* were to wait for Katya Evangeline Waters to make a choice about anything, *we*'d be dead. The only reason you are a switch and not a dominant is because you are so fucking stubborn that you refuse to take what you really want when you want it."

"You don't know me!" I shout, body stringing tight to bolt from the chair.

Close to snapping, Ez tightens his hold on my shoulders, not so much squeezing as pressing me down into the chair cushion. "You feel comfort in having a decision taken out of your hands, even if you pretend you don't. You want total control over everything except for things that are uncomfortable. It makes it easier to sleep at night, to look in the mirror, to hold Max and Clara Waters' gaze, if someone else is responsible for the hard shit. *It wasn't my fault,*" Ez mimics in a girly voice.

"Cocksucker!" I snarl, trying to free myself from the chair.

"Instead of waiting until we're long dead in our graves, I'm taking the choice from you, and giving you exactly what you need. You've been fighting me tooth and nail the entire time, just as I knew you would. Nothing you do surprises me. What would surprise me, is if you'd just do as I asked the first time, and save us all of a lot of strife."

"You're a complete and total fucking stranger to me, *Master Ez,*" I twist his name because it's not his name.

"Keep telling yourself that, sweetheart, if it makes you sleep better at night. But while you're at it, trust yourself enough to recognize me when you see me."

The more sense Ez makes, the more I thrash in my seat. Roughly wrenching my head back by my hair, he stops my fit in an instant, calming me through the clarity of pain like he owns me.

"I hate you!" I scream, voice projecting violently. But I don't hate Ez, I hate how I respond to him.

"No, you don't. But you should." He releases my hair, smoothing it, taking the sting from my burning scalp. "Do you trust me?" He whispers, freezing behind me, awaiting my response.

"Yes, dammit all to Hell!" I yell, exhausting myself. Then I breathe out, "Fuck if I know why, though."

"You should listen to that inner voice of yours more often, Katya. We are more animal than man, but those who think it uncivilized to use our baser instincts and intuition have brainwashed it out of us. If you pause and try to reason out why you think and feel as you do, instead of just reacting, you will miss the inherent truth of every situation."

Drawing in a deep breath, I close my eyes behind my mask in defeat. "I know. You're right. Why does every single one of our interactions feel as if I'm in a never-ending therapy session? I know you know I had a breakdown in the parking garage. Right or not, can't you give this girl a friggin' break?"

Sighing heavily behind me, Ez leans down, arms enveloping me in an embrace. "Many apologies, Katya. While I frustrate you beyond measure, you manage to get so firmly beneath my skin, that not only do I bend, I snap. I hadn't meant to shout at you, belittle you, or punish you."

"I bring the worst out of you because I'm toxic," I mutter, close to tears. Last night I felt vindicated when I forced Master Ez to break. Tonight I feel disgusted with myself.

"Katya… Katya… Katya," he murmurs against my cheek, and then he presses his lips to the corner of my mouth. Pulling away, he says, "To have such passion when it comes to emotion, means overwhelming passion in all areas of your life. It isn't necessarily a bad thing. Only one other person can make me lash out like I just did."

"I deserve a stubborn fool award, I guess," I ramble, remembering what Aaron had said to me in the SUV.

"I don't like this self-deprecating side of you, Katya. Some may call it stubborn, but I adore that you challenge me."

I release a series of snorts that turn into humorless laughter. "Well, that's perfect, then," flows sarcastically from my lips.

"I think we should start over, now that we've blown off some steam by screaming." Ez massages my shoulders, fingers biting deep into the muscles. I slump back into the cushion, exhausted. "Since we previously established that you trust me," Ez says wryly, a satisfied smirk evident in his voice. "I anticipated what you'd need in a submissive, and she's absolutely perfect for you." Pride and pleasure infuse his voice.

Feeling like an ungrateful bitch, "I'm sorry, Master. Thank you." Taking in a few more gasps of breath, I let the words rush out in a torrent. "Whoever you may be, I apologize for acting like a lunatic. I shouldn't have gone off like that… with witnesses," I add, muttering.

"Oh, yes. Because going postal in private is so much better," Ez turns into a sarcastic ass. "Unless you're in the commission of a crime. If so, please do so in private, as witnesses do present an unavoidable obstacle."

Confused at the odd tone in Master Ez's voice, I ask, "You're not being ironic anymore, are you?"

Ignoring me, "Come, Pet. Introduce yourself," Master Ez coaxes.

Restraint 132

Chapter Twelve

"Now, Katya, just listen to the sound of my voice," Ez chants. "You are perfectly safe. I will allow no harm to befall you, especially mentally. I understand why you were so frightened in my car this evening, which is exactly why I procured a female submissive for you. She's a good girl, kind, gracious, highly attentive. She always does as she's told."

"So, you found someone my complete and total opposite, is what you're saying, then," I grumble as comedic relief, feeling uncomfortable.

"I should hope so, Kat. To truly be dominant, means you are equipped to lead. To truly be submissive, means you trust your instincts enough to know who to follow. Neither is better or worse. It's simply a delicate balance. For without it, the world would be in utter chaos."

"What about…" I trail off, suddenly feeling out of place, especially in the world at large.

"A switch?" Ez reads my mind. "A dominant's greatest flaw is pride, while a submissive's is insecurity. Too much of either is a disaster. There aren't enough people walking this planet who have the ability to lead, while also knowing when to ask for help. Last we spoke, you said you weren't balanced because you weren't one or the other. Katya, you are the epitome of balance, as long as you don't allow your pride and insecurity to overpower your natural instincts.

"Now, Pet, please kneel in front of Katya. Be mindful of touching, please." Master Ez's tone is as smooth as silk, as if he's trying very hard to accommodate my worst fears, and it makes me respect him more. It makes me wonder how he knows me so well, how he reads me as if I'm speaking my thoughts aloud.

Senses hyper-alert, my skin is sensitive enough to feel the displaced air around me as the submissive moves to crouch in front of me. I can even hear her breathing. She's calm, as if my earlier outburst didn't bother her in the least.

"Pet, please rest your hand on Katya's knee," Ez

commands, causing panic to bubble up my throat.

"Wait!" I fling my hand in front of me to ward the girl off. My body starts to tremble as fear screams through me. "No touch! Not yet."

"Hmm, touch doesn't seem to be a problem when it's mine." Master Ez's hands slide from my shoulders, towards my breasts as he stands behind my seat. I suck in a sharp breath when his fingertips dip beneath my bustier, then the edge of the bodysuit, and sneak into my bra. His palms are filled with a handful of my large breasts.

I stop breathing. My heart begins to pound a furious beat. I don't dare move, unsure if I want this or if I don't. I'm so very frightened that I do want Master Ez to touch me– touch me everywhere. I think I'm more petrified by the fact that I am not freaking out as he caresses my breasts, manipulating them with his fingertips, rubbing his warm palms over my swelling nipples.

No one has touched my naked breasts but my doctor, not even during my rape. Mind spinning out of control, I don't even think twice about the small hand resting on my knee, doing as she was told to do, like a good girl.

"Pet is now going to massage your legs from the knees down. Think of it as a reward for working through so much tonight, and as a way to get acclimated to casual touching. Intimacy is one of your largest roadblocks, and we will hurdle that beginning tonight."

"Why do you keep talking like this is therapy?" I squeak out.

Master Ez doesn't respond. He simply begins to hum a classical piece while molesting my breasts. It's not overtly sexual, more like clinical. It's as if he knows it's unnerving me, and he wants me to become desensitized.

The girl, woman, submissive, I refuse to even call her *Pet* in my mind, seems perfectly contented to massage my calf muscles, fingertips biting deep, finding the hidden tension.

"This is so... odd," I grumble, and then a moan is torn from my throat. Ez grips my nipples between his fingers, twisting and tweaking, shooting sparks down my spine to pool in my womb. Humming, Ez plays me like an instrument, and the music he makes is lust-filled and confused.

"Casual touch is fine now, yes?" Master Ez preens into my ear, slumping forward, allowing his hands to slide deeper into my bodysuit, fingers teasing my belly.

"Your definition of casual, sure as fuck doesn't mirror mine." My voice comes thick and raspy. "I'm always the one doing the touching."

"The point was for you to hand your control over to me, Katya. The reason Pet is with us, is so that you may touch when I grant you the pleasure." Pulling back slightly, his hands slide back up to cup my breasts, palms rubbing my sensitive nipples. I wiggle around, pretending I'm not responding to their combined efforts.

"Pet and I have already discussed limits. Katya, we will push those limits," Ez warns in a slippery smooth tone. To accentuate his point, his hands squeeze tightly, tearing a gasp from my throat.

Fingers tightening and tightening and tightening, fear coils in my stomach to mix with the potent lust in my core. The sting edges into agonizing pain, but my mind is twisted, interpreting the sensation as pleasure, causing my pussy to weep and clench as his fingers press even harder.

To stop a further threat and assault from Master Ez, I decide to introduce myself to the submissive. "Nice to meet you… um?" I hold out my hand to shake and wait for her to fill in the blank.

"Nice deflection," Ez rumbles in my ear, chuckling softly to himself.

A soft, feminine hand settles into mine, slightly larger than my own. She doesn't shake, she just clasps our hands together and doesn't say a word.

Creepy.

"Pet isn't to speak as you aren't to see." Ez's voice is ominous in my ear.

"Ever?" A flash of fear strikes at the thought of never seeing Master Ez's face or hearing the submissive's voice.

"Katya, really?" The tone in his voice takes on the note of

a dramatic eye roll. "You can see me as soon as you identify who I am, and I don't just mean my name. I mean who I am to you. We will still keep the mask for playtime. My instincts tell me that you may grow fond of sensory deprivation. As for Pet's lack of a voice, that is part of our game we play. Her identity is tied to mine… so...."

"I know exactly who she is, don't I?" My voice pitches with excitement. "That's why I can't see her or hear her voice. I'd recognize it and her. But if that's the case, why aren't you nervous that I'll recognize your voice, too?"

"Ah, I feared that at first. But I'm the Boss for a reason. My tone changes to match my mood. My everyday voice is not the same as when I'm Master Ez. However, Pet's voice is very distinct."

"I… um… what? How the hell does your voice change?" I stumble over my words as the implications of what Ez just admitted sink in.

"Enough talking. It's time for you to get properly acquainted." His voice was firm, an order.

Kneeling at my feet, Pet leans against my calves, doing as her master bid. Her hands roam my thighs and over my hips. I shove back the feeling of powerlessness, knowing I need to do this to heal.

My hands move on Master Ez's command, no thought necessary because he wraps his fingers around my wrist cuffs and physically moves me like a sadistic puppeteer.

I'd hate to admit it, but Ez truly does know me all too well. I hesitated on his command, just like he knew I would. So like a seasoned dominant, he took control of my person.

Velvety soft skin slides beneath my fingertips as Ez navigates my hands. When my palms make contact with her neck and face, I begin to touch her in earnest, eager to learn her identity. With my surrender, Ez relinquishes his control over me and falls back.

As a blind person does, I use my fingertips to see. Hesitantly, I stroke her creamy skin, imprinting her facial features into my mind's eye. Her mouth opens on a moan as my fingers pass her pouty lips.

"Good girl," Master Ez praises. "She's been extremely frustrated while waiting on you to give her attention. Isn't she soft and lovely?" Master Ez's voice is lulling.

"Yes, Master Ez," I reply dreamily. Suddenly relaxed, all feelings of panic and anxiety flee. But beneath the comfort, lust is awakening.

Using my fingertips as eyes, I try to recognize her. Her silky hair is bound so I can't ascertain length. Big eyes and a pouty mouth speed my pulse. I wish I knew what color her hair and skin was, so I could form a vision of her within my mind.

A thrill shoots through my veins, adrenaline pumping into me the faster my heart beats. There is something wicked–carnal –about touching someone you can't see while they can see you. Whether it's about anonymity or not, Master Ez found the perfect way to intrigue me, to pique the puzzle-solver dwelling within me.

My hands smooth down her torso, shaping her voluptuous curves. Ez was right. Somehow he knew exactly what I liked. When I'd get lonely, I'd seek out bigger girls, loving their softness, how there was so much to squeeze and lick and kiss and suck and bite.

My hand rounds her bottom, cupping her bare flesh. The discovery that the submissive is nude has my hands shaking in disbelief. Sensing my wonder, or simply enjoying my caress, her breath shudders out, slightly gasping, and the hitching sound ignites my body into a firestorm of lust.

"So smooth," I murmur in awe as my hands glide all over her body in an endless caress. "So warm and soft."

Even while luxuriating in the sensation of her flesh beneath mine, a spark of apprehension lights. I realize I'm stroking someone I don't know, so therefore I'm not sure if it's wanted. I have no right to touch her because she didn't give me permission. I know what it's like to be powerless. If this innocent girl is under Master Ez's command, she may allow me liberties she wished I didn't take, simply because she is loyal and obedient and afraid to speak her mind.

Forever reading me like I'm an open book, "Katya, she is all yours… enjoy her." Ez reassures me.

Apprehension causes me to stammer, voice warbling from a combination of frustration and confusion. "I don't know for sure, Ez. I can't see if she likes it or wants it. How can I observe her to anticipate her needs if I can't see her?" The reality of it is, I don't want to do to her what was done to me. "This seems backwards."

"Feel," Ez flattens my palm between her very large breasts. They engulf my hand in fleshy softness. "Her heart is racing for you, is it not?" He moves my hand in a small circle and she whimpers. "Hear her. Listen to her breathing escalate. She loves it. Unlike you, she knows exactly who you are. She's here because she wants to be, and for no other reason. I didn't force her; she volunteered."

Gripping the cuffs on my wrists, Master Ez maneuvers me like he's the sadistic puppeteer again. Both hands are firmly settled upon her breasts. So luscious and full, they overflow my palms.

Ez breathes into my ear for only me to hear. "Katya, just let go. Don't think. React. Do it," he commands, giving me the permission I needed, just as he said earlier. I need someone to shoulder the blame of my conscience, because my moral code of ethics won't allow me to take what I want and own it.

Her breath hitches again, the sound oddly familiar. Her soft, floral scent fills my nostrils. But it's the breasts overflowing my hands…"Oh, fuck," I hiss as soon as I realize whose tits are beneath my palms.

I need no permission.

She is mine.

Sensing the change overcome me, Master Ez's hold releases my wrists. With his absence, he unleashes my power to be the dominant one.

I unhinge.

I'm on her in a second, yanking her to me. Needing her. Hungering for her. I hadn't realized I'd been starving as I denied myself the pleasure of her offering. I thought I had been showing great restraint, proving my potent level of control. I felt as if I gave in, I was admitting weakness, when all along I was simply doing harm to myself.

Abstaining doesn't strengthen your character, it just weakens your body, slowly draining your soul. It had been too long, far too long.

My hand flexes on her tit, causing her budding nipple to etch my palm. With a ravenous lunge, my hands seek her hair, fingertips tangling in the tendrils. I yank her closer, drawing our faces together. My mouth fuses to hers, while my tongue desperately tries to pry her lips apart.

But there is no need to try with this girl. She submits, surrenders, succumbs to anything I wish, anticipating my needs before I even feel them. Master Ez said she was my first gift, my ultimate gift: a trained submissive who longed for me to dominate her.

Quivering, a wave of joy washes over me, while a tsunami of lust rolls me under. My tongue penetrates her lips, seeking and coaxing her tongue into my mouth. Sucking, I feast, devouring her delectable taste. Animal noises rise from both of our throats as we attack one another.

Needing more of her, my hand glides from her neck to her bare ass. I push her in a carnal rhythm against my thigh, wedging my leg between hers. An erotic moan rolls up her throat to spill into my mouth when my knee makes direct contact with her pussy.

My lips travel down her neck, nipping with my fangs as I go. Oh, how she loves the bites, gyrating her mound against my knee with every press of my teeth.

Finally, I do the one thing that has rendered me mindless. Using both hands, I push her tits together, and then I merge my face between them. Soft, smooth, and smelling divine, her breasts envelope my head, rubbing against my cheeks, lips, and even my forehead as I move. Overcome, in a frenzy, I bite, lick, and suck like I've lost my mind.

"Master, may I call her by her name? Please," I beg in a voice gone hoarse with need.

"Oh, God. Katya, you're killing me." Master Ez groans, the sound flooding my already weeping pussy. "You've proven me wrong, Kitty Kat. You can definitely appreciate a gift in the spirit in which it was given."

Panting, nearly hyperventilating, I wait to use her name, even in my mind. If I say her name, it's real– she's mine. One more puzzle piece put into place. One more mystery solved. One more step closer to learning who Master Ez really is. Not his name, because the more I learn, the more sure I am. No, I'll be closer to learning who Ez is to me, and the thought petrifies me.

"Please," I beg again. I blindly grab for Master Ez's hand, quickly spilling from the chair to kneel on the floor at his feet.

Master Ez releases a husky, masculine laugh. "Katya, I am so pleased. But, no. You may not use her name yet. I know you think you know who we are. I'm not saying you're right or wrong. But you need definitive proof. Prove it, and we'll move forward."

"Fine." I slink back into my chair, unintentionally pouting. "I'm not calling her Pet. It seems disrespectful… AHHH!" I scream as a bite connects with my bottom lip, sinking teeth punishing me for my petulance. A soothing tongue stroke quickly follows the harsh pinch.

Master Ez breathes across my mouth. "Katya, Pet is a cherished term of endearment. But you may call her anything you wish, except for her given name until I am satisfied with your proof."

"Temptation," erupts on instinct. "She breaches all of my control."

A slightly evil snicker spills from Master Ez's lips, as if he knows exactly how badly she tempts me with her deliberate antics.

"Temptation? How very apt." Ez pulls away from me, leaving me feeling cold from the lack of his warmth. "All right, Kat. Temptation is all yours. You've worked her into a tizzy, and she's been such a good girl. She deserves to be rewarded." When I don't immediately respond to Master Ez's comment, he adds, "Reward her."

My eyes widen beneath my mask. He can't mean what I think he means. Surely he doesn't want us to do *that* in front of him.

Master Ez clears his throat in warning.

I guess he wants to watch.

"Temptation?" I croak out, and without hesitation, she comes to my hand.

"You may touch me..." I think about it for a second, checking my comfort level. "A little bit," I tack on as a safety precaution.

I will reward my submissive, even though Master Ez is a pervert for watching. I can't bring myself to admit her name in my head. I imprint Temptation into my memory so I don't accidentally call out her real name during her reward.

As odd as it sounds, I do what I need in this very moment. I pull her into a hug, squeezing her tightly, showing her how much I appreciate her, how much comfort she lends me, how happy I am to have her in my life. Arms wrapped around her back, my hands flow over her creamy skin.

The sensation changes, moving from comfort to frenetic. Tipping my head back, I take her mouth with mine in a long sensual kiss filled with dueling tongues and spilled moans. Without breaking our kiss, I pull Temptation onto my knees, sliding her up to my hips until she's straddling me. Once firmly seated, I widen my thighs to spread her open to my pleasure.

"Temptation," I purr huskily. "I love the feel of you beneath my fingertips, especially with the flavor of your addictive taste on the back of my tongue."

Not forgetting Master Ez's presence, but easily ignoring him, I give all of my attention to Temptation. Without hesitation, knowing she's as ready for me as I am for her, I slide my fingers over her velvety moist slit. With a squeak, she presses down on my hand, wanting more.

"Jesus," I mutter in disbelief. "You're so fucking soft... and wet." So unbelievably turned on by me and the situation we are in, Temptation's arousal drips off my fingers to cascade down the side of my hand, and I've never felt so powerful in my entire life.

I'm not a lesbian. I'm bisexual by choice. By nature, I'm straight. But those facts do not lessen the potency of this moment for me. As Temptation moves closer to me, trying to wring her pleasure from my touch, as she moans these breathy little sounds of ecstasy, I gain more of my control back. I gain so much by giving Temptation what she needs, and that transcends sexual orientation. Hell, it transcends sexuality in general. The act of dominance and submission is about something baser. At its core, it's about give and take, and there is immense power in both.

"That's a girl," I croon to Temptation as she takes her reward by steadily rocking her pussy against my hand, mashing her swollen clit into the heel of my palm. Her juices coat my hand to trickle slowly in a steady flow down to my wrist.

As if my need is tied to hers, the more aroused she becomes, the hungrier I become to give her more. With my hand stroking her pussy, she falls forward to rest her cheek against mine. Her natural scent deepens the closer she comes to climax, and I cannot resist– I have to taste her. I press my mouth to the side of her neck, lapping at a bead of sweat that's trickling down from her hairline. On impulse, I set my caps into her skin, pressing the points into the delicate flesh of her throat. Hungrily, I suck, leaving a lasting mark behind.

With an inborn instinct driving me, I mark Temptation as mine in the same manner in which Master Ez has marked me every time we've met.

Temptation's soft hand grips the back of my neck, squeezing, egging me on to suck harder, to bite deeper. She gasps and pulls my head closer to her neck.

I squeeze her breast roughly, luxuriating in the sensation of her flesh giving beneath my fingertips. From the sensual contact, my eyes roll back as a moan breaks free of my lips.

I startle when a hand touches the juncture of my clothed thighs. "Shh, it's all right." Ez whispers in my ear, and then kisses my cheek. "I'll just touch you a little bit, get you comfortable."

Lost in a fog, not thinking clearly, my only response is to nod my head yes, giving Master Ez permission to touch me sexually. His hand mimics mine as I intimately touch Temptation, causing my breathy gasps to match hers.

Master Ez holds me from behind, sliding between me and the backrest of the chair. The intense heat of his chest permeates into my back. It warms me from the outside in, all the way to the cold depths of my soul. My master's heart beats against my back, and mine slows to match the rhythm of his.

The three of us trickle as a battery, each feeding the next, connecting; breath, heartbeat, and need, all flowing continuously through us. Temptation's speed increases as she feverishly rides my palm. Master Ez's fingertips match the pace, rapidly circling on my fabric-covered pussy. We are close. We will go together as one.

Terrified, my hand leaves Temptation's breast to rest over Master Ez's hand to stop him.

"No, I don't want to come," I whimper in warning, panic leaking into my voice. "No," I cry out as if in pain.

I try to pull Master Ez's hand away, my sweaty fingertips slip on his skin. He's too strong. He doesn't stop, but he does slow. Anxiety mounts at the thought of climaxing for anyone.

Voice thready with want, breathing so laboriously that the words are garbled, Ez tries to reassure me. "Katya, it's not what you want, but what you need. Trust me. You're safe. Just let go." He gently places a kiss to my lips and I almost lose it.

With unexpected ferocity, I bite his lip– an animal lashing out. Shocked at my own behavior, I flinch. All Ez does in response is chuckle at me for having the guts to punish my own master.

"Don't come, Temptation. Not until I tell you," I warn.

She was so close, just the flick of a fingertip against her clit or the brush of my mouth against her skin, and she would have lost it.

If she goes, I will follow.

I can't follow.

Arms wrap around me from behind, holding me stationary. Ez's hands grip my breasts, then his fingertips pinch, bruising my nipples. Crying out in a combination of pain and ecstasy, my hands fly up to protect my breasts.

"No," I snarl at Ez, willing to do anything to stop him from touching me right now. Anything. Temptation is a hairsbreadth away from coming, and if Ez is touching me when she goes, I'm going to fly off the precipice with her.

I can't.

"AH!" I shriek in surprise as a sharp, punishing smack connects with my sensitive cunny. It takes less than a heartbeat before the pain sets in. A scream rips from my throat, pouring out in a mess of nonsensical words. Flames flash across my pussy lips. I look down to make sure I'm not on fire, only to realize I'm blinded. It hurts so damned bad that I'd do anything for relief. Whimpers and swear words roll off my tongue as if they are soothing balm to my burning skin.

My fingers start to rub the ache away. The sharp stinging pain changes to the sweet edge of pleasure. I almost bring myself by accident.

"Kitty Kat. I think you're loving the wrong pussycat, don't you?" Master Ez purrs, and I can hear the sardonic smile in his voice.

Without warning, Ez's hand replaces mine. I arch up into it with a groan. Moments ago, I feared coming for another human being, now I just want the release from the agonizing pressure.

My fingertips slide over Temptation's silky skin at the same time I lean in to bring her breast to my mouth. Just the thought makes my mouth water. Reality is better than I had ever imagined. Her taut little tip presses into my tongue as I suckle around her areola and sink my fangs.

Feminine hands cup my breasts, their fingertips digging painfully into my flesh, while a masculine palm rubs through my slacks, expertly grinding into the nub that's throbbing for release.

Three...

Two...

One...

"Come for me," I demand as my middle finger slips easily inside my submissive's wet, tight pussy. She's smoother than silk, and so feverishly hot that her sheath burns my flesh. I groan from the delicious sensation of her body enveloping my finger. Climax erupting, her muscles clench around me as she moans an unintelligible word at the ceiling.

Palm grinding deeper into the apex of my thighs, rubbing

the seam of my slacks over my swollen nub, nails digging in to tender flesh of my breasts, sharp teeth biting my sensitive neck, climaxing pussy clenching around my finger, and it's Temptation's release that whirls me over the edge.

Jerking, I throw my head back onto Ez's shoulder. My body seizes, waves rolling down my spine. I drag in a lungful of air, preparing for my release.

Mid-orgasm, I freeze up.

My carnal scream dies on my lips before its release.

The memories assault me, as they always do. Without fail.

Terror.

Hopelessness.

Powerlessness.

Debasement.

Shame.

Worthlessness.

Agony.

Rage.

As the emotions scroll on repeat, the memories flash at random within my rebelling mind.

Lying prone on the forest floor with a man hovering above me, I choke on my screams, refusing to surrender. Rocks dig into my abraded back and rear, fertilizing the soil with my blood. Smaller hands wrap around my wrists, immobilizing me, as a pair of larger hands trap my ankles. A set of remorseful eyes peer down at me as he uses himself to protect the others. A sadistic cackle echoes throughout the forest. The smell of his rancid breath invading my nostrils. The sound of his labored breathing against my ear as he ruts like a predator, lowering me to the level of prey. His bitter triumph flavors the air, filling me with silent rage.

Lost. Trapped. I can't flee the memories as I need, not with Temptation oblivious and Master Ez holding me in my seat. With the one who swore to protect me, the one who promised me no harm to my psyche, pressed against my back, and the most precious woman I've ever met in the throes of an ecstasy I gave her, I relive the worst moment of my entire existence, as if it's happening right this very instant in my reality.

This is why I stopped feeling…

This is why I never allow myself release.

Chapter Thirteen

How do you put the emotions back in their cage after you've released them?

You can't.

I've spent the last hour trying to center myself, and it's not working like it used to. Instead, I find myself rubbing my microfiber armrest beneath my fingertips as a way of self-soothing. At least this time I'm not visually impaired as I fondle my sofa. I dangle a water bottle from my fingers over the armrest, back and forth, back and forth, sloshing. The rhythm is as calming as a metronome.

"Are you all right? You haven't spoken since I entered the Boss's office." Aaron's worried voice breaks into my zoning-out session. This is the tenth time he's asked me that exact same question, words never deviating.

Aaron's right; I haven't spoken since Temptation came on my hand. I'd frozen in my chair, pulled my knees to my chin and tucked my face into them. Ez tried to coax me, and then I shut him out. I'd blanked my mind and ceased to feel as Ez told Temptation it wasn't her fault that I reacted the way I had. I didn't bother to look up since I couldn't see. I'd eased Temptation's mind by telling her she was perfect and I was proud of her. After that, I was given space until Aaron came to take me home. That was at least an hour ago.

"I'm fine, okay?" I try to assuage Aaron's fears, so that he'll leave– leave me alone so that I can suffer in silence, suffer in private. It's what I need. It's the only way I know how to survive. "I just need to shower and get some rest, and then I will be fine."

"Ez is worried about you, ya know? It's his job to provide aftercare when the scene's finished." Aaron leans forward to touch me, but then thinks better of it.

"We didn't do a scene," I say in denial. I'm cerebrally mind fucked. I just need a goddamned screaming, bawling fit in the shower. What doesn't Aaron understand about that? I have to be alone when it happens, because I can't have Aaron seeing me as weak.

Aaron gives me an incredulous look.

My eyes flick up, and for the first time in the past hour, I look Aaron in the eyes. "If you don't think I feel horrible for what happened back in Ez's office, then you're smoking crack. We could beat around the bush and play mind games, but we both know who else was in that room with me, and it's killing me that I let either one of them down."

"Kat, don't worry about her. Ez is taking care of her." Aaron tries to take my guilt away, but all he accomplishes is to make me feel even worse.

"Great, thanks for twisting the knife in a little deeper. I guess the only shitty dominant is me. I couldn't even take care of her because I was catatonic. Our master had to do it for me. Pa-the-tic." I drag the word *pathetic* out into multiple syllables in a flat voice.

"That's not what I meant, and you know it. You're being stubborn again." Aaron tries to get me to see reason but his eyes still hold pity. I have a laundry list of inadequacies that are racking up right now.

"Your emotions dropped when your hormones surged. It's natural. That's what aftercare is about." Aaron looks at me with pity, but he also looks at me like I'm wounded, which pisses me off.

My issues have nothing to do with hormone surges, and everything to do with human nature. Terror, pure and simple. It's my nightmarish past rearing its ugly head. The memories make me relive it every time I try to have an orgasm, and every time I close my eyes or have them open. It's in every breath I take. There is always something to trigger the memories, no matter how big or small. It could be a sound, a scent, a feeling, or a touch– *bang!* I'm on the forest floor being violated. It's inescapable, and the only thing I can do is survive.

I slump forward, burying my head in my hands. I whisper the words, wishing they weren't true. "All the cards on the table. Do you really want to know what's spinning around in my head right now?"

"Yes," Aaron states firmly. "Please. I've been staring at

the side of your face for over an hour, and you've barely blinked. It was unnerving to say the least."

"Okay, fine," I grumble. "But don't say I didn't warn ya."

"Duly noted."

"It wasn't because I was scared like in the SUV. That's not why I freaked out. Climaxing is a trigger for me. I don't want to remember the finer details because they make me feel powerless, so I'd rather forego intimacies and move on, than be stuck in an endless loop of terror."

"There is another option, Katya. You could heal," Aaron sound so innocent, so hopeful. Naïve.

"Heal? I don't have a scratch. There is no physical manifestation to explain the pain away. There is no medicine I can take. Twelve years ago I was reduced to…"

After a few minutes of dead silence, Aaron prompts me, "Reduced to what, Kat?"

Swallowing thickly, the words get stuck in my throat. "I was reduced to… nothing. Less than nothing. I looked into my rapist's eyes, and I saw nothing reflected back at me. Not anger, or lust, or even hatred. It was the expression you give to something that you don't spare a second thought. It didn't matter if I lived or died. I was no different than a squished bug, or a used tissue, or a broken rubber band. I was useless… and how do you bounce back from that? Once useless, always useless."

"Katya," Aaron breathes, tears evident in his tone. "No."

"But I survived, so others could live. I've worked hard to make a better life for my family. I've tried to find a slice of happiness amid the constant barrage of, '*It was just an hour of your life, Katya. Jesus Christ, get over it already.*'" I mock all those who have said that to me. "Then the real advice that stings just as much. '*They already took an hour of your life, infecting the twelve years after. Don't let them take a minute more.*' Sure, that sounds great in theory."

"No one will ever understand until they have been there," Aaron rasps out, and I can tell he's crying, and I hate myself because of it.

"I don't want pity. I don't want attention. In truth, I don't want anyone to know. Fuck me!" I whisper shout. "*I don't even want to know,* much less allow everyone to have an opinion about the worst time in my life. That's what I hate the most. How debased I feel, even when someone pats me on the back for being a survivor, for being strong. In truth, it's a slap in the face."

"How so?" Aaron's voice pitches with real curiosity, as if I've surprised him somehow.

"I'm trying to live my life. I'm trying to move on, even with the memories and the nightmares and the constant triggers. Even with the mental, emotional, and physical scars. So for every pat on the back, or Atta Girl, it opens up a very private wound that is none of their fucking business. I had sex. I lost my virginity. I was *fucked,*" I snarl. "Whether rape or consensual, no one in their right goddamned mind, would ask a young woman the shameful details– repeatedly –and then give her a hug."

"Jesus," Aaron hisses, shaking his head back and forth. "I never thought of it that way."

"There is a difference between awareness and none of your business. So, not only was I violated in the woods by four men, I lost the right to privacy for the rest of my life. If I say I don't want to talk about it, I'm either not moving on, because the only way to move on is to beat it to death, or I'm being a bad survivor by not championing for the cause."

Aaron just stares at me with his mouth hanging open, completely speechless, and for some reason, it makes me laugh. Eyebrows knitted together, he looks at me like I've lost my mind. "What?"

"I'm serious, dude. They all want the grisly details, and when you say they are shameful, they spew how it wasn't your fault and you have nothing to be ashamed about. Guess what, I'm not ashamed of myself. I know I did nothing wrong. But getting fucked is still not a conversation for polite company."

"Everyone's a backseat therapist. Believe me, I know," Aaron draws out, shaking his head back and forth in disgust. "I really, really know."

"So tonight, after freaking out on your ass in the SUV, and

then freaking out on *them* during what constituted as the first actual sex I've had since… maybe a girl doesn't want to be analyzed by a backseat therapist."

"You calling me that?" Aaron points at himself, looking incredulous.

"If the shoe fits, '*Mr. Are You All right?*'" I taunt, mocking Aaron's gravelly voice.

"Touché," Aaron grants. "Be that as it may, you still need to be comforted. We don't have to talk about the how or why. We don't even have to talk at all. But you just went through some major shit, so I'm not going to leave you alone. We'd both feel better if you'd let me hold you. I'm a big guy; I give great hugs."

"I can't," I mutter, tears threatening to fall. "I was supposed to be the one in control. I was supposed to be the one lending the comfort. Instead, I failed. I freaked out. Not only shouldn't I be rewarded for that, I shouldn't be allowed to be in a position where I make another decision again."

"Kat, don't," Aaron warns. "Don't pull this shit. You don't even realize it, but this is as much hormonal as it is emotional, mixing with the fact that you've been torturing yourself all fucking night. Comfort is not a reward; it's absolute."

"I just… I just need to be alone," I mumble.

Ignoring me, "C'mere and let me hold you." Aaron's voice is warm and coaxing. His arms are open in a soothing embrace, beckoning me to crawl in. I want to, but I don't deserve his kindness.

I drop my gaze to stare at my boots.

"Kat, you're acting like a child." His voice holds potency–a demand meant to be heeded. "Let me hold you," he says more forcefully than last time. Aaron has yet to close his outstretched arms.

Shit, I'm not up for a dominance challenge. I know Aaron wants to help me. Just the thought has tears building in my ducts. But if he touches me, I'll lose it.

"I need to take a shower. I. Feel. Sticky," I draw out, sounding like a skeeved out child. It's not hard to sound pitiful. I'm not lying about being sticky, either. My trousers are saturated from crotch to mid-thigh. My hands are covered in Temptation's drying juices. I can smell her and it's humiliating. I'm not ashamed of the pleasure I brought her. I'm ashamed of my reaction to being pleasured. Temptation's scent on my skin and clothing is proof that I freaked out when I would just rather play pretend.

I pull a puss-in-boots while wearing my kitten ears. Aaron laughs at my huge eyes and pouty lips. "Go shower. I'll wait out here."

***

My body may be scrubbed clean, but nothing will ever remove the filth from my soul.

"Master Ez was supposed to unlock me," I say to the reflection of Aaron. He's standing behind me as we talk through my vanity mirror. I raise my wrists up to emphasize my issue.

Patient blue eyes gaze back at me, with a sad smile playing around his lips. "Ez will. He just didn't get the time." *With your breakdown* goes without saying.

"I'll be fine. You don't need to coddle me. I'm a big girl."

"A big girl who never listens, never does as she's told, and never allowed me to hold her, even for a nanosecond, when Ez specifically told me to do so."

"A girl doesn't want a pity hug, or to have a hot guy try to hold her only because his boss told him to." I tease Aaron's reflection. "That's not very flattering."

Jaw hitting the floor, Aaron looks a '*You think I'm hot?*' in my direction. I snort at his expression, because you just can't help but be amused when an innocent blue-eyed, blond-haired guy simultaneously looks adorable and fierce.

"You can go. I'm gonna go straight to bed. I promise." I meet Aaron's eyes through the mirror again. The warmth of his body does lend me a small amount of comfort, even though he's inches away.

I want to be angry at Ez for about a billion little reasons, and a few insurmountable ones, too. But I can't as I gaze down at the gifts he's given me. Even while '*educating*' me, there is always a playful note to all of his objects of torture.

Fiddling with my mask, I try a new position within my jewelry box. It's like a puzzle. How do you make a mask and kitten ears fit into a box when irregular shapes meet a perfect rectangle? I gently shut the lid, and smirk down at the black and pink ear peeking out from the jewelry box.

With a shrug, I say, "Good enough, I guess." I look over my shoulder at Aaron. "Why haven't you left yet?"

"Let me tuck you in," sounds salacious in Aaron's gravelly deep voice, but he's looking at me like I'm a misbehaving toddler: disappointed, amused, and tender.

"Seriously? You're holding me hostage in my own home. You get that, right? Now you want to tuck me in to go night-night like I'm your child. Did I somehow miss the fact that I got a head injury that rendered me unable to crawl into bed unaided? I've been doing it for thirty plus years, I'm pretty sure I can manage."

After bitching up a storm, I still humor Aaron by crawling into bed.

"Ez is going to ask me how I do it," Aaron says as he tucks the edges in around me, and then folds the blankets under my armpits.

Feeling ridiculous as he yanks on my bedding, I ask, "Do what?"

"You always seem to obey me, but never him." Aaron tries and fails to suppress a grin. "Maybe not right away, but eventually." He leans down to give me a quick hug. "See, I even got to hold you finally. Now Ez won't have my head." With a harsh tug, my sheets are pulled tight, and then Aaron tucks the corner under the edge of the mattress.

"Now, I won't fall out of bed and bruise my hiney. Thanks," I mutter wryly.

He laughs as he moves on to my drapes, securely shutting them so that the room is cloaked in darkness.

"Good night, Kat," Aaron says, affection coloring his voice.

"Good night, Aaron. Thank you," I sincerely reply, thankful that he's leaving me alone to break down in peace.

My salutation earns me a genuine smile– Aaron thinking

my thanks was for him taking care of me, not for leaving me the hell alone. He flips my light switch and quickly strides out of my bedroom.

I roll onto my left side, just as the dam breaks, releasing the torrent of built-up emotions.

Chapter Fourteen

Eyes tearing up, a sniffle tickling my nose, the telltale sound of an invasion comforts me when it should infuriate me. My breakdown is either being cut short or will soon be witnessed. What do I have to do to get some goddamned privacy in my own home?

"Sonofabitch," I mumble underneath my breath, as bare feet soundlessly whisper across my carpet. "I'm not wearing a fucking mask of any kind," I warn. "You can just forget about that shit if you know what's good for ya. Punishment or not, we will throw down."

I'm tackled by a pajama-clad boss with cuddling on his mind. Ez lands lightly on my bed beside me, lies down, and then folds his arms around me, finally lending me the comfort I'd denied myself for the past few hours.

Shaking my head in utter disbelief, I talk to the ceiling, ignoring Ez as he nuzzles my cheek with the tip of his nose. "Aaron's going to lick my boot the next time I see him, the bastard. He hung around waiting for you, didn't he?" I accuse, but it comes out sounding amused, not angry.

Something vital loosens inside me, something that has forever been tight. It reminds me of a fist squeezing the very life out of my heart that has finally slackened enough to allow my heart to beat, to begin pumping life-giving blood throughout my system.

Master Ez, Ezra Zeitler, whoever the hell this man is… he puts me at ease. The power that radiates off of him and the playful nature he is exhibiting, almost makes me feel normal. Ez makes me feel good. I know that if I ever face a problem, he will tackle it for me.

There will always be a divide between us, because one can never forge a partnership or a friendship with someone who is so much greater: stronger, more powerful, more intelligent, and higher on the food chain. Ez intimidates me as much as he comforts me, and I don't know how I feel about that.

"I think Aaron might enjoy that." Master Ez chuckles

softly in my ear. "Mmm... you smell scrumptious, like cookies." He buries his face in my hair, inhaling deeply while enveloping me in a warm bear-hug.

"No need for a mask since Aaron secured the drapes. I don't know, though... it may be fun to *throw down*." He mimics my voice.

"Curiosity, what kind of punishment would I receive for it? The punishment may be worth kicking your ass," I taunt.

"Hmm... let's see," a purr rumbles up his throat. "Technically, it's a refusal to wear a mask. So, therefore, I would find a hideous mask and make you wear it in public."

"That doesn't sound too bad," I say before he can finish.

"In public... while I spank you," amusement heavily laces his voice, but I still cringe at the thought. No doubt he is amused because he's envisioning the punishment and it brings him great entertainment.

"But..." He pauses to arrange himself around me, leg casually thrown over my hip, as if we spoon on a nightly basis. "Throwing down would be attacking your master, which is unheard of. It would have to be an extra special punishment. I'll have to think on that one."

"I think in your spare time, you run a re-educational facility in a dystopian novel. I'll have to contact my authors and see who is willing to put that idea on paper for me. You'll be the egomaniacal leader who is destroying the world as we know it, in the hopes of saving us from ourselves."

Laughing heartily, "Nah, that position would fall to my father– birth or adopted," Ez rasps wryly. "Don't even think of asking me to explain. You'll find out soon enough."

Ez acts different than all the other times I've seen him. Relaxed, and I'd have to say this is his real personality shining through. He's no longer projecting an image. I feel differently around him, too. Now that he's seen me breakdown, I don't have to fear it. The anxiety has lessened, and I can finally let go and be myself.

"You owe me a punishment. But under the circumstances, I'll let it slide." Ez affectionately rubs his nose along my neck while squeezing me tighter.

"What did I do?" I mumble around the large lump forming in my throat. What haven't I done? I fucked the entire evening up. Tears, which have threatened to manifest for the past few hours, make themselves known at the reminder of my inadequacies.

"Believe it or not, it has nothing to do with earlier this evening," Master Ez tries to reassure me. "Katya, I'm just teasing you for threatening and swearing at me. That was a very bad Kat."

Sighing heavily, Ez pulls us onto our sides, settling my cheek against his bare chest with his palm resting on the back of my head. Before I can examine the fact that he is in pajama pants and little else, Master Ez pulls out his trump card. The phrase that is guaranteed to ruin me.

"What happened tonight? Please talk to me," he pleads.

That's all it takes... The dam breaks, and I begin to sob into his chest. I tightly wrap my arms around his body as every emotion I've ever felt rolls over me and takes me under.

Ez's hands grip the backs of my knees, forcing me to wrap my legs around his waist. His solid presence is reassuring, causing my trust in him to grow further.

This is what stupid aftercare is about. I almost went through the confusing mélange of emotions alone, and I would've never healed from it. It would have left another wound on my soul, one to join the countless others. I should have expected Ez to come to my aid. Everything he's been doing has been to prove that I should trust him, even if I don't like the hard truths he forces me to admit. When I stop being a stubborn bullhead, he won't make me face the imminent storm alone. Next time, I will trust in him and believe in him.

"Thank you, Ez. I know you will never leave me hurting. I don't know what's wrong with me tonight. I feel so... raw." I try to stem the tears, to firmly block out the past that's threatening to overtake me, but it's like I'm held wide open.

Roughly, Ez grips my hips, dragging my body along his until we are face-to-face with our eyes level. My lips rest against the slope of his nose. Gunmetal gray eyes captivate me, and I love him a little for it. It's dark in here, but this close up,

I can see his eyes. I can look into them and connect with him.

Ez trusts me.

He trusts me enough to put whatever mental game he's playing at risk, to blow his cover, and it's humbling.

I meld my body to Ez's, and refuse to blink. I refuse to break our connection. My heart speeds up, and I realize my heartbeat is matching the rhythm of his. He's breathing in short gasps. This isn't about anything I could ever understand. This moment is too intense. It almost feels of life or death, as if the man embracing me holds the keys to my healing.

"Nothing is wrong with you. I never want to hear those words uttered from your mouth again." Ez's fingers twine in my hair, as his other hand mashes my ass. I'm ensnared in the cage of his arms, but it doesn't fill me with dread and the need to lash out and fight– to escape. Master Ez's firm hold makes me feel cherished, as if he'd do anything to protect me, even from myself.

"What we do is mental, even the physical at its core is mental. We reach epic heights, and the price we pay for the high is disastrous lows. Give and Take. Light and Dark. Reward and Punishment. Life and Death."

"Balance," I breathe, trapped in the hypnotic cadence of his voice.

"Trust. The rules of humanity should parallel those of BDSM, and life would be so much easier. Trust in your partner, whether top or bottom, to balance you. We experience the same rush and descent. That is what aftercare is about, taking care of one another. Trust your partner to know what is best for you during a scene, and trust in them to bear your breakdown."

"You didn't descend," I mumble against the softness of his chest.

"Katya, don't ever assume you know what my emotions are. I ached for you when I saw you crash. When you shut me out, when you didn't trust me to shoulder the burden of your pain, I wanted to scream." Intense emotions bleed from his eyes: frustration, sadness, guilt, and ache.

My lip quivers and tears prickle my eyes. I did this to him;

I made Master Ez feel these emotions. I don't like having the power to harm another human being.

When I can't move my face to hide my tears of shame, I look away from his stormy eyes. My shame and guilt break our connection.

"No, you don't get to do that." Ez palms the back of my head, refusing to allow me to look away. "You *will* look me in the eye."

Somehow I find the strength to do as he requested, the first time he requested. We aren't in a power struggle right now. I understand he's trying to help me, no different than if he were disinfecting a physical wound.

"I can't go through this again, Katya. You didn't allow me to do the one thing I was born to do– to take care of you – because you let pride and insecurity overrule the trust you had in me." His voice changes from its commanding timber to the smoky tones I hear when he isn't Master Ez.

Slowly the real Ez is revealed to me, with his gunmetal gray eyes, the cadence of his voice, and the facets of his personality. He's giving me a rare gift, and I won't refuse it.

"I'm sorry. I just felt so ashamed. I want you to be proud of me. I didn't want you to see me like that. I didn't want you to see me as weak." My breath hitches in my throat. "I want to show you that I'm strong enough to hold my own. I don't want you to see how broken I am."

"Kat, I want to see the real you, not some fictitious version you think I want. Our jobs revolve around imaginary-land, and our play is about fantasy. But, dammit!" He grips me tighter, wrapping his legs around me as if scared I will float away. "This is raw. This is reality. BDSM isn't about play, not for the purists. It's our own tortured version of therapy. If we weren't fucked-up, sick and twisted shit wouldn't get us off. The high is amazing and the crash is therapy hell. Trust me, as I trust you, to get us through it, to move beyond it, to transcend."

"What if I... what if I can't trust myself," I stammer, feeling more confused than ever.

Ez releases a heavy sigh. "That's what I'm for, Katya. That's what I'm for. That's what your family is for. That's what that precious, metaphorical mirror is for that you're so fond of gazing into and seeing if you can stomach yourself.

"I've shown you the real me. *Me.* There is no mistaking who I am anymore. But that isn't what any of this has ever been about, Katya. My name is just a name. Who I am to you is what's important. Next time we meet, I will use the game to continue to heal you."

"I just don't understand why you even care," I murmur, having no idea why Ezra Zeitler would give a shit about a small-town girl like me.

"Kat," he sighs in exasperation. "Tonight is reality. I will tell you this much: I know you. I wanted you open and bared raw for me, with the real you revealed. Everyone modifies themselves around different people, censors themselves. I got to know you before you could do that. You've been through a lot, and I didn't want that baggage to interfere. Yes, I stalk you. I'm sure you figured that out by now." His lips quirk up into a smile against my chin.

"While you know me, I know nothing of you," I admit, feeling sick to my stomach about how one-sided this is, how I'm to open myself up to him, and he doesn't give me anything in return. "How can I trust what I don't know? Ez, I want to know you– the real you."

"Oh, Katya. You already know me. You really do." Ez playfully nips my chin with his lips. "The game is entertaining the shit out of me, but that's not its true purpose. It's for you to figure out who I am, and piece it all together. The game is the therapy that you so desperately need. I may not have shared things with you like my name or occupation, but the stories we spoke of, the memories, and the tragedies... my hopes and dreams. Those were all me."

"I... I don't understand," my voice breaks under the strain of my emotions, with confusion winning out. "I... we've never really spoken, have we?"

"Yes, Katya," Ez sounds relieved to finally admit the truth. "We've spoken often. The game, while entertaining, really is to help you deal with your issues. I want you to feel every emotion you possibly can. I want you to *feel*," he strongly draws out the word *feel*, somehow understanding how I've been walking around in a perpetual state of numb.

What Ez has told me in the past few minutes is dizzying. I will need days to work through it all. But if I could get a timeline, perhaps I could figure out who Ez really is to me.

"Since I know you won't answer why, how long have you been stalking me?"

"Almost three years," he readily admits, and the revelation stuns me into silence.

"We met at the worst time of our lives. Your pain was like a siren's song, and I wanted to use pleasure and pain to draw it from your soul." Gentle thumbs clear tears from my cheeks, tears I hadn't realized I was crying. "What happened tonight?" He gently coaxes me. "I didn't foresee it. I thought maybe you wouldn't go through with Temptation's reward, not freeze up on us."

"Can I take a pass for the night? I don't feel up to explaining." I take the coward's way out, because it's too fresh in my mind, and talking about it would make me relive it all over again. Rape may only last for a few moments in time, but you get to relive its reality over and over again. The memories feel real and in the now. An hour of your life can plague you for lifetimes.

Wiping my tears away, I mutter, "I'm not up for any more backseat therapists this evening."

"Trust me, Katya. I will never be a backseat anything, especially a therapist," Ez states, matter-of-factly. "All right, I'll let it go. But just for tonight," he allows, stressing that we will be revisiting this conversation, whether I like it or not.

"You do like girls, right?" He sounds so bewildered that I huff a laugh.

"That wasn't the issue, okay?" I blush from the memory of just how much that wasn't an issue. "I enjoyed the hell out of Temptation. It's all me," I admit reluctantly.

"So it was an issue with climaxing," he reasons out. "Do you solo play?" Gray eyes intently watch my facial expressions for emotional cues.

"Jesus," I hiss, hating the way his eyes make me feel like

I'm being examined under a microscope. "I don't want to talk about it. Trust me. My body can get off, especially when I don't want it to." Fear and humiliation make me lash out like a wounded animal.

I try to roll away from Ez to hide my shame, because he sees way too much just by looking into my eyes, the mirrors to my soul. After a pause, he lets me go, so can I roll onto my side, facing away from him.

How do you explain that the only orgasm you've ever experienced was through force, and that every time you get close to the precipice, the memories inundate your mind, leaving you in a terrifying state of horror?

"May I touch you, relieve you?" Ez whispers softly, a caress of words.

Without waiting for my answer, he draws my back against his chest, and then his hand slowly inches down my stomach, giving me time to protest. My heartbeat is wildly fluttering in my throat. My mind and body are warring, conflicted on fight or flight or surrender. When Ez's fingertips wiggle underneath the waistband of my shorts, my hand clenches on his forearm to stop their invasion. Panic slams forcefully into me, and on the heels of the panic is lust– a lust so strong that it hitches my breath in my throat.

"No... please... don't," I beg, voice thready.

I can't handle it after everything that went down. Not tonight. Maybe never. Shame swallows me whole and I retreat inside myself.

"I'm sorry I'm such a bitter disappointment. I doubt I can ever do what you ask of me. You stalked the wrong woman."

In a frenzy, I start scratching at the cuff Ez placed on my wrist, nails gouging into my flesh, drawing blood. I don't belong to him. I'm not good enough and I never will be. If Master Ez knew the truth of who I truly am, he'd hate me too.

"Katya," Master Ez orders vehemently in a cool voice. I freeze from the sound, a sharp tug on an internal leash I didn't know I possessed. Master Ez controls my emotions, my body, with nothing but the tone of voice.

"You can never deny that you belong to me. Even in

hysterics you heel to my command." Ez sits up and removes a chain from around his neck. He takes my hands, one at a time, and unlocks his cuffs that adorn my wrists. When the leather falls from my flesh, my mind is heavy from the loss.

You never appreciate what you have until it's gone. I didn't like the trapped sensation of being owned, but now with the cuffs removed, I instantly regret the choice.

"Tonight isn't the last time you'll wear these," Master Ez puts an end to my whirling emotions. "I'll put them back on you when you calm. Feel," he pushes his necklace into my hand. It is the same mystery chain used on the bracelets, with the key to my padlocks dangling from it.

"Now, feel this." Guiding my hands to a charm on his necklace, he traces my fingertips over a raised image. After several passes with my fingertip, shapes begin to coalesce into letters.

KW.

I gasp in shock. With the weight of everything pounding down on me, I snap. "Why… why would you want me? What the fuck is wrong with you?" I yell at Ez, confused. I yank his short hair, barely getting a grip. I pull his eyes into view, and shout the one question I need to have answered. "WHY?"

Master Ez doesn't react how I thought he would. But he never does. I expected him to erupt in a fit of anger because I yanked his hair and swore at him. Instead, he emits a belly-deep laugh, an infectious sound that feeds my soul. I sit cross-legged on my bed, baffled, waiting for him to either answer or educate me.

"Katya, maybe the better question to ask yourself is why I wouldn't want you. But that's not what you're asking." I flinch when Ez raises his hands, but all he does is rest his palms against my temples. "The answer to your question is in here. It'll come to you when you're ready."

Ez's hands slowly and soothingly pet my hair. His fingertips rub at my scalp, causing my eyelids to droop and a shudder to roll up my spine. Just as I'm leaning into him for more, he abruptly fists a thick hank of curls, drawing a sharp shriek from my throat.

"We will get these issues ironed out. I know all of your secrets– even the darkest ones that you think are securely hidden in the depths of your soul. All will be revealed, and then, and only then, will you be fully healed."

I doubt everything he just said, until I remember Master Ez admitting he knows everything, sees everything. I shudder from the thought of Ez knowing my deepest secret. I've never spoken of it. Only one person knows my shame, and he'll never speak of it because it's his shame too.

"I gave you a pass earlier when you swore and threatened me because of the stress you've been under. But not this time, Kitty Kat. You caused me pain and cursed me, and I cannot allow a precedent of disrespect to be established. We'll both resent you for it."

"I'm sorry," I whimper.

"You will be," Ez warns. "If you're truly repentant, you'll be a good girl and take your punishment without complaint." His voice is sharp, broken glass grating down my nerves. He's angry and disappointed in me.

Master Ez's hands close over my upper arms, and then he lifts me a foot off the bed. After holding me stationary for a few moments, he abruptly releases his hold, dropping me. I plop on the bed and bounce several times before I come to rest. The strangeness breaks me out of my hysterical state, and I huff a laugh of surprise.

"Now that your mind has cleared of that bullshit you love to obsess over, take off your shorts," he orders. "You may leave on your shirt for comfort."

Mind whirling, still processing the request, my shorts are roughly torn from my body. Stunned into immobility, I freeze.

"Snap out of it!" Master Ez yells into my face, hot breath scorching my flesh. "Think!" He claps his hands in front of my nose. *Clap. Clap. Clap.* "When I tell you to do something, do it! Don't process, just do!" Ez's hands shake sense into me while chanting, "React. React. React."

"Um… what would you like me to do? You already ripped my shorts off me." I don't mean to sound sarcastic. But, naturally, it comes out that way. I'm positive that sarcasm is a huge disrespect where Master Ez is concerned. I try to watch his body language for cues on what's coming next, but it's too dark.

"Get under the covers and get comfortable. Now!" He snaps impatiently.

Ez's mercurial moods are dizzying. One moment he's laughing and joking, the next he's trying to connect on a deeper level, and then he turns into a raging lunatic who leaves you feeling cold and bruised.

Master Ez: Dr. Jekyll and Mr. Hyde.

I scramble as fast as I can across the bed, trying to ignore my bare ass flashing in the air. I yank my covers to hide my nakedness, embarrassed by the fact that Ez is the first man to see my parts since that day... and it's not the best looking ass, either. Flabby and flat do not make a master proud or aroused.

After I get settled and calmed down, Master Ez crawls into bed next to me, and tucks the blankets around us. "Touch yourself." I jolt at the husky, lust-filled command that sounds way too provocative and intimate in the dark of my bedroom.

"What?" My eyes bug out of my face.

"Are you Twit or Kitty Kat?" he maliciously twists the words. "It's your choice."

"I don't understand, Master," I mutter in confusion, hating this side of Master Ez. He's scary, and it makes me feel like a complete and utter failure

"A twit asks questions," he says sharply. "My Kitty Kat reacts instantly to her master's commands. You said you were sorry, and I said if you truly were, then you'd listen to me. But you didn't listen. You allowed insecurity, indecision, and pride to be more important to you than I was."

"I... I never thought of it that way," I stammer out. "I *am* sorry."

A growl radiates from his throat, and it suspiciously sounds like, "Prove it."

I hesitantly skate my fingertips across my opposite arm, not wanting to touch myself, but not wanting to disappoint or disobey Master Ez, either.

"Twit! You know exactly what I mean. Stop being so

literal." He curses underneath his breath, *"Why do they always make me have to be so goddamned literal. It makes me want to strangle them."* The words and his tone of voice scream that he isn't opposed to strangulation at this very moment.

"I don't like you calling me twit," I whine, realizing all too late that calling him out will undoubtedly anger him more.

"Then don't act like one," he says flatly, like I'm a fucking moron. Easy fix: don't want to be a twit, then don't behave like a twit. "This is your punishment, not a negotiation," he growls in a tone that unfreezes me.

My hand glides down my stomach. I no longer hesitate to obey his commands, because I fear that the punishment will be far worse than just touching my own flesh. My wrist rests on my pubic mound, fingers hovering above the clit that lies below. No matter how hard I try, I can't force my fingertip down. I know that if I touch myself in Master Ez's presence, I will climax. My fear of reliving the past is far greater than my fear of Master Ez's punishments.

"I don't want to. Why are you doing this?" I plead, sounding like a child lost in the dark.

"Remember: it's not what you want; it's what you need. You must overcome this obstacle to live a fulfilling life. Either do it now, while it's just you and me in private, or I will force you to do it in front of a crowd at Restraint. It's your choice, Twit."

Body quivering, I start to cry, hiccupping on my sobs. Ez caresses my face, palming my cheek. The touch is a silent order as much as it's a comfort. It's what a master's touch does– lures you from your comfort zone, but offers you the support to hurdle over the edge into the dark unknown.

"Katya, what's your worst fear about this?" He coaxes in a tender tone, enticing me to spill the secrets he said he already knows.

"I..." *Hiccup.* "It makes the memories come back. Every time I get close to orgasm, I remember it in vivid detail. I..." *Hiccup.* "Haven't wanted to remember. I can't remember some of the parts because it hurts way too much." *Hiccup.* "I don't want it to ruin me." *Sniffle.* "I haven't orgasmed since. I just know… I just know that if I orgasm, I will remember everything as if it's happening in real time." I whisper in the dark, my voice breaking in terror. "It's the memory of the last time I climaxed that haunts me."

"You haven't since…" he trails off like he knows what I'm talking about. He slides his lips against mine, barely forming a whisper of a kiss. "I don't want to punish you harshly. Please don't force me," he pleads, as if the thought is killing him. "You won't find the crowd pleasant at Restraint. I can do the touching if that's easier," he suggests in a tone thick with hunger.

My fingertips immediately react. Master Ez's lips stretch into a wide smile across mine. Too late, I realize he manipulated me into touching myself. He knew fear would move my hand faster than an order to obey.

Slowly I swirl my fingertip around my clit. I'm unpracticed and unsure at touching myself. I've pleasured a few women, so I know in theory what should feel good and what shouldn't. But I'm dry, terror removing any threat of arousal. I try to turn my mind off and fall into my master's scent, the sound of his breathing, the warm and comforting presence at my side, but I fail.

I fail miserably.

My hand mimics the motions, creating no results. I feel nothing. No pleasure. No pain. I'm numb… and ashamed.

Master Ez senses my discomfort, and it makes me feel even more inadequate. "It's just you and me in this moment of time." Ez's words whisper across my lips, and then he kisses me.

Our first real kiss, not the platonic brushes or the punishing bites. Our mouths fuse together, lips parting on gasps, our tongues slipping into each other's mouths to mingle. Shaking violently, I realize it is Ez's body quaking mine, not my suppressed passion or fear.

Hand sliding up my side, to curve around to cup my breast, Ez draws a sharp gasp from my lips when his fingertips grip my breast roughly, tugging on my nipple. The sweet edge of pain puts me in the moment, blanking my mind to everything but sensation.

My fingertips mirror the movement of Ez's tongue as he laps at my mouth. Casting smooth circles with my fingertips, I rub my hardening clit. I huff in surprise, amazed that this man pushes away all of my self-doubt, the memories of the past, and the pain and numbness, until I feel aroused and hungry for his touch. My need plateaus as his finger slides down to join mine, dancing on my skin.

The ache in my breast increases as his nails break skin, palm bruisingly squeezing the mound of my breast. The pain elevates the pleasure and buries all thought that isn't surrounded around the man playing my body as a finely tuned instrument. Master Ez's lips travel down my neck hungrily, nipping at my flesh. A new level of agony joins the ecstasy— the sharp bite of teeth setting into my throat.

Ez's thumb joins his forefinger, pressing and tugging my clit between the pair of experienced fingertips. A sharp pinch has me muttering unintelligible words of a person possessed. The pressure mounts in anticipation of its release. I whimper, not wanting to climax, but craving it even more.

Master Ez's strong fingers enter me as deeply as they can go, slickly sliding into a body that hasn't been invaded in over a decade. Up until this very moment, penetration brought about the panic. Even a trip to the doctor's office for my annual examination or the use of tampons would cause anxiety in my wounded mind. But as Master Ez's fingers stretch me, explore me, impale me, and deeply thrust inside of me, I don't freak out. The memories don't assault me.

I fracture.

The hot palm grinding against my screaming clit while two fingers fuck me, is my ultimate undoing. My teeth sink deeply into Ez's shoulder, muffling the sound I so desperately try to smother. Master Ez's pain-filled grunt extends my climax, heightening it. It's so strong it hurts. It hurts as much as I'm hurting him. Muscles clench under my skin. Heat flashes as blood rushes in my veins. Electrical surges flow up my spine to radiate throughout my body.

I've only had one other orgasm in my entire life, and it

was nothing compared to this. The first was excruciating shame, but the pleasure was subtle, like lapping water on a shore. My second orgasm ignites my body with a firestorm of need. Once unbridled, I will need to feed the flames. I will crave the agonizing pleasure of release forever more.

I reach down to stop Ez from moving his hand, only to realize I am rocking on his palm. I still my body to stop the pleasurable torture.

"No, you're still coming. Ride it out," gasps in my ear. His palm rubs faster, his fingers flicking deeper inside.

"Oh, please. Master, stop. I can't take anymore." The pressure's still building, refusing to ebb or release. "Let me please you instead," I beg breathlessly.

"You can, and you will. Come for me, Katya," Ez commands, and I obey.

Fingertips press in just the right spot. It feels phenomenal to the point of pain. I clench so hard I'm surprised he can still move his fingers within me. The fingers that were twisting my nipple capture my clit instead, and pinch. Hard. That is the last drip in my cup, and then it shatters, taking me with it.

My teeth pierce Master Ez's shoulder again. His flesh is sucked into my mouth, and it blocks the scream that tries to escape. I almost choke myself in an attempt to stifle my cries. My body moves on its own accord: undulating in a wave, with jerky stops and starts. My eyes roll back into my head and I'm not sure if they will ever come down again. A torrent, a forceful flood pours a hot wash from between my thighs, saturating everything.

My spirit hovers overhead, glowing in the warmth of release. I transform into a non-corporeal being and stare down at my body floating in a pool of its own pleasure. My gasp of shock ricochets around my bedroom as Ez leans down to suckle my clit in silent apology for his brutality. His soft tongue thoroughly tastes me, lapping at all the moisture that still flows from my body.

"Arungh," pours from my mouth, because my mind no longer processes words.

Kind hands pick me up and place me on the dry side of the

bed. I stare up at Master Ez in wonder, and for the first time in my life, I want to make love to someone. I want to show him how much he is appreciated. I want to connect instead of endure. I never thought I would feel this deep need to connect with another human being, because I feared the memories would resurface. Master Ez just proved I have nothing to fear with him, that he will protect me from the pain.

"That was perfect. Far better than I ever imagined." His eyes are alight with satisfaction.

I hadn't realized how rewarding it was to give until I brought Temptation. The act of giving is sometimes better than the climax, which is proof-positive by the gleam in Ez's eyes.

"But you didn't get anything out of it." I mutter groggily, wondering if he enjoys giving as much as I do. Then my selfishness slams into me because I didn't take care of my master's needs.

"Your pleasure is mine, Katya. I came with you," he murmurs in a sleepy yet contented voice.

"I never touched you, and I know both of your hands were on me." I call him out.

"My God, you remind me of him." Ez rumbles the most sadistic laugh I've ever heard. "You kill me."

"What?" I'm confused, but the word just ends up sounding like a huff of laughter. Ez in a good mood is an addictive experience.

"Different things get people off. While I love physical gratification as much as the next person, I get off on making someone do what they didn't want to do, but ultimately needed to do."

"So I've gathered," I mutter dryly.

"Brat," Ez whispers near my ear, causing me to quiver from the tickling sensation. With a nip to my earlobe, "I love your bite. Your teeth sinking into my shoulder drove me over the edge." A violent tremor rolls through his body, shaking the bed beneath us.

Ez clasps my hand and presses it to the front of his pajama bottoms. I can feel the dampness from his release seeping through the thin fabric. The feel of his waning arousal beneath my hand, and the knowledge that I gave him pleasure, causes an intense aftershock to rock my body. With a hungry moan, Ez captures my lips to kiss me while I ride it out.

Ez painstakingly rearranges me on the bed since my body feels like loose gelatin. He then cuddles up against my side, arms lightly embracing me. I sigh and allow his warmth to seep into my cold body.

"I'll stay for as long as it's dark. I've dreamt about this for so long." Another quiver rolls through his body.

"Thank you," I breathe out. "I don't know if I can do this again without freaking first. I'll apologize in advance. That is if you want to do this again," I self-consciously mumble. An embarrassed flush tinges my cheeks.

Instinctively, I know that everything Ez does is for a reason. While I may know who he is, I have no idea why he chose me. I just know he's trying to heal me– heal the wounds I hide deeply inside. But that doesn't mean Ez wants me on a different level. He has never once wanted my touch in return.

My insecurities are rising, and I scream at them to shut the fuck up and allow me the pleasure of enjoying this moment, no matter how wrong it may be. My contentment quiets my fears.

Curling around me, Ez whispers in my ear. "Thank you for the two best orgasms of my life. I look forward to all the ways I imagine bringing us pleasure. Freak out if you must, but you will come again… and again… and again… even if I have to tie and gag you. Be forewarned," he darkly commands.

I pass out on pleasure as Ez's hands stroke my skin and his lips tenderly take mine. My last thoughts are of how I managed to give him two orgasms, and how I've only had two orgasms in my life: my shame and the one Ez provided.

Restraint 172

Chapter Fifteen

"Zeitler's not here today," Monica blurts out as she barges into my office, uninvited as usual. My office door slamming shut accentuates her words.

Brows knitted together, I look up from the manuscript I'm perusing for an author Edge Publishing is vetting. "What do you mean?" My voice pitches high with confusion.

As far as I know, Zeitler is around. I'm ninety-nine percent positive that Ezra Zeitler is Master Ez of the EZ persuasion. I last saw him less than two hours ago... in my bed.

Ez stayed well-past sun-up. My blackout drapes effectively cut off any infiltrating light as we laid in bed chatting about things of little consequence, simply getting to know one another on a different level.

While with Ez, I couldn't think of why it was so very wrong, not when he was telling me funny stories about his childhood. He was an endless stream of affectionate teasing about Aaron's awkward years, and how Aaron and Roarke drive him insane on a daily basis. But with Ez's absence, the regrets, the smut on my code of ethics is drowning me in doubt.

"It means... Ezra. Zeitler. Is. Not. Here. Today." Monica draws out the words like I'm being a moron for asking.

Where the fuck did he go? I want. No. I *need* to see Zeitler. I have to study him, drink him in. The anticipation is killing me.

Most importantly, I miss him already.

"I know what it means, Monica." I roll my eyes at her to make light of the situation. I don't want my stream of inner monologue to show on my face. "I just wanted to know where he went, is all," I say flippantly with a shrug, like it's no big deal.

It's a very BIG fucking deal.

"You don't have a chance in hell, fugly." Monica's evil laugh turns her warm brown eyes cold. I guess I didn't mask my face good enough.

"Dang, Human Resources is doing a spectacular job with your sensitivity training, aren't they?" The sarcasm is so thick in my voice, I could choke on it.

The woman actually flashes me a look of grudging respect for the dig.

"Don't be an idiot, Monica. You know damned well that's not what I meant. Zeitler's absence is a huge inconvenience. We had a meeting scheduled." I look down at my cell. "In ten minutes... and now is the first time I find out about it. It messes with my entire day, and you know how I love to keep an accurate schedule."

"Oh, sorry," Monica says to mollify me. She slides into my guest chair as if our uncomfortable conversation is an invitation for her to linger. "Zeitler left Friday evening with his fiancée and her family. It was a family emergency or something. Kent Preston– Adelaide's brother-in-law is huge into politics. I think he's running for Vice President," she says snootily, as if just talking about it makes her a part of their elite group. "So, Zeitler won't be back until Wednesday morning."

Disappointment and worry rush in, causing me to frown. If this is true, then my entire theory is blown to bits. While it was difficult to swallow that an affianced man was lying in my bed this morning, learning that it might not have been Ezra Zeitler next to me makes me want to throw up.

If not him, then who the fuck was I sharing my life, my bed, and my trust with?

I was excited for our meeting this morning. I couldn't wait to see Ezra Zeitler in the flesh. Knowing where *Master Ez* works, what he looks like, and what his real name is, would have been a tremendous comfort.

I wanted to look Ezra Zeitler in the eye and see Master Ez staring back at me.

It skeeved me out to think that he'd intimately touch me while he had a fiancée. But I rationalized it because he never allowed me to touch him back, so all the sexual intimacy was his odd way of healing me.

But who am I kidding, if he would've asked me to have

sex, I would've said yes without a second thought. But as soon as my mental abilities returned, I would have felt like a faithless whore and not been able to look at myself in the mirror. I wouldn't have given a shit about Adelaide Whittenhower's feelings while in Master Ez's presence. Even this morning, after doing what little we did, I feel like a whore.

Maybe Master Ez isn't Ezra Zeitler, so my conscience is clear. But if he isn't, then who the fuck is he? It's bad enough treading on another woman's territory, but it takes a real skank to have sex with a man she doesn't even know.

This out of town bullshit could be a cover story to throw me off of his trail, to complicate the game. But it's Monica happily performing the duties of Town Crier. I wouldn't believe Kayla in this instance; no doubt Ez could get her to do anything he asks. But Monica is a different story, and she's hard-headed and belligerent. She's also still angry with both Zeitler and me about Abernathy. I just don't see Monica covering for Zeitler.

"I know we don't see eye-to-eye most of the time." Monica begins, and I flash an incredulous look in her direction. She leans forward, getting into my personal space, and cautiously places her hand on my forearm.

"I believe it's because we are so much alike. And… well… I can be a bit of a bitch." We share a grin at that revelation. "Katya, please take my advice. You don't have to admit it, but somewhere in that head of yours, you're thinking about our boss in a bad way."

Monica said I don't have to admit it, so I don't. I do, however, admit that I have it bad for Master Ez. They could be one in the same, or completely different people, that's a huge difference.

"I have no thoughts of our boss, except that I have to upset a new author, whose dreams will be crushed unless Mr. Zeitler gives the okay to publish her."

Not buying it, Monica just talks over me. "Ezra loves Adelaide. They've been together for six years, and they went to school with each other from kindergarten on. Their prominent families are connected. Nothing will break them up," Monica warns. "Especially you."

I have to love Monica, while trying to make me feel better, she insults me.

Priceless.

Typical.

Much needed advice.

Noting my wounded expression, Monica leans back in her chair. "I know you've heard the rumors, but I'm not with Abernathy anymore. After nearly three years, he just dropped me with absolutely no explanation. I was good enough to spread my legs every time he wanted me, and then the next time, I no longer was."

Monica looks away from me, true pain marring her face. It's sickening of me to think, but seeing Monica as *human* has me seeing her in a new light. An anguished Monica is a beautiful sight.

"Maybe Zeitler's interested in you, or maybe he's not. But after playing with you, he will drop you, too. Men like that don't want women like us," she warns.

"And what kind of woman is that, exactly?" I ask, voice tight, trying to restrain my erupting anger. Monica is hitting way too close to home for my comfort.

"The smart and strong women. The women who demand more out of life. Women who act and think like men. Powerful men may play with us to get their cheap thrills, to get a high from the challenge of bending us. But they will always marry the easy to manage, pretty little things, and then house them in gilded cages to raise their perfect children. They look great on the front pages of newspapers during charity events while holding the hands of their pedigree offspring, and they smile sweetly during political debates."

Swallowing the bile rising in my throat, I nod my head in agreement. "Women like us," I repeat, "Can't keep our mouths shut. We'd want to be the ones up there debating the assholes with backwards policies."

"Exactly. Powerful men don't want to be shadowed by more powerful, opinionated, intelligent women. They just want to fuck us because we're a wild ride, while their wives prepare their seating charts and dinner menus."

Looking me dead-to-rights, Monica and I are bared raw for one another. "We're their dirty secrets– their wives and children are their *lives*," she stresses.

Feeling dead inside, I know I don't even have to ask, but I do anyway. "Abernathy's married, isn't he?" Monica nods in assent. "I'm sorry. I really am. But I'm not that stupid."

"You're already that stupid, Katya. It's too late," she issues an ominous warning.

Sounding in denial, "I have no intentions on Zeitler. His absence not only screws up my day, but at least the rest of the week. Kayla's going to have a fit rescheduling all of the authors I'm vetting."

"Fine, be that way," Monica sighs out, knowing full and well that everything I just said was utter bullshit. She looks disappointed in me, like she was hoping we could connect for a few minutes, or maybe the part of me that hungers for friends is projecting. "I guess our five minutes of truce are over."

"Thanks, Monica. It actually does mean something coming from you," I respond, being genuinely appreciative.

Olive skin blushing a pretty bronze, "Don't get all mushy on me, boss. I'm still after your job, ya know?" She flashes me a wicked smirk filled with promise.

"Oh, of that, I have little doubt," I drawl, smiling just as wickedly. "Good luck with that. I'm curious to see what you'll do next. Now, get out of my office and get your bony ass back to work… and if ya see my assistant, tell her to get her plump ass in here. We have some schedule rearranging to do."

The conversation with Monica hit me hard. It's the first time I saw her as a person rather than an annoyance. I think I could actually like her, if we could only get over the animosity she holds for me, and if she'd leave my job alone.

It was wrong of Monica to have an affair with Abernathy. Obviously he wasn't going to leave his wife for her, because if he was going to leave his wife, he would've done that before cheating. Monica may not have been cheating on anyone when she was with him, but she lowered herself to his level when she slept with him. It was disrespectful on so many levels.

If Master Ez is Ezra Zeitler, then I'm doing the exact same, stupid-ass thing as Monica. He's engaged to a rich, educated, influential woman. Aside from the fact that I'm none of those things, why would I lower myself by having an affair with an attached male?

I'm worth more than that.

All women are worth more, no matter their station in life. We all deserve equal respect.

But, Zeitler's vanishing act blows my theory out of the water. If he's been gone since Friday, just after I saw him at the elevator with Adelaide, then who in the hell did I spend most of my weekend with?

I lean back in my chair, close my eyes, and plot…

A long while later, "Ms. Waters?" Kayla's soft, hesitant voice jars me from my thoughts.

I glance at my assistant, mentally sizing her up. My hands remember every inch of Temptation's luscious body.

"You look lovely today. Is that a new scarf?" I compliment her, and I've never done so previously. I do so now because I want to see her reaction, and she doesn't disappoint. Kayla flushes a beautiful pink as a shy smile spreads her lips.

God, Kayla's perfect.

"My boyfriend bought this for me yesterday." Her fingertips graze the material knotted at her neck, drawing my eyes.

Hmm… boyfriend?

Either Zeitler and Kayla aren't Master Ez and Temptation, or somebody's really stepping up their game. It takes less than a heartbeat before realization strikes. If Master Ez is fooling around with me, then he's surely fucking sweet Kayla.

A tortured sound wheezes out of my throat. I lean forward, gripping the edge of my desk, sightlessly staring off into space.

Fuck men!

Fuck 'em, and not in a good way. My God, I'm a stupid bitch. I need to stop obsessing about hearts and flowers, and rainbows and dog shit, and get down to the business at hand. Who the hell is Master Ez, and what does he have to do with me?

I don't trust anyone anymore, especially myself. But I do trust facts. In the four weeks I've worked here, not once has Kayla mentioned a boyfriend, nor has she ever worn a scarf. I'm sure my teeth marks are embedded in her skin beneath that knotted silk.

Logic overpowers the agony. "It's truly a beautiful scarf. Your boyfriend has *amazing* taste," I flatter.

Facts: Are Kayla's buttons fastened higher than usual? It appears so.

"I need you to rearrange my schedule for the rest of the week. I'm sorry, but Zeitler's absence has a domino effect on everything. It's too bad he took his sabbatical during Edge Publishing's Author Drive."

I study Kayla's reactions. Either she's a very good liar, or she's not Master Ez's submissive. Pet. Temptation. I'm getting more confused by the second.

Restraint 180

Chapter Sixteen

I believe in being proactive. I won't sit on my ass and wait for Master Ez to make his next move or for Ezra Zeitler to show back up on Wednesday morning. My mind has been spinning furiously, trying to light on anything that makes a bit of sense.

My mind kept stalling on Ezra Zeitler, the owner of Edge Publishing, and how I hadn't seen him for the first month of my employ. It glared so brightly that I finally figured something out.

I was hired for the top position at Edge Publishing without ever meeting the owner. I have a staff beneath me, and an assistant of my own. Kayla is highly professional, efficient, organized, and task-minded, and I share her with my most important minions. Monica is tasked to handle my work overflow, and when I have nothing for her to do, she is to assist Alec with the promotional aspects of the business. There are a handful of employees I personally supervise, but Edge Publishing also has a large group of work-at-home employees: copyeditors, proofreaders, and other various taskmasters. Edge Publishing takes up the entire fourteenth floor of The Edge Building.

After thinking over how Edge Publishing operates, an important fact came to light.

Ezra Zeitler has no assistant. He has no jobs to perform, other than okaying who and what we publish. There was a reason I never met him in the hallway, and why all of our communications were either via email or through Kayla.

I met Ezra Zeitler when he was ready to meet me.

It's amazing how thinking of committing a crime brings to light how my boss doesn't have an assistant. A very welcome oddity that I don't have to make up excuses or try to sneak past them to break into my boss's office.

Kayla's like a beautiful, champion show dog chained to my office door. Even I can't go in or out without her knowing my every single move. She's currently getting my lunch, where I purposely sent her ten blocks away to order me an ice coffee at an obscure coffee shop.

Preemptive strike.

Ninja Kat is in action. I stalk down the hallway, sticking to the walls, wishing for shadows that do not exist. As I ghost, I feel like a criminal. I look guiltily over my shoulder every few seconds, feeling prying eyes I cannot see.

Thankfully, the hallway is desolate. I had to wait until it was in the middle of lunch hour, with most of the employees either out-to-lunch or tucked safely away in their offices. The time of day dramatically cut down on non-employee foot traffic, but upped the chances of my coworkers milling the halls.

My office is several hundred feet down the hallway from Zeitler's. The elevator is directly in the middle of that space. My eyes keep cutting back to the elevator doors while my ears tune in for the telltale sound of the elevator on the move. It would be just my luck that those doors would open up and spit Zeitler out, just as I commit my first crime.

I wait, leaning against the wall, examining my chipped fingernail polish all nonchalant-like, looking like I belong where I rest. Nope, I'm not contemplating breaking and entering– wouldn't dream of it.

I creep silently down the hallway, eyes on the lookout for coworkers who will rat my ass out. Zeitler's office lies straight ahead, beckoning me with its hidden secrets. I quickly sprint the last twenty feet, and then I lean my back against Zeitler's door, catching my breath. My hand slowly creeps, seeking out its prize. My fingertips quickly twist the doorknob.

Drat!

It's locked

I drop to my knees, yanking a pin from my hair as I move. I unsurely poke at the lock. All the while I hear an imaginary timer going off in my mind. If I don't get this door unlocked within a minute, I'm going to have to hightail it back to my office in defeat.

Years of snooping on my older sister comes in handy. Living in a one bathroom home with a mother and a teenaged sister was always a challenge. I learned how to pick the lock on the bathroom door, because it was either that or piss outside. Who knew it took three hours to pluck your eyebrows, which is why I am not a girly-girl. Years of being the tomboy is also why it takes less than thirty seconds before I hear the snick of Zeitler's door unlocking.

Movement over my shoulder draws me from my crouch. Mailman Rick strolls towards me, happily whistling his usual cheery tune. The obvious is the unobvious. I make no excuses for my presence. I wear a smile and innocently wave as he strides by.

The moment Mailman Rick turns the corner, out of sight, I turn the knob on Zeitler's office door, and step inside. I silently pray the office is vacant. What a shitty Ninja Kat I would make if I break into an occupied office... I'm mean, c'mon, really?

I breathe a sigh of relief that a six-foot-tall towhead isn't sitting behind the maple desk. Dragging oxygen into my lungs, tasting the scent in the air on the back of my tongue, I can smell him in here: smoky, spicy, and warm. It's the same scent that is infused in my sheets. I enjoyed the fragrance of his skin as I laid in bed this morning, procrastinating before I went to work. I'd know that scent anywhere.

I lean against the door and take a few brief moments to survey the space. I try to imagine the man, Ezra Zeitler, working in here. Even more insane, imagine Master Ez sitting behind that desk. Neither seems possible.

The room has absolutely no personality, bland and lifeless. The lack of an assistant is a huge tip-off, but the absence of the usual detritus screams that this office is just a formality. The place is spotless, and I don't just mean clean. Nothing is out of place, no personal effects, no mementos from sandy-beach vacations, not even a potted plant. Everything feels staged.

Spurred into action, I push away from the door and scope out the place. The desk, office chair, and guest seating are exactly as mine. However, I do not have a picture of Adelaide Whittenhower smiling on the beach framed on my desk. Nor do I have a photo and announcement of my engagement to said woman hanging proudly from my wall. Blonde, blue-eyed, and waifish, Adelaide pleasantly taunts me from the pictures.

Resentment coils in my gut. If Zeitler is Master Ez, and I'm now ninety-nine-point-nine percent positive he is, then I'm officially as stupid as Monica said I am, and I should be punting myself in the cunt. If Ezra Zeitler isn't Master Ez, then I hate my boss on principle. The lucky fucker has everything I don't have: happy life, a beautiful spouse-to-be, and gobs of money to take insanely expensive vacations.

Snap out of it, Katya. You have a game to play and information to find. Emotions will only sidetrack you. Shut it down and stick to the facts.

I yank open the drawers to his desk, finding absolutely nothing– as in *empty* drawers. A large pile of mail sits atop the desk, drawing my attention. I grab a handful, and quickly leaf through it, checking the mailing dates. It appears my boss hasn't gone through the pile since Friday, lending validly to the out-of-town story.

Hmm… what do we have here? *Men's Health* and *GQ* tell me absolutely nothing. As for *Mental Health Weekly*, that is a different story. Holding the magazine in my fingertips, I check to make sure it's his and not a mistake.

The mailing label says **Dr. Ezra Zeitler**.

What the fuck?

The publication falls from my fingertips onto the desktop with a loud thud, scattering envelopes onto the floor.

Magazines say a lot about people. My *Writer's Digest* and *RT Book Reviews* say that I'm an avid reader, perhaps in the profession. *TV Guide* and *Entertainment Weekly* say I love information on shows, movies, and pop culture.

You wouldn't read *Parents* if you didn't have kids. You wouldn't read *Cigar Aficionado* if you didn't love a good stogie. Why would you read *The Game Informer* if you didn't play video games?

I can see Zeitler loving the first two magazines in his pile by the shape of his body and his fondness for designer labels. Curiosity, what does a book publisher need with psychiatry magazines? And most importantly, what kind of M.D. is Zeitler?

I do the first thing any smart woman should have done. I

finally admit that I am a reformed stupid girl. I whip out my cellphone and Google Dr. Ezra Zeitler.

I don't dare go into a major search while in the commission of a crime. The first item on the Google search is a phone number listing.

Dr. Ezra Zeitler: licensed Clinical Psychiatrist specializing in repressed memories, PTSD, and mental trauma. #1456 North Avenue. The Edge Building #112. Dominion, New York.

"Motherfucker," I snarl as I quickly dial the phone number listed for the office on the first floor of this very building, smart enough to use Zeitler's *'fake'* office phone to call his *'real'* office.

You have reached the office of Dr. Ezra Zeitler. Please leave your name and number, and I will return your call to set up a consultation during office hours.

I don't recognize the deep, manly voice, but if Ezra Zeitler is *my* Master Ez, then I know for a fact Aaron Frost and Roarke Walden take turns babysitting him. Perhaps the owner of this voice belongs to Roarke.

Eager to vacate before I'm caught, I make my way to the door before I go postal, irrational female on my boss's office. Hand on the doorknob, a framed picture catches my notice.

Judging by the clothing styles, the photograph is ten to fifteen years old. A group of waspy kids, ranging from young adults down to a little guy, are surrounding a tiny girl holding a *'Sweet 16'* party hat. The birthday girl looks decidedly uncomfortable as she glares daggers at the camera. Ezra Zeitler and another young man are bookending the girl, their arms thrown over her shoulders as they look to one another over her head.

Dread settles in the pit of my stomach. I ignore the fact that a young Fate is resting against a young Queen's shoulder, while the pair of them grin down at an angelic little fellow, and a gangly Aaron is smiling broadly at the camera...

I ignore all of them in lieu of the bookends. One is obviously a young Ezra, with his white hair and pale skin. The other is Ezra's perfect counterpart: tan skin to Ezra's light.

Dark hair to Ezra's white. But everything else is identical: gunmetal gray eyes, the way they hold their tall, lean bodies, and the same exact smile twisting their lips that somehow denotes different emotions. Ezra's smile is sardonic, while his counterpart's is mischievous.

Which begs the question...

Why does a psychiatrist own a publishing company?

What relationship does suit-guy from the front of Restraint have to do with Ezra Zeitler?

The questions have one answer: A best friend would buy their best friend a company to publish his books.

*Ez*ra Zeitler and Cort*ez* Abernathy.

Are there *two* Master Ezes?

***

I slink back to my office, feeling rather smug after my B&E's success, but heartsick over the facts I found.

One step into my office, and something feels different– off. Wrong. It's almost as if I can feel a disturbance in the air surrounding me. Someone was in here while I was in Dr. Zeitler's office, I know it. My eyes rove over the entire room, noting changes. But nothing is out of the ordinary.

I stiffen at the grotesque sight in the center of my coffee table.

Sweat emerges, beading along my spine, and adrenaline floods my veins. My heart goes into hyper-drive, fluttering in my chest. I creep towards my table, looking left and right over my shoulders. My eyes tell me I'm alone, but the sensation creeping up my spine screams differently.

I can feel eyes on me. Eyes I cannot see.

I flump down on my sofa cushion with an exhausted huff, and I just stare wide-eyed at my coffee table.

Bewildered. Lost. "Fuck me," is forced out between my clenched teeth. "You've got to be fucking kidding me." A hysterical giggle bubbles up my throat. I just stare in awe, shaking my head back and forth... back and forth... back and forth. "Fuck," I breathe.

The BDSM hedonistic chessboard is proudly displayed in the center of my coffee table, with all the pieces set into position. An ominous note is resting between the warring sides: black vs. white.

I gingerly retrieve the folded piece of paper from between the kneeling submissives, and flatten it out on the tabletop. Holding the note, my hands shake so badly that I can barely make out the words.

~My devious Kat burglar~
Do you not appreciate the chess set? How can we play if it's hidden beneath your desk? I want the board to stay right where it is, Katya. I've removed two of your submissives from the board, overtaking them during the game. My little sneak, you've removed one of mine by your expedition this afternoon.
How you please me.
-Forever your Lord & Master-
The Boss– Ez

"Motherfuck!" I shout to the empty room. I can almost hear Master Ez's calm, patronizing voice in my ear as I read the words. I inhale deeply, hoping to catch his scent lingering in the air, proof that he was in here, whoever the hell he is.

I can't leave the board set up in the middle of my office, not with a constant stream of meetings set up over the next few days. I'm not going to allow Edge Publishing to go down in flames because of the whims of its owner and/or author.

"It's not what you want, Master. It's what you need." I smirk down at the creepy chess set. "Do you really need the game *this* accessible?"

Since I cannot do anything with the information I just obtained, I do what I can. Inspiration strikes. My fingers pluck up a black pawn submissive and set it off to the side. I move the white pony-playing Knight into position. The obscenity isn't lost on me: my pony-playing knight rises above the kneeling submissive pawn in front. Master Ez is a perverted motherfucker, and I kind of love him (them?) for it.

Chuckles bubble up as I make my real play. "Game on, bastard."

Restraint 188

Chapter Seventeen

This is the most difficult moment of my night. I hate dredging up the past, wallowing in it for the sake of healing. It seems contradictory. Shouldn't I move forward with my life, not fall backwards? Trying to relive every second of my violation seems counterproductive and regressive.

What is so wrong with wanting to forget?

I curl up on the sofa while wearing fuzzy pajama pants and a hoodie, and I'm wrapped up in a fleece blanket. These sessions always drain the will to live right out of me, and I need the comfort. I have a carton of black raspberry ice cream, a bag of plain potato chips and French Onion dip, and a package of Oreos on standby.

I log onto my biweekly therapy session with my laptop. Many patients go to their psychiatrist's office, sit on a sofa, and pour their hearts out. Many don't say a word, or clam up, or lie. How do I know this, you ask?

Simple, I used to be one of them.

I'd go to my sessions and freeze up. I'd feign memory loss and sit there like a stone. My past is humiliating– my own personal hell. Why would I share those moments of torment with a complete stranger who is silently judging every word I speak?

That's exactly what it feels like. Judgment. Because that's exactly what it is. The therapist is staring at your face, watching your every expression, as if you are a specimen under a microscope. They dissect every word you speak for hidden meanings, all the while never saying anything as you answer their hypothetical questions.

I was attacked, violated, and abased like an animal. But I lost something more valuable that day. I lost my right to privacy. Everyone forgets that you are a human being in their quest to help you, as if they have a right to every thought you make. Not only did I have to tell the authorities, my family, my doctors, my lawyers, the judge, the jury, reporters, random strangers… I now have to share my nightmare with countless therapists until the day I die.

Why, I ask again, is it wrong to want to forget?

At the last parole hearing for Raymond Hunter, I went catatonic, refusing to speak. The judge was upset, almost releasing my rapist. Even knowing how important it was to have a voice, I just couldn't say the words out loud again. It's like repeatedly being violated, only it's by those who say they want to help you.

I now have a court-appointed psychiatrist. The judge granted my request for anonymity to lessen the humiliation. No in-person sessions. No phone-in sessions. No Skype sessions. I screamed that he either do it my way, or he could throw me in jail for contempt of court, because I was not speaking the words out loud another time for the rest of my life.

Judge Paxton didn't want to risk looking like a judge who would prosecute the victim, so we reached an agreement to online sessions. But the judged stressed how badly I was in need of therapy since I had the audacity to question his judgment in the middle of his courtroom.

For the past three years and some change, I have engaged in therapy sessions with Dr. Jeannine twice per month. The relief I feel in the ability to type the words to the psychiatrist is astounding. She cannot see me and I cannot see her, and it makes this horrible situation bearable, tolerable, yet so very un-fucking-comfortable.

KitKat411: I'm here, @liv2heal

liv2heal: logging on…

liv2heal: How have you been since our last session?

KitKat411: Struggling, but there's nothing new with that.

liv2heal: I can't help you if you deflect. Has there been a change since we last spoke two weeks ago?

KitKat411: The memories partially resurfaced. It's always the same shit. My feelings don't change. You said I would gain a different perspective, that the regressive memories would resurface and I could finally move on with my life. It's not happening, and I don't see what the big deal is about remembering. Trust me, it's overrated. I'd rather be in the dark than be in an endless loop of self-torture.

liv2heal: You went through a tragic event. It changed you at the core of your personality. It takes time. As you heal, the perspective WILL change. You cannot heal what you don't acknowledge. Ignoring it will not make it go away. You're stronger than that, Katya.

KitKat411: If I've said this once, I've said it a billion times: I do not understand WHY I need to remember something my brain is blocking as a way to protect me. I trust my mind's decision. If I subconsciously don't want to know, then I don't need to know.

liv2heal: There is a reason you've blocked out some of the events, while others are brightly spotlit. Your mind is protecting you, and when you are ready, it will reveal itself. I understand moving forward, but your mental block says we need to go backwards and work through it before we can move forward into the future.

KitKat411: Are you aware that you've repeated that same bullshit line twice a month for the past thirty-six months? It's like you just copy/paste from our previous sessions, and then plug in the responses depending on how I respond. I'm not getting better. I'm getting worse. And you are not helping me at all. This is a total waste of both of our times.

liv2heal: You are light-years ahead of where you were when we started our sessions. You are getting better, even if you don't realize it because of the delicate subtlety.

KitKat411: I went to a BDSM club. I have a man stalking me, and I'm pretty sure he is my very engaged boss. But even then, I'm not so sure. He could also be my married client. Or he could be a combination of the two. Clearly, I'm not getting any better since I allowed him to touch me sexually, knowing he was cheating on his significant other. I play these games, and for some unexplainable reason, I get off on it. Is that healing? Is that sane? I don't fucking think so! It's morally bankrupt.

liv2heal: You've never been sexually active before, so that is a major step in a positive direction for a woman at your age. While it is amoral to have an affair with an attached man, it's commonplace for someone with your background.

KitKat411: You've got to be smoking crack with one hand and typing with the other.

liv2heal: DEFLECTION.

KitKat411: Did I anger you? Shouty caps, much?

liv2heal: You've never been able to stand the touch of a male, or even the females you've used for gratification. Textbook behavior of a victim with intimacy issues. You chose the attached man because he is unobtainable. It is a safety mechanism.

KitKat411: Trust me, I had no choice in the matter. Did you miss the part where I wrote STALKER? Mind you, I seem to enjoy it, so I'll own that shit.

liv2heal: Progress, owning your decisions, whether right or wrong. Another very poor decision is that he is your boss. You need to think of your career first, his fiancée second, and your own self-respect. You mentioned your client as a possibility as well: the same advice applies.

KitKat411: I'd feel better if you'd just call me a faithless whore and be done with it. Then I could own that, too.

liv2heal: Katya, I'm only mentioning this now to stop you. I will NEVER engage you when you exhibit childish behavior. Your decisions. Your consequences. Own them, and then move on from them. Your choices shape you; they do not define you.

KitKat411: I bet I piss you off. My psychiatrists in the past didn't last long before I broke them, made them crack a smile, roll their eyes, sigh, or curse at me. I wonder if you love the anonymity of online therapy more than I do. I bet you're hurling expletives at your laptop screen from the privacy of your own home. Dr. Jeannine, do you and your doctor friends sit around once a week over wine and trade horror stories? Does my behavior put you as a shoe-in for the most problematic patient award?

liv2heal: While you are behaving as a woman of your own age, you need to examine why you're acting out.

KitKat411: Doctor, don't you think that by not engaging my childish behavior, it's simply ignoring a problem? Isn't that what you always tell me, how we have to acknowledge a problem or we can't heal it? How are we to heal my childish behavior if you ignore it?

KitKat411: You're screaming at me right now, aren't you? You hate that I just threw your own psycho-babble bullshit right back at you.

liv2heal: As for the BDSM club, I think it's a good idea. Perhaps someone could teach you some manners.

KitKat411: HA! I bent you a bit, right there, didn't I? Admit it. I didn't break you. But I most certainly bent you.

liv2heal: You changed the day you were physically attacked. It mentally wounded you. You can never come back from that and be the person you once were. You may have gained the BDSM cravings from your ordeal. The power exchange this offers is not unexpected for a woman with your background. I sense a great need to be in control, which is why you keep deflecting by baiting me during our sessions. But I also sense your underlying need for me to put you in your place, which is making you lash out because I refuse to engage in that destructive behavior.

KitKat411: Point taken. But I get so sick of you spouting off about how everything I do is directly tied to my attack. One hour of my life DOES NOT have to impact every hour that follows. Everything doesn't have to be nature vs. nurture. Maybe my '*ordeal*' only strengthened needs I already possessed, or I wouldn't have enjoyed certain, debilitating parts of my ordeal. I shouldn't be chatting with you, paying to listen to your psycho-babble bullshit. It only makes me more confused, even more unsure of myself, and it makes me feel worse.

liv2heal: The needs which took you to a BDSM club, most certainly manifested with your attack. It is not in your nature to act in such a manner. As for your '*enjoyment*', it was your body's only recourse in order to protect your mind that afternoon. Biologically, a punch hurts, just as sex feels good. Even if you want to be hit, it's still going to hurt. Even if you don't want to have sex, your body is still going to respond as if it felt good. Our minds protect us when we can't handle what's happening to our outside bodies. Yours chose an unconventional method to protect itself.

KitKat411: Would it kill you to just say what you mean? Just say, "You enjoyed your rape." I accept it. I own how I got off, how I had an orgasm while being violated. Now you need to make peace with it, too. And fuck your nurture views. My nature is to enjoy this sick shit. I started this long before my rape.

liv2heal: Please explain.

KitKat411: Nurture: I was the second and youngest child to a set of parents who have been married for forty years, who took the best care of me. I was not molested or abused in any way. Nature: I played rape fantasies as a child. I wasn't even ten years old yet. I was the attacker, and I would chase my friend down. She was just a little girl, too. She was a few months younger than me. She was a little girl who was being molested by the men in her family: her father, her uncle, her brother and his friend. So she was always really scared when we played this game. Instead of calling the authorities and saving her, I played with her mind. I was too young to feel anything about the sex, but not too young to enjoy her fear. I'd chase her, bring her to the ground. We played it, but never went past the capture. It's only fitting to be the victim after always being the victimizer, don't you think? My NATURE is sick!

liv2heal: Is this true?

KitKat411: FUCK YOU & FUCK OFF!

Chapter Eighteen

Plotting for the game, in which I am not a player but the actual pawn, takes my mind off of my therapy session. Or so I lie to myself. I've chatted with Dr. Jeannine since the court appointed her to my case when Raymond Hunter was up for parole three years ago. It's hard to let go after such a long history, but I'm done with these one-sided conversations with a faceless antagonist. In Dr. Jeannine's defense, I haven't told her everything.

No shit, that's an understatement.

The last bit of info I shouty-caps-locked at Dr. Jeannine was epic. It enraged me when she thought I was lying. No one lies about shit that sick.

I wasn't lying. I grew up in a home that was the epitome of the American Dream: start out dirt-poor, work your fingers to the bone to feed your family and put a roof over their heads, love your wife and children as if your life depended on it, and then succeed in your endeavors.

I was never abused in any fashion, and I have absolutely no idea where these sick fantasies came from. But I've had them for as long as I remember. But I will say being gang raped cured me of them.

I used to hunt and stalk my friends and cousins. It never turned sexual because I didn't know how to make it sexual. My body had needs I didn't understand. Even as young as four, I was lurking around the fringes, waiting to pounce on my loved ones. I was a sweet and quiet child, overly sensitive and could cry at the drop of a hat. But there were times I felt truly evil. What I just admitted to Dr. Jeannine is one of my biggest and darkest secrets, and it has put a taint on my soul.

I'd always wondered if my stalking, hunting, and raping were God's way of paying me back for the way I spent my early childhood. If so, then I've learned my lesson, and I've learned it well.

Pushing away the pain of my past, I begin act two of my investigation. Internet searches on Dr. Ezra Zeitler and Cortez

Abernathy.

Ezra and Cortez, who I will now call the Ezes, grew up on a huge estate named Shadow Haven. The estate is on the fringes of Dominion, in a gated community known as Crestview. While I was unable to find a familial or financial connection between the Ezes, Shadow Haven has been their mutual address since birth. They attended school together until their graduation from Hillbrook Preparatory School, where they parted ways with Ezra going to Harvard and Cortez beginning his writing career.

Ezra Zeitler comes from a long line of *Old Money*. Old money that was invested over and over again, creating a *lot* of new money. According to tax records, he is listed as the owner of Restraint and Edge Publishing, as well as self-employed through his medical practice.

Most of the interesting information came from society pages filled with Adelaide and Ezra's vacations, celebratory occasions, and gossip. Balls, charity functions, humanitarian efforts, awards and ceremonies, Ezra has Adelaide on his arm in all of the pictures. He couldn't have been more than twenty when they began dating.

One of the largest affairs was when Cortez Abernathy married Divina Hastings, Ezra's first cousin on his mother's side. It was the wedding of the decade according to the website I was perusing, and it featured dozens upon dozens of photos of Cortez and Divina, as well as Ezra and Adelaide. Every other bit of information I found on Cortez was book-related: fan pages, reviews, and promotional and sale pages.

Ezra Zeitler is something of a media darling himself, being called the billionaire bachelor. He's not shown in a light as being a playboy, more reluctant to be tied down.

I have no words to express how I'm feeling in this moment. I'm almost numb. Almost, because there is a quiet rage simmering beneath the surface. I have no idea if Ezra and Cortez are tag-teaming me. But I do know for a fact one or both are Master Ez, since there is no other plausible explanation.

It's the why that is bothering me the most, the

disingenuousness of this entire situation. Why me? Why make a fool of me?

Ezra Zeitler and Cortez Abernathy are rich men suffering with ennui, and I am a challenge who fits into their criteria: broken enough to intrigue the psychiatrist, with a passion for the written word to fascinate the writer.

I'm not as daft as Monica. Yes, in my heart of hearts I believed it to be Ezra who was Master Ez, and I felt a deep connection with the man. Even now, thinking about it hurts me as much as it makes me miss him– need him. Not once did I ever believe my life would turn into a storyline ripped straight out of the pages of a contemporary romance: rich playboy heals the wounded small-town girl.

Utter bullshit.

Wealthy men marry affluent women and create pedigree children, while they play games with lesser men because they are so rich nothing has any value. You only appreciate that in which you earn, what you have to work for, what you gain through challenge. If you have enough money and power to buy the world without lifting a finger, then there is no cost to anything.

In this scenario, I am not the wife, or even the mistress. I am the disposable distraction of no worth.

I've never wanted to cunt-punt myself as badly as I do now. Any way you look at it, if it's one or the other man or both, they turned me into a faithless whore. They made me go against my beliefs by touching me while they're committed to another. Worse, I've betrayed myself, because whoever the hell Master Ez truly is, he's turned my life upside down and ass-backwards.

I want Master Ez, and that makes me sick.

Mind fucked.

The most powerful word in the English language is **WHY**.

When anything happens, good or bad, the first thing we always ask is *why*. We will go to the ends of the earth looking for the answer to that particular question.

Why is *why* so powerful? Because without the answer, we will never have closure, and it's always someone else who holds us in suspense. They have all the power as long as they hold our truths. We will always wonder, and it's always curiosity that killed the Kat.

I wouldn't be able to walk away now, even if I tried, because I have to know why. I need my questions answered, even the ones I never knew I had. I must take my power back from the Ezes by retrieving *my* truths.

I've been manipulated and coerced. I've had the carrot of truth dangled before me. I've been given my wildest dreams: the career I've always wanted. The ability to be touched by a man, and want to touch him in return. I've found my sexuality beneath the hands of an adulterous cerebral fucker.

I'm walking the knife's edge between being able to look in the mirror and like who is reflected back, and the curiosity of learning why.

I can always get more therapy to help myself sleep at night. I can always apologize to those I've hurt. I can promise myself I will never do those destructive behaviors again.

I can repent.

But I cannot live a life of asking myself why until the day that I die.

Chapter Nineteen

Reckless.

The longer I go without seeing Master Ez, I'm either experiencing clarity or a warped sense of reality. I find myself wanting to fuck over Master Ez, to lash out. I simultaneously want to ignore him, but at the same time I want to get his attention.

As the hours pass, I find that girl I've buried deep, the evil, naughty part of me. I've always had the ability to see the insecurities held within someone and exploit them– kick them where it hurts. I loathe this part of myself, always believing even though I've never acted upon these dark thoughts, Karma still punished me for thinking them in the first place.

I've always been logical, respecting all those around me, treating them as I wished to be treated. Yet, I've been lowered time and time again. The vengeful girl is slowly erupting, wanting to behave badly just because she can, because it doesn't matter either way.

A good girl was raped in her sacred place. A good woman is being stalked in her new home. Being good never got me anywhere but harmed.

A smart woman protects herself by stalking back.

It's sixteen hours before I do something stupid– irreversible. I don't know what, but I know I won't be able to take it back. It's Tuesday afternoon, and all of my time is spent counting the hours until Wednesday morning. Waiting to see Zeitler in the flesh reminds me of high school, where you'd sit in class waiting for your crush to arrive, but he never showed.

The day feels empty– unnecessary.

The reckless part of me is gaining strength without proper supervision. I now find myself lying in wait for my assistant, to steal one of my truths back.

Tuesday has been a lonely day, indeed. I've yet to see Kayla at all today. She didn't even come into the office this morning, feigning an appointment.

I hear the knock on my office door as much as watch it

reverberate, since I've been staring at it for hours… waiting.

"Enter," I call, anticipation boiling in my blood.

Kayla slinks in wearing that scarf again. I'm not exaggerating about the slinkage. She rolls her hips as she walks, sashaying across my office. It's as sexy as it is unnerving.

Something akin to revenge takes me over. I may not have any control when it comes to Master Ez: Dr. Ezra Zeitler and/or Cortez Abernathy. Whoever the fuck the guy is, or guys, as the case may be. But I know without a shadow of a doubt that Kayla is Temptation.

I'm not going to harm Kayla. I'm going to teach her a lesson, and if I'm right about her being Temptation, she will find the punishment more of a reward.

Walking across my office, jouncing her tits and shaking her ass and twitching her hips, she's challenging me to prove she is Temptation. Begging for it. I'm about to give her a taste of what she wants.

"Come in and lock the door," I order low from my throat, followed by a husky sound that pours out, surprising us both.

Bless Kayla's heart. She does as I ask; locking herself in my office with me while I'm obviously in a mood, proving my Temptation suspicions.

"Katya, what is it?" She looks confused, tiny blonde brows knitting above her ever-trusting eyes. God, I hope she's acting, because in my current state of mind, this could get messy.

I stalk towards her, swaying my hips as I go, seeing if my body holds any allure. Kayla's eyes dart around wildly like a spooked animal. Her uncertainty ignites me, forcing lust to pour through me. It makes me do the things I'd usually avoid– the stupid, stupid things.

"Mmm… you wore the scarf again. Lovely." As I finger her silk scarf, my intensity backs Kayla up until she is pressed between me and the door. "Did you wear it just for me?" I purr in a sultry tone, tugging on the ends of the scarf, teasing that I'm going to remove it.

"Ms. Waters," Kayla gasps out, and we're back to Ms. Waters when I was Katya a moment ago. "What are you doing?" Her blue eyes are huge, glistening with anticipation.

Good question. What am I doing?

I can't test Dr. Ezra Zeitler since he won't show up to work– coward –and I have no idea how to find Master Ez. I could stalk Restraint, but he'd tan my ass raw for that. However, little Kayla, she will do as I ask, and she is right here, right now. If she fights me, it's all the better.

A quiver begins in my toes, waves over my body, almost undulating me. The force of the potent sensation leaves my scalp tingling, and then surges back to my feet. It's like my childhood, chasing my friend. No matter how wrong I know it is, I can't find the strength to stop myself.

Kayla is so soft and supple, so sweet and juicy, and she will never say no. I just hope I'm not wrong about her being Temptation. Because even if she isn't Master Ez's multipurpose submissive, Kayla will still readily bend to my will.

"I think you did. You wore it just for me, because of me. Didn't you?" I pluck the buttons of her blouse, one at a time, exposing her lacy bra.

"Yes." Kayla's breath shudders out and her body trembles under my hooded, predatorial gaze.

I act on instinct, on want, without a thought or care for consequences, because that's what you do when you embrace temptation. Holding Kayla's wide gaze, I cup her lace-covered breast in the palm of my hand. The weight of the flesh is exquisite. I give it a gentle squeeze, fingertips pressing in and dimpling her breast, loving how responsive Kayla is to my touch. Never taking my eyes from hers, I graze her nipple with my thumb, and it pebbles for me as if eager to obey my silent command.

"Ms. Waters, what are you doing?" Kayla stammers out in a breathy voice. Her aroused tone belies her slurry of confused words.

Ducking beneath my arm, she slides from between me and the door, no longer trapped. "Don't do that!" she whispers, yet the words slap me as if she shouted. Her feet take her across my office, away from the door. Away from safety.

As Kayla tracks across the carpet, I keep pace with her, never overtaking her. Stalking. Seeking. Hunting my prey.

It's sick to admit, but I've never felt so exhilarated. My body thrums with life, with excitement and anticipation–boiling over with lust.

Head cocked to the side, holding her in my sights, I drawl out, "Oh, Kayla, don't flee. It excites me so," I warn in voice that screams *RUN!*

Panting wildly, luscious tits rising and falling beneath her abrupt intakes of air, as well as jiggling from her poor attempts at escape, I swear Kayla's trying to tempt me, not thwart me. With a whimper, she rounds my desk, putting it between us, believing it makes her safe.

Leaning forward, I place my hands on the edge of my desk, with the short expanse between us. "Mmm… forget what I said. Excite me, Kayla. Ignite me, Kayla. Run, Kayla, and let me chase you. I want to see where it leads. Flee from me… run from me… let me chase you…" I chant.

Subconsciously obeying, Kayla moves left. I feign right and circle back towards her. She is breathing in little pants, gasping, causing her flesh to pink beautifully. It builds my excitement to intoxicating levels. She makes a dash around the desk, a poor attempt at fleeing, and adrenaline rushes through my system from the thrill of the chase and the impending capture.

"Don't move," I order in a throaty voice.

Kayla freezes, tits jiggling from a sharp gasp while she tries her damnedest to remain at rest.

"Good girl. Peeerrrrfect," rolls off my tongue, a raspy growl barely sounding like a word.

I watch Kayla visibly fret. She's feeling uncertain, mulling over if she should continue the chase by running to the door, essentially giving me what I want, or obey me by not moving. The calculating glint in her eyes makes me so damned proud. Master Ez taught Kayla well. She's smart, anticipating what I want, what I need.

If Kayla wasn't Temptation, if she wanted to leave, she would've escaped already. She wants this as much as I do, the little tease.

I round my desk until I'm even with Kayla's trembling body. "Don't fight me," I warn. I lean forward, using my body to press my assistant into the desk. Holding her gaze, issuing another silent warning, I run my hand up her skirt, finding soft, perfectly plump flesh.

Palm skating up her inner thigh, skirt hooking on my forearm, I knead her bare flesh as I go. My eyelids shutter, becoming hooded from the sensation of her feverish skin beneath my fingertips. Perfect.

"Ms. Waters. Don't do that." Releasing breathy little gasps, Kayla faux-struggles to get away. Her small slaps connect with my shoulders and back, barely brushing my skin in her attempt to not anger me as she pretends to fight back. The combination of it all causes my body to flash with liquid heat.

"Calling me Ms. Waters isn't doing anything but exciting me more. Disobeying me excites me, too." I dig my nails into her tender thigh. "I told you not to fight me, not to move. Yet you disobey. Keep it up and we'll see where it leads," I warn in a voice gone husky with lust.

Kayla fitfully struggles in my arms, more for my benefit than for true escape. She's playacting the scene, feeding my hunger.

"Yes, fight me. Struggle more. Disobey me, Kayla," I purr her name into her ear, nipping the lobe with my front teeth. Her moan informs me how I've won the battle of wills.

With quick, forceful movements, I shove Kayla over the arm of the guest chair, ass up with her face resting upon the seat cushion. I fling her skirt up, until her panty-clad, round rear is revealed.

"Oh, God," I groan, hungry. Kayla's plump ass is covered in tiny, white lace panties. Her rosy pink skin is delectable, bitable, begging for a teasing smack.

"Naughty, Kayla." I tear her panties from her body.

The harsh sound of renting fabric pools moisture between my thighs, dampening the seat of my panties. I expose Kayla's ass to my viewing pleasure– plump and round, perfectly swat-able.

Without conscious thought, I find myself swatting Kayla's behind.

Once…

Twice…

Thrice… four times until Kayla's skin glows bright red and my palm is outlined on her ass. Her moans, sobs, and cries turn me on like nothing ever has before.

My God, the power!

I gasp through the heady sensations wracking my body. "I have a theory. Two things happened recently: I was gifted with the use of highly trained submissive and your behavior changed. I ignored it yesterday. But, beauty, it was the same today. For a month, you've teased me until I throbbed and ached. Yesterday, you showed up all covered instead of your usual teasing attire. The temptation to rip your clothes from your body was worse. So I did."

I swat Kayla's ass again just to hear her squeal, the reverberating force stinging my palm.

"I think this scarf is for me, too." I abruptly tug the silk tied securely around Kayla's throat, nearly choking her. But she is calm beneath my touch, trusting me infallibly.

I wrap my hand around the front of Kayla's neck, lifting her until her back meets my chest. She is a few inches taller than me, a larger girl in all aspects. But this works to my advantage. Nose nuzzling her hair, I set my teeth into the silk covering her neck. I bite over the scarf, knowing exactly what I will find beneath it– evidence. My tongue fishes underneath the fabric… and I feel exactly what I was seeking.

"Oh, my temptation, beauty," I moan in ecstasy. I gently squeeze my hand on her throat, while my other hand smooths down her body, inching her skirt up in the front, and dipping between her trembling thighs. My fingers easily enter her wet pussy, slipping in and out, making a *squish-squish* sound... and then I bite her.

Hard.

Kayla's generous body quivers beneath my touch. Moans, pleas, and whimpers flow from her lips as she climaxes for me.

The louder her moans, the faster I thrust my fingers inside her, until I'm fucking her sopping wet pussy with four fingers.

"Say it!" I demand while Kayla comes on my hand. "Say it!"

"Yes, Mistress. I'm your Temptation," she breathes reverently.

Gripping Kayla's hips, I haul her onto my desk. I prop her heels onto my shoulders, and I reward the world's most perfect submissive by feasting between her thighs with my lips, tongue, teeth, and fingertips. I hold her in place with a hand wrapped around the scarf that covers my bite mark. The bite mark I gave Temptation at Restraint...

Afterwards, I'm thoroughly content running my lips over Kayla's neck and cheek as I hold her on my couch. I close my eyes and visualize the chessboard. Kayla earned me another move— another truth. A satisfied smile twists my lips as I lean forward to move the pieces. White pony-playing Knight overtakes Black penis-shaped Bishop. I'm progressing nicely.

Restraint 206

Chapter Twenty

I've been running on pure adrenaline for the past sixteen hours– the high from taking control of Kayla and the thrill of the hunt.

I understand Master Ez better now, recognizing how he was doing to me what I've always done to others, showing me how frustrating it is. I've always been in control of my female conquests, giving them pleasure and refusing to allow them to do the same to me in return. Master Ez fed me a taste of my own medicine over and over again, and I hated the flavor.

Even while saying I craved the need to submit, I longed to take over by touching Master Ez in return. Not that I should *want* to touch him. Not that he wants me to touch him. But that doesn't change the fact that I want to touch him against my better judgment, but that could just be the high talking.

I was shocked when I didn't hear from Master Ez last night. I thought for sure he would want an update on our little game. Plus, I'd uncovered Temptation's true identity. No question that it was definitive proof. I thought for sure Kayla would run her satisfied little rump right back to her master and gossip about me.

I might be disappointed that I didn't receive a pat on the back for a job well done, but I'll deny it.

My heart beats rapidly in anticipation. The suspense is killing me. Time has slowed to a crawl as I waited for Wednesday morning to approach. I sit in my office like a junkie waiting for their next hit off a crack pipe. My hands shake so badly that it reverberates up my arms and down through my body. Sweat beads on my skin, sliding down my spine. A few chance meetings with Master Ez, a sighting of Cortez Abernathy at the front of Restraint, and one hallway bump and a real meeting with Dr. Ezra Zeitler, and I'm a fucking mess.

Wednesday is finally here. The need to see Zeitler and Abernathy is a building tempest inside my body, building and building in pressure until I feel like I'm going to implode. I must see them with my very own two eyes. I need to prove my suspicions correct.

Refusing to be bulldozed, I had Kayla set up a meeting between Zeitler and Abernathy, stating that if the elusive author didn't get his ass into my office, then I was making an executive decision to drop him as an author at Edge Publishing. Amazingly, the Ezes complied with nary a complaint.

Another level of power descended upon me when Kayla confirmed the meeting, making my mind spin in heady intoxication. Finally, the wait is over, and my heart is going to burst beneath my breast.

Standing in the center of my office, the frenetic energy roiling through me offers me no rest. I stare at the open door, never daring to blink. Waiting… always waiting.

"Katya, the members of your meeting have arrived." I lick my lips at the sight of Kayla. The little submissive is dressed to please. I give her a wink as I turn towards my guests.

Zeitler walks into my office first, seeming reluctant, sheepish in fact. I can't stop myself, I openly stare at him— devouring him –cataloging every single detail about him. His pale hair is trimmed short to his scalp. Is that the hair I yanked in anger? His pale skin warms beneath my gaze, pinking handsomely. Is that the same flesh that spooned me while I slept? His eyes latch on to mine, refusing to look away. Are those the same gunmetal gray eyes that connected with mine, trusting me as much as I trusted them? Are those long, tapered fingers the ones that thrust deeply inside my body, bringing me to climax? Are those supple lips the same that kissed me tenderly, but attacked my pussy like a fiend?

"*Dr.* Zeitler," I greet, stressing his title. "Thank you for meeting with me, especially on such short notice," I say wryly, since he missed all of the meetings I had scheduled with our prospective authors. My only action was to think he didn't care, and I took vetting new authors as my ultimate decision.

Polite, refusing to blink, Zeitler's eyes seem to drink me in as well, reading me as if I spilled my deepest, darkest secrets at his feet. "Ms. Waters?" He looks a question at me, a question I don't understand so therefore I have no answer.

"This is Mr. Abernathy," Zeitler gestured to a man standing in my doorway.

My breath whooshes out of me in a torrent because I'm right. I didn't want to be right, but I am.

Tall, dark, and dressed to kill… The suit man from the entrance to Restraint is none other than the infamous author, Cortez Abernathy.

Unable to stop myself, I catalog Abernathy as well, all the while comparing him to Zeitler. A luminous smile flashes an invitation as well as a silent warning as I drink him in. His tan skin is gorgeous– touchable. Black hair, cropped tightly to his skull, in exactly the same style as his counterpart's. Eyes the exact same shade of gunmetal gray gaze at me in expectancy and curiosity. Their height, weight, and the way they hold their bodies is identical. The only difference is what they emote.

Dr. Ezra Zeitler is calm, assured, and stoic.

Mr. Cortez Abernathy is mischievous, taunting, and slightly antagonistic.

I have no clue which is Master Ez, or if they tag-team me, since they both exhibit characteristics of the Master Ez I've come to know.

"The elusive Mr. Abernathy has finally graced me with his presence." I say grandly as I walk forward to greet him, keeping up with the charade these two fucks are playing on me. "It's a pleasure to meet you, *again*." I acknowledged our first meeting in line at Restraint.

Zeitler flashes a look of curiosity at both of us, wondering what I'm speaking of. I guess they don't share *everything*.

"Perhaps we can get to know one another better, Ms. Waters." Abernathy eagerly takes my hand in his. But instead of shaking, he clasps my palm between the pair of his and doesn't let go. "I do so hope we will."

Normally, I can't tolerate the touch of a man I don't know, one I've just now met. Under other circumstances, the contact with a stranger's skin would have freaked me out. Instead, it's comforting. The sensation would have confused me if I hadn't realized that he may or may not be Master Ez. Cortez

Abernathy cradles my hand in his, and it just feels good.

Blinking away the confusion, "Ah, shucks! Are you flirting with me because you know I've butchered your book?" I tease and threaten him simultaneously, while blushing for real.

Abernathy laughs, smoky, warm, and deep… and it sounds so much like Master Ez that I have to turn to Zeitler to make sure he doesn't have his hand firmly shoved up Abernathy's ass and is playing ventriloquist with the author.

Deep down I'd hoped, *needed* to believe that Ezra was Master Ez, and that the Cortez connection was just a coincidence because they are the best of friends. But now, my heart is breaking because I was so naïve, stupid, and not just because of my childish hopes and dreams. At some point, probably while lying in bed listening to childhood tales, I allowed my heart to join the game, and now I'll suffer the consequences of its breakage.

"Ms. Waters," Abernathy laughs my name instead of speaking it. "I'd flirt with you in spite of my book. Maybe we could get a drink while we talk over what I need to improve to meet Edge Publishing's new standards of perfection," he charms me, flashing a panty-melting smile.

Using their personalities as a gauge, I flirt with one and ignore the other. "I'd enjoy that, Abernathy." I bat my eyelashes, flirting back. My eyes dart to Zeitler, who looks confused by my behavior. That is the point. I need to throw everyone off their game and see where they land. "But only in the professional setting of my office. How is Mrs. Abernathy fairing?"

"Lovely as ever, my Divina," he says with genuine affection, face softening. His eyes dart to Dr. Zeitler, and I swear he whispers '*cock-blocker'* underneath his breath.

"Please, call me Cortez," he says cunningly. His eyes pierce me to the depths of my soul. "Or, if you prefer, please call me Cort, as a friend would."

I slowly pull my hand back, smiling politely when in actuality I want to knee him in the junk. Cort. Cortez Abernathy is *that* Cort. The one Aaron is jealous of and finds sick delight in calling Piggy. Yet another puzzle piece drops into place.

I gesture to my sofa for the Ezes to take a seat, while I occupy the lone chair in my seating area. Ezra and Cortez, the Ez twins with gunmetal gray eyes, chat on my sofa about the manuscript, while they seem to be having an entirely different silent conversation, judging by their body language and intense eye contact. Only a fool would look at this pair and miss the palpable connection that was wrought over a lifetime.

Aaron, Roarke, and Kayla, I need to figure out how they are attached to the Ezes. I assume Aaron and Roarke are Ezra's assistant/bodyguards, seeing as how Roarke's buff body is hanging out in the hallway across from my open office door, fingers clicking on his cellphone. But the brute could be here for either of the men, I suppose. Kayla is a submissive at Restraint, where I saw Cortez, but she works at Edge for Ezra.

I'm so confused, my mind is whirling. It's a matter of either/or or both. ...Then there is that wicked laugh. They chuckle, snicker, and laugh identically. It's creepy, and makes it impossible to figure out which is the real Master Ez.

I sit, not listening to a thing the pair discusses. My mind reels as I try to find a new plan, but I can't seem to come up with one. *Operation upset the boat, part two: disrespect Ezra by flirting with Cortez.* Neither is my usual M.O. Either man will find this disheartening if they are the real Master Ez.

Will the real Master Ez please stand up?

"Ms. Waters suggested that you should completely scrap the draft and start again." My name draws my attention. Truths to unfold or not, I do have integrity, and the moment work is brought into the conversation, I can't help but respond. I think I can still flirt while I serve shitty news, or give it the good ol' college try, that is.

"I'm sorry, Cortez," I smile to soften the blow.

"Please, call me Cort. Remember?" The man prompts, womanizing player wafting from his pores. While this isn't a core personality trait of Master Ez's, it does lend to the validity, since Master Ez is cheating on his significant other, no matter which man is playing the leading role.

"Cort," I allow with a curt nod. "To be completely honest, your manuscript is nothing special. The title is horrendous, and nothing happens from page one to the end." As I lean forward to place my hand on his knee, my elbows press into the sides of my breasts, lifting and creating a provocatively appetizing view. The Ezes hungrily eye my cleavage.

I smile to myself. Men and women alike, can't help but stare at breasts, even if they aren't that great. It's like a car wreck; you just can't look away. *Boobies!* Pushup bras are an amazing invention, just don't look at my saggy tits once the supportive bra is removed. Ugh.

Zeitler looks worried by my strange behavior, while Cortez looks intrigued. I give a reassuring squeeze to the naughty author's knee, and then draw away to rest my back on my chair cushion.

"It needs some major reworking, but I am confident that you *will* make it another best seller for Edge Publishing and your *pen name*," I stress, meaning he'll either fix it, or Edge Publishing will *not* publish it, best buddies or not.

Both of the Ezes flash me inquisitive looks, silently asking what I meant by my pseudonym comment. Abernathy is not Cortez's birth name. I'm great at research, finding Ezra Zeitler's birth name of Holden– his mother's maiden name. Ezra was adopted by his mother's husband when he was a young teenager. Aaron's mother's cougar of a boss. Aaron was trying to help me out through our seemingly innocent conversations by giving me logic puzzle-worthy information. I was unable to locate Cortez's birth name, seeing as how his records were sealed– another oddity.

Cortez, with his hand pressed to his chest, looks for all the world crestfallen, but I don't miss the telling look that transferred between the Ezes. "I won't argue with you, Ms. Waters. I've just been so distracted lately," he says, almost angrily, as his eyes dart in his co-conspirator's direction.

"Maybe you could breathe new life into your book, instead of outright abandoning it. It will be a lot of work… if you could get over your distractions, that is."

"Why, yes… if only," Cortez whispers, a funny little

smirk flirting with his lips. "May I call you Katya? Perhaps Kat, if we could be friends?"

Without permission, Cortez reaches over to finger a few strands of my hair, which have escaped my up-do to fall past my shoulders to lie against my chest. The backs of his knuckles graze my nipple as he twists my curl around his pinkie.

I close my eyes and breathe through my nose. Either my last session with Master Ez cured me, or Cortez is Master Ez. The more disturbing thought is that all dominants in general have this potently sexual, scary as fuck effect on me. Obviously Cortez is a dominant, or he wouldn't have been at Restraint. I just can't see this virile man kneeling on the floor and submitting.

"Of course, Cortez. Please call me Katya," I purr. I surreptitiously pull my hair from his fingers, all the while hammering home how we are *not* friends. No Cort and Kat.

Zeitler breaks into our syrupy sweet, albeit mildly threatening, flirting by clearing his throat. "That's an interesting box," Zeitler says roughly, like his mouth is dry. "What's inside it?"

My boss comments on my solution for the explicit chess set, which is sitting atop my coffee table. It's right where Master Ez placed it and told me never to remove it. Because the chess set deserved nothing less, it's secured in a mahogany box, which is shaped like a tiny trunk shined to a glossy finish. The game is safely nestled inside, underneath the key-coded top.

As an extra challenge to the game, I want to find out if Master Ez is crafty enough to hack the code so he can move his pieces.

My lips break into a wide grin. "You remember the chess set I received from my secret admirer?"

"Why, yes," Dr. Zeitler says. Lips quirking up at the corners, "I believe you called this person your stalker."

"Ah," I breathe, stifling a laugh. "Well, it's a long-term game, and I didn't want anyone to accidentally move the pieces on us. It's safer this way." My voice is pure passive-aggressiveness.

I can't help it, a snicker spills from my lips. Ah, that created a reaction. Dr. Zeitler tries to suppress a grin, but fails.

"Well, it's a gorgeous box. Perhaps you and I could play soon. Over a working dinner? We have a lot of authors to sort through. How about we meet at your apartment, and we can narrow down the prospects followed by a game or two of chess?"

Eyes narrowed and leveled on Zeitler, Cortez stands abruptly. "I'm sorry to bail, *Kat*," he twists the nickname I didn't give him permission to use. "But I have an appointment to make." Turning to Zeitler, "I believe you were to accompany me, Ezra. *Now*," he orders, suddenly furious.

"Hmm... I wonder where we're going. Some place fictitious, I'll wager." Zeitler stands, joining Cortez, and the pair sighs in unison– a sound I know all too well.

The grin Abernathy flashes his friend is filled with jealousy and malice. "We were having lunch with Adelaide and Divina, remember?" Cortez's words are polite yet cutting, and directed solely at me. He wanted me to remember they were both attached.

"Ah, so we're going down *that* path? The fictitious one?" Zeitler bites out, suddenly as furious as Abernathy.

Cortez bends down to grab my hand, squeezing gently. "I'll work on the manuscript over the next few days, and I'll call Kayla to set up our next meeting. Give me less than a week, and I'll bring by the first five rewritten chapters."

"Excellent," I say, happy to have some progress, even if it's only for Edge Publishing.

Straightening, Cortez says to Ezra, "Ready?" Before my boss can tell me goodbye or set up a time to discuss our prospects, Cortez is halfway to the door.

"Of course." Ezra pulls his cellphone from his trousers, and begins to dial. "Just let me call my cousin, and while I'm at it, how about my mother. If we're going to say we're having lunch, we might as well truly do it. I'm sure you'd love to share a meal with Ms. Whittenhower... and perhaps my father, too."

Mid-step, Cortez stops, body convulsing in a strong

shudder, and then he walks straight out of my office and into the hallway beyond. My boss raises an eyebrow while smiling to himself, and then pockets his cellphone– call never made.

"Hmm, so much for lunch," I mumble to myself.

"Lunch? If Cort is going to test my patience, I'll drop his ass into the middle of a living nightmare... one he'll never forgive me for."

"Who in that scenario is Beelzebub?" I ask, and then instantly regret it. Regret how I seem to gravitate toward my boss, not even realizing I'd moved. I find myself standing next to him, facing him while Roarke and Cortez openly stare at us from the hallway.

Huffing a laugh, "Individually they are perfect angels. But if you place Adelaide and Cort in an enclosed space together, Cort becomes the Devil himself."

"Ah, he's one of *those* types of friends," I murmur to myself. "One who thinks you can only play with him." Now I understand Aaron's animosity towards the author.

"Precisely," Zeitler purrs, eyes never leaving Cortez, and then he turns to me. "I have a fundraiser this evening, supporting my father. I'd like to meet tomorrow night if that would be agreeable."

"After hours?" I ask, and then tack on, "In my office, not my apartment, and no sustenance. We will narrow down our prospects, and that's it," I stress.

"Of course," Zeitler says, looking like a fallen angel with his pale skin and white hair. "I'll meet you here at six o'clock tomorrow night."

My boss leaves me, without ever touching me so I could balance how I felt when Cortez versus Ezra versus Master Ez touched me. More than disappointed, I watch as Zeitler joins his retinue. Cortez immediately starts whispering furiously, while Ezra tries to calm him down.

"Great," Roarke says, flashing me a look like it's somehow my fault. "There goes a peaceful afternoon."

Chapter Twenty-One

I can smell Master Ez wafting around my office, driving me into madness. The one who inhabited my bed, the one who made me think of silly bullshit like making love and pouring my soul out– his scent lingers like a punt to the cunt.

The smoky intoxicating scent is imprinted on my being. But since they came in here as a pair, I can't even hazard a guess as to which it belongs: Ezra Zeitler or Cortez Abernathy. You can throw a voice, a laugh can sound similar to another's, genetic traits are shared, but a scent belongs to one individual.

Even if they are tag-teaming me, I want to know which one belongs to that scent, and then I want to kick his ass for making my heart beat, for making me feel emotions I'd rather forget, for baring me raw, and for making me feel like a whore because he touched me while attached to another female he obviously has no intentions of ever leaving. Not that I would expect Master Ez to leave her. Not that I'm hoping for that. Not that I could look myself in the mirror if Ezra left Adelaide and chose me instead.

I'm a goddamned liar, especially to myself.

Kayla finds me a while later, drumming my fingers on my desk, completely lost in thought. "Katya, may I get you a drink? You've been quiet for a few hours." Her voice is meek, scared, and I don't like that.

"Really? It's been hours?" I ask in surprise.

"Yeah, it's been just over two. I didn't know if I should disturb you or not, so I've checked on you a few times." She looks worried, and I hate it. I should be the one taking care of her, not the other way around.

"C'mere," I murmur, needing some sort of affection to anchor me– a soft touch as a soothing balm on my injured emotions.

When Kayla is within arm's reach, I grab her by the back of her neck to draw her to my mouth. I kiss her gently, softly. The kiss is at complete odds with the aggression flowing throughout my system. Our lips dance for a moment. The touch is out of mutual comfort, not an ounce of sexual heat or passion, just friendship.

I draw back and whisper against Kayla's lips, "Thank you." I thank her for clearing my head and offering me solace, for stabilizing my thoughts. Staring into her wide, blue eyes, an idea enters my head– a light bulb moment.

I smile against Kayla's lips. "Tell me Restraint's phone number, please." She freezes beneath my hands. I know she's worried that I'm doing something wrong, and going to get us both into trouble with Master Ez. I'll take the blame if he's angry.

"Don't worry, beauty, I'm just calling a friend." I reassure her.

With a shaking hand, Kayla transcribes the phone number on my notepad, and then pushes it towards me. Within seconds, she's hightailing it out of my office, not wishing to be privy to whatever I'm about to do.

Smart woman.

I punch in the phone number, unsure what I'm going to say or ask, and wait as it rings a billion times. Just as I'm about to hang up and yell at Kayla for giving me a bogus number, someone answers.

"Restraint, this is Kristal speaking," echoes from the other end of the phone.

"Is Queen or Fate available to speak?" I ask cordially while swallowing my own heartbeat. Why am I so nervous? Oh, it could be that I know I'm going to get an ass whooping for this. Yeah, that's why.

"What do you think this is? A hotline?" Kristal practically spits into the phone. She's such a sweet, submissive girl. "Some of us have work to do, ya know? Some of us are at their second job. Why are you calling this number? This is for in-house calling only."

"Um," I stammer, feeling like a moron. "I don't have their personal numbers, and I need to speak with one of them, please."

"This better be a fucking emergency, or I will reach through the phone and tear out your tongue." The last part is a menacing whisper. I shiver at the thought. Before I can answer, she's talking again, "Who is this, anyway?"

Cranky bitch!

"Kat," squeaks out. Then I gather my courage and continue. "Katya Waters," I announce, owning it. "Either put Queen or Fate on the line, or give me their personal numbers." When I finish, I sound hostile with Kristal's mood influencing mine.

"Kat, why didn't you say that to begin with? Hold a moment please," Kristal finishes sweetly.

Does everyone at Restraint have multiple personalities?

Why, yes. Why, yes, I think they do– myself included.

"Kat?" Queen breathes harshly into the phone, panting as if she ran to answer.

I'm actually relieved Queen answered me and not Fate. By that picture framed on the wall in Ezra Zeitler's faux-office, I know they both have known the Ezes for a more than a decade. I just feel Queen will be more forthcoming of the pair.

"I hope you're out of breath because you ran to the phone, and not because I'm interrupting you," I say in amusement. "Please tell me you weren't doing a scene."

"No, it's all good. I was just making sure we had enough security for the evening. I was walking a new guy around Restraint. I ran because I was on the floor, not near a phone."

"Ah," I breathe, acting as if I understand when I really don't. "Sorry it's such an odd hour to call. Are you free for a few minutes to chat? I need to ask you a few questions. But only answer the ones that won't get you into any trouble."

"Ask away," Queen offers. "Besides, I like trouble."

"I'm sure you do," I say with a smile. I like Queen. She feels like a kindred spirit. "I'm going to cut straight to the chase. Who is Master Ez? Ezra Zeitler, Cortez Abernathy, or both?" I list off the first question in my mind.

"Ah, good God, girl!" She chuckles into the phone. "Can I tell you I don't know?"

"No, you can't, because I'm not stupid," I grumble, feeling bad because everyone I've met is attached to these assholes, so therefore they are not trustworthy. I'm also sad because I'll never find a friend, even if I feel the spark of connection, because their loyalties will always lie elsewhere, no matter what.

"Queen, I can tell you're lying, and I assume you were ordered not to tell me specific things. So just say *'I can't answer that because I don't know, or because I do and I was told not to.'* Okay?"

"Fair enough, but I doubt I will be able to help you much." Sighing, Queen pauses for a moment to gather her thoughts. "I do know who Master Ez is. At least I can tell you that you are correct. He is one of those men, or both."

"Thank you," I say immediately, and I genuinely mean it. "It's not a comfort under the circumstances, but at least I know that much."

"You're welcome," Queen says, but she sounds hesitant.

"Is Kayla screwing Ezra and Cortez? What about Aaron and Roarke?"

"Wow." Queen snorts. "You don't fuck around, do you? You're like a goddamned bulldozer. So not what I expected."

"Should I apologize for that?" I mutter, feeling stupid.

"No, definitely not. You'll need that set of titanium balls to survive them. Now this, I can answer. Kayla has had sexual contact with Aaron, but not Roarke. Kayla was brought in by Master Ez to heal Aaron of his issues, but that hasn't gone so well. However, Cortez appreciates the girl's ability to take him on. Ezra only touches her in a nonsexual manner."

"So, Master Ez is so high-handed he tried to give Aaron a girlfriend. Why am I not surprised," I muse to myself, but earn a chuckle from Queen. "What can you tell me about their sexual habits? They seem pretty unfaithful to their women."

"Whoa, Nelly. Give me a second." A tapping sound flows from over the phone.

Furious, I snap out quickly. "No fucking way, girlfriend. Drop the cellphone. Either answer me straight away, or say you can't. But do not fucking text those bastards, because technically they will be the one answering me. I want to hear it from you."

"God, you guys are going to destroy each other. Fuck,"

Queen hisses. "He's going to kill me for this. I have to tread lightly."

"I realize that. So, really, just say you can't answer if you can't. Okay?" I implore, hoping her inability to answer specific questions will be more of a clue than whatever answer she would have given. "How long have you known them?"

"Harmless enough. I met them both at Hillbrook. It was the end of my senior year, and the middle school graduates were visiting for their freshman orientation. I've known them off and on since, cropping up in my life when I least expect it, and often times when I wish they hadn't."

I just pick a question at random, knowing Queen can't answer most of them anyway. "Why is Aaron jealous of Cortez?"

"Because Cortez is a jealous asshole and makes our lives miserable because of it. Aaron's not jealous of Cortez; he wants to beat some sense into him," Queen snarls out, obviously just as annoyed.

Confused, I mutter, "What's he jealous about?"

"I'd tell you if I could, Kat. But on this I cannot speak. I will tell you this, Cortez is a loyal bastard. If he deems you worthy, he will keep your secrets, no matter who asks. He's also the biggest slut on the face of the planet. No, he's not unfaithful to his wife: cock-in-pussy-wise, he doesn't believe that's cheating on her. As for faithful, Cort loves Divina with all of his heart, is loyal to her, respects her, and takes the utmost care of her, and he always will. Cortez Abernathy is a good person, just one I want to poke with a Spork."

Not knowing how to lead after that, I stammer for a few seconds, feeling like a complete and total dolt. "What do they want with me?"

"Can't answer that," Comes before I'm even finished asking my question. "And even if I could, I wouldn't. That is for you to discover, Katya."

"Do they want to hurt me?" I whisper, voice breaking as I begin to shake.

"No," Queen whispers just as softly. "They don't want to hurt you, but they will. It's inevitable. They will be sorry, but that won't change a thing, now will it?"

"No," I breathe. "It won't."

"Listen, I was firmly against this– the way Master Ez is doing this. You need to be careful, Katya. There are a lot of people involved with this, some you haven't even met yet. Yes, it is for your benefit, but it will leave you in pain when it's all said and done. I wasn't exaggerating. I'm relieved you've got balls of steel. You'll need them."

"What do I do?" I ask, knowing she can't tell me.

"It's Master Ez, sweetheart. There is absolutely nothing you can do but let him have his way. It's how it's been done for nearly three decades. **No** is not in his vocabulary. It's safest to say yes immediately. Safer and saner for *you*."

Chapter Twenty-Two

I curl up in bed, staring up at the dark ceiling, after another unsuccessful cyber search. I looked up both Ezra Zeitler and Cortez Abernathy again, this time trying to be more comprehensive. Yes, they have been friends since diaper-hood. They grew up in the same house, that is if you can call a massive estate a house, especially when it's surrounded by hundreds of acres of private, wooded land.

Cortez Abernathy and Ezra Zeitler have lived at Shadow Haven Estates their entire lives. One look at the photos of the estate, and I knew I was way out of my league. There is no way I am anything other than a distraction in their bored lives, one they will toss away like trash once they've broken it.

They attended prestigious school after prestigious school together, until Ezra went to Harvard to become a psychiatrist and Cortez settled into a life of writing. Since no one at Edge Publishing has ever called our boss **Dr.** Zeitler, I thought it was top-secret. But it's common knowledge, according to the web and newspaper articles.

Ezra was Cortez's best man in his wedding to Divina Hastings– Ezra's cousin. The three of them were raised as close as siblings, and Aaron, too. Aaron Frost was prominent in many of the articles and postings. He has been their lifelong friend. Aaron's mother is Shadow Haven's housekeeper. Even though he is a few years younger, he grew up side-by-side with Ezra, Cortez, and Divina, going to all the same schools with them, simply shadowing a few years behind.

It just goes to show how the rich and influential's minds work. If you raise your servants from birth, you can control their educations, so the endless expanse of time spent with them won't be a bore. They will be your intellectual equal, and as such, your entertainment and confidant.

I was surprised when I stared at the pictures of the married couple: Cortez and Divina. Utter devotion blazes from their eyes when they look at one another. I searched for newer pictures to see if the expression had changed over recent years.

Monica said she and Cortez were lovers for well over three years. Surely the look of devotion changed in that time frame, or else why would Cortez feel the need to cheat? I found a picture taken a few days ago at a charity fundraiser. Divina is genuinely laughing, and Cortez looks thrilled to be the one who amused her.

Ezra and Adelaide's engagement party photos from six years ago, show Cortez and Divina in the background smiling proudly. That picture made me sick to my stomach. At this point, it doesn't really matter which man is Master Ez, because they are both faithless bastards.

I checked their records, not even a parking ticket as adults. However, their juvenile records were sealed. I found this suspect. You only seal something that exists. Good little boys don't have juvenile records. Even guileless Aaron has a sealed juvenile record.

Ezra Zeitler is famed for being the Billionaire Bachelor. He is well-loved by the media for his philanthropy. The media darling is most gossiped about for his extended engagement to Adelaide Whittenhower. Theories range from homosexuality, on the parts of both Ezra and Adelaide, to a failed business merger marriage between their high-profile families. Ezra is in the media more often than most movie stars.

Cortez Abernathy has a huge following of fans for his books. I had a hard time finding information on him that wasn't related to reviews, book signings, and fans screaming he is a rockstar.

All the while during my search, my instant messaging software pinged constantly. My therapist, Dr. Jeannine, and Kimber, my online friend from a violence support group, have pestered me relentlessly all evening long.

No, the irony was not lost on me. While I cyber-stalked my stalkers, my therapist and another victim wanted to check-in on my mental health status. Yeah, I see nothing wrong with this picture, either.

My mind will not shut off as I wait to see if my stalker will slide into bed with me. I'm torn. I want Master Ez to lie beside me. But at the same time, I never want to see him again.

Neither one of them is a good idea. It's just as Monica says; they are taken. I would just be their dirty little secret. Cortez is married and Ezra is in a long-term engagement to be married.

Sickeningly, that doesn't change how I feel about Master Ez. How low I've stumbled down off my perch of self-righteous ethics. I miss the days when I was the master of my emotions. Now I have no control over anything, and I hate it as much as I crave it.

I long for the comforting sensation that flows over me when I'm around Master Ez. There haven't been many people in my life who truly made me feel safe, even my parents failed at that. With my past, it's a miracle to want to be touched, to share intimacy, to find a level of trust to make love to someone.

Why did my dark and damaged mind choose someone who is bad for me? Someone who isn't available? Someone who will ruin me?

Yes, the Ezes belong to and/or own a BDSM club, and engage in those activities. But that doesn't mean I have to demean myself by lowering to their poor standards. Don't get me wrong, I want to play, too. There is also nothing wrong with playing if it's by the rules. Except I want rules where everyone knows the consequences. These men are playing while the other half of their lives are in the dark. That isn't honesty, and that isn't someone I want to hand my trust.

My skin chills from the depressive direction of my thoughts. A full-body tremor wracks me. I rub my hands up and down my forearms, trying to warm myself with friction. Even though I am cold down to my soul, I get up for an extra blanket. It may not warm my frigid heart, but it will comfort me like a teddy bear comforts a child.

My apartment came fully furnished with everything I'd ever want or need, and mysteriously in a style that would please me— a style which was reflected in my office as well. It was move-in ready, with me moving from my parents' home with only my personal items, clothing, and books. I'd be stupid to think otherwise, because I have a very good idea why this is the case.

Master Ez thought of everything when he furnished my apartment, I'll give him props for that. Evidently my height was a cause for his concern. Folding stepstools are strategically placed in rooms that have shelving that is too far to reach.

I snicker to myself as I climb up the stool to get my blanket out of the closet. I stretch my body out, just reaching the blanket with the tips of my fingers. I grunt a bit, trying to get that extra inch to gain my prize.

I'm a stupid girl.

A wide, disbelieving smile splits my lips when a warm hand settles on the small of my back to support me. I shake my head back and forth.

Speak of the Devil, and he shall appear. In this case, think of the Devil.

"Well…well…well, if it isn't Batman," I purr in a mix of amusement and annoyance.

I turn to face Master Ez, but a firm hand stops me. Immediately a mask is snapped into place across my face from behind, effectively blinding me. Strong hands curl around my hips, gripping to lift me from my perch. Fabric slides across my arm as the blanket is dragged by to settle at my naked feet.

"Kneel," his voice commands, huskier than I remember—more powerful. Not to be denied. A fog of confusion descends, so thick I cannot think through it, forcing me to submit immediately. Before I can even think to move, I find my ass resting on my heels.

Using bravado to cover the confusion that has washed over me, "Well played this afternoon, Boss. Who would have thought there'd be two Bruce Waynes to choose from? Maybe I will surprise you and play with both," I twist the words, flirting with malicious intent.

"Mmm… don't tempt me, Kitty Kat. You may just get what you ask for, only to find out it was something you never wanted in the first place."

I'm taken aback by the cold calculation in his voice. Usually Master Ez either has a playful or patient edge to his voice, but not tonight.

"Are you angry with me, Ez?" My voice warbles, and I

hate myself because of it.

"No, Kat. I am not angry with you," his voice softens as his fingers rake through my hair, exposing my ear. "In fact, I like you very much. I didn't want to like you, which angers me greatly," he whispers menacingly in my ear, sweet breath scorching me.

"I don't understand." I try to pull away to stand, but his hand tightens in my hair, fingers knotting in the strands, roughly yanking my head backwards.

"I said kneel. Did I say you could get up yet?" Harsh fingertips pinch my nipple through my thin t-shirt, punishingly so. A yelp is forced from my mouth, as the pain is sharp and everlasting. The sting goes on for long seconds before dissipating into a dull ache.

This is the side of Master Ez that frightens me. The side that isn't trustworthy. I now attribute these mercurial moods to the fact that there are two Master Ezes. Which one is gracing me with his angry presence right now?

The idea thrills me as much as makes me sick. I want to comply, but at the same time I want to fight back. But then Queen's words flood my mind, and I decide it's best to trust her instead of my faulty intuition and ridiculous emotions.

*"It's Master Ez, sweetheart. There is absolutely nothing you can do but let him have his way. It's how it's been done for nearly three decades. **No** is not in his vocabulary. It's safest to say yes immediately. Safer and saner for you."*

"Good Kitty. If you listen to me, we'll have a nice time. If you go deaf to my requests, it won't be pleasant. Do you understand, Katya? KitKat? Kitten? Or is it Kat?" he asks, mocking me beyond belief for a reason I cannot decipher.

"Yes, sir," I mutter in an emotionless voice. "Understood."

"Good. Very, very good. This is why I like you–"

I cut him off against my better judgment, "Even though you wish you didn't."

"See, you do comprehend very well, Kat. Which is exactly why I like you so much. I have a reward to give to you," he purrs, fingertips clenching against my scalp. "Your game has drastically improved over the past few days. Bravo on the keypad on the chess box," he murmurs slyly in my ear. "Too bad I figured out the code already."

"Why am I being rewarded, then?" I ask in confusion as fear slams into me out of nowhere. Every other time I've been with Master Ez, I felt safe, even when he was '*educating*' me. But not this time. Something outside of my control set him off, and he's going to take it out on me.

"Oh, Kitty Kat. It's *my* reward," he barely breathes the words. But they sound more terrifying said in near silence. "I could pound nails with my cock. Ever since I watched you take our Kayla, I haven't been satisfied. I've fucked and sucked and jacked off, but nothing takes the ache away– the hunger I have for you. Damn, the way you stalked Kayla... It made me so fucking proud," he growls like a wild animal.

Did Master Ez just growl, '*ever since I watched you take our Kayla?*' Watched? No one was in the room with us. I would have noticed. A shiver of trepidation wracks my body, and it's not the kind of cold that a blanket can ever comfort.

"It's not very flattering, you telling me how much you want me. But the statement is on the heels of you admitting how you've fucked constantly for the past few days," I grumble snidely, annoyance thick in my voice. "Why would you even tell me that?"

"Do not speak unless spoken to," Master Ez bites out fiercely, tone bordering on violence.

Self-preservation kicks in and I do as I was told. I worry what the consequences would be if I didn't. I really hate this side of Master Ez, the side that four deadbolts can't keep out. If I was really worried, I would have gone to a hotel instead of waiting in my bedroom for him to show up.

Bad, Kat! You deserve everything you get for being such a dumb cunt.

The unmistakable sound of metal-on-metal, the grinding noise of a zipper sliding open, has me freezing in panic. My breathing picks up as fear rushes through my veins. A gasp is torn from my throat when the silky flesh of a cock glides across my bottom lip, leaving slick wetness in its wake.

I've never sucked a cock. Hell, I've never even touched

one. I've never even changed the diaper of a baby boy. I may have been raped by two penises, but I've never held one in my hand. When my private flesh was violated by them, it took away all of my curiosity.

I should be scared over what Master Ez is asking of me. I should examine how this is a horrific idea that will plague my conscience for the rest of my life. I should worry over how he will be disappointed in me for being so inept. But all I can think is how my master wants this from me, and how I will give it to him willingly. Consequences be damned, because the only consequences that should matter are the ones my master provides.

"Suck me," Master Ez moans from the depths of his chest. "No hands," he orders, voice thick from undisguised lust.

A smooth, slick cockhead swivels between my lips, asking me to open, teasing and taunting– coaxing me to suck.

To delay the inevitable, I ask, "How is that a reward? It's more for you." As I speak, he squeezes salty liquid on my bottom lip, and then taps his head on it while humming a warm sound.

Unbiddenly, my tongue dabs out for a taste. A sigh breaks free as I experience my first taste of a male. I don't want to like it. I don't want to feel excitement over what is happening. This isn't what I dreamed my first oral sex would be like. But I cannot deny the heady power that is flowing through me, intoxicating me. I don't feel lowered. I feel higher than ever.

"No speaking," he reminds. "Sucking."

I'm Master Ez's passenger. I wait, unsure what to do, how to do it, or what he wants me to do. Instead of allowing my ineptitude to destroy me, I use it to gather patience.

"Get to sucking," he chants hypnotically while swirling his cockhead against my bottom lip. "Ah, lap it up, Kitty Kat," he purrs salaciously.

I give Master Ez's cock an experimental lick, groaning at his intoxicating taste. My tongue flicks out again, following the curve of the head to run along the edge of a thick vein. Master Ez shudders, body swaying into mine.

Power.

Pure unadulterated power floods me at the feel of his smooth flesh sliding against mine, knowing I'm bringing him pleasure.

I cannot believe Master Ez is finally allowing me to touch him in return.

His voice is wry yet overshadowed by intense hunger. "Good Kitty. I'm rewarded as your master, because you've done so very well. Your reward is to enjoy me."

"Are you saying your cock is that impressive?" I huff a laugh, and Master Ez uses the opportunity to rub my tongue with his cockhead, feeding me more of his tonic.

"Yes, that's exactly what I'm saying. Impressive isn't the word I'd use. Exquisite is more accurate." I wait for a chuckle. But when one doesn't come, I get scared.

"I doubt I'll even fit between your lips, Kitty Kat. Pretend I'm Kayla, and lick me off," he orders, fingers wrapping tightly around strands of my hair. "Or... we could just find out."

With a tight fist, my hair is wrenched violently at the roots. The sharp pain is instantaneous and intense, causing my mouth to open on a silent scream of shock.

I'm gagged.

I'm gagged by a huge cock impaling my lips and bumping the back of my throat. Nudging my tonsils, I cough, choking around the cock blocking my air supply.

Impressive isn't an accurate word, yet neither is *exquisite*, unless you add *torture* to the mix. Exquisite torture. But still, I have no word to describe the piece of flesh suffocating me.

I start to panic, body involuntarily trying to protect itself, to escape– to survive. My flailing arms are caught quickly by one strong hand braceleting both of my wrists.

This isn't what I imagined for my first blow job. There is a vulnerability to kneeling on the floor while a man fills your mouth. He holds your life in the balance. He could take his pleasure and harm you if not careful. He could leave you feeling more than breathless. He could suffocate the very life from you.

I thought I could trust Master Ez.

I was wrong.

Petrified, I start to weep uncontrollably, tears sliding down my cheeks to drip from my chin. It's been so long since I cried– not even *then*. My emotions fracture. I'm being violated, only this time it's my mouth instead of my cunt, and it's by someone I trusted.

Without fail, men always invade our bodies as if we are lesser beings. It's their way of lowering us, controlling us, as if they have a right to penetrate us with their flesh. It's why I chose women in the past when I was flesh-starved.

I have no say in this act. But yet again, I put myself into this position. I am at fault. I could have stood up and tried to walk away. I could have told him no instead of worrying about disappointing him, or I could have taken the punishment for disobeying him. But I knew from past experiences with Master Ez, the punishment is always far worse than the initial request. He's also never frightened or harmed me before.

This experience also hurts because I'm compromising my morals. The man who is fucking my throat is either engaged or married, and I'm an accomplice to his adultery simply because I never said no.

The worst, if Master Ez had been kind, sensual in his request, I would have freely given him pleasure, and enjoyed it. I would have been enlivened by it. I would have been secretly pleased that he wanted me to touch him, and I would have beat myself up over the moral laws I broke at a later date. But since Master Ez is being violent, I change my mind, and that is all on me.

I am at fault.

"Breathe out of your nose, Kitty," he instructs in a kind voice, and that is what flips the switch in me, lessening the panic. I push out a large gust of air through my nostrils. "Yes, just like that... mmm... take more," he croons, pushing farther down my throat as I try to breathe past the invasion. He speaks to me with affection, his voice sounding all wrong to my ears.

Master Ez holds me in place by palming the back of the head, while he pushes his cock into my mouth. His fingers edge up to the hinge of my jaw and massage, opening me further. I swallow that much more of him, until he's bumping the back of my throat with every thrust, and I can sense that I'm nowhere near the base of him.

I long to use my hands to see how big Master Ez is, anything to distract me from what's truly happening. I need to know what it feels like, the flesh that is rubbing me raw, chaffing me, burning me with friction. It seems wrong, not knowing what it looks like. Since I'm blinded, I want to see by touch. My hand moves out of its own curiosity, slipping from Master Ez's grip around my wrist.

I elicit a sharp shriek, the sound ricocheting around my bedroom. A hand palms my entire breast and crushes it like a vise. I scream long and loud, the harder he grips and twists, bruising me. All sound diminishes into deafening silence when it's cut off by a cock rooting itself into my throat so deeply crinkly pubic hair fills my nostrils.

Master Ez abruptly pulls from my body, and I almost vomit from the need to gag. I swallow back the urge as I draw air into my burning lungs, scalding my tender throat as it floods by.

"I said no hands. I will bind you," he warns in a cold voice. "Don't force me. Punishment is involved."

Punishment? This isn't what he calls punishment? I do as Master Ez asks, yet he violently punishes me anyway. Violating me, both my trust and my body.

With a brutal shove, Master Ez's cock slams past my gag reflex, thrusting deeply down my throat, as if it's my second cunt. He fucks my throat and mouth like you would punishingly screw a pussy. Tears leak from my eyes, mixing with the saliva dripping from my chin.

I'm reduced to the level of an animal. Oxygen. Food. Water. That's all I need to survive. I'd do anything to breathe. Anything. It's either find a pleasing rhythm for both Master Ez and myself, or suffocate as a consequence.

I inhale when Master Ez pulls out, and exhale through my nose when he plunges back in.

Inhale. Thrust. Exhale. Thrust. Inhale. Thrust. Exhale. *Trust*– trust that both Master Ez and I will continue with this rhythm, for his pleasure and my survival.

"You have no idea how frustrated I've been, with all the things I couldn't control in my life weighing down on me. All I wanted to do was spend time with you, get to know you, and I wasn't allowed. Denied. Denied. Denied."

I gurgle, close to throwing up from the need for oxygen, as Master Ez tries to hold a conversation while fucking my face.

"Then I had to watch you take Kayla in the manner you did, but I couldn't join." Master Ez's body shakes violently, his cock enlarging, and then a small amount of cum is released to ooze down my throat. It helps to lubricate the cock that is injuring me while soothing the burn.

"All the progress you've made, and I can't take any credit for it. It was supposed to be about all of us. So goddamned selfish!" Master Ez shoves deeper, impaling me, bruising me from the inside out. The more he talks, the less control he uses. His hips jerk wildly, slamming into me, rocking my entire body as he palms the back of my skull.

"The shit you pulled during the meeting. It took all of my control not to bend you over the chess treasure box and fuck you until you screamed bloody murder. The satisfaction I would have earned from making *him* watch."

Master Ez is impaling me faster and harder, making it impossible to keep a rhythm of inhale-exhale. Just as I think I will pass out from the lack of oxygen, his orgasm hits.

"K...a...t...y...a," he screams at the ceiling as jets of scalding cum shoot down my esophagus to fill my belly and leak out around his thrusting cock. The front of my t-shirt is saturated from the moisture trailing from my chin: tears, saliva, and cum.

Master Ez curls around my body, pressing deeper, filling me. Eye mask or not, blindness is closing in around the edges and stars are erupting in my peripheral vision. My body loses its fight to stay upright.

I am suffocating.

Dying.

Suddenly I can breathe. I gasp in large breaths of cooling air while choking on the viscous fluid filling my throat. Ez holds me upright while I kneel on the floor, maintaining my balance until I get my equilibrium back.

"Eat all your cream, Kitten," Master Ez purrs in a tight voice, sounding guilty yet jealous yet angry. "Take all of your medicine." His thumb brushes across my bottom lip, and then plunges in, delivering my medicine.

Supportive hand disappearing, Master Ez just walks away, leaving me where I fall. I roll to my side, retching and convulsing, choking on much-needed air as my belly empties its contents on my bedroom floor. Gasping breathlessly, I lay on my carpet in shock, not understanding what just happened.

The blowjob wasn't a reward for him or for me.

It felt like punishment. Like Master Ez was punishing us both.

It felt vindictive and wrong.

My skin crawls with every bad emotion one can imagine. My fingers curl around the edge of my nightstand as I struggle to pull myself to my feet. I take a large breath, silently praising myself.

That was nothing, Katya. You've lived through worse. It was just ten minutes of your life… that's all. It was only ten minutes. It's nothing compared to an hour.

I tell myself comforting, pretty lies as I hobble into my bathroom to step into a scalding hot shower. Ten minutes was far worse because it was at the hands of someone I trusted, especially because I allowed it to happen.

The only one at fault was myself.

Chapter Twenty-Three

I do what I'm best at when I get knocked down: I drag myself off the ground, stand back up on shaky legs, and dust the shit off my ass.

I survive.

I have a long list of things I have to accomplish, and a confusing, painful, ten minute blow job and the lifetime of consequences that follow, will only compound if I lie down and die. After I came up for air from crying, throwing a fit, plotting revenge, however long that all might take, I'd still have a life to lead and responsibilities to deal with.

Last night reaffirmed my stance that the only person I can count on is myself, and I cannot let the people down who have come to count on me. I have a publishing company to run, employees who need my leadership, and new authors who have earned the right to see their names written on covers. I have a family to support with my earnings.

As much as I'd love to lie down on the sofa and read a syrupy sweet, contemporary romance while indulging in a crying jag, I don't have the luxury. As the day has progressed, I've ticked the to-do items off my list that have been plaguing me. One of which I've tried to avoid for weeks on end, and it's time to relent and get it over with.

I've held Kimber off for the past three weeks by telling her I'm still acclimating to my new life, so I don't have time to chat. My guilt is getting the best of me, and I bite the bullet. As an added bonus, Kimber will occupy my time by taking my thoughts away from what happened last night.

I don't have to physically speak to Kimber. Riddled throat or not, my fingertips are perfectly adept at typing out my replies, so I no longer have a good excuse.

I'd met Kimber in an online support group for survivors of violence. We hit it off immediately with our shared miseries. Kimber is one of the only people I've truly opened up to about my past, more so than with my family because there was no pressure. The ease of being an anonymous person hiding behind a username and a laptop screen was a major relief. I felt like I could tell Kimber anything, which is exactly why I've avoided her as of late. She'd recognize the change in me just by how I type a simple reply, and then I'd have to acknowledge the change myself.

I'd love to meet with Kimber in person one day, except her fear rules her. She and her two friends were kidnapped by a very bad man, where she was made to watch one of her friends forced upon the other repeatedly. She didn't think they would make it out alive after the sickening things they were forced to do to each other and to other people, all the while being psychologically terrorized. She's never been the same since, even going as far as to use the username **Lunatic**.

Kimber no longer leaves the house. Agoraphobia, they call it. She lives her life in a virtual world, while I live mine in an imaginary one. Neither of us embraces reality– a friendship too good to be true.

Lunatic: Kat? Do I need to put out a cyber APB on your behind? C'mon, girlfriend. I've missed you. Are you still here? Did the big, bad world swallow you whole?

KitKat411: I'm here. Sorry it's been so long. I've been busy with things, especially with work. I want to show my boss I was the right person for the job, probably biting off more than I can chew in the process. Plus, I have a minion who is a bit bitchy that I need to get in hand. So, enough about me. How's the virtual world been treating you?

Lunatic: KAT! You're alive! I've missed you!! I thought aliens abducted your ass. It's been so long.

KitKat411: I know. I know. I said I was sorry!

Lunatic: I'm just yanking your chain. Honest. There's nothing new with me, since nothing ever changes around here, you know that. I sit in my cave, writing new programs and creating and upgrading websites for clients. I make sure my ladies behave and bring me food when I'm hungry, lest I'd starve to death. I'm very proud of the growth of my company. I may have to hire a larger staff to handle the influx. The three of us are not enough anymore.

KitKat411: WOW! That is fantastic news. It seems like

you've been busier than I have been.

Lunatic: The rest is just boring coding, which I won't bother going into. It would go right over your head, kind of like when you hit me with big words. So, how's your apartment? How's the job? Do they appreciate your Grammar Nazi ways? Your love of the English Language? How is your boss? Coworkers? Any new friends?

KitKat411: Slow down, Kimber! LOL! I like my new place. It's comfortable, and suspiciously exactly as I want it. The job is great. I have three people who work directly for me. One is a pain in the ass, but we understand each other. If she didn't want my job, I think we could be friends. The others do as I ask, as soon as I ask, so the only issue I have is trying to do too much at once to prove myself. My boss... I'm pretty sure is the actual BOSS. Don't ask! I met a woman who I'd like to try to befriend, but that depends on whether or not I can trust her. Her name's Queen. I feel connected to her for some inexplicable reason.

Lunatic: Aww! I bet Queen feels connected to you, too. You're so easy to get along with.

KitKat411: Ego-stroker! You know damned well I can be a bit of a bitch, and that is online. Imagine how I am in person.

Lunatic: I know why you turn cranky, so it's all good. This Queen person would understand if you let her, I'm sure. So, you were really excited to hit the scene for real. Did ya ever gather the nerve? Dude, I'm too terrified to leave my cave, let alone venture into a BDSM club.

KitKat411: Brave, I am not. But I did finally branch out and visit the club. I'm confused. I don't know how I feel about it. It's exciting, and for the first time in a very long time, I feel alive. But I thought it would be filled with rules and structure. You know how much I need that sort of thing. How do you let go if you don't know where you'll land when you fall? I don't have that much faith in anyone without boundaries and structure.

Lunatic: I'm always on my computer researching stuff. Why don't you tell me what you mean & I'll look it up for you.

KitKat411: All of James Atwater's books were filled with stringent rules. Do A, expect B. It was negotiated upon beforehand, and completely voluntary. Then there were safewords for when you were uncomfortable and needed to stop. I've found none of that at all. I have no choice, and it's confusing me, making me rethink whether or not I even want to be around that sort of thing.

Lunatic: I'm confused, because I thought that was how it was as well. I mean, can't you say stop if you don't want to do something? Just get up and leave?

KitKat411: It felt like that to begin with. If I didn't obey my master's orders immediately, he would punish me, saying it was an education to teach me a lesson I needed to learn. For the most part, I agreed. I'm a bit of a bullhead, so I'll be stubborn just for the sake of being spiteful. But the reward and punishment system changed. I thought you got rewarded when you earned it, and punished when you misbehaved because you needed to be educated with a lesson. I found out that wasn't the case.

Lunatic: Um… Kat, what did you do? I always took you for a good girl.

KitKat411: I didn't do anything, honest! I also didn't think I did anything that garnered a reward, either. We're playing a game, and when you win a battle, you move these chess pieces on the board we have set up. I won, and moved the chess piece. I thought that was the end of it…

Lunatic: Oh! So you were rewarded. That's awesome. From what I've read, masters do stuff like that. They aren't supposed to punish you for no reason because that would be confusing. But rewards are different. It makes them happy to give their submissives nice things and to do nice things for them. I believe that's what being a dominant is all about. I'm not in the lifestyle, but I can assume it's how I feel about my employees. They love waiting on my ass, and I love buying them an endless stream of packages from Amazon Prime.

KitKat411: I wish it was something as simple as goodies from online shopping. The thing is, he said it was a reward. But it was HIS reward.

Lunatic: Don't you want to make him happy? My

employees seem very content with waiting on me, doing little things for me, because they know it makes me happy.

KitKat411: I do. I really do want to make him happy. But his reward went against all I thought I knew about the rules, while breaking my own moral code of ethics. I thought we both were to get something out of it.

Lunatic: Everything I've read says that. So you gave him a reward and didn't get anything out of it? That's not too bad, Kat. I thought submissives were supposed to want to please their masters. I know you're not a submissive. But I assume a switch would have a similar connection to their master.

KitKat411: It's not like that at all. It was out of the blue, and for no reason whatsoever. He said my reward was my master's pleasure. Yet his pleasure was my punishment. I know punishments aren't supposed to leave lasting damage, but in order for him to get his reward, I was hurt. It won't go away for a long while. It hurts in a multitude of ways. I feel violated: mentally, physically, and morally.

Lunatic: Katya! What did he do?

KitKat411: No. I don't want to say. It's too embarrassing. Just know that I'm having second thoughts. Hell, third or fourth or millionth thoughts. I can't trust what happened. I can't even trust my own emotions and intuition anymore. I'm fucked– everything is going haywire and wonky on my ass. But I do know I don't want to do this anymore. There is no balance, and it was the promise of balance that drew me to BDSM in the first place. I don't think he is the right master for me, but I don't think he will just let me walk away, either. Just forget it. Forget I said anything…

Lunatic: I'm not forgetting shit, Katya! We're friends. I care about you and your well-being. Tell me what he did, so I can get off this computer and kick his fucking ass! I'll shove his nuts down his throat!

KitKat411: You don't even know who he is or where to find him. Plus, you don't leave the house. I appreciate it. & Kimber, you are my only real friend. I'm so glad I have you to confide in, and I'm sorry I've avoided you for the past few weeks. I just didn't want to admit to you what I didn't want to admit to myself. When I talk to you, more comes out than with Dr. Jeannine, and I avoid you to avoid therapy.

Lunatic: Please tell me so I can fix it. I beg of you!

KitKat411: I will. When I'm comfortable, I'll tell you. It's just too raw right now. Okay? I would have done it for him regardless. If he would've only asked, I would have said yes. I wouldn't have been morally comfortable, but I would have done it just the same. I wanted to make my master proud. It was the brutality of the act. It felt vindictive or something. I don't know... But I'll be okay. I always am.

Lunatic: Katya, please tell me exactly what happened. Everything.

KitKat411: Don't worry about me. I'm good. Tell me more about your company. It's called Empowerment, correct? You must be so proud to be adding more employees.

Minutes go by without a reply. I strum my fingers on my desk, hoping Kimber is all right. She never leaves the house, so why would she get up from her computer mid-conversation? After twenty minutes, I start to get frantic.

KitKat411: Kimber! Where did you go? Are you okay? You're scaring me.

Lunatic: Ah, Kitty Kat. I do understand. You can come to me for anything, anytime. Always! You realize this, don't you?

KitKat411: What, say again? What did you just say?

Lunatic: Katya, I typed it out, silly. You can just reread it. But I'll type it again just the same. You can come to me for anything, anytime... Always... I will be here for you!

My heart beats so fast it may explode. I've heard those exact words recently. I didn't read them. I *heard* them. But where and from whom?

No. Please, no. Don't let this be true. Tears trail down my face and my body shivers with hurt. I prepare for the ultimate betrayal. Worse than being gang raped and humiliated. Worse than a ten minute skull-fuck.

Lunatic: KitKat? What's wrong?

KitKat411: White Rook sweeps Black Knight, motherfucker! How could you? Stalker or not, this breaks some kind of covenant. Worthless piece of shit!

DR.Lunatic: Katya, calm down. I told you we all censor ourselves to different individuals. This was the only way. My story was real, with the exception of the agoraphobia, even the attack. Everything said was true emotions. I mean it, Katya. I will always be here for you. & I know what you've been through better than anyone.

I smash my laptop shut with such force, I crack the plastic frame. I stare down at my shaking hands, muttering over and over, "This cannot be happening. This cannot be real. This cannot be happening. This cannot be real."

"Katya, what's wrong?" Kayla asks from my doorway, but I don't look up at her, choosing instead to stare at my smashed laptop. "Are you all right? I heard a noise?"

Kayla must have heard the wounded animal sound I was involuntarily emitting from my chest.

Master Ez is Kimber. I don't know if that means Ezra Zeitler, Cortez Abernathy, or a combination of the two. Kimber felt like a woman. She *really* felt like a woman. She felt *real*.

Kimber isn't real.

My body is wracked with uncontrollable sobs as I learn another of my truths.

Truth: Master Ez is Ezra Zeitler and/or Cortez Abernathy.

Truth: Kayla Cummings is Temptation.

Truth: Kimber isn't real. She's Master Ez.

Real or not, Kimber just died for me. She really was my only friend, and she was just a figment of my stalker's imagination. How sad is that? I've never felt as alone or broken as I do now… and I've been so low that death sounded like a sweet release from the misery of life.

Kayla's hovering– mothering –forces another layer of guilt to wash over me. She is mine to take care of, not the other way around. I point at my throat. I doubt I will speak again. My throat is a fiery torture brought straight up from Hell. I tried to eat and nearly fainted. Thirst equals drinking shards of glass. Forget about talking. I can't even whimper from the pain. My master's pleasure is my reward. Is my master's pleasure another word for punishment by torture?

I quickly wipe the tears from my cheeks and flash a wan,

reassuring smile. I kiss Kayla's forehead, and then I take her hand to lead her to my office door. This isn't her cross to bear.

I take a few minutes to collect myself, and then I head for my boss's office on the first floor– his *real* office. It takes me the elevator ride down fourteen floors not to break down and die, but I manage to compose myself.

Survive.

Chapter Twenty-Four

Dr. Ezra Zeitler's office is easy enough to locate, thanks to the fact that my recent obsession had me memorizing his office number. No one stops me as I traverse the building, being as I am an employee and a resident of The Edge Building. The dozen or so security guards I pass, all nod politely in my direction, almost as if they sense the mission I'm on. I walk directly to Ezra's office, encountering my only roadblock–Aaron.

I yank open the door to Zeitler's real office, only to find Aaron sitting behind a reception desk. His huge body overpowers the tiny desk and chair where he is stationed. He looks up to see who arrived, pen poised over paper as he writes something in an appointment ledger.

My eyes flick around, noting my environment. The small waiting room is innocuous with its pale gray walls adorned with woodland prints. Four cushioned chairs line one wall, creating a waiting area with magazine-covered end tables, with the opposite wall hosting a snack station with coffee and pastries. Classical music trickles from hidden speakers, giving off a sense of calm welcoming.

Unlike the surroundings, I am not welcome and Aaron is not innocuous. He stares up at me, wide-eyed and confused, looking for all the world as if he was caught red-handed.

I just shake my head at Aaron, communicating that it isn't worth fighting me over. The expression on my face speaks volumes, because he just stays seated at his desk and doesn't move. I doubt he even breathes.

"Enter," comes Zeitler's muffled voice through the door just as I'm turning the knob.

I move into Ezra's office, expecting to see him sitting behind his desk, looking self-important. I wait for the punch to the gut sensation to return, only now realizing it never fled me to begin with. I'm on the edge of tears, refusing to look at the man I sense openly gawking at me, when with a shock of surprise, I spot the other occupants in the office: Cortez and

Queen.

A sense of intense betrayal descends upon me, one far greater than before. Queen, of course. Kimber felt like a girl because she *was* a girl. I wanted to be friends with this woman, and she was toying with me all along.

Queen freezes when she notices me hovering in the open doorway with Aaron ghosting behind my back. I can tell by her body language that she was arguing with both the Ezes, and my arrival took them by surprise.

None of them knew it was me who opened the door. This afforded me five seconds to observe their unguarded interaction. All three were in the middle of an intense fight, no one taking a side, judging by how they are glaring at each other with their muscles taut and their fists clenched.

I stare at them, and they stare back in a mix of abject horror and guilt.

Which one brutally violated my throat?

Which one played Kimber?

Ezra?

Cortez?

Queen?

All three?

Maybe they took turns… who the fuck knows? They do. I don't. That's the problem.

What they don't understand is that this isn't just about the betrayal. Kimber died moments ago. She was real for me. Three years of conversation, of pouring out my soul, and it was all forged. Fake or not, the perception of Kimber died for me. How apropos that I said she lived in the virtual world while I lived in an imaginary one. True, Kimber never existed in reality because she never really existed at all.

Kimber was the imaginary one, built to feed me a false sense of security and phony friendship.

I grieve deeply, and my throat is punishment for my stupidity as I drag air in at a steady rate. I stare at them, not bothering to hide the emotions that flash across my face.

I examine the Ezes again, needing to know who was whom, which one was with me and when. Whose cock was thrust down my throat, and who held me while I slept? Because without a shadow of a doubt, they were separate entities of Master Ez.

Ezra and Cortez are similar in stature. The only notable difference is skin tone and hair color. Ghostly pale skin and cropped white-blond hair makes Ezra devastatingly handsome. Cortez's flawless skin is the color of caramel, and his jet-black hair gives off an exotic energy. Both men have the same haircut, so I would have to run my fingers through their hair to compare the texture.

I hold Cortez's eyes. I have no need to with Ezra. I know his eyes are stormy gray. My shoulders slump as I absorb the fact that their eyes are indistinguishable, with the only difference what they emote.

Which one made me think about making love for the very first time? Which one made me regret ever feeling that way? I brush tears from my face on that fleeting thought.

Master Ez is correct about one thing. We all represent ourselves differently in certain circumstances. It was an out of body experience to take Kayla in my office. Everything about me came alive. These men have two identities: normal for everyday activities and dominant for when the mood strikes. I bet both of their voices change with the metamorphosis. But how can they sound exactly the same?

I gently place my gift to them on the desk, and then step away abruptly. I almost stumble into Aaron, my back hitting the solid wall of his chest.

"Katya?" Zeitler asks cautiously, fear lacing his voice.

I shake my head while pointing at the offering.

Ezra picks up the Black Knight and raises his eyebrows in question. It was the play from a few minutes ago. It's the piece I removed when I figured out Master Ez was Kimber. I wait for him to read, and then share my note with Cortez.

~Master Ez~
Ezra & Cortez
I know there is no backing out of the game. It's in motion and will not come to a rest until the final move– until I learn all of the uncomfortable truths, I will wish for the rest of my

life I never learned. I know the rules are ultimately up to you (both?). Rules you seem to make up as you go along.

I have a request. You always say it's not what I want, but what I need. Well, I need consistency. The Dom/sub relationship is built on consistency and trust. If I do A, then I expect B as a result. (You) broke those rules, and I believe there should be a consequence for that. Unless you feel trust only flows one way, as if it doesn't matter if I trust you as long as I obey you out of a sense of fear.

Kimber was outside the spectrum, a betrayal of the deepest order, and that broke my trust in a way I doubt I will ever forget, let alone forgive. Compounded upon that, my reward last night breached consistency. (You) harmed me for your own pleasure in the name of reward. For my reward is my master's pleasure. I suffer the consequences of such a reward. The gift of torture that keeps on giving.

I do not wish to associate with people who lie, breach trust, break promises, and harm me because they can. With what I've already suffered through, I believe I deserve better. I realize at this point, that my life as I know it is directly tied to Master Ez: my job, my home, my co-workers, and the tentative friendships I've tried to develop.

With that being said, I will play your game under one condition. If I win, I am released from under your control, where I will go back to my family and live my life in peace and tranquility, as I should have from the very beginning. No job is worth this. No truth is important enough to lose your sense of self. I also realize that a person(s) who has treated me as you have, may not stick to the word he has given. Call me naïve, but I'm hoping you will.

If I lose, I will stay under duress as I make your life a living nightmare.

Last night the game changed for me. It's no longer a journey of self-discovery. It's for my freedom.

~ Game on, Bastard Ezes~

I wait as Zeitler reads the note. When he finishes, he looks up and runs his gaze over my body, looking for signs of visible trauma. From one blink to the next, his cautious expression changes to pure fury. When Ezra fists my note in his hand, looking on the edge of exploding, I back away towards the door, pushing Aaron with me.

As I turn to leave the office, I catch sight of Ezra smashing the note down in front of Cortez on the coffee table. The last sight I see before I bolt through the door, is Queen holding Cortez down on the sofa while Ezra hovers over the pair.

I dart, moving as fast as I can, trying to outrun more hard-to-swallow truths. Aaron follows me a few steps behind, never getting in my way or intervening as I make my way back to the only safe haven I have– my apartment. I don't even protest when Aaron walks in behind me. He secures the four deadbolts on my door, and then turns to me. I even allow him to hold me while I try not to cry.

Restraint 248

Chapter Twenty-Five

I pull away instantly, not wanting comfort from Aaron. I've never hated myself as much as I do now, because even after all of the bullshit Ezra has pulled, I still want him to be the one to comfort me.

Not offended by my refusal of his affections, Aaron drags a chair from my dinette set and places it on the left-hand side of my door. He sits down, pulls out his cellphone, and ignores me as a way of giving me privacy. The young man was born and bred and educated to serve while blending into the background, affording his charges a false sense of privacy while giving them a very real sense of security.

I know without a shadow of a doubt, Aaron will only allow one man to enter my private space. I trust Aaron to protect me against everyone save that same man, who he is undoubtedly texting with my whereabouts.

Proactive.

Survivor.

I could dwell on all this bullshit, or I could take care of the issues at hand. My throat is on fire. I spend the next few minutes ignoring my emotions while I locate anything I can think of to soothe the fiery agony. I gather my ingredients and sit down at my dinette set, trying to muster the courage to take my medicine.

Movement draws my attention, but I don't bother to look up from my remedy. I do wonder why I never heard the locks engage, or why Ezra brought another bodyguard. I suppose Aaron was contacting Roarke via text since he was with me and not protecting their precious cargo. I continue to ignore everyone as another chair disappears from my kitchen table, no doubt flanking my door.

I'm under no illusions. Roarke and Aaron are not here for my protection. They are here for two very real reasons. One: to trap my escape. To force me to sit here while Ezra explains or doesn't explain. Two: to protect Ezra from my slowly simmering wrath.

I ignore Ezra as he settles into the chair across from me and sighs a long-suffering, miserable sound from deep within his chest. I still don't look up, refusing the give him the satisfaction of my attention. Especially since the only question written across my face and held within my gaze would be....

WHY?

I feel like a mixture of MacGyver, Bill Nye the Science Guy, and a drug addict. I smash four ibuprofens on a sheet of paper with the bottom of my tumbler. I don't bother using it in its spray form: I pour an ounce of Chloraseptic into my tumbler, and then I add the pain medicine by folding the paper into a funnel. Swirling my glass, I stare at the concoction for many long moments, working up my nerve.

My shaking hand reaches and falls back... reaches and falls back... reaches and falls back. I repeat this process several times, always coming up empty-handed.

Ez's voice breathes through my mind *'don't process, just react!'*

"Katya," he says, firm yet commanding.

My eyes snap up to meet Ezra's. I knew who the real Master Ez was the moment I turned to leave Ezra's office. The eyes holding mine left me with little doubt.

Dr. Ezra Zeitler is Master Ez. *Only* Ezra, with a violent episode courtesy of a jealous man-child.

"Drink!" he softly commands.

I do.

I don't process. I react. I toss back the contents of my medicinal concoction, and as a brutal consequence I do not deserve, I suffer by burning in living hell. My fingers curl into claws and dig into the edge of my kitchen table, leaving my fingertips pure white. No sound escapes from my silent scream. My neck strains and arches. The worse it hurts, the faster I breathe, the more the pain increases. It's a torturous cycle of Hell.

Ice water flowing into my mouth rouses me when I hadn't even realized I'd passed out. I find myself tucked on my sofa with Ezra curled up next to me, embracing me with one arm while the other rubs an ice cube on my lips.

"Hold this in your mouth. It should help some as it melts. I've never experienced this firsthand, but I've taken care of someone who has," he murmurs softly.

Acquiescing, I open my mouth, allowing Ezra to place an ice cube inside. I look my question at him. The question I will be asking until the day that I die for a multitude of reasons.

WHY?

"Just so we are very clear. I did *not* do this to you." Ezra's voice sounds strained with barely leashed violence.

Embarrassed and ashamed, my eyes seek out Roarke and Aaron, who are most definitely listening in with one ear but not looking at us. Flanking my front door, sitting in my dining chairs, Aaron is reading a well-read paperback that appeared out of nowhere, and Roarke has a tablet clutched in his hands as he plays a game of some kind.

I roll over on top of Ezra and bury my face in his chest, inhaling the scent that has become my greatest obsession. My addiction. Needing reassurance that he's truly the Master Ez who held me in my bed, my fingers make quick work of the top buttons on his shirt. I reach in, clutching his necklace in my fist, seeking my charm. My fingertip etches over the **KW** of my emblem, and sobs of relief spill from my chest. A key swings from the chain– the key to my bracelet. My fingertips light on other charms on the necklace. The **C** is obvious to me now. Cortez Abernathy. However, the **Z** stumps me, but I'm too exhausted to care who or what it means.

"Cortez is not dead, but he is very, very sorry," Ezra promises.

I shake my head no as I slide up Ezra's body until our faces are even. I look him dead in the eyes and mouth, *"He's mine."*

"Fair enough," he allows. "However, I did have to punish him. I gave Cort a taste of his own medicine. It's doubtful that he will be able to talk for several days." Ezra sounds so menacing that I shiver. His arms come around me, holding me, trying to warm me when he was the one who made me feel cold.

I look my question at him. *What was the punishment?*

Looking me straight in the eyes, Ez shamelessly deadpans, "I skull-fucked him." He says this with no remorse or embarrassment, and absolutely no emotion, like shoving your cock down another man's throat is nothing.

A silent laugh bubbles up my throat, scraping it raw. Surely Ez is joking.

"No, Katya. I did to Cortez what he did to you. Exactly as he did to you." Ezra is dead serious.

How can Ez do that? He'd have to enjoy it in order to do it. It's a biological impossibility to perform *that* act without being aroused.

Reading my thoughts as if I'd spoken them aloud, "The private things I said to you when I was acting as Kimber were very real. I have no issue with taking Cortez's mouth. It wasn't the first time, nor was it the thousandth time that he's sucked me off," Ezra says this as if he's ordering a coffee, not admitting that he's gay, or admitting that he just brutalized his friend's throat, and he doesn't feel badly about it, either.

"Are you gay?" I mouth, eyes darting to the guard dogs, worrying I've crossed a line, and I'll upset Ezra for asking a highly personal question that is none of my business while two men listen in.

"I've always thought of myself as gay, yes," Ezra replies without hesitation. "I want to explain why Cortez did as he did. I don't want you to hate him. I want you to forgive him, but I don't expect you to forget what he did. I'm not making excuses for his abhorrent behavior. Cortez is the most emotional human being on the planet."

Movement catches my eye: Aaron shaking his head up and down rapidly, while his partner in crime is trying his damnedest not to laugh out loud. They share a look, and then pretend they aren't listening in. If anyone ever wanted to know a secret, these men would be the ones to seek.

"I'm two months older than Cortez. We've spent all of our lives together, with the exception of three torturous days. Days I explained to you when I was speaking as Kimber— my abduction. So, I see Cort as an extension as myself. Sometimes I look at him, and I'm amazed I'm not thinking, feeling, tasting, or seeing what he is– that's how tightly we are wound. So, it wasn't that odd for us to be sexual from the time puberty struck. Touching Cort is the same as masturbating, only it's heightened by a thousand fold."

"Cortez gets jealous?" I croak out.

Roarke's loud guffaw has Aaron joining in with him. A death glare from Ezra has them trying to school their expressions but failing miserably.

"I've always known Cortez was the one for me," Ezra admits, and it kills something vital inside of me to hear it for some reason. "But, sometimes, we don't get what we want. Sometimes fate is cruel. I'm gay, and Cortez is not. Just so you know, the jealousy flows both ways. My teenaged years were torture, because Cortez noticed all the girls around us had grown breasts, and he loved how it felt to sink in between their thighs. I doubt there is a beddable woman within these city limits that that man has not penetrated."

Ezra laughs, a sound filled with amusement, pride, and pain.

"Our jealousy is odd. We've found a happy medium. We both acknowledge we are life partners without sexual connotations. We haven't been lovers since we were sixteen. Sometimes it gets the better of us and we snap, engaging in violent, brutal sex that leaves us in more pain than before. Our rules are simple: Cortez leaves men alone, and I leave men and specific women alone."

"But," I rasp out, confused. "Not fair."

"I didn't make that rule up, our jealousy did. Cortez is very angry with me. I'd promised to share you with him, and I don't mean sexually. Your time. Your attention. Your affection. We were to share the Master Ez title, but I was selfish. Cort snapped, thinking we had been lovers."

"Oh," I breathe as realization dawns.

"In Cortez's defense. He was doing to you what he enjoys most, not realizing you might not enjoy it. It's something I refuse to engage in with him. Jealous, thinking I'd been touching you in that manner, he took it out on you to hurt me. Cort was punishing me while sending a message."

"Heard loud and clear," I force out.

"Explicitly so," Ez agrees. "Cortez and I share a life, and I was keeping you from him, and it wasn't fair. In a way, the punishment I just meted out was his ultimate reward."

"Cort doesn't play well with others," Aaron mutters in our direction. "I tried to warn you."

"Understatement," Roarke adds. "Remember when Cort kicked Caleb in the head during soccer, pretending he was aiming for the ball. Tore the kid's head up with his cleats, all because Ez was invited to a sleepover and he wasn't."

"Fat fucker was too lazy to play soccer, anyway," Aaron grumbles, suddenly pissed off.

"Cortez is an incredible human being," love and affection and silent warning flow from Ezra's lips. "And he isn't *fat*."

Aaron scoffs, "He used to be," while Roarke makes a face of agreement, nodding his head yes while mouthing the word. Ezra chooses to ignore them both.

"We're extremely stressed out in this stage in our lives. We've reached a pinnacle. We have to find a way to live together in peace, or finally cut the cord and move apart. The thought is terrifying and depressing. Cort can't be happy with only me because he loves women. So we either find a common ground or we move on. I've been simultaneously doing both, because I refuse to live in this limbo anymore, and the transition has been rather difficult."

Frustrated, Aaron spills, "Remember when I said Master Ez was dealing with two blockheads?" and that's all he has to say about that.

"And one of them was himself?" I croak out.

"Ha! Good one!" Roarke rumbles a laugh.

"I'm sure you're asking yourself why I'm telling you all of this," Ezra says, ignoring the litany of negativity rolling back and forth between his buddies, as they trade horror stories about Cortez and Ezra's antics, and Aaron keeps injecting some of mine into the mix.

"Last night was inexcusable– unforgivable. I don't want you to hate Cortez. I know the two of you could be very close if he would get over his jealousy and if you could get over the violation. I don't want either of you to miss out on getting to know one another. You have a lot in common, just with your love of the written word alone. I was being selfish, keeping you all to myself to begin with, and had I known this would happen, I wouldn't have. I regret that."

"Why?" I try to say, '*Why me? What is going on?*' but I only have the ability to rasp out a single word.

"Attraction isn't based solely on sexuality, or else Cortez wouldn't be obsessed with me. I'm a psychiatrist, and even I cannot explain why we feel the emotions we feel. I am truly gay. I look at men and feel the stir of lust. But I've also been with women. Not many, mind you. Enough to fill the fingers on one hand minus my thumb, yet I've been with fewer men."

"I wonder why?" Aaron muses. "Perhaps because of Single White Female Cortez threatening to hack off your dick in your sleep."

"Hmm… we must be living life by different scripts," Roarke adds. "Because I'm not sure who would be the stalker in this scenario. Cort does not stalk. He retaliates immediately. Whereas someone else we know bides his time, lying in wait to destroy you."

"Roarke… Aaron…" Ez sighs out, having enough. "As I was saying. Attraction is a mix of chemicals, emotional reactions, and environmental stimuli. There have been a few women in my life that I truly wanted, wanted as much as I've ever wanted any man: emotionally, mentally, and physically. They pinged everything that intrigued me. So do not stress over the fact that I'm gay. Forget about it actually. I don't advertise the fact for obvious reasons."

"I. Will. Keep. Your. Secret." I force out, wishing I hadn't when the flame reignites in my throat. Ezra reaches over to the coffee table, long, tapered fingers lifting a piece of ice from a glass. He gently swabs my bottom lip, coaxing me to open.

"I trust you," Ezra murmurs as he places an ice cube on my tongue. "Or I would have never told you otherwise. Anyway, after you left my office, I decided I'd better watch the security feed to see what happened. Did you honestly believe Cortez was me?"

The disappointment in Ezra's voice makes me sob. Not only did I mistake someone else for him, but he witnessed my violation.

I sob harder when I realize the stalking fucker hid cameras inside my apartment. I have absolutely no privacy. Always being watched, every moment of my life inside this building is a violation, whether it be a violation of my privacy or my body. I live and work in a giant maze of a mousetrap, specifically designed so he can observe me as a scientist would watch a wild animal. The broken part of me intrigues Dr. Ezra Zeitler.

I stop sobbing and start laughing hysterically when I realize that I feel like I cheated on my master with his lover, that I cheated on my faithless master with his faithless lover. The whole lot of them has absolutely no morals, and it's insanity that I'm behaving and feeling as I am.

Ezra soothingly strokes his fingertips against my cheek, causing me to flinch when he hits the fingertip bruises along my jawline. The joint feels cracked, or at least displaced.

Always reading my mind, "Cortez is an extension of me. If you touch him, it is not a betrayal, Katya. Do *not* feel ashamed. You aren't the first person to mistake one of us for the other, nor will you be the last."

"Kimber," I breathe the word as an agonizing wave of grief inundates me out of nowhere.

It was definitely Ezra who played Kimber in the beginning. Kimber's story was how she and her friends were abducted as teens, brutally raped, and made to rape one another. It's a story that will stick with me for a lifetime. I'd thrown up after I'd read the sickening details of Kimber's account. The only way I had dealt with it was to pretend it was a fictitious story and not reality. I feel ill knowing that Ezra, Cortez, and Aaron all starred in the events that were reality. It was bad when I thought it was three girls. I don't know why, but it's somehow worse because it was three strong, intelligent, influential boys being victimized.

"I told you my story was the truth," Ezra says softly, a hint of sadness filling his voice.

I wrap my arms around Ezra and hug him tightly. All is

not forgiven, but I understand where he comes from. I know the pain and shame of being a victim. I know how it makes you feel weak, and how you will do unmentionable things to remove said weakness.

I can understand how a man would pretend to be a woman while retelling his story, using the anonymity of the internet as a shield. I don't have the ability to empathize with how emasculated Ezra, Cortez, and Aaron must have felt after their ordeal. It's difficult to admit, but as women, we are inherently created to be penetrated. Gay or not, being a strong man meant to protect himself and others, reduced to the level of a defenseless, helpless animal, it would have had an immense emotional toll.

"Queen?" I croak out.

"Don't blame Regina," Ezra mutters, sounding guilty. "Shit. Never call her Regina, or else she will kill me. Yes, she played the part of Kimber when I was busy. It was easier in the beginning when you'd respond to me. But when you finally moved here, there was no schedule, and I didn't know if I would be online or not to chat with you. Regina is a cyber-genius. She is the owner of Empowerment Internet Solutions. She didn't make anything up when she spoke with you, either. She is also one of the only people I trust. I thought you both would enjoy one another. So blame me, never her."

I don't know if I have the capacity to get past any of this, I think to myself, unable emotionally or physically to voice the words aloud.

"I know you well. So nod if I am right. When Cort came to you, you thought he was me, but his voice sounded too hoarse." I shake my head yes in response. "Did you figure out that it wasn't me when he took your mouth or when he offered you no Aftercare?"

I mouth the word, *"Both."*

"You were worried that we were both playing Master Ez, and we were switching back and forth, tricking you." I don't even have to answer that one. Ezra draws me tighter in his arms and sighs deeply.

"I need you to know that this game we play was never

about learning my name. It has always been attached to my identity, but it's not whether or not I am Dr. Ezra Zeitler or Master Ez. It's about who I am to you. Who *we* are to you," Ezra stresses, shaking me a bit. "Every single thing I have done has been for your benefit. I have never wanted to harm you. My only goal is to walk with you through the healing process. In the end, you are the only one who can heal yourself, but you have to trust me to prepare you for the end of the journey."

Chapter Twenty-Six

My feet pound the ground with such force it reverberates up my legs and trails up my spine. The sharp snap of twigs breaking under the impact echoes in my ears, along with the deafening tattoo of my panicked heart. My terror-filled breath saws out my lips, exhale clouding the air across my face as I run—

Run for my life.

A looming pine tree is a taunting, solid barrier, directly in my path of escape. Precious life-saving seconds are lost as I veer around the tree, or else risk smacking headlong into it. Upheaved from the ground, gnarled roots catch my toes and upend my balance. I catch my fall with outstretched palms upon the pine-needle-laden ground, bruising and tearing my flesh. With a forceful lunge, I propel myself forward to gain momentum.

Droplets of blood nourish the soil from deep cuts welling on my hands. Branches slash my cheeks and thorny vines snag my skin and clothing, almost as if they are offering aid to my hunters. My mind is clear of all thought, except for the inborn flight reflex of someone desperate to survive.

Self-preservation forces my muscles to maintain their wild run, even as my body protests the movement with bloody and bruised, burning limbs. My hands instinctively rise and fall, protecting me from the brutal violence of nature.

Four hunters stalk me as if I were a wounded animal— their prey. They gain on me steadily, even if their visages are blurry to my tear-stung eyes. With rapid movements too quick for me to register, they converge, charging me from different directions— herding me, running me to ground as a pack.

Territorial rage explodes through the simmering fear in my blood. As their target, not only am I being assaulted, my sanctuary is being violated right alongside me. I've hiked this wooded lakeside trail since I was a child. When I was small, I'd venture out farther, creating a larger boundary of my own backyard. As an adult, the lake and the wooded trail surrounding it, are my home. We're being invaded, and I'm powerless to stop it.

I know every dip, curve, and incline of the landscape. Up until just moments ago, this was where I went to clear my mind and seek solitude. Childlike dreams of the future were forged here, right alongside the adult decision of what I would major in in college. My bubble of safety, the trust I have in my land to protect me, and the courage I have to protect it in return, bursts on the whims of ruthless men.

Now, I run for my life, hoping my lifelong knowledge of the landscape will pull me through to the other side— safety.

In tune, somehow connected as pack animals, they hunt in perfect synchronization: breathing in harmony, legs moving with the same graceful fluidity, intuitively knowing where to head me off to push me towards their partners and propel me to their destination.

If it weren't me versus them, I may have found their symmetry breathtakingly beautiful.

I speed up on the descent down a steep ravine, drawing me closer to the lake and its imminent comfort. My sneakers skid on soft dirt, pebbles rolling me, making it nearly impossible to stay upright. I catch my fall several times by sightlessly grabbing for roots and branches. Thorns jab into my flesh with my hold, only to tear my skin as I pull away. I acknowledge no pain from my wounded palms as they rapidly beat with the pounding of my heart. Falling backwards, head hitting a rock with a great, jarring force, I fear I'll be rendered unconscious, unable to protect myself. Inertia has other plans for me, causing me to slide down the embankment on my rear while I regain my senses. By the time I reach the bottom, my shorts are shredded by the earth and damp from the blood seeping from the resulting wounds.

Rolling to a stop, I crawl to all fours. In shock, I barely wince as the jagged edges of river rock and the grit of ballast from the long-ago railroad bed embed into my knees and palms. I try to right myself on stable ground, but my energy is waning. Agile footfalls catch my notice, driving fear and adrenaline to flood my system, fortifying my survival instincts.

With a deep, pain-filled keen, I propel myself to my feet, and take off towards safety.

They allow me no rest as they close in from all sides, like the shadow of darkness creeping across the land every sunset— sure and swift, and unavoidable. They try to pull me off course by rerouting me with their movements. Driving me like an animal, they prove their adept hunting skills by forcing me off the hiking trail. Separating me from any other hikers we may encounter, from the safety of the known, I'm now parallel to the path, going away from it at an abrupt angle. The one in charge is wordlessly maneuvering me to his destination, and I am powerless to stop it.

The primal, animalistic side of my brain already recognizes its capture. I can see it playing out in my mind's eye: the four hunters felling my body, tearing into me like lions on a fresh kill, stripping my dignity away along with the last vestiges of my cherished innocence. My system floods with adrenaline. A vicious quaking rocks my entire body, slowing my pace. I shiver in the cold of impending doom, even as my body erupts with a feverish sweat.

My logical brain, the part of me that holds self-preservation above all else, overpowers my fears. From my depths, I scream, "I will not give up! Never surrender!" I will fight to my very death just so I can wear my pride as a badge of honor in the afterlife. Furiously, my mind spins escape routes and defense plans as I am led, pushed, and driven by the unit.

My only salvation is the lake. If I can get to the water, I can swim to safety. Like the trail, I know everything about the lake: the inlets, the currents, and the boat-tied docks. As a balm to my soul, I can feel the caress of its chilled water welcoming me into its promise of safety and comfort. The tree canopy overhead casts rays of light for my path. The crystalline waters glisten invitingly, beckoning me towards its secure embrace.

Half in the now, half inside my fantasy of escape, I'm taken aback when the leader comes into sharp focus just off to my right. I stumble when I see the fierce expression on his face,

the look of triumph as he gains on his prize.

"It won't be long, boys," his smug voice projects, filling the woods with his victory. The shrill cadence of his voice sounds like broken glass to my sensitive ears.

In a futile dance of survival, I go left, and then right. Left, and then right, panting wildly as I look for a hole in their defenses. My injured foot slips on a patch of moss, situating the leader in easy reach of my bleeding arms. In a pitiful, last ditch effort, I veer to the left, away from his grasp, only to miscalculate the trajectory of the other hunters.

Arms enclose me from the side. Startled, yet not surprised by the inevitable, I close my eyes in defeat. "I'm so sorry," a young, somber voice whispers softly against my hair.

I wake to a blood-curdling scream…

Chapter Twenty-Seven

The memories are back. I've managed to keep them at bay for almost twelve years. I've only spoken them twice, and never in their entirety: once at the trial, and the second time was reluctantly at the parole hearing. Both times were unemotional accounts of the event.

I've lived my life avoiding all things that bring the memories to the fore. I've never cried or screamed or lashed out for the injustice dealt to me. There was no reason. It was all said and done. Justice was dealt to my rapist, and then I was left to pick up the pieces of my destroyed life. There was no sense in lying down and dying when I had so much work to do to live for those who needed me. My only option was to survive– to endure. To give in to the emotions threatening to destroy me would mean they won. I was victimized for an hour of my life, but never a victim because I didn't break.

Twice the memories have corroded my thoughts in just a few short days: during my almost-orgasm with Kayla, and in the wee hours of this morning. That is my issue: their reoccurrence, not the memories themselves, or so I tell myself. I just want to put them back in their box and never let them out.

I'm never without the thoughts of my rape, but they are blurry copies of the actual event. I see bits and pieces with a film cast over the image. Yet out of the blue, a scent or a sound will bring on five seconds of my ordeal with perfect clarity.

The reality of it is, I don't remember my time on the forest floor. Oh, I know what happened to me, but my mind protects me from the minute details of it. I am thankful for my subconscious. This morning's nightmare was the first time I was thrust back to the forest floor and made to relive the event as if it were happening in real time.

It's what Dr. Jeannine has been pushing me to do. It's what I've refused to acknowledge. She says I will never heal without accepting the details. I think she is wrong, and my subconscious agrees.

I blame my stupid yet courageous actions on my lack of sleep and my frayed emotions. Both make me extremely ballsy. I've had a few days to come to terms with the truths Ezra has shown me thus far, but apparently I'm too daft to get to the heart of the matter and solve this equation, as he says we're still playing our little game of destroy Katya from the inside out.

Ezra Zeitler is Master Ez, who thinks himself my ultimate keeper. He provided me with a job, with a home, with faux-friends, and with a faux-submissive, all so he could gain complete and total control over me.

Once you hold dominion over the necessities– sustenance, shelter, currency, friendship, affection, mind, heart, and soul – you essentially own the person. He managed to do all of this while watching my every move through surveillance, his minions, and while pretending to be Kimber to promote his stalking. The psychiatrist examined my actions and reactions to all of his stimuli, and he got off on it.

I have no idea why.

WHY?

Ezra is manipulative and controlling, and I hate that. But what I hate even more is how drawn I am to his caring, giving, and calming nature. I hate how Ezra makes me feel bad about myself, even while he manages to make me feel better– healed.

The reckless part of me is surfacing again, and she is pissed the fuck off.

My mother gave my sister and me some good advice as we were growing up. I was four years my sister's junior, so I heard the advice way sooner than most. As a mother raising two daughters, we were taught the sister-code from an early age.

Rule #1: All males are assholes until they transform into real men– some die as assholes. Any asshole your sister had first is not the asshole for you. If he treated her poorly, he will treat you poorly. If he cheated on her, he will cheat on you. No, you are no better than your sister. You cannot reform a bad boy asshole. He is just an asshole, and the love of a good woman will only make you an asshole lover.

Rule #2: If the asshole somehow convinces you to break

rule #1, with or without your knowledge, then it is your duty as a woman to tell your sister she is with an asshole, and then grovel for forgiveness while you heal from the fingernail scratches.

Rule #3: How do you teach an asshole a lesson? Fuck his brother. Preferably if the brother is a real man.

My mother wasn't referring to biological brothers and sisters. Woman to woman. Man to man. You have a duty not to denigrate your sex by your piss-poor behavior.

Obviously Rule #1 and Rule #2 are negated by Rule #3, because more often than not, the brother is attached to one of your fellow sisters. But why should women be held to a higher standard, while the men go wherever their cocks lead them?

While turn the other cheek, dignity, and humility sound good in retrospect, nothing is as satisfying as revenge, even when you regret it later.

My mother said the regret of inaction was far worse than the shame of action. Sometimes an asshole needs to be taught a lesson. Harm an asshole's pride, and the humbling will change him into a real man faster than love ever could.

Master Ez is an asshole, and that is the only explanation I have for my actions.

I've had to look and act innocent for four days straight– a magical feat reserved for unicorns and fairies. While working my ass off for Edge Publishing an average of eighteen hours per day, I've managed to do some recon myself. Mailman Rick had to deliver my mail, and he had to take my mail, and he had to read the tiny notes no surveillance camera could ever detect. This afternoon's mail had just what I needed.

It's been four days. Four days of healing. Four days of planning. Four days of circumventing security cameras, minions, and the ever-watchful eye of Master Ez. Four days of missing his cerebral fucking.

It's the missing part that truly fuels my actions. A sick part of me wants to wreck Ezra's relationships so I can have him all to myself, and that is disgusting. I've never felt so close to my brethren before. This is my first act as a scorned, irrational female under the guise of Rule #2.

As I ride down the elevator to the first floor, I convince myself I'm not trying to sabotage Ezra and Adelaide's relationship. I'm simply doing my duty as a fellow sister; a woman should know when her fiancé is a faithless asshole. Especially when the woman in question is a refined, educated heiress who works as an art curator.

Pedigree, blue-blood breeding and my jealousy aside, Adelaide Whittenhower should know.

I enter Ezra's real office to find Aaron and Roarke splitting a pizza while playing a round of *Skip-Bo*. The both look up at me in surprise, and then flash me identical grins, like they aren't about to stop me from whatever foolishness I'm about to commit.

As I open the inner-office door, I kind of wish the bodyguard/assistants would have stopped me.

Ezra stares wide-eyed at me from his desk, completely floored to see me materialize before him. I get off on how stunned he is, because I finally got one up on him. I want to feel disgusted with myself, and I know I should. But the vengeful, reckless woman inside of me is gleefully high from the rush.

Adelaide stands behind Ezra with a possessive hand on his shoulder. Their framed engagement announcement and picture hangs directly behind them on the wall. What a beautiful couple they make. How phony to have the same exact images, in the same exact frames, hanging in the same exact locations on the wall, in both the fake and real offices.

I wish they would have left me out of their relationship, and then I wouldn't be having to suffer through this while in denial. But somewhere deep inside me, a lonely girl cries, and she is screaming out her pain. She never feels like she is good enough– always someone's dirty little secret.

Any part of Adelaide that touches Ezra, needs to fry in acid.

Great, my inner bitch is territorial.

"Ezra. Adelaide," I say in greeting as I flop down on the chair facing his desk.

I'm wearing a skirt, and neither has to imagine what my

panties look like. The black lace flashes like a billboard '*Open for Business.*' My conscience is thrilled that my lacy panties are boy-shorts instead of a thong. Yeah, even on days when I want to act like a skank, skank panties do not manifest in my dresser drawers.

"Are you feeling all right, Katya?" I almost lose my nerve hearing the concern in Ezra's voice. Almost.

"Well, you see. If someone is going to treat me like a whore, I thought I should at least dress and act the part. I had a rough night last night," I purr salaciously, like I was out whoring around when nothing could be farther from the truth.

My rough night included nightmares of running through the woods while being hunted by gang rapists. This is why Master Ez doesn't frighten me. I've already lived through the worst, everything else pales in comparison. Even the sound of that in my own mind gives me pause. I'm losing it. I should abort my mission. *Operation game over.*

"Did I miss something?" No doubt Ez is wondering if he should be reviewing the security footage as a full-time occupation at this point, knowing I could be up to mischief or getting skull-fucked when he's not paying close attention.

Ezra's eyebrows meet his hairline and his mouth drops open when I lean forward. I strike a trashy, skanky pose: legs spread, elbows on knees, chin in palms, panties and bra on display. Adelaide's gaze glues to my ample décolletage and her mouth drops open.

"You must be the *Boss's* woman." I emphasize the word boss.

"Yes, I'm Ezra's fiancée." Adelaide's voice is filled with pride, but it has a shrill edge, annoying. She's very haughty. I wonder if Ezra gags her during sex. I would, I couldn't stand the sounds she would make. Then again, I'd never fuck her— too skinny.

All right, inner bitch, I let you out to play, but shut the hell up inside my head! I feel disconnected, like I'm dealing with multiple personalities, and not a one of them seems to like Adelaide Whittenhower.

In less than a heartbeat, I forgive Cortez for his violations.

I can understand how jealousy is a wicked mistress; how it makes you do the stupidest shit on the face of the planet, all because you want to hold onto something that doesn't belong to you.

"So, what do you have to do to get this man to actually tie the knot? Six years is an extremely long time for an engagement. What are you, engaged to be engaged?" I flash an evil smirk in Ezra's direction.

Ezra leans his head against the back of his chair and releases a deep, long-suffering sigh. When he's satisfied that he holds our undivided attention, he looks me dead-on as he places his hands on his blotter. Ezra is completely resigned to live through my antics, whatever they may bring.

What do I have to do to get him to tell the truth? I am insulting his fiancée to her face, and Ezra looks like he's a perfect angel sitting in a church pew.

Adelaide looks back and forth from Ezra to me, over and over again. I see the light bulb burn to life in her mind. She glares at Ezra when he remains silent– smart man.

"What? Do you think he's waiting for you, of all people?" Adelaide says dramatically. "All men cheat. This little stunt means nothing. When you leave here in a few minutes, I'll still be his fiancée, and you'll still be nothing more than a trashy whore."

"I'll be a trashy whore with a clean conscience, which is why I'm here to tell you that Ezra has been dipping his fingers where they don't belong, treating me and making me feel like a whore, all the while disrespecting you."

"I could care less. You're probably just an assistant to lower management who's looking to suck her way up the ladder." Adelaide's voice is snide, but her expression tells me she knows exactly who I am.

Adelaide knows I'm the object of her fiancé's stalking. I see deep-seated knowledge glare at me from her light blue eyes. She knows what I want Ezra to tell me. She knows what I *need* to know. If I can't piss Ezra off enough to get him to spill, maybe Adelaide will.

"Ah, that hurt." I fake a hit to the chest. I swear Ezra's lips quirk up at the corners, but the movement is gone instantly. "Actually, I head Edge Publishing, but you already knew that. I bet you even know my social security number and my birthdate. Now, why is that?"

"Ezra wouldn't touch you. You're disgusting," Adelaide spits, like the words leave a bitter taste in her mouth. It takes everything in me not to mention that it was Ezra's fingers deep inside of me just a few days ago, making me come. Better leave that unsaid. I just shrug. My presence will annoy Adelaide more than my words.

I feel bad, because I am using Adelaide to get to Ezra. She is his fiancée, and I'm going above and beyond to get his attention. Technically, I'm the other woman– the interloper. Now that I know Ezra Zeitler is Master Ez, and Cortez Abernathy is his 'partner', neither of them are intimately touching me while they are attached to someone else.

I was raised better than to be someone's whore. My parents raised me to be someone's wife and mother. I have more self-respect than I am exhibiting. I will never let my master touch me sexually as long as he's engaged to another woman.

I'm not the skank I'm playacting right now. I'm just thankful that our intimacy never reached sex. I'm not even sure that Ezra likes me in that way, since he would never let me touch him back and he admitted he was gay.

Ez did say he was attracted to a few women. Four he said by my mathematical deductions of *'the fingers on one hand minus a thumb.'* The odds are not in my favor, since one of those four women is undoubtedly engaged to be married to him. Adelaide is the woman standing at Ezra's side. She is the woman who doesn't care that he cheats, because she knows he's not going anywhere– least of all with me.

It hurts me to know that this well-educated, rich woman lowered her standards in order to put up with a man who cheats on her and stalks prey. Her gorgeous, blue eyes scream that she is frightened of me, that she knows exactly who I am. It also bothers me that Ezra doesn't see Adelaide or myself as good enough. Neither of us meets his needs, or else he wouldn't need two: one who is cultured for the society pages, and one who is stalked for shits and giggles.

Maybe Ezra is waiting for Cortez to cut the cord on their partnership, after which he will marry Adelaide in the ashes of his ruined relationship. Who knows? All I know is that I don't factor into any of this. It's none of my business, but Ez dragged me into it just the same.

I feel bad, but it isn't stopping me from self-destructing. Maybe I'll annoy Adelaide enough that she'll leave Ezra. I don't want her to leave him for my benefit. I wouldn't want a man who would take me as a consolation prize. I want Adelaide to leave Ezra because she is worth more than this.

I'll feel guilty after the game is finished when I try to look at my reflection in the mirror.

"Why do you put up with Ezra cheating on you?" I ask, curiosity getting the better of me. "I don't understand it. Why does Divina put up with Cortez cheating on her? Is it something you learn in prep school: how to accept your husband's mistress 101... intro to infidelity... doormats anonymous?"

Ezra's laughter echoes around the room, husky, smoky, and spine-tingling. I hate myself a little bit because it warms my heart and soul. The cheating bastard wipes his eyes on a hanky, chuckling to himself.

Adelaide stomps her designer stiletto and shrieks in frustration. "Why aren't you married? You're in your thirties. My guess is that no one has ever wanted you." She looks proud of herself, like she just scored a point.

"I'm not married because the thought of a cock near me makes me puke a little in my mouth." Her flinch makes me smile. What I don't expect is the curious look that follows. I've piqued Adelaide's interest and intrigued her.

I stare Ezra down, silently pleading with him to end this debacle. He's the only one who can. He gazes back at me innocently. *You dug this hole... you will crawl out of it.*

"You're a lesbian?" Her shocked outburst doesn't sound as if it's a bad thing to be a lesbian.

Adelaide Whittenhower is a strange one. I expected her to

throw a fit, not look interested. She turns away from me as if the very sight of me burns her eyes. But not in a bad way, and it makes her feel ashamed of herself.

"Not liking cock doesn't make me a lesbian by default, ya know? It just means I haven't found one that doesn't make me choke." I grin wickedly at a wincing Ezra. It will be a long time before I stop reminding him of Cortez's skull-fuckery.

I go in for the kill. "But, then again, I haven't seen your fiancé's prick yet," I taunt the couple.

I wait for it…

Adelaide rushes across the room and tries to slap me. I catch her bony wrist in my hand before it makes contact. She stills instantly, staring down at me like she's seen a ghost.

I hammer the final nail into the coffin by staring Ezra down while holding his fiancée's wrist. "What do ya say, Ezra? You already treated me like a whore, you might as well finish the job. Whip it out, and let's see if it will dampen my panties or make me gag a bit in my mouth."

Ezra hesitates. I think he's actually contemplating it. I snort at him when he uncomfortably shifts in his chair. I realize he's aroused by the thought. Ezra wants to know which result I would give. I can see the force of his control as he tries not to unleash his cock.

We are locked in our own private world; everything else is on the outside. Both of us are trying not to laugh as we ignore Adelaide's tirade. She's screeching at us in the background.

Sorry, Ezra, I'm pretty sure Adelaide hates you right now. We simultaneously break our stare and look to the frantic woman in the room. I almost feel bad. Almost.

"Just tell me what you want from me, and this all ends," I say to Ezra while gesturing to a pissed off heiress. I'm thoroughly exhausted on so many levels. "I'll call her off," I offer. "If you don't actually tell me the truth for once, I'm going to Divina next," I threaten. "I know you don't respect your fiancée, but you love your cousin."

Ezra stiffens, drawing in air to reply, but Adelaide's words sink in and strike me deep first.

"If you won't touch a man, how do you expect to have

children? But then again, who in their right mind would ever want to share their genetic makeup with a lunatic like you?" She says the one thing guaranteed to defeat me.

Adelaide's words pierce like a dagger to the heart. I wheeze, as all the air in my lungs expels in one long keening sound. I try to stand and turn before either can see the anguish cross my face. My deepest secret wants out of its box, clawing its way out– screaming.

I'm going to irreparably fracture.

"Go!" Ezra orders, and my numb legs obey.

I woodenly rise from my seat, deep in the throes of an epic panic attack. My chest is tight, as if my heart is trying to forcefully beat its way out. My lungs burn with the need to breathe as I go from breathless to hyperventilating. Darkness creeps along the edges of my peripheral vision, but it's nowhere near as dark as my thoughts.

"Katya, stop!" Ezra demands.

I stop.

I'm locked in my master's demented version of the children's game *red light/green light*.

"Get the fuck out, Adelaide. Now!" Ezra releases his fury as the door opens. The force of his scream echoes back to us, and I know that it carried into his waiting room.

"Don't touch," I say as I feel Ez hovering near me. "If you do, I will break. It will all flood back– all of it." My voice is dead with panic. "I don't want to remember. I'm not ready."

"I will only settle my palm on the small of your back, okay? I need to direct you to my bathroom." Ezra speaks quietly and calmly, making sure I don't spook.

I don't look up, but I nod my head in agreement. I don't have the energy to reply. I'm focused on the panic that flows over me and rolls me under.

Ezra's palm hesitantly rests on the small of my back. It's a warm comfort as his heat seeps into my body, loosening the panic. He leads me towards the door in the corner of his office. I don't watch as I walk. I just close my eyes and follow his lead.

Chapter Twenty-Eight

I fold onto the tile floor, the coolness on my legs grounds me to the here and now. I rest my cheek on my knee, embracing myself in comfort. A cool, wet washcloth is draped over my head and neck, blinding me.

I welcome the darkness.

"Katya, I don't know if I should applaud you or punish you for this stunt. This was beyond my scope. You never cease to amaze me." Ez releases his patented sigh as he settles on the floor next to me. "This isn't going to end the game. Getting me to snap isn't going to earn you your truth. You have to reach the finish line yourself, and it isn't through me."

"I'm sorry. I probably ruined your relationship with Adelaide. I have a good excuse, though," I offer meekly, and he snorts a laugh in reply.

"Ah, now *this*... I am curious to hear." Ezra's amusement relaxes the tightness in my chest.

Admitting the truth isn't life or death. Would it be so bad to count on someone for a change, to have them shoulder some of the burdens that suffocate me? Ezra is the man I know, the man who comforts me. He trusted me with his private horrors when he pretended to be Kimber, and I should do the same in return.

I finally open up and trust Ezra, because I have little choice.

"I could deal with everything, but not when it's compounded by my nightmares. The memories are coming back, and I don't want to remember." I sob into the washcloth. "It scares me to death. I'd rather pretend it never happened. It's easier. Admitting it out loud feels like a little death. I don't know if I can survive living through it again... sometimes I think the memories are worse than the actual experience. They haunt me," I whisper.

"Hey, now. Hush," Ezra says soothingly. "It's going to be okay, I promise you. You'll never heal if you bottle it up. The fear will choke you to death."

"But you don't understand," I breathe.

"I understand a lot more than you realize, Katya. Cortez, Aaron, and myself, we were in your position. We're still in your position. I know all about horrific memories haunting your waking hours, just as much as they do your nightmares. It's why I *need* to help you," Ezra says with such strong conviction that it emotionally exhausts me to hear him speak.

"I have a secret," breathes out past my lips. I say it before I can stop myself. I've never uttered those words before.

"You have many secrets, just not from me. I think this may be one, though. Is it not? Tell me and you will feel better. I can't help you if I don't know everything." The tone of Ezra's voice lulls me into compliance– proof that he is my true master. Ezra pats my back gently and croons soothing noises against my hair.

"There is no way you could ever know everything that has ruined me." I peek out from beneath the edge of the damp washcloth to meet his stormy eyes. "My secret is bad... very bad," I breathe. "But it's so precious that it was the only reason I survived."

Ezra exhales a breath and waits while maintaining our eye contact. His patience is astounding. He studies me for a few moments, as if weighing his words before speaking them.

"I know about your past, Katya. I know the details of what happened to you, and it's not because I pretended to be Kimber. I know how your mind ticks. I understand why you will only touch women. I even know why your climax brought the memories back, and I think it would be a good thing for you to remember. You *need* to remember. I think I know all of your deepest secrets, unless you have more to tell me."

Ezra is sitting next to me on the floor, but he slides me across the tile until we are facing one another. Slowly the washcloth is lifted from my face. He peers down at me and smiles like an angel, his white-blond hair a glowing halo atop his head. That smile is what makes me tell him my secret.

"Only a few people know my secret," I say of my family: my parents, my sister, and my secret. I draw in a deep breath and breathe out, "But they would protect her to the death."

The moment the words are released, a heavy weight lifts from my soul. But the relief is short-lived, because a second later, it is replaced with anxiety. Especially as I watch Ezra crumple to the floor in a state of shock. His face is blank, but his muscles twitch beneath my fingers. I know what he is feeling. I've had enough freak-outs to recognize the symptoms. He is living in his own private hell. I just don't know what I said to set it off or how to fix it.

After a few minutes, Ezra hoarsely whispers, "Whose is she?"

I automatically reply with, "You don't know my secret." However, his stormy gaze screams that he does. On the spot, I understand that Ezra does know me– all of me –except for this. His stalking didn't garner this truth.

"I do now," he mutters, sounding incredulous. "Is she from the man who raped you, or did you have a child later on in life?" His face is a blank, emotionless, expressionless. "But I know you've never let another man touch you."

"How did you know what I meant?" I whisper. Ezra stares hopelessly down at me in reply, and shakes his head as if suddenly exhausted. "I had a daughter from my rape–"

I cut off the rest of my sentence because Ezra erupts into a vicious panic attack. I watch Ezra rock back and forth in a trance-like state. He keeps repeating the word '*monster*' as his face pales even more as it drains of blood.

Ezra makes the most pitiful sound I've ever heard come from man or beast– a sound that will haunt me for the rest of my life.

"Ezra, are you all right?" I shake him, but he doesn't notice.

He's borderline catatonic. I should be the one freaking out. It was my secret to tell. I was the one panicking just moments ago, needing someone to help me shoulder the burden. But seeing a strong man reduced to a mumbling mass of panic, yanks me from my own miseries. I drag Ezra to my lap and wrap my arms around him. He feels so cold to my touch that I'm frightened he's entering shock.

Ezra is supposed to be the strong one.

Ezra is our rock, the foundation that supports Cortez, Aaron, Roarke, and Kayla... and I'd hoped he'd support me, too. But if he falls apart, none of us stand a chance.

"I don't understand why you are so upset. Please calm down," I beg him, voice warbling from worry.

"How can you live as if nothing has happened? How are you not insane? How can you raise that monster's child?" His voice is filled with disgust and bitter self-hatred.

"Ava is not a monster's child," I hiss. "She is *my* child, and she's perfect." My voice warps with silent fury. I try to push Ezra from my lap but he holds on tightly. "What kind of man are you to say that about a child to her mother's face?" I accuse, furious.

"Ava?" Ezra hisses sharply. "Your daughter's name is Ava? It's not about the girl or you... it's about that *monster*," Ezra twists the word until it sounds more menacing than the word Satan.

"There were circumstances I never told anyone," I defend my daughter and her father. "My daughter's father wasn't a monster."

"What do you mean, circumstances?" He asks, sounding hopeless and lost. The words are muffled from where he's pressing his face into my lap. "How could her father not be a monster? He raped you and left you for dead."

"I... I... never told the whole story about that day. I always omitted one vital piece of information. I just... the truth was worse than I could handle. To this day, I can't remember the minute details. But... Oh, God, Ezra," I desperately cry, finally ready to admit the truth I've kept hidden for almost twelve years.

"I was run down by four men– three of them were very young, younger than I was. One of them was just a boy, to the point that in my memories I almost see him as a child. I protected them when I gave my statement. I said the boys just held me down because the man made them, and that they ran while he raped me. I lied."

"I know," Ezra admits gravely. "It's in your records that the monster said his son went first, and that no one corroborated his story."

I suck in a gasp of air at Ezra's revelation. I didn't know that Raymond Hunter confessed the truth. I don't know why I thought he would protect his son. He probably tried to push the rape off onto the boy. My secrets weren't as hidden as I'd hoped.

"Ezra, I don't like that you read my files," I hiss, feeling violated all over again. "I haven't even read my files. I just… I just couldn't handle reliving it, seeing my violation on paper. Knowing that an account of what happened is out there for public consumption, and that you've read it, it feels like another assault. I would scream about boundaries, but you'd never listen," I grumble warily.

Ezra wraps his hands around my upper arms, holding me at arm's length. He stares me dead-to-rights and asks, "Your daughter, Ava, is she the son's child or the monster's?"

"My daughter is not a monster, and she wasn't created from my rapist. Ava's father is the son," I reveal.

Ezra squeezes me tighter, as if he lessens his hold, he will break apart. He's breathing hard and his heart beats rapidly against my palm. He's quaking so hard that my body rocks from the force.

"How do you know it's his?" Ezra asks, lips barely moving as he speaks.

"Raymond Hunter never finished… he never finished inside me," I stammer out, simultaneously ashamed and relieved. "He was interrupted when he figured out the boys escaped, and he immediately chased after them… He never finished."

I've thanked God for that saving grace, every single day since my assault.

Abruptly releasing his hold on me, Ezra sprawls onto his back on the tile floor, with an arm covering his face.

"Any more shit I don't know?" he asks in utter disbelief, and I can't fathom why it's such a big deal for him. But Ezra prides himself on control. This is information he didn't have, so therefore he wasn't in control.

"Seriously, are you trying to intentionally kill me?" Ezra

mutters, voice twisting with wry humor as he wipes tears from his face.

Ezra releases his patented heavy sigh, and then reaches over to yank me into his arms. He holds me, and neither of us speaks as we seek our mutual comfort. It's not about sex, or my truths, or dominance and control; it's just about connecting to another human being. It's about understanding their pain and wanting to remove it. But sometimes it's about dwelling in the pain– nothing bonds people closer together than mutual torment.

Master Ez or Ezra, whatever name you call him, he is my strength. I feel lighter. Just saying the words out loud lifted some of the weight from my soul. We remain in each other's arms for a long while, until I'm staring at the insides of my eyelids, drifting in and out of sleep.

"Take Katya back to her apartment and lie with her while she sleeps, okay?" Ezra rubs soothing circles on my back as he talks to someone who just entered the bathroom. I don't have the energy to care who.

"Are you sure that's for the best. It should be you, Ez. Kat may freak out on me." Aaron. It's Aaron's gravelly deep voice.

I relax further, feeling safe.

"A new development just materialized and I must fact-check it immediately. Just hold Katya, and make sure she can smell your scent. Comfort her. The last hour has been a stressful one," Ezra makes the understatement of the year.

"What is more important than Kat?" Aaron sounds furious.

"A mini-Kat," Ezra freely spills my secret, as if it's his right to tell.

Aaron's stunned gasp echoes throughout the bathroom, removing all animosity that surged inside me.

"Okay," Aaron breathes. "I see your point. What's this about scent?"

"Some things are ingrained inside Katya's psyche. We may sound different or look different, but we smell the same."

"What?" I garble out, but with the fading panic attack mixed with my revelation and the earlier stress, I'm quickly fading out. It's either sleep it off or pass the fuck out. The mind can only handle so much shit, and sometimes it quits before the body is ready.

"If that's true, shouldn't it terrify her?" Aaron asks in a tight voice, sounding incredulous.

"One would think so. But after I figured out that it had the opposite effect, I've employed it a few times to calm her, so she would sleep. Katya associates it with safety. Please take her," Ezra begs. "It's killing me, because I want to be with her, but this cannot wait."

Chapter Twenty-Nine

Aaron is becoming a master caregiver, and I feel guilty for putting him through it. It's not his responsibility to coddle my ass, but he's doing it like a champ. I'm showered, fed, and tucked into bed with Aaron leaning against me.

I'm resolved. No matter what I remember, what is thrown at me, I will not breakdown again. What I did in Ezra's office earlier was inexcusable. Guilt shames me for how I treated Adelaide. She is a human being and has done nothing wrong. She has been wronged, not only by Ezra but by me. I can deny any culpability up and until I figured out how Ezra was Master Ez, but everything after that is all on me. I would love to blame Ezra for allowing it, for perpetuating it. But I am at fault.

Only I control my actions and reactions.

I had promised myself as I laid ruined in the woods that I would never break. I debased myself today, and not in the cathartic sort of way that one achieves through a BDSM scene. I sunk to a whole new low, and I am more ashamed than I care to admit.

My bad behavior aside, I'm glad I finally admitted the truth. I feel lighter. I just hope that I didn't confide in the wrong person. Ezra doesn't have the best track record: controlling, stalking, spying and recording, micromanaging, and faithlessness.

My God, I'm so fucking stupid for spilling my secrets to him. No way can he be trusted. I'm not entirely sure he's sane at this point.

Shaky and unsure, I take Aaron's hand in mine and twine our fingers. I need the connection to find a sense of comfort. Aaron has been respectful of my space, only leaning against me and not touching my skin. I appreciate the gentlemanly attempts, but I need touch.

"So, you have a daughter, huh?" Aaron says conversationally, but I can tell he's floored. "Tell me about her."

"What would you like to know?" I volley back, finding it

odd to discuss Ava with anyone outside of my family or her teachers.

"How come none of us knew about her?"

"I wasn't exactly keeping Ava a secret." I snort at the ridiculousness. "Contrary to popular belief, I am a very private person, and I don't feel comfortable walking up to complete strangers and giving them my life history. If you're speaking of Kimber, we met in a support group for survivors, so I kept our conversations centered on that. The only reason I told her about my move was because I wouldn't be available to chat as I had been."

"Kat, I'm sorry about Kimber." Aaron sounds genuinely sincere, causing me to hide a sniffle. "I can understand not wanting to spill your life history out. But I'd think you would have to tell your employer."

"Men and women aren't looked at in the same light, Aaron. No one asked, so I didn't volunteer. A boss assumes a mother won't put all of her effort into her job because she'll be worried about her children. A boss assumes a single woman will eventually marry and procreate. They never worry about a man being or becoming a father, assuming he won't care about parenting. I thought it best that I didn't say anything, in case I was going up against a guy for the position."

"Do women really have to think about shit like that?" Aaron asks, sounding stunned.

"Absolutely. It's a damned if you do, damned if you don't world for a woman. A strong woman is a feminist bossy bitch, who secretly wishes she was a man. A working mother is a bad mother, because she's selfish for putting the almighty dollar first. On the opposite end of the spectrum. A weak woman is a doormat who allows a man to walk all over her. A stay-at-home mother is lazy because she doesn't work and uses her children as the excuse. There is never a happy medium with this bullshit. We are criticized constantly, no matter what we do, and more often than not, it's not by the men. It's the women who are the opposite of us who tear us to shreds. My policy is to never answer questions I'm not asked. It's safer that way."

"I'm glad I have a penis, and I'm glad I never had to decide what I was going to do with my life."

"I'd just settle for not being judged, because as a single mother, my only choice was to work. But, even if I was married, I still would've chosen to work. It's just who I am. That's my point. It's an individual decision that every woman has to make– a decision every woman has to defend on a daily basis."

"Don't you miss your daughter?" Aaron hedges, like he's worried he's insulting me.

I squeeze his hand, letting him know I'm not offended. "Of course. I talk to Ava twice a day. She and I both lived with my parents, in the only home we've ever known. Ava's surrounded by family, going to the school she's been in since Pre-K, with the same friends. We decided as a family for me to move to Dominion, to try to better my life, so in turn I could better the lives of my entire family."

Aaron's ever-so cautious, as if he never questions anyone, so used to always being the one asked to do something. "So, you were going to just leave your daughter with her grandparents?"

"No, but it will kill my parents when Ava moves here with me. The separation will be brutal. Ava is gifted, highly intelligent– scarily so, actually. I was saving up for her first semester in Hillbrook's middle school program." I snort, rolling my eyes. "The irony is not lost on me, Aaron. I hadn't known it was your alma mater at the time. Ava chose Hillbrook before I accepted the job at Edge."

"Wow," Aaron breathes. "So your daughter is scary smart, huh? What is she like? What does she look like?"

"Ethereal. Intimidating. Demanding. Manipulative. Controlling. *Fuck*," I hiss out, realizing how bad that sounds. "Ava is an eleven-year-old tyrant. But she is also loving, affectionate, and compassionate. It's the moments when Ava behaves as a child I cherish the most– when she laughs or does something silly. She's the smartest person I've ever met, and she utterly terrifies me."

"I take it she's bored back home in that small town?"

"Academically, I would have had to send Ava somewhere very soon, and I would have followed her. But that isn't what was pushing me for a change of address. Old rumors have a way of coming back to haunt you. Everyone in town knows what happened to me, and they know Ava was the result. My biggest fear was telling her the truth of her conception. But worse, of someone telling Ava what they thought was the truth."

"Does she ask about her father?"

"Yes, and I tell her all I know, which isn't much. I can't even remember what he looks like. I've blocked those details out. I only have the emotions he left me."

"My God, Kat. That must be impossible." Aaron tugs my hand, drawing me into his side, lending me more comforting support.

"I don't look at my daughter and see the product of my rape. I look at my daughter and see the reason I survived. Ava was not a mistake. She was a gift. I endured hell to bring her life, because Ava was created to make a difference in this world."

"Shit," Aaron croaks out, turning his face away from me. I squeeze his hand tighter, but I don't comment about the sniffles. "Sorry. It just. It just brings up my own shit, ya know?"

"Oh, boy howdy, do I ever," I say to make Aaron laugh. "How can you be around all this craziness? It isn't healthy for you."

Aaron is a big guy, but he reminds me of a teddy bear–sweet and innocent. I don't think being around Ezra is a good idea for him. I wouldn't look at it as running away, more as retreating for sanity's sake.

"Did it ever occur to you that we need each other, and that includes you, Kat? We feel immense comfort around one another, even during an avalanche of stress. One's sanity is the next person's sanity," Aaron chants cryptically, saying so very much, but making absolutely no sense... and sounding vaguely insane as he says it.

"I don't understand," I mumble out of confusion.

"I know," Aaron breathes as he rests his cheek against mine. "Ah, Katya, what are we going to do with you." He chuckles heartily, a happy yet sad sound. "You shocked us all today. I can't believe you did that. It was so out of character. What must have been going through that head of yours to make you behave in such a way?"

Embarrassed by my own actions, I change the subject. "How did you meet Ezra?"

"Well, I know you've been snooping on our histories, so I'm sure you already know," Aaron says wryly, causing me to blush. "Roarke knew Ezra longer, going to grade school with him, and I met him when I was a little guy. But when I was twelve, my mother was employed by Diane Zeitler," Aaron says fondly. "Ezra's mother. Mom became the housekeeper of Shadow Haven Estates, and we moved in with the family."

"Tell me more, please. I don't want to think about my own mess." My tone is just short of begging. "Please distract me, Aaron."

"All right. All right," Aaron chuckles warmly. "Story time!"

"Thank you," I say, being genuine.

"I had a good childhood, chasing after the guys. We did what boys do, played video games, got into trouble, hiked around the woods, and goofed around. I was a couple of years younger, so I idolized them. See, Ezra and Cortez were inseparable. Cortez didn't like that Ezra warmed to me so quickly– jealous *prick*." Aaron says the word *prick* with affection lacing his voice. "Cort would snub me and could be kind of nasty towards me. But he eventually got over it when he figured out Ez saw me as a kid brother. We had a couple of good years together," he trails off.

"What do you mean?" My voice is tinged with confusion. "You're still together now."

"Ah, shit." Aaron rolls over and buries his face into my hair. "I see what Ezra means. I remember your smell." His comment makes me uncomfortable. I try to pull away so I can't ask what he meant by that, but he tightens his grip on my hand.

"I got to have fun with them for around three years. If we

thought it, Ezra bought it. If we wanted to go somewhere, we went. We had a lot of fun picking on Divina and Faith."

"I know you were raised with Divina, but who is Faith?" I ask, but he doesn't answer me. Must be another relative.

Aaron just talks over my question, as if he has to spill the words or he'll choke on them. I know the feeling. "It all crashed down when Ezra went missing." Forgetting all pretenses of boundaries, Aaron engulfs me in a hug. "Cortez went insane, savage. Seventy-two hours of unadulterated torment." Aaron laughs without humor. "Ezra's dad, Marcus, he couldn't even control Cort, and he controls the universe."

"Oh, Aaron," I cry, tightly embracing him back.

"The worst was not knowing where Ezra was, or if he was still alive. But we didn't have to wait too long before we were taken, too. Up until then, none of us had a concept of what real pain and torture was. We learned rather quickly."

"How long were you gone?" My voice breaks as I realize I'm not the only one holding an immense wealth of pain. Aaron's admission validates all that Kimber had told me about her abduction. Kimber is Ezra. A small comfort that Ezra hasn't lied with every breath he's taken, at least some of it was truth.

"A week to the day of Ezra's abduction, we were rescued by an unlikely person. Cortez and I were only gone for four brutal days, but Ezra endured a week. Ezra, he always gets us what we need, he always protects us, and this was no exception." There is a soul-deep reverence when Aaron speaks of Ezra.

"Ezra had to sacrifice a part of himself to save us from a similar fate, and we used that distraction to escape. Can you believe it was Ezra's eighteenth birthday? What a way to start his adult life, huh?"

"I can relate," I whisper.

"Oh, no doubt you can. So, yeah. We had a couple of good years. Yes, nothing ties a greater bond than tragic circumstance. But our bond is now sick, poisoned– diseased. There is a need that wasn't there before, and it's never satisfied... and it's Ezra's need," Aaron whispers in a bone chilling tone, just as I drift off to sleep.

***

I hold my agonized scream, swallow it and choke on it, as my captor's leg sweeps mine from beneath me. I fall to the ground, expecting a hard impact, but he takes the brunt of the fall.

I thrash my arms and legs, trying to break free from his hold. My punches and slaps land with a hollow thump to reverberate down my arms. With the solid connection of my elbow to his chest, his sharp grunt of pain lights satisfaction throughout my body. I may not win, but he's going to hurt, too.

Breathlessly, I lash out as an animal would, fingers curling into claws, sounds of pain spilling from my throat. The more panicked I become, the less effective my struggles are. I fight for my life, but it does me no good. It doesn't rescue me from my violent fate.

More hands join my captor's, holding me down to the hard-packed ground, trying to subdue my struggles. Their fingers slip in the blood and sweat slicking my skin, making it difficult for them to contain me. With the pass of their flesh along my injuries, I falter from the severe pain that strikes me like a physical blow.

Whether in reality or in remembrance, I can never place a face to the young men. My mind withholds this knowledge, whether it's to protect me, I do not know. Their faces, their bodies, every detail about them is blurred, everything but the hands that hold– the hands that ultimately harm me.

Three sets of medium-sized hands. Neither boy nor man.

Head jerking from side to side, I frantically search until my eyes land on the leader. He stands proudly, watching the scene unfold before him with smug satisfaction. Now, him, I never forget. I remember every detail in Technicolor. He's a tall, lean man, who is well-dressed and handsome, except for his expression of malice and the aura of madness radiating off of him. He is a man, who if you saw him on the street, you'd think he was a gentlemen. But all too late, you'd discover the sickness leaking from his soul mere moments before he attacked.

I lie helplessly and hopelessly on the forest floor, an animal caught in an inescapable trap. One male leans on my feet with his hands on my shins, restraining me. Another pins my arms above my head, his smaller hands barely able to contain me. The third, the one who ultimately captured me, is petting my face. It's his sick and twisted way of calming me. The intimacy of it makes me wish he'd just punch me instead.

"Well, which of you wants to go first? She's definitely ready now." The leader speaks of me as if I'm truly an animal. Meaningless. I no longer have a purpose, other than to be defiled for their entertainment. Once broken, I will be utterly worthless, even to them— especially to them.

"No," the third orders. "You aren't going to subject her to all of us," he growls with authority.

Blessedly, the third turns my face to the side so I no longer have to see their leader. But it's a sadistic trick, one designed to inflict maximum damage, just as how his soft touches somehow felt crueler than a violent strike. My mocking view is of the lake. Its crystalline water, which promised safety, now taunts me. I try to reach out to the water for help, fingertips unfurling, trying desperately to touch it. A whimper escapes my lips when the lake doesn't envelope me in its watery embrace.

"Well, son, this is your first hunt. I thought we'd share in the spoils, and then dispose of the body in the lake after we've broken her." A sinister laugh bubbles up from his chest, pure evil anticipation.

My body tries to shudder, but it's immobilized by two of the boys, but nowhere near as immobilized as I am by my fear. Terror rolls over me and takes me under, rendering me incapable of rational thought. Panic wraps me in its darkness. It leads me to a place that can only be described as Hell. The dark recesses of my mind are far scarier than my violent reality.

"This way we can do anything we want and no one will hear us." Madness leaks from the leader's voice. "We can take our time. And look at that lake… no one would find her for days. I planned this perfectly."

"Katya, snap out of it!" Strong hands press my arms into

my mattress, while a fierce shake jolts me out of the nightmare of my past.

I rouse to find my face buried against a manly chest, no longer pressed against the damp, moss-covered ground. My teeth are locked on his flesh, smothering my high-pitched screams. I abruptly pull back, thankful that I don't have my caps on. They would have left a lasting scar. I breathe a large lungful of air, catching his familiar scent.

Aaron.

"Oh, God," I groan. "I'm so sorry, Aaron. Did I hurt you?" My panic returns for a new reason. My hands flutter about, checking to make sure I didn't harm him.

"No. No, I'm fine." Aaron's voice is gravelly deep and gruff, with a tinge of embarrassment bleeding through. Aaron awkwardly slides off me, turning his hips to the side to hide his reaction. I don't want to examine that too closely. I just hope he likes being bitten, and isn't some kind of freak who gets off on other people's torments and nightmares.

"I'm sorry. I told you the past fucked us up, too." Shame is evident in Aaron's voice, and it makes me feel badly for silently judging him. We can't help how we cope with the past.

"Um… it's all right. I think," I stammer out. "What time is it?"

Groggily, I look to my clock, noticing it's morning already. I'm due for work in less than an hour. I'd slept the entire night away with Aaron at my side, keeping me safe and sound. Other than the resurfacing memory, I actually feel pretty, dang good.

"Ya don't have to talk about it with me. Um… you were screaming in your sleep, so I know what was happening." Aaron backs away from me, moving towards my bedroom door. I try to reply, but he cuts me off. "Uh– um… I don't want to remember it when you're in the same room with me. I need the bathroom."

Chapter Thirty

It amazes me how we can look at others and think they have their shit together. I know differently. On the outside, I appear happy. My profession is one that I'm passionate about. I am healthy. My family is alive and well. But on the inside, a fundamental part of me is broken. Aaron's behavior this morning brought this to light. Is anyone whole on the inside?

The happy trio is ruined on the inside, but not torn apart. Their bond is so strong it can't be severed. Even well-put-together Monica is fractured. I can smell her inadequacies like a bloodhound. If I were less of a person, I would exploit them.

Kayla is the only one of us who is genuinely happy. But then again, who in their right mind would play with the twisted trio? Hell, she plays with me, and I know I am not right in the head.

No one is whole. We can only strive for contentment. I could let my past strangle the life out of me by playing the victim, but I am no victim. I'm safe. Nothing can harm me as badly as my past. Once you've lived through the worst, everything else is a cakewalk.

I breathe deeply and make a circuit around my office.

You are in control, Katya. No matter what you remember, it will not break you. You've lived through it once, now it's time to accept it and move on. Maybe Dr. Jeannine is right. You must remember the repressed memories in order to be able to overcome your past and move forward into the future. You are in control.

I repeat this mantra to myself over and over as I pace my office. I don't know how long I go through this process, but eventually I make my way back to my desk. As I sit and decompress, I feel the fissures slowly repair in my psyche. None of us are normal. I must accept myself as I am, and them as well.

"Katya, this arrived for you a moment ago." Kayla sounds hesitant as she stands in my doorway, half in my office, half out in the hallway.

I motion her over with my fingertips. I study Kayla as she moves towards me. Her thick blonde hair and big blue eyes make her look innocent and fresh. Her pink skin glows with good health. Her soft body says she lacks for nothing. She radiates like the sun. Is she okay on the inside? Is she broken?

"Is everything okay, Katya?" Kayla drops down on her knees at my side, resting her hand on my forearm.

"Are you okay?" I ask instead of answering. I study her face, looking for signs of distress.

"Yes," she smiles as the word passes her full lips.

"No, I mean in here?" I press my palm in between Kayla's breasts over her heart. "Why are you with us? What created your need?"

Kayla cocks her head to the side and thinks about what I just asked, really thinks it over. Her emotions play out across her face as thoughts skip through her mind.

"Sometimes we're just born this way," she says in a voice tinged with seriousness. "You were born to lead, and I was born to serve. I need someone to take control for me in order to feel safe– that's all. It's nothing scandalous or dirty. I just want to feel safe and comforted."

"You mean it's in your nature to behave in such a manner. No specific event created you." I say to Kayla what I've been trying to tell Dr. Jeannine about myself. "You're submissive because you were born to submit. Like I'm dominant because I was born to lead– to offer the wisdom, comfort and safety a submissive needs. But at the same time, I feel the need to be comforted by someone stronger than myself, for them to shoulder some of my burdens. It's what makes me a switch."

"Yes, exactly that." Kayla smiles brightly. "No matter how many times I tell Master Ez, he just doesn't believe me." She rolls her eyes at the memory. "I'm perfectly fine... sane... happy. I have no repressed childhood nightmares. I grew up in an amazing home, and I love my family to pieces. I am who I am, and I'm good at being me."

"Nature versus nurture sounds like my therapist. She won't believe that my needs started long before the attack. Maybe Master Ez and Dr. Jeannine went to the same university," I muse.

Kayla rises, and then kisses me sweetly on the cheek. She taps the letter on my desk, and then leaves me to my privacy.

~Katya~
Aaron will accompany you to Restraint this evening.
You will have no need for the mask this night. The mask is solely for your sensory deprivation now that you know my master identity.
I will not be at Restraint until later in the evening, so Aaron will show you the Dungeon and our private room at the club. You've been under a great deal of stress, and I wish to reward you with a new experience, one in which you've waited ever-so patiently. You seem to trust Aaron in a different manner than you do Cortez, or even me, and I understand why. I trust Aaron to keep you safe in all ways, and I believe you sense this as well.
I realize how enticing it is to be hit with the hunger. The sights, scents, sounds, and sensations at Restraint can be hard to overcome. If inspiration strikes, you may play with Aaron-only. Enjoy yourself. Truly. Play. I want you to feel satisfied. That is an order from not only your master and your boss, but from your friend. You need some stress relief.
Ava is an extraordinarily beautiful creature.
Thank you.
~Ez~

I still have no idea why Ezra is so fixated on me, to the point of seeking my daughter to check on her well-being. I have a feeling the psychiatrist has an obsessive need to know everything, to ferret out all the details, or it will mentally vex him until he has all the knowledge he can retain. I'm not surprised. I've already ascertained he's not right in the head. No sane person uses fake identities to stalk victims, draws them into their life, only to place them under constant surveillance.

The only reason I'm not running for the hills is the fact that I don't sense malevolence from Ez. When my intuition is firing properly, I can sense a person's intention, and Ez has always felt genuine in his efforts. Everything he is doing is for my healing. I believe him when he says it, and I notice it when he shows it through his actions. With that being said, I hate the method of delivery, and he pisses me off more often than he pleases me. It's too bad my stupid heart doesn't notice the difference.

I smile pleasantly to myself, feeling hopeful for the first time in a very long time. It is a huge relief to voice my fears and secrets, and to have someone shoulder my burdens. That is what Kayla was speaking of, support and guidance. Just saying the words aloud released the pressure building in my soul.

Ava isn't a dirty secret, and I was treating her like one in my new life. Back home, I raise her as any mother would. It's a small town, so all rumors are heard as they spread like wildfire throughout the community. But my family keeps to themselves, are hard-working, and are good to the community. By the time Ava started school, the rumor mill had died down, but I could sense its rekindling as my daughter grew into a lovely young woman.

I had survived my attack for my daughter. When the opportunity arose to better myself, I took the chance. I wasn't running away from my daughter. I was creating a stable and secure future she would join, one I would thrive in when she left my nest to create her own. We can't live for our children, because if we lose them, we are left with nothing. We will always lose them, because they must grow up and move on to live a life of their own.

I was taught to better myself, to reach for contentment, so I would be strong enough to give my daughter all she would ever need. Sometimes selfish acts are born from selflessness. Leaving my daughter was for her own good, because a healthy Katya was necessary to give Ava an attentive mother.

I didn't tell anyone at Edge about Ava because I didn't want to explain who her father was, something that is highly uncomfortable and none of their business. I also didn't want my boss to feel like he had to give me special treatment because I am a mother. I wanted to prove my worth first, and when I was settled, have Ava join me. I'm thankful every day that I have the most supportive parents on the planet.

The reoccurrence of the memories screams that I'm going to have the breakthrough Dr. Jeannine promised. I'm thankful that I am not with my family when it happens. Ezra is still a stranger to me, and there is less to lose if a stranger sees me fracture. It would hurt my parents and my daughter to see me in immense pain, something I've always hidden from them. So I'm thankful they won't witness it, and hopeful for a calmer future once this passes.

I don't know what type of life I will lead here, but I know that specific people will be in it, whether I want them to be or not. Kayla and I have a good rapport. Aaron and I have bonded over pain and our mutual adoration for Ezra. Ezra and I have a lot of kinks to work out, because I hate his evasive and stalking behavior. But there is one person left who I need to get to know so we may live peacefully, and he and I have some unfinished business to attend.

I sent Cortez Abernathy a message when I got to the office. He should have been here moments ago, and I fear he will remain elusive.

"I figured you wouldn't show," I murmur to the man casting a shadow over my desk. I look up and smile at the charming bastard. I want to hate him for violating me, but I can't. I thirst to know why he did it, and I can't find that out unless I ask.

"I've been called many things, and most of them are very bad, but never a coward." Cortez slowly leans in, gunmetal gray eyes never leaving mine, and tenderly kisses my hand. He leaves his lips on my skin for an inappropriately long time. I stifle a shiver, and get pissed at myself for enjoying his touch.

"We need to call a truce," I announce.

"I wasn't aware we were battling, and I'm not the one who's playing a game with you. So," he spreads his hands as if to say '*why do we need a truce?*'

"So…," I draw out, feeling mighty uncomfortable with the direction the conversation must take. "You skull-fucked me. I've never done that before, and I'm not sure I want to do it ever again!" I slam my hands on my desk and stand.

We are eye-to-eye. I'm furiously panting, shocked at how

quickly my mood shifted. The bastard has the audacity to laugh at me– a smoky sound, thick and rich and completely intoxicating. Cortez stormy eyes twinkle with delight as a rosy blush tints his cheeks.

"I could just say I'm sorry, but I'm not." He smirks at my outrage. "I could promise never to do it again, but that'd be a lie, too."

I bug my eyes out at him and speechlessly stare with my mouth agape… and the bastard kisses me… an open-mouthed kiss, tongue snaking between my lips as it tries to coax my affections. I smack his chest and try to pull away, but he bites my bottom lip and won't let go. My arms flail, either trying to hit him to release me or just to hear him grunt in pain.

Cortez abruptly let me go, and I breathlessly fall into my seat. I sit, stunned and confused. I liked it, and I shouldn't have liked it. That stolen kiss aroused me. The man innocently sitting across my desk from me, I want him, and it's a really bad idea.

What is wrong with me?

The two men who light a fire in my belly are unavailable, even if they don't think they are.

"Still want that truce of yours, Kitten?" Cortez sits across from me, smirking and blushing, all proud of himself. He crosses his legs, and rests his palms on his knee.

"Why are you being so mean to me?" I whine pathetically.

"Oh, I'm not being mean to you, Kitten. This is just me. I am an acquired taste. Some people can't take me," he says sarcastically.

I instantly know why my staff was split on telling Abernathy that his book was trash. Meek Kayla is scared of him, and Monica is intrigued by him. I shake my head at the bastard.

"Truce," I mutter again. "We need one right this goddamned second, you and I. We need some ground rules and boundaries, because we both know Ezra is going to do whatever he wants, to whomever he wants, whenever he wants, and we will have no say in it whatsoever. I'm going to need you to get off my back so I can survive the lunatic."

Cortez's lips spread in the widest smile I've ever witnessed, and then he floors me. "I like you, Kat. In fact, I like you very, very much. You're not blinded by Ezra like the rest of them. You see him as I do, and you still find him intriguing, but you refuse to be his disciple."

"Yeah, that pretty much sums it up. I no longer operate on blind faith. But I feel Ezra thinks he's doing the right thing for the right reasons, I just don't know why or what."

"I'm sorry," Cortez states, sounding sobered by shame. "Truly sorry. I will never touch you unless invited."

"You won't be invited, Cort," I mutter, and for the life of me I can't figure out why he smiles broadly since I was denying him my affections.

"Kat!" Cortez shouts, clapping. "You called me Cort. We're finally friends!"

"Oh," I mutter, rolling my eyes. "Having your penis shoved down my esophagus means we bypassed friends a few days ago. Never again," I stress. "I will not be the other woman. I will not be disrespected. I will not be your mistress, or tolerate being treated like a whore. I will never engage in sexual activity with an attached person. *Ever.*"

"Hmm…" Cortez leans forward, gazing at me like he's finally seeing me clearly and he likes what he sees. "Has Ezra been informed of this new development? He said you hadn't had sex *yet*. But the use of yet implies intent, correct?"

"I refused to be disrespected like that, Cort. I *refuse*, no matter what my mind, body, or heart wants. *No.*" I look away from his very perceptive gaze, scared of what he may see. "Besides, it's a non-issue since Ezra likes dudes and is apparently totally into his fiancée."

Cortez releases an honest to God growl. The feral animalistic sound echoes around my office to reverberate down my spine. "I hate that cunt. I'd kill her if I could."

"About that jealousy," I say before he makes me an accessory to premeditated murder. "Don't go shitting on my doorstep with that bullshit. I want no part in that. You have no reason to be jealous of me. I care for Ezra, but at the moment, he pisses me off more than endears me. As I said, it's a non-issue anyway."

"I'm not jealous of you, Kat. Not now that Ezra isn't running interference. Ezra made a promise and broke it. One of many. Each one more painful than the last. But this promise was the last straw."

"I understand your history is very complicated. But I don't appreciate being put in the center of it, especially when I don't belong there. It won't happen again," I warn.

"Just so you know, I wasn't the one who missed those meetings with you. Your assistant listens to Ezra over me. I was stonewalled. Monica finally contacted me, wanting to know what the hell was up, and that was the only reason I met you."

Cortez takes a moment to compose himself, to dampen down the fury. "The day we met, I realized Ezra broke his promise. I was so overcome with fury that I enacted his punishment without concern for you. I realized when I was done, that it could be likened to a child breaking his friend's toys, just so no one else could play with them. I feel remorse, because you would be a favorite toy," he purrs salaciously, while gazing at me with a naughty glint in his eye.

"I'm a human being," I remind him.

"I enjoyed the skull-fuck, Katya. But had I known it was your first, I would have romanced you so you'd be willing to have a second taste."

My eyes take a slow route over Cortez's body, traveling over his expensive V-neck t-shirt, which showcases his nice chest, to roam up his bitable neck, to caress his kissable lips, and to finally light on his gorgeous, tan face. There is a softness to Cortez that Ezra lacks. You can tell Cortez is quick to amuse, quick to love, and passionate in all things.

Cortez will love you with his entire being, just as he will hate you with everything he has in him.

"I like you, too," I purr while a flirty grin plays along my lips. Cortez's copper-toned skin blushes pink, and he looks pleased that I find him to my liking. "Are you still married as of this afternoon? Did you get a divorce since last we met, by chance?"

Confusion muddling his expression, "No," he draws out.

"Then no. No first, or second, or third tastes. No tastes of anything," I command. "I understand how you and Ezra are a package deal, how no matter who you may find yourself attached to, you will ultimately belong to the other. Wives, fiancées, girlfriends, they are a deal-breaker for me. An absolutely never. Do I make myself clear?"

"Crystal," Cortez mutters, looking awestruck. He's got a little bit of a switch in him. I suspect he enjoys being told what to do. "Good luck getting Ezra to abide by a rule he himself didn't create. Just so you know, if you fuck up and let Ezra touch you, I'm sneaking in some more kisses."

Snorting, I lean back in my chair, all the while shaking my head in disbelief. "Nice. I feel so flattered that you threaten to touch me in retaliation, when I just said there would be none of that jealousy bullshit between you and me," I remind him, voice dipping low into growl territory.

Looking mystified, Cort mutters, "It would be because I want to, not because I'm being a shithead."

"Maybe I'm confused, but I thought being gay meant you only wanted men."

"I. Am. Not. Gay." Cortez pounds the side of his fist on top of my desk, causing my coffee mug to slosh and my pens to roll around. "Ezra thinks he is, but his dick seems to home in on pussy more often than ass. Trust me on that one."

"Again, I feel flattered that the sexually confused is using me to piss off their equally sexually confused partner. So just leave me out of that bullshit, okay? If I suddenly find myself in need of sex, I'll look elsewhere."

"Good luck with that," Cort grumbles, appearing shamefaced for blowing up. "If you won't have him, he'll pick someone else. You'll think it was your decision, but it won't be. Best learn how Ez operates now while it's early. Life lesson: Ezra always gets his way. If he wants your lips wrapped around my cock, I can guarantee you'll be sucking my dick before the month is over."

I do what you do to a child, ignore them. I will not be taken off course with dirty talk, and I will never suck Cortez

Abernathy's dick again. A full body shiver rolls over me as the remembered panic. My throat aches and my lungs burn in remembrance of the blowjob from hell.

"What does Ezra really want from me?"

"No, those answers are forbidden of me to speak. But I might be persuaded to give you an answer or two if you were to crawl on your hands and knees, and then wrap that tiny, hot mouth around my cock. I want to watch you suck me off, Kitten. I want to fuck you so badly. For that, I'd tell you everything. But my punishment will be severe, so you better make it worth my while," Cortez warns, and he's deadly serious.

"I'll figure it out myself, you lecherous bastard," I growl. "How can you cheat on your wife so easily?"

"Perhaps it's not cheating if it's a marriage of convenience," Cortez says without shame.

"Yeah, it is, and you know it." I sigh and roll my eyes, because there is no arguing with this charming bastard "You're incorrigible."

"Ah, I've heard that many times before, as well," he says with wry amusement. That intoxicating, heady laugh rumbles up from his chest, and it's pure torture to hear the amazing sound.

"You and I will be best friends. Mark my words, Kitten," Cortez threatens as he rises from his seat, ending our conversation on his own terms.

My only reply is to roll my eyes at him. Cortez waves as he leaves my office, his anticipatory laughter following in his wake.

Chapter Thirty-One

"Are you ready to go in, Kat?" Aaron shies away again and blushes. He's been standoffish since he picked me up at Edge, after he bluntly asked if I was up to playing around in the dungeon with him. He smoothly walks to the entrance of Restraint, hips rolling invitingly.

After being around Cortez's sexual magnetism and missing Ezra's comfort, I need a distraction from the confusion and pain in my mind, and my mind has chosen Aaron for some unknown reason. I blame my increase in lust on insanity and stress. Yeah, it has nothing to do with the fact that Aaron is every girl's wet dream. He is an *available* wet dream, one without strings attached, or a fiancée, or a wife.

My mother's advice is screaming in my ears, and I'm trying very hard to ignore it. I accidentally broke Rule #1 when Ezra brought me to orgasm and Cortez took my mouth, so I enacted Rule #2 with devastating consequences. It's taking everything in me not to send Adelaide Whittenhower an '*I'm sorry*' note and a bouquet of flowers.

My mortifying remorse is making me rethink my mother's rules on womanhood. But there is something right about Rule #3 that is enticing. Ezra and Cortez were caught in the act, Ezra's fiancée was told the truth, but neither was held accountable for the consequences of their actions.

Aaron isn't a consequence, but he is the epitome of Rule #3.

How do you teach an asshole a lesson? Fuck his brother.

Aaron is a good guy: sweet, caring, innocent, and smoking hot. We would both enjoy whatever mischief we get ourselves into. It would be without awkwardness, and it would be pleasant because I trust him.

Who I really want is off-limits, and it is so wrong to use another human being in their stead. But maybe I'm sick of always being the better person. Just once I'd like to not take the moral high ground and get into some trouble of my own making.

The reckless bitch inside me is preening, trying to sex herself up, because the thought of making Ezra eat his pride is more intoxicating than knowing all I have to do is ask Aaron to fuck me and he'd do it. The power is heady. I want Ezra to regret. I want Ezra to wish he wasn't with Adelaide. I want him to leave Adelaide for everyone's sake, and then I want to turn him down.

Jesus, I'm fucked in the head.

Am I really thinking about doing this? Shouldn't my past be swimming to the surface to stop me with the sheer force of my panic? The fact that I'm smiling, comfortable, and horny, suggests that this is something I really, truly want to experience.

"Hold up, Aaron." I clutch his thick wrist, pulling him to a stop before we reach the entrance to Restraint.

As Aaron swings around to face me, he blushes again. "What's up with you being all shy?" I'm not sure why, but his behavior makes me want to tease him, to devour him. He flushes a beautiful pink, reminding me of Kayla's skin.

"Ah." Aaron smooths his big palm over his skull-cut hair. "This morning…um… are you okay with how I behaved?" His baby blues dart away when I try for eye contact.

Oh! Aaron was in the bathroom for a while. I hadn't realized until now what he had been up to in there. I can't help it– a snicker escapes my lips. Now I'm embarrassed, too. I grind the toe of my boot into the pavement and stare at the ground. I flash Aaron a wicked smile as I look up at him through the lace of my lashes, teasing him.

Aaron's lips part on a gasp. Ah, that's sweet. I've never had anyone crush on me. I full-out laugh and mock punch him in the arm like I'm a twelve-year-old girl, where you hit and taunt your crushes instead of just spitting out the truth. Something tells me innocent crushes were an experience we both lacked in our childhoods.

"Come on, Stud, let's go feed our needs." I can't help but trail a laugh on my way to the entrance.

How ironic: childlike crushes in the parking lot of a BDSM club. I notice that Aaron is frozen in place, so I call over my shoulder, "Put that damned dimple away, sweetheart, before I spank it off ya."

Aaron plugs his big hands in his front pockets and sulks over to the door, face bright red with embarrassment. He flames brighter when he spots the bouncer.

"Roarke? You're back?" Aaron sounds shocked to see him, and then it dawns on me. If Roarke is here, then so is Ezra.

Disappointment simmers in my blood; a feeling I knew would follow in Ezra's wake no matter what. Ezra is pushing Aaron off on me, not that either of us is complaining. Ezra wants to be my master by giving me advice, educating me, and micromanaging my life, but that doesn't mean he wants me to be *in* his life.

Irrationally, I want Ezra. But he doesn't want me back. He's incapable of wanting me back. A calming balm settles over me, and it feels like resolution. Aaron isn't my second choice; he's my friend. Friends play together, especially at Restraint. It doesn't equate a relationship. It just means you're letting off some steam.

Aaron tucks his chin to his chest, hiding his burning cheeks, trying to pretend he didn't invite me here to fool around a bit. Roarke releases a deep guffaw at his buddy's embarrassment as he opens the door for us.

I wrap my hand on the back of Aaron's neck, drawing his ear down to my lips. "Boy, you're in for it now," I whisper into his ear over the din of the music.

I'm in a strange mood– a good mood. I feel free. Something about Restraint puts a wicked smile on my face and makes me want to be naughty. It must be the pheromones flavoring the air.

Aaron is on the menu tonight as my willing victim.

"We need drinks. At least a few." Aaron's hand snakes around my waist, and he gives me a little squeeze. Normally I would have frozen at the casual touch, especially from a man. The look of surprise on Aaron's face tells me it's new for him, too.

Before we even approach the bar, Kristal is patiently

waiting. I arch my brow at Aaron in silent question.

"Being number two has its privileges," is his answer. "If Ezra is the boss, then Queen and I are boss two and three. Ezra may own this joint, but I run Restraint, with Queen lending me support when need be," he offers casually.

"Wow," I say in surprise. For some reason I thought Aaron followed Ezra around like a servant. I'm glad to learn Aaron has a life outside of Ezra Zeitler's.

"Two magnum shots and a pair of sevens," Aaron orders Kristal.

"Those are some mighty powerful drinks. Are you trying to get me tipsy?" I tease Aaron, and I'm startled to realize I really love teasing him. There is something inherently innocent about Aaron, even as he's staring at you with eyes filled with a depth of sadness and wisdom.

"I hate beer. I'm good for a drink or two a night, and sometimes none at all," Aaron says with a shrug, but I can tell there is more to it than that. "I think I'm gonna need some liquid courage around you tonight, though."

Aaron eyes the length of my body, lingering on my chest, proving that he's feeling what I'm feeling. It's like my lust is feeding his lust, and his lust is feeding mine, in an endless loop of unfed hunger and untapped sexuality.

"Here, let me take this for you," Aaron offers, as he pulls the ribbon to my cape.

When his eyes take in my outfit, I blush from my toes to my hairline. Look who's getting embarrassed now? I'm encased in a bodysuit made out of silk fibers, resembling spider webs. The only other clothing covering me is a black, silk sheath. My girly bits are barely covered.

Aaron's blond brow arches as his eyes feast on my lack of clothing, and then those damned, little boy dimples reemerge as a wicked grin splits his lips.

My whole body lights up like a fireworks finale. What is up with this trio? Why do they ignite me as no others do?

Aaron is like a fat-free treat. You can have a taste without guilt or shame, and you're good with just one serving. I have a feeling Ezra and Cortez are like decadent sweets laden with fat and sugar: once eaten, they will stick to you forever and it will take a lifetime of work to lose the craving for their flavor. They are not a dish I can risk tasting.

"Are you trying to kill me?" Aaron's hand slides down my arm to my wrist, searching. "Don't leave my side, and make sure your bracelet is visible at all times. If you leave me for a second, not only will I punish the shit out of you, Ez will murder me. Understood?" The intense look in Aaron's eye seizes my lungs.

Breathless, speechless, the only thing I can do is nod my assent.

Aaron lets his inner dominant out to play for the night. He must have been hiding it, because he's strong enough to give Ezra a run. I blink in surprise as he hands Kristal my cape for safe-keeping, and in return she flashes me a look of shock. I guess Kristal didn't know Aaron was stronger than he appeared to be, either. All I can do is shrug back at her.

"Pound it back in one swallow," Aaron orders as he hands me a shot glass.

I don't process. I react. I take the shot glass from his outstretched hand, and then I suck it back. I inhale fire. I would cough or choke, except my lungs refuse to function.

"Are you trying to kill me?" I gasp out, and receive a wink in reply.

"Oh, just give it a minute," Aaron says knowingly, patiently waiting for what, I have no idea.

Jesus, my body warms to the rocket fuel running through my veins. Instant buzz. Wahoo! Let's party!

I step to the side and teeter a bit. "What the hell was in that shit?"

"Trust me. You don't want to know," Aaron murmurs, and then laughs at my annoyed expression.

"How come you guys don't have bracelets?" I jingle mine as I ask.

"Who in their right mind is going to mess with me?" Aaron runs his hands down his stacked chest. At six feet and some change, Aaron is well over two hundred pounds, and most of them are muscle. "I think I will take my chances."

"Do you have a necklace?" I reach over and feel up Aaron's broad chest, lingering a bit. I groan when an excited nipple buds underneath my fingertip. Aaron rolls his eyes at me, knowing full and well I'm using this as an excuse to fondle him. I get down to the business at hand.

Bingo!

I extract a necklace from Aaron's shirt, and it's identical to Ezra's. "What's this?" I ask about the charm dangling from it, but I'm unable to discern the initials.

"You know very well what it is, Kat. Here, drink this down." Aaron hands me the seven-and-seven, just as my fingertips graze a key on his chain.

"Hey! This better not be what I think it is." I actually stomp my foot.

My answer is a husky chuckle as he downs his drink.

"Sonofabitch!" Aaron had a key to my freedom this entire time.

I open my throat and swallow my drink whole. I pucker up my face as the alcohol hits my stomach and fire breathes up my throat.

"Ugh," I groan through it. "Kristal doesn't fuck around, does she? I doubt there was any soda in my drink at all. Restraint is going to go belly-up with Kris manning the bar."

Aaron's eyes dance as he gazes back and forth between Kristal and me. "Kris knows the value of green better than anyone I know. Who do you think balances Restraint's books? Anyway, I think she likes you, or she thinks you're cute when you're plastered."

"Ha-ha!" I mock laugh. "Hey, you lied before when you said you couldn't unlock my wrist cuffs," I accuse.

"Couldn't... wouldn't... same difference," Aaron drawls. "Ready to dance, Kat?" He grabs my hand and tugs before I can answer.

"Ah. I've never danced with a guy before. I don't think I know how," I self-consciously mutter, and Aaron's response is to tug me closer to the dance floor. I lose my footing and almost go ass over teakettle. Whoa, I think I'm a sip away from smashed.

Aaron hauls me against his chest, helping me regain my footing. His fingertips tickle as they move my hair away from my ear. "Lightweight," he breathes in my ear.

Aaron's touch elicits a full body tremor out of me, curling my toes. He's hooked me now. I'll do whatever he wants tonight.

Aaron and I join the group mating dance. We grind, gyrate, and flow across each other in a poor excuse for dancing. We depict the act of sex on a primal, carnal level.

"I fucking love the way you smell." Aaron groans a hungry sound against my hair. His hands palm my face, tilting my head backwards. Aaron holds my eyes for a split second before he leans down and bites my neck savagely.

"Ah... fuck..." I moan, shuddering in bliss. My eyes roll back in my skull and my body loses the ability to support itself. A wide palm rests on my ass, bracing all of my weight. Then he squeezes, nails tearing the webbing of my bodysuit.

I lose it.

My forearms hook behind Aaron's neck to lift myself up to his level. Lips-to-lips. I attack his mouth with single-minded desperation: biting and tugging, and finally drawing his bottom lip into my mouth.

"You really are trying to kill me," he groans in agony against my mouth.

"Hey, you're alive, that's all that matters." I teasingly nip his lip, and then I slide down his body. My eyes widen when I figure out why he sounds so pained. "In need of the nearest bathroom, baby boy?"

Aaron looks shocked; wide blue eyes gaze down at me in unadulterated lust, and then a husky laugh rumbles up his throat. The laugh is no less intoxicating than his counterparts', but instead of smoky and deep, it's husky and gravelly. Knowing I'm the one who's causing Aaron's happiness, something bright flares inside my heart.

Aaron tucks my hair behind my ear and softly yet seductively whispers to me, "Inside you, Katya. I need...to be... inside you." Anticipating my reaction, he tightens his arms around me or else I would've collapsed to the floor in a puddle of lust.

Uncomfortable with the screaming reaction my body releases, I swiftly change the subject. "Is this the anthem for Restraint?" I yell over the song in question.

"Dirty babe…" Aaron croons to me. "You see these shackles?" He kisses my bracelet. "Baby, I'm your slave… I'll let you whip me if I misbehave…. It's just that no one makes me feel this waaaay," he sings in my ear.

"All right, fella, for the rest of the night, you will only be known as Justin," I tease Aaron. "You brought my sexy back, J.T."

I issue a tiny giggle, feeling a decade younger– thrust back into an era I never got the opportunity to enjoy.

Aaron chuckles with me, somehow understanding me on a baser level. "Tour time!" He takes my hand in his and leads me towards the back of the club.

I catch a glimpse of Queen on the way by, and I note her open expression of wonder. "I just want to say hi to Queen," I project to Aaron over Restraint's loud music.

"Okay," Aaron yells back. "I'll wait over by the wall."

"What's up with the strange looks you're throwing my way?" I ask Queen as I pull her to the side, away from listening ears.

"I've just never seen Aaron so… social. Um… be careful. They're like a pack. If you play with one, expect the other two," she warns.

"What's that supposed to mean?" A perplexed tone laces my voice.

"Ah." Queen taps her chin with a short, cherry red fingernail, choosing her words wisely; no doubt from a prewritten script courtesy of Ezra.

"Ez is very territorial. There isn't a person on this planet who is as jealous as Cort. I'm just issuing a warning. There is no way you could have forgotten Cort's nocturnal skull-fucking so soon."

"I'm sick the fuck of this cloak and dagger bullshit, *Regina*," I twist her name so she knows I know exactly who she is. "Or should I call you Ezra's relief-pitcher Kimber."

"Christ," Queen snarls, looking away from me, angrier than I've ever seen another human being. "If you haven't figured it out yet, Ezra has a way of forcing you to do things you don't want to do. I played Kimber because it was my version of a wellness check, making sure Ez wasn't harming you."

"I'm sorry, but I cannot thank you for that, even if you were coerced or trying to take care of me. At any time, you could have messaged me the truth of it all, but you didn't. So instead of thinking I owe you a thank you, maybe you owe me an apology instead."

"Mary, virgin mother of Jesus," Regina spews, showing signs of her catholic school upbringing. "It's like… watching a fucking train wreck, that's what it's like."

"Then get me off the tracks by telling me the cocksucking truth!" I shout.

"You think I don't want to? Seriously? Things are not always as they seem. Please, Katya, I'm not trying to be mean. I'm not saying they don't want you to be with them. I'm just trying to warn you. You may not like what you find when this '*game*' concludes. You're going to get hurt, even though they don't want to harm you."

"I get it, okay? I know I'm just a broken toy Ezra wants to fix because of some compulsive, psycho-babble bullshit. I'm a challenge for the doctor. I also hold no illusions that they want me as their partner. They already picked the women in their lives, and I won't touch Ezra or Cortez while they are attached. It's a well-known fact."

"You can tell them what you expect, but Cort will just smile and do whatever he wants anyway, just like a spoiled child. Worse, Ezra will look you in the eye while he manipulates you into thinking what he wants was your idea in the first place. I've watched them systematically destroy every single person they've ever touched."

"I don't know if I can trust you, Queen. You've lied to me just as they have. I can't be real around you since you won't be real around me. I can't take your advice until you stop hiding whatever it is you're hiding from me. I can sense it. I want to trust you. I want to be your friend. But if you won't bend a bit by telling me the truth, then my friendship is *your* loss."

Queen just shakes her head at me sadly. "Kat, with Ez between us, we can never be friends. I like you. I really do. I got to know you well over the past year as I played Kimber. The details I gave were either mine or Ezra's. The emotions were real."

"I'm not going to say thank you or apologize for anything that was out of my control, especially when I was the one getting tricked." I stare at my feet, unable to meet Queen's eyes. I don't want her to see how painful all of this is for me.

"I know you believe you're safe from Ez and Cort because you said you wouldn't touch them if they were '*attached*'. But just know, if you touch Aaron tonight, you'll be fair game. It doesn't matter anyway. Cort could charm the faith from a nun, and Ezra never takes no for an answer." She speaks from experience.

I suffer a shiver at the memory of Cortez using his cock to scour my throat. I rub my jaw in remembrance. "I'm pretty sure it's Cortez who doesn't take no for an answer," I say underneath my breath.

"That was out of the ordinary for Cort," Queen mumbles, looking uncomfortable. "He never has to take since everyone wants to give him what he wants."

"Listen, I just want a night that is fun for once. When I was a kid, I had to go to school and to work. Then I was attacked, and my life changed. I then had to go to school, work, and raise a child. My life has always been about living everyone else's lives. I was never allowed to relax and enjoy myself. Every breath I take has a consequence I must pay. I've never been free. I've never gotten to act my age. Just for tonight, I want to experience that. Aaron makes me feel like the young woman I never had the chance to be. So if that is wrong, I'll pay for it tomorrow."

Sighing, Queen closes her eyes while running her fingers through her shorn, strawberry blonde locks. "I understand, Katya. I do. But you will pay for it sooner rather than later. Just be careful."

"I promise to be careful. Besides, Aaron is very sweet." I glance over at him, to find him leaning on the wall, watching the crowd.

"I'm not worried about Aaron. I'm worried that Ezra and Cortez will see your willingness to touch Aaron as the greenlight to take whatever they want from you."

"I'll heed your warning, Queen. Really." I squeeze her hand in reassurance. "I'm stronger than I look. I can take care of myself. Some things you learn the hard way. It's not all physical strength. It's your constitution, your will to survive, and your emotional control. I will be okay."

As soon as I start towards Aaron, he walks towards me. "What is Queen so upset about?" He wraps his hand around my waist and directs me to the door hidden in the corner.

"Queen's worried about me being around you guys, especially Ezra and Cortez." I answer honestly.

"Hey, you're safe with us. I promise you nothing will ever happen to you again. No one will ever harm you, especially us." Aaron's bright eyes hold me captive like a deer caught in headlights.

"Cortez already showed me what he was capable of, and I don't want a repeat performance. I'm not a total masochist. Asphyxiation by cock isn't my thing," I say slyly.

"Cort paid for that, and he apologized, and you've half-assed forgiven him already. It won't happen again unless you want it to."

"What happens next time he gets jealous? Huh? I really don't feel like being taken by force," I blurt out, suddenly angry.

"It will never happen again." Aaron holds my gaze, a serious expression marring his boyish face. "Because Cort added you to the short list of people who makes him see green, and I don't mean he'll be jealous *of* you. He'll be jealous *over* you. The next time Cort touches you, it won't be a fit of mad jealousy. You'll want it."

After I figure out Ezra's true motivations regarding me, I hold no misconception that I will ever be a part of their group. There is too much history between the three of them. I could never compete. I'm not sure if I want to, or if it's even worth it.

"I won't ever want it again." Denial rings in my ears. "And Cortez will never be jealous over me. I'm just a distraction. I'm not a part of your group, Aaron. I don't fit in with you guys."

I don't know if I imagined it or not, but it sounded like Aaron whispered '*you're the center of it*' underneath his breath.

"Are you ready for the dungeon?" Aaron prompts as we stand near a heavy steel door. "There are rules involved."

"I love rules," I say with conviction.

"I know," Aaron says wryly as he punches a four-digit code into the door's security keypad.

"When I know what the rules are," I add.

Chapter Thirty-Two

"Welcome to the dungeon at Restraint!" Aaron flings his arm out like a game show host, huge grin spreading his lips and denting his dimples.

Several sets of eyes swing our way, check us out, and then go right back to what held their attention prior to our arrival. A sense of rightness descends upon me. I step over the threshold, into the large, open space of a world devoid of judgment.

Aaron moves me to the side, away from the doorway, and then he wraps an arm around my shoulders. He gives me time to acclimate to my surroundings.

Restraint's BDSM dungeon is reminiscent of an abandoned factory: concrete floor, concrete walls, and a high ceiling with steel beams and cables crisscrossing it so randomly that they can't possibly hold a functional purpose. The area is windowless and doorless, save the single door at my back. The dungeon is a lengthy oblong room with a hallway at the rear. It's very frigid, not in temperature but feeling.

I close my eyes to heighten my other senses. Sounds: the snap of a whip, the clink of chain, moans and grunts, a high-pitched scream of pain, followed by a guttural release. Scents: the sharp tang of sweat, the sweet edge of arousal, the taint of wax, cloying perfumes, and the musk of sex. The room is stifling hot. You can almost feel the humidity beading your skin with moisture. The air is permeated with pheromones, need, and possibility.

I pop open my eyes and catalog my surroundings. Stations— if you can call the areas designed specifically for BDSM activities as stations —line each side of the room. Each station is being used by people seeking the fine art of BDSM in its various forms: Bondage. Discipline. Domination. Submission. Sadism. Masochism.

The center of the dungeon is narrow and completely devoid of objects. Strange contraptions, which I have no name for, accompany spanking benches, stocks, a cage, several St.

Andrew's crosses, and hanging restraints. The end of the room houses a wall of equipment, or rather, instruments of pleasurable torture. Each station is occupied with eager members. The narrow area in the center is crowded with voyeurs and several men and women wearing Restraint's security t-shirts.

I turn to ask Aaron a question, only to find him gazing raptly at me. It's as if he's judging and savoring my reactions to the new world being laid out before me. My eyes are glazed with hunger. My skin is beaded with sweat. Eager, I pant, drawing in the smells of sex deep into my nose. Moisture pools between my quivering thighs. It's like I've finally found my home, a place where I truly belong. It's a heady, mind-bending sensation.

"Why do you have the club in the front if the members are in the dungeon?" I ask breathlessly. The concept is foreign to me. I ask an inane question, because I'll do anything to lessen the strange awareness overpowering my being.

"Fresh meat." Aaron chuckles as he bashfully runs his hand through his skull-cut hair. His face turns an appetizing shade of pink "Uh... you can only get back here if you're a member or accompanied by a member. We need to recruit new members to keep it fresh in here. Plus, a lot of our members are exhibitionists. We need people to watch them exhibit."

"Um...why isn't there any seating or comfort?" I look around, wondering if I may have missed it. "It's rather odd," I mumble, thinking the first thing I would change in here is the ambiance, not that I will ever have a say in it.

"Well, the majority of our members are masochists and submissives. We have a shortage on dominants. Even stranger, we do have one master who happens to be a masochist," Aaron says this like it's an odd combination, but none of us are a flavor of normal.

"This is Master Ez's personal rat maze, isn't it? He hides out in his office with his security camera feeds, analyzing the shit out of the membership. Admit it," I taunt.

"I can't say for sure," Aaron mumbles, blushing redder than Hades. "Most of the time he's working."

"I'm just fucking with you, Aaron," I act as if I'm teasing when I'm not. "The lack of comfort just feels like something Ez would pull to see how people react to its absence."

"Well, the no seating *is* a punishment of sorts. We wouldn't want someone to have a seat on the couch and take a nap. This place is about control. You have to be alert to maintain control. We also don't want to encourage loitering. If you really want to be here, you'll stand as you watch."

"What if you don't like to be watched?" I don't think I'd like playing in here with all these people watching. It seems impersonal and cold.

"See that hallway back there?" Aaron points to the far end of the room. "There are rooms back there for privacy. All of Restraint's Masters have their own private rooms, as well as first-come-first-serve rooms for the membership. What are you interested in learning about?"

"Oh!" My eyes dart everywhere, never lighting on one thing. "I... um..." I blush.

"That's okay. It's overwhelming at first. I completely understand." Aaron scans the area, as if he's looking for something specific. "You've met Dexter, right?"

"Dexter, the sadist?" I squeak out, and receive a chuckle for my description.

"Dexter's not a bad guy. He's actually one of the nicest guys you'll ever meet. He only does the pain thing because he sees it as a gift he's giving a masochist. It goes hand-in-hand. Usually Dexter just gives the sub whatever they need. He really is quite gentle. I won't lie, he loves giving pain to those who need it. It's his specialty, and he's highly skilled and controlled. He does get off on it, though."

Aaron rubs his palm against his skull-cut, and it makes me want to reach up to see if his hair feels like crushed velvet. I'm learning this habitual gesture means Aaron's uncomfortable with something.

After a long pause, Aaron finally says, "We all have something we don't want to admit to that gets us off." I raise an eyebrow at that. What does Aaron like that he's freaked about?

As Aaron pushes me through the crowd, he wraps both arms around me and draws me to his chest as we walk. It's odd, but I quickly realize why he does it. Several revelers get handsy on our way by. A hand appears out of nowhere and grips my breast, forcing a pained squeak of surprise out of my throat.

The man who groped me drops to his knees and apologizes profusely. It all happens so quickly that I don't understand what's going on. I look over my shoulder at Aaron for some help, since I have no idea what to do, only to find him glaring down at the fallen man. Aaron's expression is scary enough to make the Devil pause.

"Apology accepted," I say to stop the impending storm.

"If you touch her again, I will rip your hand off. Are we understood?" Aaron spits.

"Yes, sir! I'm sorry, Aaron. I didn't know she was with you," the man apologizes profusely again.

"Katya is off limits. You better be thankful it was me who caught you, and not the hoods." His voice sounds cold, devoid of the Aaron I've grown to know and like.

"I–I– I'm sorry, Aaron. I will make sure everyone leaves her alone." The man scurries away into the crowd so fast I can't track him.

"How come Ez and Cort wear hoods? I'm assuming that's who you just threaten him with." I ask to redirect Aaron from what just happened, hoping to calm him down enough to get *my* Aaron back.

"Hmm…" he mutters absentmindedly as we squeeze our way through the crowd, eyes peeled for more groping hands. "I would think that the son of an heiress and a billionaire mogul, and a bestselling author, wouldn't like to be outed as deviants who dabble in the BDSM culture."

"Since when are you sarcastic? It doesn't suit you," I chastise. "How come you don't wear a hood?"

"I'm the son of a housekeeper and a bodyguard. My father isn't in politics like Ezra's is. No one gives two shits what the servants do in their spare time. I had two choices on my future profession, dependent on my sex: housekeeping or security.

My dad watches over Ezra's aunt, Divina's mother, and I was given to Ezra."

"And here I thought my choices were limited by being born in a small town," I drawl out, amazed at Aaron's family dynamic. "Do you hate it?"

"No, not at all," he says in all sincerity. "I told you I was glad I was born with a penis. Housekeepers don't get to be educated alongside the 1%, nor do they shadow rich people who tend to shower them with attention and gifts. Since Ezra thinks he owns the world, he has both Roarke and me, so we have spare time to do as we wish."

"And that is?" I prompt, avidly sucking up any information I can get. My name is Kat for a reason. I'm curious by nature.

"Roarke's a retired police officer, who spends every ounce of his spare time playing FarmVille2, and I took Restraint on as my own. I like my life, even if I was born to serve."

"The serving must be difficult to deal with because of your dominant nature," I muse.

"You have no fucking idea," Aaron draws out. He pulls me closer to whisper in my ear, "I only serve one man in all things, and I'm lucky he puts my needs above his own."

"What about Cortez? Why does Ezra need all this protection while Cort runs around free as a bird?"

"You do remember who Ezra is, correct? He's the guy who is sitting in his office right this second, eyes on a laptop screen filled with security feeds from no less than ten different locations. Cort is well-watched, and nine times out of ten, he's with Ez anyway."

"HA! I knew it," I gloat. "I knew Ez wasn't in his office working."

"He *is* working," Aaron stresses. "He's a psychiatrist with OCD and a plethora of anxiety disorders, all stemming from the fear one of us will be abducted again. He is only calm if he can see us, no matter where we are or what we are doing. That laptop is in his possession at all times, so he can look at his loved ones and take a deep breath."

"Wow," I gasp. "I thought I was fucked up."

"Come, let's see what Dexter's up to." Aaron pushes me towards the very end of the dungeon, near the hallway.

All thought of anything else flees my mind when my eyes connect on a small woman hanging from the ceiling by her wrists. Ah, that explains the weird wires and metal bars on the ceiling. They support the hedonistic activities of the members of Restraint. A thin metal chain is secured to a beam by a pulley system. The woman's hands are connected to the chain by leather cuffs on her wrists.

Absentmindedly, I rub my wrists, remembering how it felt to wear Master Ez's cuffs. My heart skips a beat, aching.

The first thing I notice, is that there aren't many watchers on the far end of the dungeon. A few stand off to the side, but not too close. Saw horses are set up, creating a barrier from the crowd.

Leaning into Aaron, I whisper my guess. "Dexter doesn't like people too close during a scene?"

"Very observant, Kat," Aaron praises me, suddenly sounding like a deviant teacher. "No, Dex doesn't like anyone in touching distance. Sometimes it's hard to keep people back. They try to make it a group activity. He also needs room to swing his whip without fear of hitting bystanders. It's a spectacular sight," Aaron says, and his eyes glaze over in remembrance.

"Why not use a private room," I mutter in confusion. "If you don't want people watching or getting in the way…"

"The girl," Aaron points at the woman hanging from the ceiling supports. "Heidi, she likes people watching. That girl is a voyeur's dream. She also can tolerate moderate pain. There aren't many masochists around who are willing to play with Dexter. He's too intense. So Dexter and Heidi have compromised: Heidi gets to be watched, and Dexter gets to hurt her, and then fuck her."

Aaron leads me to the wall and leans back against it. We are close enough to see everything, but far enough away that we aren't crowding Dexter and Heidi or the other watchers.

Dexter isn't much larger than I am. I doubt he hits five and a half feet in height. He's very slight in appearance, but it's the power radiating off of him that makes him feel immense.

Dexter stands in front of Heidi, and slowly peels his shirt off. She can't take her eyes from him, and neither can I. Like a magnet, I'm attracted to him. It makes me reevaluate my sexuality: I like soft females and hard males. Dexter is surprisingly muscular for his size. His chest and arms are corded with lanky muscles that flex as he moves.

Dexter prowls– that is the only way to describe the rolling gate Dexter uses when he walks. He prowls over to the wall, and then pulls on a chain. Heidi rises slowly, until her toes barely touch the ground. She sways for a moment before coming to a rest. Dexter stalks around her in a circle, gradually closing in. He reminds me of a large jungle cat. A jaguar– deadly, fast, and powerful. As soon as he is within arm's reach of Heidi, he grabs the front of her dress, right between her breasts, and rips it from her body. She releases a sharp shriek of surprise, as her body sways on the chain from the force of her dress being rent away.

"I hope that wasn't her favorite dress," I murmur to Aaron out of the side of my mouth.

Sluggishly, Aaron turns his face to gaze at me, and something inside me wants me to flee. His eyes are dilated, almost no color remaining. His irises are completely eclipsed by his pupils. His nostrils flare wildly as he draws my scent into his lungs. His lips are parted on a pant as his breathing increases. A pink tongue darts out to moisten his drying lips, and my body instantly reacts to the sight.

I turn back just as I hear the swat of the riding crop hitting Heidi's thigh. I expected another shriek, but she is surprisingly quiet. Her face is lax as she watches Dexter's every move.

"So do you top people often?" I ask to distance myself from the scene, and I hope conversation will bring Aaron back from the brink.

A giggle edged in hysteria bubbles up my throat. To me, my question lamely sounded like, *'do you come here often?'* I'm so out of my depth.

I hear another groan, and it's not Heidi's. It was Dexter's guttural reaction to his *'art'*. He's enjoying himself in a way a man enjoys being *inside* a woman, but all he is doing is slicing leather through the air. My lower belly tightens at the deeply sexual sound.

"No," Aaron says, voice deep and husky.

No.

Just no.

No other information. *Jeez.*

"Why not?" I still don't dare to look at Aaron. I can feel the heat radiating off of him, and it frightens me in a good way. It's a feeling I'm not sure I want to explore in the middle of a dungeon.

"When we got back," Aaron pauses, and I know he means a long time ago– the abduction. "We tried to be normal by going back to how it used to be, but we couldn't recapture it. Cortez wouldn't touch Ezra, and nothing could get him to do it. Not bribery, guilt trips, jealousy, cheating. Nothing. Our abductor made Cortez… use me, and he made Ezra watch as the ultimate punishment."

"Jesus," I hiss, heart bursting with the empathy I feel for these men.

"Yeah, one act of sex fucked us all up. I was only fifteen. Cort was seventeen. Ezra was days away from eighteen. Cort didn't want to do it any more than I wanted him to, but he made it okay for the both of us since it was either that or… I refuse to say."

"I'm sorry," I breathe, reaching out to grip Aaron's hand.

"I should be the one apologizing to you," he mutters. "Ezra feeling powerless is not a pretty sight. He was powerless to help us. Cort started fucking every single female he came into direct contact with while refusing any form of affection from Ezra. I was petrified of Cort because I was reacting to him. We were just beyond fucked up."

Aaron shifts closer and pulls me up against him. A scream cuts through the air, causing my head to snap up. Heidi has a bright, red welt on her left breast. I look away, just as Dexter swipes her gorgeous peaches and cream breast with the flat of his tongue.

A heavy weight is slowly building in my tummy. When it

crests, I don't want to be in this dungeon. I've never felt this way before. The sensation is close to being high, or maybe craving a high. A high you're unable to deny.

"Ezra's dad was having similar issues. Marcus is the ultimate Alpha male, and he found solace in BDSM as a way of regaining his power. Marc and Dexter pulled Ezra into it as a way of helping us deal."

"Did it help?" I ask, but not because I want the answer, even though I do. I want to distract my attention away from Aaron's seeking fingertips trailing up the back of my thigh. Combining his touch with the sounds emanating from around the dungeon, it's an elixir for sex.

"Yeah, especially for Ezra. Not so much for Cortez. I think he behaved worse afterwards, actually. I have a lot of shame and guilt I needed to have worked out of me, and Ezra found a way to do it without sex being brought into the equation," he quickly tacks on, blushing red in embarrassment.

"What about you, though? I mean, you're a dominant acting like a submissive. That must be difficult."

"I was fine suppressing my dominant urges until recently, like I'm just now coming into my own. I haven't pursued any girls– I never have. So Ezra began to worry. I'm not gay. I don't want men at all. But that shit with Cort fucked up my head, because a part of me enjoyed it. Then there was all the bullshit in my head about how I was born to serve Ezra, to protect him from harm, and he was taken during my watch, and harmed while we were all together."

"You were only fifteen," I cry out.

"I know," Aaron whispers. "But guilt is never rational."

"Truer words have never been spoken," I breathe, never feeling more connected to another human being as I do now. Aaron gets me. Truly gets me, because we've both been there. It's the same reason Ezra sought me out.

Like seeks like.

"I like girls, and it's getting harder to ignore it." Aaron firmly grabs my hand and presses it to the front of his pants. His fingers curl over mine, grasping his bulge under my palm.

I whimper because I love the feel of Aaron's arousal in my

hand. I've never intimately touched a man before. Just a quick brush over the front of Ezra's pajama bottoms and when Cortez crammed his cock down my throat. I never count my rape as part of my sexual history. It was not consensual.

"So, Ezra brings us Kayla. He says he picked her out for you, since he was getting closer to bringing you home–"

"Bringing me home?" I cut Aaron off.

What the fuck does that mean? I try to remove my hand, but Aaron tightens his grip. He's throbbing under my palm, jerking and spasming. I've never felt anything like it before, and it feeds into the craving that's screaming inside my lower belly.

"I told Ez I wanted to wait for you." Aaron keeps talking as if I hadn't interrupted him. "Ezra made me be with Kayla."

My eyes widen when Aaron's bulge starts to jerk under my hand, wetness leaking through to my palm. Breathlessly, Aaron pants and moans deep in the back of his throat as he climaxes against my hand.

Wide-eyed, I stare sightlessly into the dungeon as I experience a man coming in my hand for the very first time.

"I know how sick I am, getting off on the thought of being forced, so don't judge," Aaron gasps, shame lacing his tone.

"Ah. Far be it for me to judge you on that particular subject," I quickly utter in shock.

"You're right... sorry," Aaron mumbles as if he knows what I meant.

"I thought we were doing our usual thing, where Master Ez helped me work out my issues. Instead, Ez tied me down and brought Kayla in. You get the general idea of what happened next. I mean, I didn't argue. I did as I was told while she rode me."

I snort, shaking my head back and forth. "I cannot believe I'm about to say this, but I am not surprised by anything that man does anymore. I should be flabbergasted, but he's somehow manipulated me to the point that these outrageous acts of therapy seem normal. Fucked. Up."

"Ezra never allowed any of us to be normal. Be thankful you had twenty years before he showed up in your life unexpectedly."

"Thirty, actually. Thanks for making a woman feel young. Wise move if you want a steady stream of pussy."

"Sure, thirty," Aaron drawls out like he's humoring me. "I told Ezra I didn't want to have sex like that again. We compromised. As long as I got my dominant urges out in a scene, he wouldn't make me have sex with Kayla. Cortez really liked that idea, since he always had a girl on hand to play with. Kayla prefers Cort's experience to my ignorance, anyway. I'm learning, though."

"You didn't like having sex with her?" Sweet Kayla is perfect.

"I really care for Kayla, so I loved every second of it. But just because I wanted to be with a girl, didn't mean any girl would do. I want to choose for myself. I probably would have chosen Kayla after I worked through my shit. But the way Ez did it, it made me want to rebel. I may be his servant, but I'm not his submissive."

Aaron pulls my back against his chest until my ass is even with his groin. I close my eyes against the sensation. It's wrong to want sex while we are having this conversation. But it's difficult not to think of sex while Dexter is circling Heidi again. Only this time he is stalking around naked, and he's not at all proportionate.

Tilting my head to the side to be sure, "Jesus," I hiss in awed wonder. "How the hell did Dexter grow that… thing? It looks like a third leg." My eyes enlarge in wonder.

Aaron barks a laugh just as Dexter slides a good ten inches into Heidi. Baby boy is rousing behind me again. Phenomenal.

"Ezra kept to his word. But he forced me to explain myself, as is his way. Someone I saw during our abduction, I want to be with them to make it right. It's completely irrational. It was my job to protect Ezra against what he was forced to do, and I failed to do so. Somehow in my mind, I've warped it until it makes sense. Ezra understood after I explained it to him, leaving me alone. I knew he was waiting for the same thing, so it felt wrong, like I should bow down to Ezra and give up my own needs."

"You're a good person, Aaron. You shouldn't miss out just because someone else wants the same thing. It's not about money or dominance; you just deserve it."

"I know that," Aaron murmurs, not at all sounding convinced that he is deserving of his own life. "You don't know what Ezra has done for us. I felt like he should get what he wants first, even though I know he isn't selfish. So, Ez was upset with me for not confiding in him sooner. If I had trusted him with the truth, he would have never forced Kayla on me."

Heidi's moans cut off all conversation, but it's Dexter I can't take my eyes off of. He is a very small man, but watching his muscles cord as he thrusts– a work of art. Sweat beads on his flesh, glistening in the light. His hips piston, thrusting deeply into Heidi. Her moan is a continuous keen of pleasure.

"I want to show you something, Kat." Aaron's fingers grip my chin and turn my face to the side, giving him access to my mouth. I moan as he runs his tongue along my bottom lip, tasting me. Aaron has to hold me upright because need weakens my knees as lust pools in my lower belly.

Aaron stops abruptly, and says, "Follow me," in a husky voice deepened with hunger.

I follow Aaron down a narrow hallway until we reach the very end. The sides of the hallway are lined with doors. Each door has a nameplate. I read the plaques as we walk by: Alexander. Dalton. Queen. II. Syn. Dexter. A blank plaque. These doors have heavy locks. The rest say *Member*, and the doors don't lock.

"Why do some of the doors have a name listed, and others simply say Member?" Interest laces my voice.

"The masters earned their own rooms, since they went through our training program Dexter and Marcus provided," Aaron explains. "The blank door is our meeting room, and the other rooms are by reservation-only for our members."

"Oh," I mumble, thoroughly engrossed by the inner-workings of Restraint's dungeon.

At the end of the hallway is a door marked *PRIVATE*. This door has a keypad like the one from the main club to the dungeon. Since Restraint's Masters' rooms only have a regular lock, I assume this takes us to another part of the building. After a series of beeps, the door disengages. Aaron swings it open and gestures for me to enter as he had before– game show host style.

Restraint 326

Chapter Thirty-Three

I enter a small dungeon-like apartment. It's the width of the main dungeon, but much shorter in depth. I stare in awe at the room's contents. It's like walking into a fetish dream world to indulge my curiosities.

On the right-hand side of the room is a small replica of Restraint's main dungeon: Lining the length of one wall is a spanking bench, a cross, stocks, and weird furniture that looks to be customizable. Chains and straps hang from the ceiling support beams. Half of the back wall has either toys or torture devices, depending on how you look at it, and they are categorized and organized by type and function. I'm impressed.

On the left-hand side of the private room are the comforts of home: a king size bed draped in a cloud of steel-blue bedding, a designer leather sofa, a pair of matching chairs, and there's even a coffee table and end tables. Everything is in hues of blue and gray, matching the concrete room. Near the sofa is a small refrigerator sitting atop a cabinet. They thought of everything.

The room is huge and opulent. I'm almost afraid to touch anything, as if I don't belong in this room, like I'm invading someone's private space.

"Whose is this?" I ask in awed wonder.

"Ours," Aaron says with great pride as he wanders over to the sofa to sit down.

"Who does '*ours*' pertain to?" I ask, tone warping with sarcasm over his vagueness.

I turn to study Aaron, to see how he reacts to his environment. He's relaxed, at home, as if he's spent a great deal of his time in this space.

"Ezra, Cortez, me, and Ezra's dad, Marcus. We all share this space. We like our privacy. It's yours now, too," Aaron happily offers, and it confuses the hell out of me.

"Why is it mine now, too?" I mumble, eyes seeking the dungeon side of the room. My feet long to walk over there and touch everything.

"Make yourself at home. Explore!" Aaron says excitedly, gesturing with his hands.

As I wander, I wonder why Aaron is here with me and not Ezra. This feels like something Ez should have introduced me to. I assumed that he would be the one to usher me into the lifestyle.

Well, ya know what that say about assuming. It makes an A.S.S. out of U and ME.

Ezra had forced his mastery on me. I have his bracelet clinking on my wrist as proof that I'm supposedly his. Yet here I am, with his number two. Before I allow myself to wallow in rejection, I pull up my big girl panties.

I should be grateful for Aaron. He's been here for me every time I've had a breakdown. He's lightened my mood. He's given me a gift I thought never to regain. The free feeling of youth I'd lost, or maybe never even had.

I'm positive Ezra is otherwise involved at the moment. He doesn't need another soul who is dependent on him. He already has Cortez, Aaron, and Kayla. I don't know what Ez's friendship with Queen is like. He also has his family and Adelaide. He doesn't need me leaching off of him for support, too. I need to move on from the fantasies I've been pretending I don't have. I have to acknowledge how I want Ezra in order to forget about wanting Ezra– that doesn't even make sense in my own mind. I'm just a befuddled mess.

A door in the back corner of the comfort side, beckons me forward. I peek inside and find a fully loaded bathroom fit for a king: a large, black granite two-person shower, with a seat and multiple showerheads. A deep bath with a bazillion water jets. A long granite vanity with double sinks. This bathroom is twice the size of the one in my apartment, and it's just a private bath in a BDSM club. You could have sex orgies in this room.

Jesus, think of the possibilities.

I leave the bathroom, my mind clouded by a whirling fog. It's as if I stepped into another world from the one I used to inhabit. I grew up in a three-bedroom, one-bath ranch house, situated in the woods. Everything was nice, sturdy, built to last, but never extravagant or over-the-top. If it didn't have a functional purpose, we didn't need it.

People like me have second homes: dilapidated hunting cabins, campers, and tents. We do not have fourth homes which function as sexual playrooms.

My old world seems safer than the one I'm lingering about on its fringes. We all have a purpose. None of us were put on this planet to entertain those around us. We work as a cohesive unit to survive, and when we lose someone, the loss is devastating. In this new world– the world where nothing has value because you have too much of everything –no one is necessary. Once thrown away, your loss will never be missed, because you're instantly replaced.

As I trail my fingertips along the soft, silver and navy Egyptian cotton bedding, I wonder how many people have fucked in this bed. This room doesn't really scream sex and torture, but I find it hard to imagine anyone making love in this room.

The shelving on the '*Spanks for the Memories*' side draws me like a moth to a flame. Whips, canes, floggers, cats, and things I cannot fathom a name, hang organized on hooks. I shudder at the pain they have inflicted on countless victims. My fingers move before my brain registers, and I'm opening small drawers in an apothecary table. Everything is well-organized in the creepy, little drawers.

"Is this sanitary?" My OCD springs to the fore, and I shiver at the thought of dirty toys.

"Katya," Aaron says to gain my attention. He's watching me intently, judging my every reaction and expression. When I meet his blue eyes, he continues, "This is *our* room. No one has been in here except for us, not even Kayla."

"Us? Why not Kayla?" I turn from Aaron's inquisitive eyes, and start rummaging through several drawers, suddenly feeling like an overzealous squirrel at the base of an oak tree.

"Yes, *us*: Ezra, Cortez, Marcus, and me," Aaron stresses. "Queen has been invited in here before. Other people have walked in here, but never to play."

I flinch when Aaron's hand envelopes my wrist. I didn't

feel him move. "And now, *you*."

Only using his fingertips, Aaron lightly brushes my hair away from my neck, and then he leans forward to place a gentle, open-mouthed kiss to the nape, directly over my Chrysalis tattoo.

My eyes slip shut, as a shiver runs up and down my spine, before it finally settles in my womb. Aaron curls around me, as if he can sense my insecurities and he's trying to reassure me. But he's also emoting a potent cocktail of lust and need, which is doing odd yet welcome things to my body.

"Kayla is our submissive," Aaron explains. "But she is not one of us– at least not yet."

I remove a clamp from one the apothecary table's drawers, and I play with the metal object to distance myself from the uncomfortable conversation. I don't know why I feel so damned confused. My emotions are firing in every direction. I just feel disconnected.

"I'm not one of you, either," I murmur sadly. "At least Kayla belongs to the trio of you as a submissive. I could never be that for you. I'm nothing to any of you."

Lost in my destructive thoughts, I pinch the clamp on my pinky, tearing a yelp of pain from my mouth. I quickly remove the clamp from my throbbing pinky.

Man, if this clamp is for a nipple, I would scream like a banshee.

Aaron turns me in a circle until I'm facing him. His expression is serious, but it softens when he sees me sucking on my injured finger.

"This," Aaron takes the clamp from me, and then returns it to its proper drawer. "Is not for fingers." He laughs at me, a pleasant rumble of a sound. "I will be happy to demonstrate its actual purpose later, if you'd like. Now, what's the matter?"

"I… I'm confused as to why it's you with me tonight. I thought Ezra would introduce me to this stuff." Aaron's face flashes hurt, but he covers it quickly. "No, it's not about you, Aaron. I really enjoy your company. Actually, I'm happy I'm here with you instead. It's less pressure. It's just… after all the '*I am your master*,'" I say it in a poor facsimile of Master Ez's voice. "I thought he would be the one to... you know, master me."

"Well, you answered your own question," Aaron drawls out. "If Cortez were here with you tonight, it would be what he wants. Ezra, or rather, Master Ez, would give you what you needed, even if you wouldn't enjoy it. You and I can relax, explore, and just experience." He shrugs.

"So... um... what do ya wanna do, then?" I ask hesitantly.

Aaron's earlier shyness returns with a vengeance. His face heats up and his baby boy dimples reappear. "I can answer questions you are curious about– up to a point," Aaron stresses.

"How come you are more forthcoming than Ezra? He doesn't explain shit," I say in an annoyed voice.

"Ah..." Aaron glides his hand through his barely-there hair. He must be nervous. "Ezra is a little intense–"

"Ya think?" I cut Aaron off, and he laughs in reply.

"Yeah, like that– Master Ez would have kicked your ass for interrupting." Aaron shakes his head in mystification. "Anyway, I was told what I couldn't say, so everything else is fair game. I think the more informed you are, the better. It won't be such a shock when you figure out why Ezra has done this for you. But he plays things closer to the vest than I do, because he wants you to work your way through things, not be told them."

What an understatement.

Aaron picks up the clamp and fingers it. He locks his eyes with mine as he says, "I want to play with you. We don't have to do a scene or anything. Just have fun, and see where it leads. Okay?"

I shake my head up and down like an idiot. My voice left me the second Aaron looked at me with heat in his eyes.

Aaron abruptly drops to the floor to lie on his stomach. My eyes almost pop from my skull at the sight of brawny, innocent Aaron lying at my feet. He flows smoother than water.

Whoa!

"Wwh... what are you doing?" My mouth dries up

instantly, and I have to lick my lips to moisten them in order to speak.

"Well, I believe your exact words were, '*Aaron's going to lick my boot the next time I see him, the bastard.*' Now seems like the perfect time, don't you think?" He rolls his vibrant blue peepers up to gaze at me through his impossibly long lashes.

Aaron's pink tongue darts out to dab at the toe of my boot, leaving a wet patch behind. I shuffle uncomfortably on my feet. I close my eyes against the sight, but a visage of Aaron's tongue is imprinted behind my eyelids. Something soft is sliding up my calf, and then the side of my knee. My eyes fling wide open when I feel dampness left in the sensation's wake.

"Ah-fuck," slips past my lips when Aaron nibbles on my inner thigh, teeth barely grazing my skin.

"Mistress Kat, I believe that makes us even." Aaron looks at me in a way no other ever has. He looks hungry– a starving man, and I'm sustenance after a long famine.

"Yes... Yes, I believe we are even now." My voice is husky with need and shaky from nervousness.

Aaron flows to his feet like water, and then he clasps my wrists together in one of his palms. As he raises our arms above my head, a flash of memory flits across my mind. I close my eyes, trying to bring it into sharp focus, but I lose the thread. As my eyes flutter back open, I'm immediately captured by a pair of bright blue headlights, and then the memory surfaces with the force of an earthquake.

I'm lying prone on the forest floor, surrounded by the heat of my captors. Several sets of hands are trying to hold me down to the ground as I struggle to escape. A warm palm clasps my wrists together, trying to stop me from harming myself and the others, drawing my arms straight out above my head. A fingertip strokes my pulse point in a soothing, circular rhythm, trying to ease me, to calm me. I wrench my head backwards, trying to see the face of my consoler. Oversized eyes set into a young face captivate me– bright blue.

A look of relieved satisfaction crosses Aaron's face. My mouth opens on a gasp as my mind reels, trying to sort out what I just experienced. Never have I remembered that moment, but it is an integral part of me.

Aaron leans down and attacks my mouth before I can speak: tongue piercing my mouth as his lips fuse to mine, his fingers fisting the back of my hair as he draws me closer. We turn into feral animals. Hungry, urgent noises erupt from our connected mouths.

My nails twist in the front of Aaron t-shirt, to tear and pull until I've ripped it from his back. My mouth immediately seeks the beautiful landscape of Aaron's muscular chest. I feast: bite, lick, and tease his chest with my tongue and teeth. I suck his small nipple in my mouth and bite down, marveling at the masculine taste and the feeling of my teeth sinking into flesh that is hard.

I whimper in relief. I've played with women for so long, fear and numbness turning me away from what I really desired. Finally, I am feeding my baser urges– the need all straight women have for men.

Aaron's hand palms the back of my head and fiercely yanks me back up to his mouth. Growling, feasting at my mouth, he abruptly slows his pace, and then pulls away from my lips.

Aaron peers down at me with an expression of pure satisfaction on his face. An expression that warps into a devious look, which makes me want to run.

Aaron's fingers locate the hidden zipper on my shift, and then drag it down agonizingly slow. Ever-patient, he looks into my eyes, waiting for me to deny him. When I don't pull away, Aaron takes that as consent. He skims his fingertips along my shoulders, and then he slides my dress down my arms until it falls to pool at my feet.

Raw and exposed, I try to catch my breath as I stand naked before Aaron in just a webbing of silk. He gazes at me with a devotion I've yet to earn, and it perplexes me.

Aaron winks playfully, and then he bends down, drawing my nipple into his mouth through the silk of my bodysuit. The rasp of his tongue on my heightened nerves pulls a groan from my throat. He sucks hard while his fingertips tweak my nipple's twin. His mouth switches breasts, and instantly, a sharp pinch radiates from my nipple to spread across my breast.

I shriek at the pain, my eyes darting to the source– the clamp.

Aaron gazes up at me through the lace of his lashes while he suckles me. He's so beautiful that my stomach clenches and my heart hurts. A quick flick of his pink tongue has me so mesmerized that I don't register the flash of metal until I feel its sharp pinch. I want to jump around from the intensity: it stings, pinches, and burns my sensitive nipples.

"Just breathe through it. It'll be worth it," Aaron promises, flashing me a reassuring smile.

I slow my breathing and concentrate on anything other than my screaming nipples. A few moments pass, and then all I feel is a slight pressure on each breast and a dull ache surrounding my nipples.

"I would love to take this slowly and play around with all of this stuff." Aaron gestures around the mini-dungeon. "I want to see how you'd react," he says gravelly deep. "But I can't wait. I need to be *in* you. Right. Now." Aaron groans the words, an edge of sharp desperation infusing his voice.

Aaron drags me a few feet, picks me up, and then roughly tosses me onto the bed. I bounce several times before I come to rest in the center of the mattress. A sharp giggle is torn from my throat– a little bit manic and a whole, helluva lot confused.

"I've never had sex with a guy willingly," I admit. "I'm–" I am at a loss for words.

I've wanted men off and on, but I was so terrified that I turned to women instead. I was always frightened that my past would tear me apart during the act. But I've never felt as heated with desire as I do for the trio. Something about them makes me crave things I've never allowed myself to desire.

"I understand, Kat. Don't worry," Aarons says as he tenderly caresses my cheek. "If you freak out, that's okay. You can trust me to take care of you."

"I do trust you," I whisper, and I even mean it.

"I know, and I'm honored," Aaron murmurs as he gazes

down at me. "We have this in common. I'm not sure how to make love to a woman, and you're not sure how to make love to a man. So we make one hell of a pair, don't we?"

Aaron's eyes change from that of a comforting friend to a starving man. The dominance and power radiating off of him flips a hidden switch inside of me. I suddenly feel safe, and within that safety all fears dissolve, and in their place is pure desire.

When Aaron's fingertips reach for the button on his jeans, a thrill flashes through my entire body. I start to pant with lust-filled anticipation. I clench my thighs against the ache that's fiercely building– an ache I must relieve.

We reach the point of no return as I watch Aaron strip out of the rest of his clothing: boots thudding to the floor, and then the pants, boxers, and socks quickly follow.

Aaron is a work of art. Created as protection, his taut, coiled muscles were honed through physical activity. He stalks me on the bed, crawling on all fours. He glides like a wild animal intent on its prey, either to fuck or to kill.

The fight or flight instinct bursts through my veins, making me feel invigorated. Instead of giving into my baser urges, I fight myself instead. I force myself to stay still, to push the encroaching panic away. It's time to face my fears head-on, not to run in a blind panic. Maybe what I fear the most is what I need to feel alive.

Awed, I freeze like a rabbit snared in the sights of a wolf. Aaron stalks me across the bed; the proud jut of hard flesh and the potent, heavy weight dangling below are a silent threat of what's to come.

"We can either take this slow or fast." Aaron releases a seductive growl. "It's your call."

Aaron settles himself on top of me: warm, heavy, comforting, and sexual. My mind flashes to all the reasons I shouldn't do this and to all the reasons why I should. I close my eyes and just feel. My skin absorbs the heat of his. My nose drinks in the masculine scent of his skin. My sex weeps at the feel of his arousal pressing and seeking for its way inside my body through my bodysuit.

"Fast," I say before I can stop myself. "I just don't want to freak out and change my mind."

"Don't process. Just react." Aaron chuckles. "Yeah, now's probably not the best time to bring up Ezra's mantra when we're this close. But it fits perfectly."

Aaron's palms smooth down my thighs, fingertips massaging during their journey. When he reaches my ankles, he removes my boots, one at a time. They thump to the floor with finality.

He presses his chest against mine and slowly circles, using his body to work the clamps. The push and pull on the nipple clamps makes me gasp. The sensation shoots straight from my breasts to my clit, in a line of agonizing fire. I widen my thighs, subconsciously begging Aaron for attention.

Aaron abruptly sits up, using his knees to widen me further. His gaze captures mine as his fingers seek the fabric acting as a barrier between us. Digging in, twisting it around his fingertips, Aaron rips the crotch of my bodysuit, shredding the webbing. I gasp, watching Aaron rent my clothing from my skin, until I am laid bare to his sight.

Seeking fingertips make contact with my screaming flesh, sliding from my clit to dip deep inside my body. I arch up into his hand, needing more.

My eyes are forced shut, the intense pleasure making my eyelids flutter. I turn into a moaning mass of quivering flesh beneath Aaron's hot touch.

The sensation changes. It feels so much better than moments ago. Smoother. Warmer. Larger. Velvety softness glides through the wetness of my folds. I slit my eyes and look to Aaron's, but they aren't focused on my face. I follow his rapturous gaze and release a gasp of shock.

Aaron stares intently at his hand, the hand that is leisurely dragging the head of his perfect cock back and forth against my pussy.

Skin-to-skin.

Aaron's eyes roam up my body before they finally connect with mine, glowing a reverence which humbles me. "I need this. Do you? Are you ready?" he hoarsely whispers.

"P l e a s e," drags past my lips, edging into begging.

I'm panting in anticipation, remembering how my first time felt– the odd moment when I began to trust the man inside me, just as my body began to betray itself.

I know this moment with Aaron will be better, healing, because I said yes. It will be better because I trust him. It will be better because he is Aaron, and he is my friend.

Enthralled, I watch as Aaron has the good sense to roll on a condom. His thick fingers shake as he impatiently covers his cock with latex.

"I've dreamt of this moment every night for the past twelve years," his voice breaks from intense emotions.

Before I can even ask what that means, Aaron flexes his hips and enters me. He stretches me, and I lose all capacity for thought. The full feeling has me arching off the bed. Unintelligible words rumble up my throat. I whimper, wanting more of the satisfying sensation.

Aaron's eyes glue to the juncture of our bodies. An odd expression crosses his face. One I've never seen before. His expression is almost pained. He starts to move, rolling his hips in a circle, while his eyes never leave where we're joined together.

When Aaron finally meets my gaze, his eyes are glittering with tears. I start to panic until a funny little smile twists his lips.

"Katya, this is better than my imagination could ever create." Aaron's voice is thick with emotions I cannot name. "Reality is so much better."

Suddenly, Aaron's fingers pull down on one of the clamps compressing my nipples, releasing a sharp, "Aaaahh," from me. It is an agonizing pleasure– a burning that shoots flames to my core, causing my body to grip and clench around Aaron's length. He toys with both clamps for a few moments as he gently rolls into me, enjoying my body's reaction to the pain.

Leaning down, Aaron takes my mouth with his lips, causing us both to issue a relieved moan on contact. He thrusts his cock deeply inside of me to the hilt, with his sac pressing tightly to my ass. Needing to experience all of him, I wrap my arms around his shoulders, fingernails biting into his back, with my legs around his hips.

"I need to feel all of you. Deeper," I moan.

I'm no longer the numb creature who only ever felt pain and loss, while refusing to let in the softer, more sensual aspects in life. Now, all I feel is the pleasure Aaron is gifting me, and I know without a shadow of a doubt, I will never be able to turn the emotions off again.

Aaron reaches between us to pinch the clamps, releasing my nipples simultaneously. I experience a moment of pure relief as the pressure ebbs. I sigh… and then the blood floods into my thirsty flesh, and I scream to the ceiling as sensation returns to my nipples.

My voice echoes around the room, causing a continuous keening sound. The pain. The hot-burning and the cold-prickling of my skin being nourished from the blood it was long-denied. My nipples experience what my soul has endured for over a decade: the agony of going from pain, to quiet numbness, back to experiencing pain, and finally the glorious sensation of feeling alive.

A warm, wet, suckling mouth offers me succor– first to one nipple, and then the other. The pain changes to exquisite pleasure as Aaron laves at my sensitive flesh.

My inner muscles clench around Aaron's pulsing cock as I reach the precipice of orgasm. The combination of Aaron being thrust deeply inside me while he suckles at my aching breasts is what ultimately fractures me.

I wrap myself around Aaron: my legs anchored to his waist, my ankles cross with my heels digging into the globes of his perfect ass. My hands grip his cheeks, nails digging in, urging him to move with me as I counterthrust. My mouth latches on his shoulder to muffle my sounds of pleasure.

Aaron's thrusts pick up. The force of the movement drags us up the bed until I have to grip the headboard to keep from braining myself. Guttural sounds emanate from the both of us: grunts, groans, growls, and moans. We sound more animal than human.

Aaron's size increases inside me, and begins to throb,

beating with his heart and erratically jerking in starts and stops. He slows his pace as we climb to our mutual climax.

Aaron takes my face into his palms and connects our gaze. Both of us are wide-eyed and breathlessly huffing in air.

We come apart together.

His name, "Aaron," whispers as a prayer from my lips. Never taking my eyes off his, I still as I feel him find his release. I savor the sensation of giving and receiving mutual pleasure.

"Katya... Katya... Katya..." each time he calls my name softer and quieter– a benediction.

We settle on our sides to catch our breath, still wrapped in each other's arms and connected by mind and body. A slight movement catches my attention. On the couch– just mere feet away –Ezra sits with Cortez's head resting on his shoulder, with content smiles stretched across their faces. Ezra turns his head as Cortez looks adoringly up at him. Their eyes are glinting in the darkness.

Ezra whispers, "That was beautiful," and then he affectionately kisses Cort's parted lips.

Chapter Thirty-Four

My feet pound the ground with such force it reverberates up my legs and trails up my spine. The sharp snap of twigs breaking under the impact echoes in my ears, along with the deafening tattoo of my panicked heart. My terror-filled breath saws out my lips, exhale clouding the air across my face as I run—

Run for my life.

A looming pine tree is a taunting, solid barrier, directly in my path of escape. Precious life-saving seconds are lost as I veer around the tree, or else risk smacking headlong into it. Upheaved from the ground, gnarled roots catch my toes and upend my balance. I catch my fall with outstretched palms upon the pine-needle-laden ground, bruising and tearing my flesh. With a forceful lunge, I propel myself forward to gain momentum.

Droplets of blood nourish the soil from deep cuts welling on my hands. Branches slash my cheeks and thorny vines snag my skin and clothing, almost as if they are offering aid to my hunters. My mind is clear of all thought, except for the inborn flight reflex of someone desperate to survive.

Self-preservation forces my muscles to maintain their wild run, even as my body protests the movement with bloody and bruised, burning limbs. My hands instinctively rise and fall, protecting me from the brutal violence of nature.

Four hunters stalk me as if I were a wounded animal— their prey. They gain on me steadily, even if their visages are blurry to my tear-stung eyes. With rapid movements too quick for me to register, they converge, charging me from different directions— herding me, running me to ground as a pack.

Territorial rage explodes through the simmering fear in my blood. As their target, not only am I being assaulted, my sanctuary is being violated right alongside me. I've hiked this wooded lakeside trail since I was a child. When I was small, I'd venture out farther, creating a larger boundary of my own backyard. As an adult, the lake and the wooded trail surrounding it, are my home. We're being invaded, and I'm powerless to stop it.

I know every dip, curve, and incline of the landscape. Up until just moments ago, this was where I went to clear my mind and seek solitude. Childlike dreams of the future were forged here, right alongside the adult decision of what I would major in in college. My bubble of safety, the trust I have in my land to protect me, and the courage I have to protect it in return, bursts on the whims of ruthless men.

Now, I run for my life, hoping my lifelong knowledge of the landscape will pull me through to the other side– safety.

In tune, somehow connected as pack animals, they hunt in perfect synchronization: breathing in harmony, legs moving with the same graceful fluidity, intuitively knowing where to head me off to push me towards their partners and propel me to their destination.

If it weren't me versus them, I may have found their symmetry breathtakingly beautiful.

I speed up on the descent down a steep ravine, drawing me closer to the lake and its imminent comfort. My sneakers skid on soft dirt, pebbles rolling me, making it nearly impossible to stay upright. I catch my fall several times by sightlessly grabbing for roots and branches. Thorns jab into my flesh with my hold, only to tear my skin as I pull away. I acknowledge no pain from my wounded palms as they rapidly beat with the pounding of my heart. Falling backwards, head hitting a rock with a great, jarring force, I fear I'll be rendered unconscious, unable to protect myself. Inertia has other plans for me, causing me to slide down the embankment on my rear while I regain my senses. By the time I reach the bottom, my shorts are shredded by the earth and damp from the blood seeping from the resulting wounds.

Rolling to a stop, I crawl to all fours. In shock, I barely wince as the jagged edges of river rock and the grit of ballast from the long-ago railroad bed embed into my knees and palms. I try to right myself on stable ground, but my energy is waning. Agile footfalls catch my notice, driving fear and adrenaline to flood my system, fortifying my survival instincts.

With a deep, pain-filled keen, I propel myself to my feet, and take off towards safety.

They allow me no rest as they close in from all sides, like the shadow of darkness creeping across the land every sunset—sure and swift, and unavoidable. They try to pull me off course by rerouting me with their movements. Driving me like an animal, they prove their adept hunting skills by forcing me off the hiking trail. Separating me from any other hikers we may encounter, from the safety of the known, I'm now parallel to the path, going away from it at an abrupt angle. The one in charge is wordlessly maneuvering me to his destination, and I am powerless to stop it.

The primal, animalistic side of my brain already recognizes its capture. I can see it playing out in my mind's eye: the four hunters felling my body, tearing into me like lions on a fresh kill, stripping my dignity away along with the last vestiges of my cherished innocence. My system floods with adrenaline. A vicious quaking rocks my entire body, slowing my pace. I shiver in the cold of impending doom, even as my body erupts with a feverish sweat.

My logical brain, the part of me that holds self-preservation above all else, overpowers my fears. From my depths, I scream, "I will not give up! Never surrender!" I will fight to my very death just so I can wear my pride as a badge of honor in the afterlife. Furiously, my mind spins escape routes and defense plans as I am led, pushed, and driven by the unit.

My only salvation is the lake. If I can get to the water, I can swim to safety. Like the trail, I know everything about the lake: the inlets, the currents, and the boat-tied docks. As a balm to my soul, I can feel the caress of its chilled water welcoming me into its promise of safety and comfort. The tree canopy overhead casts rays of light for my path. The crystalline waters glisten invitingly, beckoning me towards its secure embrace.

Half in the now, half inside my fantasy of escape, I'm taken aback when the leader comes into sharp focus just off to my right. I stumble when I see the fierce expression on his face,

the look of triumph as he gains on his prize.

"It won't be long, boys," his smug voice projects, filling the woods with his victory. The shrill cadence of his voice sounds like broken glass to my sensitive ears.

In a futile dance of survival, I go left, and then right. Left, and then right, panting wildly as I look for a hole in their defenses. My injured foot slips on a patch of moss, situating the leader in easy reach of my bleeding arms. In a pitiful, last ditch effort, I veer to the left, away from his grasp, only to miscalculate the trajectory of the other hunters.

Arms enclose me from the side. Startled, yet not surprised by the inevitable, I close my eyes in defeat. "I'm so sorry," a young, somber voice whispers softly against my hair.

I hold my agonized scream, swallow it and choke on it, as my captor's leg sweeps mine from beneath me. I fall to the ground, expecting a hard impact, but he takes the brunt of the fall.

I thrash my arms and legs, trying to break free from his hold. My punches and slaps land with a hollow thump to reverberate down my arms. With the solid connection of my elbow to his chest, his sharp grunt of pain lights satisfaction throughout my body. I may not win, but he's going to hurt, too.

Breathlessly, I lash out as an animal would, fingers curling into claws, sounds of pain spilling from my throat. The more panicked I become, the less effective my struggles are. I fight for my life, but it does me no good. It doesn't rescue me from my violent fate.

More hands join my captor's, holding me down to the hard-packed ground, trying to subdue my struggles. Their fingers slip in the blood and sweat slicking my skin, making it difficult for them to contain me. With the pass of their flesh along my injuries, I falter from the severe pain that strikes me like a physical blow.

Whether in reality or in remembrance, I can never place a face to the young men. My mind withholds this knowledge, whether it's to protect me, I do not know. Their faces, their bodies, every detail about them is blurred, everything but the hands that hold— the hands that ultimately harm me.

Three sets of medium-sized hands. Neither boy nor man.

Head jerking from side to side, I frantically search until my eyes land on the leader. He stands proudly, watching the scene unfold before him with smug satisfaction. Now, him, I never forget. I remember every detail in Technicolor. He's a tall, lean man, who is well-dressed and handsome, except for his expression of malice and the aura of madness radiating off of him. He is a man, who if you saw him on the street, you'd think he was a gentlemen. But all too late, you'd discover the sickness leaking from his soul mere moments before he attacked.

I lie helplessly and hopelessly on the forest floor, an animal caught in an inescapable trap. One male leans on my feet with his hands on my shins, restraining me. Another pins my arms above my head, his smaller hands barely able to contain me. The third, the one who ultimately captured me, is petting my face. It's his sick and twisted way of calming me. The intimacy of it makes me wish he'd just punch me instead.

"Well, which of you wants to go first? She's definitely ready now." The leader speaks of me as if I'm truly an animal. Meaningless. I no longer have a purpose, other than to be defiled for their entertainment. Once broken, I will be utterly worthless, even to them— especially to them.

"No," the third orders. "You aren't going to subject her to all of us," he growls with authority.

Blessedly, the third turns my face to the side so I no longer have to see their leader. But it's a sadistic trick, one designed to inflict maximum damage, just as how his soft touches somehow felt crueler than a violent strike. My mocking view is of the lake. Its crystalline water, which promised safety, now taunts me. I try to reach out to the water for help, fingertips unfurling, trying desperately to touch it. A whimper escapes my lips when the lake doesn't envelope me in its watery embrace.

"Well, son, this is your first hunt. I thought we'd share in the spoils, and then dispose of the body in the lake after we've broken her." A sinister laugh bubbles up from his chest, pure evil anticipation.

My body tries to shudder, but it's immobilized by two of

the boys, but nowhere near as immobilized as I am by my fear. Terror rolls over me and takes me under, rendering me incapable of rational thought. Panic wraps me in its darkness. It leads me to a place that can only be described as Hell. The dark recesses of my mind are far scarier than my violent reality.

"This way we can do anything we want and no one will hear us." Madness leaks from the leader's voice. "We can take our time. And look at that lake... no one would find her for days. I planned this perfectly."

"No," the third repeats. "This is my first time and my first hunt. I will not share." His voice sounds strong, but his body betrays itself. His hands shake against my face. He rolls his eyes to meet the gaze of boy number one, and hold for a moment– silently communicating.

"No, I wouldn't have wanted to share on my first time, either. Since it's his birthday, he should get to pick," boy number one says, as he's stationed at my feet.

"Son, what exactly do you propose? My patience is wearing thin with your petulance." The leader's voice is softer when he speaks to number three.

"Just me. The others go into the woods at a distance. I don't want an audience. No harming her, either. She's just a girl." He strokes my face like I'm his pet. I try to ignore the calming, affectionate gesture, but it overpowers everything else.

"Fine, you have a choice. We all get a turn, and then I end her life when we're through, or we go with your plan, but I get to have a go. I promise that she will live, but I doubt she will wish she had when I'm finished," he gloats threateningly.

"No, just me," the third boy hisses at his father's face.

A slap reverberates from his jaw down through his fingertips. Its force shakes my face.

"Take it or leave it, son. This is not a negotiation. I didn't go to all the trouble of making you, getting you back, and bringing you your friends, only for you to disrespect me like this in front of our catch." His voice is cold and detached.

With a swift kick, a boot connects sharply with my ribs,

eliciting a crack to wrack my body. I bite my bottom lip to keep the building scream from erupting. The pain is excruciating, sharp and burning agony– fire races across my ribs and flows down my spine. It's difficult to breathe. Every breath shoots painful stabs up my side. I bloody my lip to keep the wounded sounds at bay.

I count slowly and breathe shallowly. Eventually I am able to concentrate on the feel of the moss beneath my cheek, the damp scent of the ground, the lapping of the water on the shore, anything except my circumstances.

Hands disappear from my body, signaling that the negotiations have ended. A pair of young men slip into the woods just out of sight. Detachably, I realize that this means I get to live. They chose the option where I get to live when this is over, but I may wish I hadn't.

I release a heavy sigh, and then draw in a lungful of clean, fresh air. My lungs fill to capacity, and my rib protests the pressure. My body eases with the realization that I may get to see another day. I know the leader thinks I will regret his son's choice, but as long as I have a tomorrow, I can endure today.

Self-preservation wins out over the fight-or-flight response. Instinctively I know that if I try to fight back, if I try to run, they will catch me within seconds, and then the leader will have no issue crushing the life out of me as if I were an insect.

I lay numbly on the ground, not moving, barely breathing, heart pounding so loudly it deafens me. I don't fight as the third boy unbuttons my shorts, draws the zipper down, and then slides them off my hips along with my panties.

My heart rate goes into hyper-drive as he spreads my thighs and kneels between them. With gentle hands, his fingertips dig into my hips as he lifts me, anchoring my thighs with his own, and then places my bunched up shorts underneath my bottom as a cushion.

"Look away," he orders his father in a scratchy rough voice.

"Now, son, where would the enjoyment be in that?" You can hear the wry, evil amusement bleeding through the

leader's tone.

I close my eyes and tell myself to let nature take its course. It will be less violent if I submit– surrender. Number three is being surprisingly gentle, reluctant, as he rubs my tummy, trying to calm me.

"Son, do I need to show you what to do? I know this is your first time with a girl, as this incarnation. I've had much fun with you and your friends, but it's time the gay side of you enjoyed a woman. Come on, you have a minute to do it, or I will," the leader threatens menacingly.

"I'm doing this. Don't do anything rash," he says to his father.

"You aren't making love to the girl. Just fuck her and get it over with. I know you know how to fuck," he spews in disgust.

The metal-on-metal sound of a zipper lowering has my eyes squeezing shut tightly. If I can't see it, it's not really happening. Betraying tears leak down the sides of my face to wet the hair near my ears. A warm, heavy weight lies on top of me, covering my body. His hand reaches forward, cupping the back of my head, to pull my face against his chest.

"There... there... Shh... He can't see any part of you with my body hiding yours. I promise," he murmurs softly, but his voice breaks in fear. I know it's not a promise he can keep.

I start to shake uncontrollably. I'm too smart to think the thoughts most people would dwell on. 'This isn't supposed to happen to me.' 'I can't believe this is happening to me.' 'What did I do wrong to deserve this?'

I know there are no guarantees in life, and I find no comfort from the thought. My life or death is in the hands of the leader and his son. There is no escape, no rescue, no reasoning or pleading my way out of this. My only option is to endure and pray that I will live through it.

I try to distance myself as I had during the negotiation, but I can't find the switch in my brain. I start to panic. I bite my lip against the terrorized scream that is threatening to spill from between my lips. I'm frozen in fear. I can't even move my fingertips.

"Can I at least enter her without you hovering?" The son whispers.

"Fine. I'll be back in two minutes. I have to make sure the boys didn't run off. If they run again, I'll kill them this time," he threatens.

"I know. They know." He speaks as if he's heard the threat a thousand times before, and he's bored with it.

"I'm so sorry. I don't want to do this to you. None of us do. Well, I'm positive he does," he says snidely about his father. "He kidnapped us. First he took me from my home, from my bed, and then he went back and took the others. I know he's capable of exactly as he said... we've seen him in action over the past few days. I'm so sorry," he repeats like it changes a damned thing.

He shifts his body until I feel the hot, firm press of him against my sensitive flesh. I whimper in fear as I try to press my back into the unyielding ground beneath me to get away.

"I'm sorry. It has to be this way. It's the only way I can protect the others. He's already taken so much from my friends; they'll never heal from this. This way you'll have two less people inside you, and they can keep what little innocence they have left. I am so sorry," he cries in shame.

With the flex of his hips, he enters me with searing pain, tearing through my innocence. Penetrating. Impaling. He pushes deep where nothing has gone before. My eyes pop wide open and my mouth forms a silent scream. My fingernails claw into the compacted earth and dig, breaking my nails until I feel the wetness of their blood spill.

The switch flips over in my mind as he slowly rocks into me. I process very little with the exception of his control. He holds so much back in an effort not to harm me.

My eyes hold wide with fright as I concentrate on the wisps of clouds peeking through the voids in the treetops. I stare at the canopy instead of feeling the sensations rocking my body. I zone out and watch the magnificent beauty of nature instead of experiencing the brutal nature of man.

A sinister cackle draws my focus to the middle-aged man holding my wrists above my head. His nails bite into the thin skin, leaving crimson crescents filling with blood. His pale, clammy skin is revolting, but not as vile as the lewd, evil expression on his face.

The sensations rush into my system as he leers down at me. The pain throws the switch wide open. I see more clearly than I had before. I finally register what the boy looks like, his musky, masculine scent filling my nose, his touch on my flesh, his taste on the back of my tongue, and our bodies connected at our sexes. Pain and terror mix, racing my heart and creating a chemical reaction in my blood. Adrenaline rushes through my body as I try to fight. Every movement causes the nails to dig deeper, to draw more blood.

"Look at me, not him." My eyes flash to the husky, smoky voice. "That's right... look at me," he coaxes.

Gunmetal-gray eyes captivate me. A boy around eighteen is rocking into me from above. He is tall and slight, as if he hasn't filled out into the man he will become.

"No son of mine stops before he's finished," the leader hisses at the boy when he slows his thrusting.

"It's just you and me. Don't look at him." His voice holds sympathy, and I remember how badly he fought his father. How he was forced to take me, sacrificing us both to save his friends.

"Stay with me," he murmurs. His pace increases, and I whimper from the ensuing pain, and for another sensation I don't want to admit.

"Let go of her hands," the boy seethes. "She's not going anywhere. You'll get your turn. This is mine. Step back." His anger terrifies me, reminding me of animals fighting over a fresh carcass.

I freak out, struggling in earnest, no matter how badly my wrists are bloodied.

"Shh... I've got you. Just look at me," he croons, trying to soothe me.

My hands are released, and I flex my fingers, but the boy instantly recaptures them. I startle and cry out.

"I just want to hold your hands. I won't hurt you or hold you down. It's okay. Stay with me," he begs. He draws our *clasped hands between our bodies and settles them at our chests.*

"It's just you and me. We're all alone. I saw a pretty girl walking the trail, and asked her to join me at the lake. We walked and talked. When we got to the water, we kissed, and then it turned into something more. Now, it's just you and me, making love next to the sparkling water. Imagine it with me," he coaxes me into his fantasy world. "It's just you and me..." he moans. "Stay with me," he draws me deeper into his fantasy.

I no longer feel the agony and terror. I fall into his eyes and I'm swallowed by his imagination. He whispers words of comfort to keep me with him. We lock eyes and block out the rest of the world.

The pain turns to an unfamiliar ache. My legs part and my hips angle up, completing a deeper connection. Shame slams into my soul as I feel pressure build and heat spread throughout my body. The boy's face echoes back his own displeasure with our bodies' reactions.

Green and gray eyes fuse together, dual victims and victimizers as our bodies betray us.

I try to restrain myself as little whimpers sneak past my lips. The boy bends down. His lips feather against mine as he speaks, "Call me-." But stubbornly my mind refuses to process what he says.

My body releases the ultimate betrayal as he pours inside me. I tighten all of my muscles against the need to writhe. I bite into the chest above me, teeth sinking deep into his flesh, drawing blood to fill my mouth, as I repress the sounds trying to escape my throat. My fingers squeeze his, and his squeeze mine in return.

Moments pass as we freeze in our shame. A throat clearing brings us back to the present. The leader's expression is awed. For once he is speechless. Even with my body broken and violated, the thought of unnerving him brings me vindication.

"Good job, son. She was a virgin, wasn't she?" He's pleasant, not at all like the rapist he is.

"Yes," the son says in shame.

He slowly eases out of my body. The movement causes me to wince and dig my fingernails into the backs of his hands— and it's not from pain. The boy looks down at me with a similar expression: a mix of shame, guilt, and pleasure.

He brushes my hair from my ear and whispers, "I'm sorry for what I'm about to do. If you survive, I promise I will find you and always protect you. We will be together again," he swears.

The absence of his body chills me to my soul. I know what's coming next. I don't need any pretense. My life is in the balance. If I manage to survive, I may be broken beyond repair. I see it in his eyes, how he thinks leaving me is cowardly. He is sacrificing me to save himself and his friends. I am to distract the disgusting man as they run. I can only pray they will get me help along the way.

"I can't watch you take her," he grits out, voice breaking on every word. "I'll wait with the boys while you finish up." He stands, secures his pants, and then moves to the side to give his father the space between my thighs, as if I'm just a vessel you penetrate. Worthless.

"Now, c'mon. I want to show you how it's really done." The leader drops to his knees, pants already undone, with his manhood a violent threat.

"They will scream, fight, and beg," he gloats, hoping I do the same. "I need to show you how to fuck. What you just did was too gentle. I'll give you thumbs up on making the little slut come. The look on her face as she tried to fight it and the sounds she tried to suppress, I will cherish that memory for the rest of my life."

I hold the son's eyes as his father roughly enters me. He starts to move in jarring strokes. He fills me so deeply, it tears my insides. I feel no pain as the wetness of my blood and the son's spendings drip from my body. I make no sound because inside I am silently screaming. I don't move because I am frozen in terror. I don't hear the forceful grunting of the man rutting in me because all I hear is the pounding of my blood through my breaking heart.

I just hold the son's eyes. The orbs are the only thing anchoring me to sanity.

"I can't watch this," he says again, with his hands fisted at his sides. His knuckles turn white from the strain. I concentrate on that minor detail to distract myself from my brutal reality.

"Fine, be a fucking coward, and go run back to your lover. I'm positive raping all those whores and your little friend cured him of his gayness. If not, we'll go through this again and again until it works."

Furious at his son, he thrusts so violently that I slide a foot on the ground. A jagged-edged rock deeply slices into my back, as roots gouge into my thighs and behind. The wounds feels cold against the earth.

I watch as the boy's back swiftly retreats into the trees, taking my sanity away with him. I resume my cloud watching as I'm brutally violated. I feel no pain as the father punches me in the face, his knuckles cracking against my cheek and eye, while shouting at me to fight him.

I lie completely and utterly numb as he beats me within an inch of my life, repeatedly punching any part of me he can reach while still penetrating me.

Darkness is fading in around the edges, promising to take the pain away, but the steep price is how I will never see tomorrow...

I hold on, staring at the wispy clouds in the bright, sunny, afternoon sky with one eye, long ago losing the ability to see out of the other.

Moments later, as he's rutting on me, he bellows, "----!" The word still doesn't process in my mind— its way of protecting me from the truth. The leader pulls from my body before he finds his release. He draws upright, trying to refasten his pants with great difficulty since his hardness is in the way. "Those little cocksuckers," he growls to himself.

"You bastards have better not run. When, not if, I find you, you are all dead. I will fuck your corpses!" He screams at the top of his lungs when understanding dawns. His son used me to distract him so they could flee.

After a brutal kick to my ribs, because I preoccupied him long enough to lose his victims, he charges off into the woods on a rampage.

I pull my shorts back on with shaky, numb fingers. I have great difficulty, not able to get them to slide up my sticky thighs covered in blood. I get my shorts as far as my knees and leave them there.

I keep repeating, 'I will survive this... I didn't break... I will survive this... I didn't break... I will survive this... I am still alive...'

I drag myself several hundred feet from the site of my violation on my hands and knees, my shorts impeding my escape. The blood trail is nearly fifty feet long, with my knees leaving drag marks. I push myself up to my feet, self-preservation giving me the strength.

When I'm satisfied nothing points out my location, I wedge myself into a thicket of scrub brush, trying to hide out of sight. If he returns, he won't be able to find me. I curl into the fetal position and pray.

The numbness is fading– slowly replacing it is pain. The pain my body is firing is nothing compared to the agony deep within my soul, my mind, and my heart.

The only thing that keeps my animalistic keens at bay is the thought that I didn't scream, beg, or fight. Even though he took my body, I didn't give him the satisfaction of my pain or pleasure. He didn't break me. If I survive this, nothing ever will.

***

"Hold Katya down so she can't harm herself!" Ezra's harsh command is tinged with fear.

A sound pierces the night, an agonizing primal scream is sharply ringing in my ears. Over and over, like an alarm. It takes me a moment to realize it is *me* emitting the terrorized sound. *Me* thrashing on the bed. *Me* clawing, kicking, punching, and flailing at anything my hands and feet can connect with. Voice lost, energy drained, I fall lax to the bed while laboriously panting.

"What's happening? Did I hurt Kat somehow?" A naked

Aaron freaks out as he kneels on the edge of the bed, his hands trying to protect me, to ward off whatever is plaguing me.

"No, Aaron," Ezra softly sighs the words. "I thought this might happen. I'd *hoped* this would happen. Katya couldn't be told. She had to remember on her own... and now she is remembering." Ezra explains to comfort Aaron.

But I find little comfort in the words. I've remembered my torturous past in lifelike detail, experiencing it again as if it just happened. But I still cannot grasp the tentative thread– that tiny thread of knowledge that I intuitively know is somehow pivotal to my healing.

My eyes snap open when I finally come to terms with the fact that I'm no longer trapped in the past. I'm lying on a bed deep inside the recesses of Restraint. I am not hiding out in the scrub brush, with thorns snagging my already wounded flesh.

Aaron's hands barely restrain me as they slip in the sweat that sheens my body. "I'm okay. You can let go." All hands disappear on my word. Mind foggy, I realize something devastating.

"God, Aaron. I'm so sorry," I mutter in a panic. "Did I freak out during?" I grab his hand, so badly wanting him to understand it wasn't his fault; there was nothing he did wrong.

"No, Katya. It's okay. You were both napping for about twenty minutes before your nightmare started." Ezra speaks near my head as he leans a hip on the edge of the mattress. "It's all right, you're safe here with us."

I'm overcome with an insane need to bury my face against Ez's chest and bawl like a lunatic. I look around for Cortez, finding him standing at the foot of the bed, looking utterly petrified.

"What's the matter?" I ask Cortez.

"I...I... do you remember everything?" He looks like a frightened child, and I experience an overwhelming urge to comfort him.

"What do you mean, Cort?" I ask, tone showing my confusion.

"Um... I guess not. May I sit down, please? You scared the shit out of us. I guess we have a reprieve until you go batshit crazy on us again." He flops on the bed and exhales a heavy sigh.

"What did you remember, Katya?" Ezra's voice is soft, yet commanding– a mandate I must answer.

"My rape. Some things are fuzzy. I still can't see faces, and where names were spoken, I draw a blank. It's the most I've ever relived." I shiver, and draw a blanket around myself.

"It will come. Soon. You'll remember very soon, I think," Ezra guarantees. I give into my urge to press my face into Ezra's chest, an inhale his comforting, smoky, musky scent.

"I need to speak to Dr. Jeannine," I rasp out numbly.

Chapter Thirty-Five

After a lot of coaxing and reassuring, I'm finally alone in my bedroom. Cortez seemed frightened *of* me, and Ezra seemed frightened to be around me, so they were easy enough to avoid. Aaron, however, he is on guard duty, with all three of them in total agreement that I shouldn't be left alone.

Aaron took me home, and then refused to leave, even after I assured him that I was fine. I argued how I refused to speak with Dr. Jeannine if he was still with me. Spilling your soul, your deepest and darkest fears and secrets, should be done in private. It's about as personal as you can get.

Our compromise was for me to inhabit my bedroom with my laptop, while Aaron camped out on my sofa with a James Atwater Uncorrected Proof Copy he stole off my desk.

I wanted to contact my therapist immediately, but I couldn't bring myself to actually do it. My confusion was overwhelming. My mind was mush. No matter how much I concentrated, I can't hold a solid thought. So I took a long, hot shower, made Aaron and myself a meal, where we ate in companionable silence, and then I cleaned my entire apartment while Aaron pretended not to be in my way.

The cathartic nature of the menial did nothing for my mental state.

Three showers later, I decide a conversation with Dr. Jeannine is an absolute necessity. No matter how many times I shower, I cannot get the leader's filth out of my mind and body. I try to conjure images of making love to Aaron to cleanse my mind, yet fail. Raymond Hunter dominates every thought and emotion I have.

KitKat411: Dr. Jeannine?

liv2heal: Katya, it's been awhile. How is your progression fairing?

KitKat411: First, I would like to apologize for lashing out at you during our last session. It wasn't your fault, and I took it out on you anyway. I'm sorry.

liv2heal: Accepted. Obviously, I did nothing wrong. What has happened? You only contact me when forced.

KitKat411: I know I'm not very professional when it comes to our interactions. I realized that you were right, and I was fighting it. I repressed the memories because it was too painful to relive. I'd rather live in denial than face what truly happened to me. Being debased and violated is not something that is easy to admit. Now I understand how I must remember the past in order to have a healthy future.

Live2heal: Katya, you are not my only patient, and you are not the only one who behaves in such a manner. The majority do, because it's human nature to act as such. I know how to read a person's motivations, and that is why I am a good psychiatrist. Never feel shame about how you react. I take no offense, because I know your reactions are never about me. I'm here to heal you. It's all about you, Katya. While I appreciate your apology, it wasn't necessary. Now, what has happened since our last session?

KitKat411: A lot. For the first time in my life, I had consensual sex. It was with a friend, and it was nice. But I did freak out after it was over. I drifted off to sleep and entered a nightmare, remembering everything. Every smell. Every pain. Every sound. I can't remember the name I heard, but I know I heard it. The boys' faces are blurred. Other than those two very important details, I remember everything as if it just happened to me hours ago. I feel raw and exposed, and now I can't get it out of my head. It's like a building tempest, and when it crests, I will either remember the truth or I will break.

liv2heal: Katya, just breathe, and know everything will focus into sharp clarity when you can handle it. You will remember when your mind feels safe and secure. I promise. Soon. You'll remember soon.

KitKat411: I am so frustrated. I want to scream! I feel like if I could just overcome this block, then I could finally heal. I could finally move on.

liv2heal: This is major progress, Katya. Major.

KitKat411: I know. I can't believe I had real sex for the first time with a man tonight. I never thought I'd trust someone enough to let go, even for five seconds.

liv2heal: Do you believe that is what brought about the progress? How do you feel about that, Katya?

KitKat411: Yes. No. I don't know. Memories have swamped me since I started exploring my sexuality. I didn't freak out during the act as I had always feared I would. I was in the moment, not thrust back into the past. It was afterwards when the memories resurfaced in vivid detail, waiting to haunt my sleep.

liv2heal: I'm never one to prescribe sex, but clearly this is working. You need to overcome this block to heal. Focus all of your concentration on the details surrounding the fuzzy memories. Just go a few seconds before the blur, and try to discern every single detail, no matter how big or small. It might flow into the void, developing the repressed memory into clarity. When your mind determines you are ready, it will clear.

KitKat411: What if it never clears? I can't live with this suffocating feeling. The memories are assaulting me, but the blankness is strangling me. I feel crazed. It's insane to hate what I used to cherish. Before I didn't want to know, but now I do. What should I do?

liv2heal: Concentrate on a phrase, a scent, a small sliver of the memory that borders the fuzzy parts. This will be difficult, and undoubtedly painful. Calm yourself and focus until a part of the memory becomes sharp with clarity. The faded parts will slowly manifest when your mind realizes that the detail isn't going to harm you. This is a progression. You can't force it. This is a part of you that is locked away inside your mind. Only you can release the memories. I apologize, Katya. I must go. Please contact me with your progress.

KitKat411: Thanks for the help. Bye.

liv2heal: …logging off.

Restraint 360

Chapter Thirty-Six

The boys kept to their word by leaving me alone for the duration of the weekend. My mind feels like a hamster in a wheel, spinning and spinning, and going absolutely nowhere in my escape.

I did my usual: clean, cook, organize, workout, and primp. My cathartic routine still left me drawing a blank, no matter how much I focused around the haze.

Monday mornings are usually soul-suckers, but this is beyond a Monday. I feel dead inside, worse than the comforting numb I lived with for almost twelve years. Now I feel too much, sensitive to everything and anything, in or around me.

I must jump this hurdle, or I can run no farther. What was locked up nice and tight in the denial box has escaped and refuses to return. It's screaming to be heard. I feel like I did just after my rape. It's as raw and real as if it happened over the weekend, not a decade ago.

Making matters worse, I can't depend on the boring continuum of routine, where you do your job and nothing else matters. Kayla is a ghost, asking nothing of me, cancelling all of my meetings, leaving me to my own devices. I assume the boys told her to leave me alone, since she isn't even in the building. Monica and Alec are conveniently staking out book signing locations around Dominion, and won't be back until the end of the week. It's just me, the worker bees I never interact with, and Mailman Rick milling the halls. I'm desperate enough to bother the rest of Edge's employees, but I fear being a wrench in their well-oiled machine.

The largest shock is what's missing from my coffee table. A large mahogany box would be hard to sneak out of my office. I'm sure if I look in the obvious location, I will find it. I guess our chess match is at its final stages, where I'm left with the final move.

Who is Ez to me, and why can't I remove the blockage from my memory? Their answers will be my own personal checkmate.

I haven't been able to get one phrase out of my mind for days. It plays on repeat, demanding its mystery solved. The hamster continues to run its wheel, screeching the metal, grating on my nerves with mind-bending annoyance.

Soon. You'll remember very soon.

Over and over this phrase spins uncontrollably in my mind. The hamster's speed increases, the metal grinding continuously. The pressure in my mind is building. I grab my forehead and squeeze against the agony, as if the phrase itself is causing a fissure of truth to assault my memory.

Soon. You'll remember very soon.

Remember what? The past? I'm working on that, if only my mind would cooperate. My brain screams at me that I am not hearing it– not perceiving its gift of information correctly.

Soon. You'll remember very soon... Soon. You'll remember very soon... Soon. You'll remember very soon...

I kneel on the carpet, panting as the pressure builds, hands gripping the sides of my head. The pain is pounding, excruciating. It rivals any migraine that came before it.

Think! Dammit, think! Think! Remember!

Just as a scream boils up my throat, clarity overpowers me, removing the agony from my mind. It's not about remembering the past; it's about deconstructing the present. All roads always lead back to one man.

My body uncoils in unadulterated fury as I rise to my feet. If I thought my mind hurt, it is nothing compared to the betrayal that slams into my heart, or the shame over the fact that I'm yet again being a stupid girl.

How could I be so blind? How could he manipulate me in such a manner that I couldn't see the truth before me? How could he turn an intelligent woman with a heart of stone into the creature who exists today?

I don't like myself right now. But worse, I hate him.

To protect me, my body overpowers the ache to fill me with vengeance.

I experience a rush so addictive that if I could bottle it, I would make billions. I find myself on the first floor, just outside of Ezra's office, and I don't remember moving my feet a single inch. I'd run from my office to this very spot, and I remember nothing.

A rage blackout.

Roarke takes one look at my face as he sits behind his desk, and he raises his hands in the air as if I hold a gun pointed at his chest. He surrenders, not even calling out to the man he was born to protect.

Seeing red, I fling Ezra's office door open, and catch it with a single fingertip before it rebounds off the wall to bash my skull in.

Lunging, I jump to Ezra's desktop in one move, landing inches from him. Never have I moved so fluidly, so quickly. I feel more animal than man. A wash of shock crosses Ezra's face– jaw-dropping distress.

Crouched atop Ezra's desk like a feral animal, I lock stares with him. I coil all of my fury into my muscles, and then launch myself at him. I knock Ezra out of his chair, the harsh thud forcing the air out of both of us. The momentum propels us forward, and I ride his body several feet across the floor until the wall stops our path of travel. When we come to a rest, I'm already pummeling Ezra with my fists to the chest, the neck, the torso, upper arms, shoulders, and face.

Seething, nonsensical words flow from my mouth rabidly, as I beat Ezra into submission.

A hand tries to stop me, wrenching my head backward. But they made a fatal mistake by getting too close to my face. While pounding my fists, I jerk forward, biting the hand trying to restrain me.

The skin tastes soapy, clean, as my teeth sink in. Cortez. I hadn't realized he was here, but why wouldn't he be? Cort is always shoved up Ez's ass.

"Don't!" Ezra commands, and I almost stop. "Let Katya get it out. We deserve it!"

"You fucking B A S T A R D!" I scream in Ezra's face like a homicidal banshee, as my arm cocks backwards. With a forceful snap, I punch him in the face hard enough to draw blood.

"Katya, please stop. You're going to hurt yourself. You can't punch Ez's hard head with your tiny fist. You'll break it." Cortez sounds oh-so reasonable. "Your hand, not his head. Others have tried and failed. Ezra is indestructible."

Cortez is the least reasonable of the merry fucked up trio, living off of pure emotion. But now he's sounding rational, logical, which should be the tip-off that I'm not acting as I should. I'm not thinking clearly. But I can't muster the strength to care. All I see is red, and I want to enact my revenge.

"How could you? Do you have no boundaries? This is beyond human!" I scream.

"I had to save them at any cost," Ezra cries out. "It was life or death!"

Ezra's response momentarily stuns me. My readied fist falls to my lap as I sit perched on Ezra's chest. I'd been beating his handsome face with my fists. Blood drizzles out the corner of his mouth– blood I spilled.

"Katya, why don't you tell me what Ezra has done now," Cortez says calmly. He tries to pull me off of Ezra, but I don't allow it, gripping my thighs tighter around Ezra's chest.

"Is it punishment you're looking for? If so, this isn't how it's done. You could be like Ez, and mentally destroy your opponents. You could be like Aaron, and pretend it didn't hurt and turn the other cheek. You could be like me, and go batshit crazy. You don't want to be like me, Kitten. It hurts to have regrets."

"Punishment," I growl, staring into Ezra's eyes. "No one should have the power to run around and destroy lives just because they can. There must be consequences."

"All right, then. I will help you beat Ezra in the dungeon later. Good?" Cort tries to placate me. "We'll even have Aaron help. That's how it's done."

Cortez tries to pull me away from Ezra again. He clasps my fists in one of his own, making sure I won't hurt myself by beating Ezra. My knuckles are bloodied and bruised. He also puts a palm to my forehead, making sure I can't strike out with my teeth.

"This isn't the place for this. Our colleagues can hear."

Cortez is back to sounding oh-so reasonable again. "What if one of Dr. Zeitler's patients arrives? They aren't exactly stable to begin with. Some are criminals. They would go after you for harming the good doctor."

"Good?" I snort out.

Cort gently strokes my hair and whispers soothing words to me, most of them calling Ezra a ruthless bastard who needs to be taught a lesson. Soothing words of revenge. Cortez treats me like a wounded animal, or maybe a psychiatric patient.

Ezra is frozen beneath me, his eyes tracking my every movement. He says nothing, just patiently waits to see what else I will inflict.

"Ezra pretended to be my therapist, Dr. Jeannine," I utter without taking my eyes from Ezra. Shock flashes across his face. "I… I just can't believe the lengths you went to in order to invade my privacy. I would have told you if you'd asked. But no, you made up people who didn't exist. You had me bond with them, and then you came in like God and took them away."

I hit Ezra in the chest with my fist– it barely lands yet he still flinches from the contact. My punch was more out of frustration than the need to hurt him.

"Kimber was my friend," I sob, breath hitching in my throat. "She was real for me, and I grieve for her. Jeannine was my doctor, who I told very private things. I can't believe neither of them never really existed. My emotions don't know that, though. They were very real for me, and now they're dead," I sob out the last word. "My narrow world just lost two people in a matter of days."

Ezra continues to stare up at me with shame filling his eyes. Speechless, he just breathes and bleeds while allowing true emotions to wash across his features.

"You should have just come to me as yourself, as Dr. Zeitler, and as Ezra. I would have trusted you if you were real. I would have loved you as you are."

A maniacal laugh bubbles up Cortez's throat, scaring me to the core of my being. "If this is how Kat reacts to this, she will never speak to us again when she gets the rest of the truth,

Ezra. You really should have just told her three years ago. Yeah, Dr. Zeitler knows best. I don't fucking think so," he says snidely, continuing to laugh without humor.

"I can't trust you. I don't trust you." A keening noise erupts from me, and I use all of the emotional control I possess to smother it.

Dr. Ezra Zeitler will not break me. Nothing ever does and nothing ever will.

Ezra looks me in the eye as he clenches his fists in the back of my shirt. "Listen to me, Katya," he orders, and I comply. I calm as my green eyes meet his stormy gray.

"I am a psychiatrist. I know what I am doing. I went into this field because I'm mentally ill, have been since I was twelve years old, way before I was abducted. I can relate to my patients, because I am someone else's patient. I know what they are going through. I know what you are going through."

"Ez, that may be true," Cort whispers. "But you would kill the first person who fucked with you like you're fucking with Kat. You wouldn't stand for it, and neither should she."

Ezra ignores Cort, talking right over him. "I made the decision to become a psychiatrist long before I was abducted and harmed. After that, it was the only thing that kept me sane, knowing I could help others. Three years ago, when I finally found you, I wanted to tell you the truth, but that wouldn't have helped you– healed you. This game between you and I has been an intense therapy session meant to draw the memories that you've been denying yourself. You need to heal, and I'm healing you in the only way I know how. I'm sorry that it was unconventional, underhanded, fucked up, and wrong. But I never said I wasn't any of those things."

"I... I don't even know what to say about that," I half whine, confusion thick in my voice. "All this was in the name of therapy?"

"Yes and no. It was for our *mutual* therapy, not just you and me, but others as well. We all need to heal from the past, from events not of our making, events out of our control. We all need to regain our power. You've yet to truly remember, and until you have, you cannot heal. When you finally give in to the memories, then and only then, will I allow you to push me away and hate me. But until then, you'll do what I say for our sanities' sake."

"I…" I don't know what I want to say, but Ezra silences me with a fingertip to my parted lips.

"No, I've explained all that I can. The rest is up to you, Katya." Eyes flicking to the man standing behind me, "Cort, please take Katya to her apartment. Do not leave her alone for a second," he says, and then he returns his gaze back to me and continues. "I'm giving you a few hours to think. Tonight. The dungeon. We'll work this out. You can punish me for our trespasses. But you still need to remember," he warns.

Cortez drags me off Ezra, but my legs won't support my body. They trail like dead weight as I'm pulled away from my master. The sobs I'd suppressed, finally bubble up as my heart breaks. I'd say it breaks into two, but no– three. It's killing me inside.

Cortez finally gives up on me finding my own footing, and hauls me into his arms. "Kiss her goodbye," Cortez orders Ezra.

"Cort, I don't think that's such a good idea," Ezra murmurs, sounding guilty. "Lest you forgot the teeth marks embedded in your hand."

"Don't be a coward. Do it. Nothing is irreparable. It's a miracle we're all alive. As long as we live, forgiveness is possible. C'mon, kiss Kitten goodbye. If she bites, at least I will have something to laugh about." Cort flashes a sly smirk.

Ezra slowly approaches me, as if afraid to spook me. He cups my face in his hands tenderly, as if I'm made of spun glass. When his lips connect with mine, I sob and clutch my chest against the sweet-edged pain.

Warm drops hit my face, and at first, I think they are tears from my eyes until I look to Ezra. Liquid emotion streams down the sides of his face, and it's my undoing. I kiss him gently, just a brush of lips. Ezra trembles at the contact, and then sighs, as if in agony as he pulls away.

"You both have the afternoon to think up something creative. Make the punishment brutal. I deserve it." Ezra looks to Cortez and me with his face full of shame and anguish.

Chapter Thirty-Seven

"I'm going to take a shower," I call to Cortez as I weave my way through my living room. I try to lose him in the hopes he has proper manners and won't follow me into the bathroom.

I'm raw, as if my psyche is an open wound weeping from the collection of recent and not-so recent tragedies. I just want to be left alone so I can deal with it in peace, and maybe plot my revenge.

For once, I want my pound of flesh. I've earned it. I deserve it. Why should I always have to turn the other cheek? Maybe people like Ezra would stop harming others in their egomaniacal quests if they knew what the bitter tang of betrayal truly felt like.

Cortez's fingers wrap around my forearm before I can make a break for it. "Hey, I think we need to talk about this. You've got a lot going on right now. Let's work it out. Okay?" Cort asks, sounding hopeful, trying to use his charm to get me to do as he asks.

I stare Cortez down. The animal is still in control. I no longer hurt: mentally, physically, or emotionally. I feel more clear-headed than I have in almost twelve years. I am no victim. I endured an hour of hell in my favorite place on Earth. I've held the consequences of that hour ever since. I've brought a person into this world, and she will never feel these far-reaching consequences wrought upon me.

Ezra did what he thought was right, what he was trained to do. He tried to slowly pull my issues out until I could face them. He tried to coax my repressed memories gently. I may understand it, but he was wrong in his execution. He should have come to me as himself. Whether it was Dr. Jeannine or Dr. Zeitler, it would have played out the same, only I wouldn't feel the sting of betrayal right now. He will pay for that mistake. It's about time someone pays the price of their betrayal when they destroy me.

"Ah, Cortez... do you want to hold me while I break?" I purr seductively, yet a snide flavor warps my voice. "Do you think I need to be coddled and cuddled? Do you want to hold my hand while I cry?" Sarcasm twists the venom dripping from my voice, making Cortez unsure what emotion is fueling the words. "News flash– I won't break. I. Never. Break."

Taken aback, Cortez's hand drops as he says, "That's not healthy. We all needs someone to shoulder our burdens from time to time."

"Don't pull Ezra's psycho-babble out on me, Cort," I warn. "I've cried enough on you guys' shoulders, back when I was dumb enough to trust you. I was cold and smart, and then Ez manipulated me into feeling warm and safe again. I'm no longer that dipshit of a woman I've been for the past two months."

Cort tries to be the voice of reason again. Scary thought. "Kat–"

But I cut him off. "I never lie down and wait for help that will never arrive. I won't be passive. I take matters into my own hands and save myself. That's what smart people do."

"Smart people also recognize the person standing before them as someone who they can trust, someone who is only here because they want to help. A smart person knows when to ask for help instead of being stubborn. Maybe I should have Aaron tell you this shit, since I'm usually the one he smacks in the face with reality."

"I don't need your help right now. I need to regroup, to plan my next course of action," I bite out.

"And out of everyone you know, who the fuck do you think is the best person for that job?" Cort snarls. "I'm a goddamned writer. *Your* writer." Cortez gestures to his body, not only talking with his hands, but screaming with them. "I'm the motherfucking plot master! So let's go plot, Kitten."

"I don't know if I can trust you," I whisper.

"Trust this," Cort breathes into my face, getting angrier with every word spoken. "I've been with Ez since birth, and he's fucked me over time and time again. He's left me feeling just as bereft, raw, betrayed, and wounded as you feel right now. Worse, actually. So trust that I want to punish Ezra more than you could ever imagine, even if I have to use you to do it.

Trust *that*, Kitten."

My throat clenches– a remembrance of how far Cortez Abernathy is willing to go to teach Ezra a lesson, even if he has to use me to do it. *That*, I can trust.

No soft touches between us as Cort looks into my eyes, knowing the exact direction of my thoughts. He doesn't apologize. He doesn't shrug or nod. He doesn't even smirk. He just keeps staring at me with blatant honesty and a need to seek his own vengeance, even if he has to use my pain as an excuse.

"Ezra never apologizes to you, does he? He never allows you to punish him, does he?"

"Never," Cort breathes; eyes glossy, fists clenched. "Not once. Ez hits me where it hurts the most, using mental tactics I can't avoid. The sick thing is, he doesn't even realize he's harming me in the process. The few times I've hurt him, it was nothing compared to the pain he's dealt me. So, what's the plan, Kitten? We *both* need this."

Cortez looks at me as if he's seeing me for the very first time. We've been around each other a few times, and I've never felt as if I ever really got to know him. Yes, being skull-fucked was enlightening. But reading Cortez Abernathy's books had given me even more insight into him as a person. Of all the conversations we've held so far, this moment is the first time I've understood Cortez on a human level.

I look back at Cort as well, truly seeing him for the person he is, and liking what I see. Cort is my mirror image, more like me than anyone I've ever met.

Aaron is childlike in his pain. He's severely loyal to Ezra, which is a detriment to his other relationships. I'm not discrediting him for it. I love him in spite of it. Aaron will always put Ezra above all others, no matter the consequences. Which means I can only trust Aaron if Ezra has my best interests at heart. My lack of trust in Ezra means Aaron's loyalty is not a chance I'm willing to take.

Ezra reacts all right, but on his own terms. He is selfless because he takes care of Aaron and Cortez first, but selfish because he does it to punish himself. The air around him is permeated with self-hatred. Doesn't Ezra realize he can't truly love someone else if he can't love himself? He'll always doubt their love, because why should they love what he hates?

Ezra is a martyr.

Cortez sees to his needs and wants first. It sounds selfish, but it's not. How can you help others if you can't help yourself? You must be at your strongest to tackle what life throws in your path. You cannot allow someone else to leach your strength, to drain you, or else you can't shoulder your own burdens, let alone someone else's. Cortez doesn't break. He doesn't wallow in his pain. He knows he's fucked up, and accepts that fact with open arms. His attitude allows him to accept everyone else despite their problems. It's a simple way of living– ruthless and practical. I accept them all.

"Are you going to go take a shower and cry like a little bitch, or are you going to grow a pair and help me plot?" Cort challenges me, more so with his unflinching attitude than with his words. "You with me?"

"I'm with ya," I utter, never breaking his stare. My mind forms our plan in an instant. "We're going shopping, and then we're setting up the dungeon. I need you to do a few things for me, like get people rounded up. This will go down in history as a phenomenal punishment."

"You're not really going to hurt Ezra, are you?" Cort looks at me like I've lost my mind, causing a wicked smirk to pull at my lips. "I'm not sure I'm comfortable with that," he breathes out.

"Says the man who used me to punish Ezra. Yeah, I ain't buying your bullshit, buddy," I taunt as Cort chokes on a laugh. "Oh, Ezra will hurt, all right. Just not physically– much. We're going to hurt him where it matters. Cerebral fuckage, Dr. Ezra Zeitler-style."

"Just hearing that made me spring wood," Cort sighs, eyes slipping shut as he shifts the growing bulge around in his pants with the heel of his palm. Groaning from the contact, I realize I better distract Cort before he fucks himself. He's shameless enough to masturbate before me, of that I have little doubt.

"Ezra made a mistake. While he was studying me under his microscope, I was learning him as well. I know his weaknesses, and we're going to prey upon them. Most importantly, no one knows how to hurt Ez as much as you do."

We share a conspiratorial smile for what's to come.

"I like you, Kitten. I feared all I'd feel was jealousy when Ezra brought you back into our lives, like you were my replacement. But honest to God, I really, *really* like you. You fit in; you were meant to be in our group, because we all complement one another in perfect harmony."

Cortez stalks toward me, his naughty, anticipatory smirk backing my ass up. I keep moving away as he tracks me across my living room. Something snaps in the man as I act as prey. He turns predatory. Hunting. Seeking. Not allowing my escape, Cort yanks my hair hard, tightly wrapping his fingers in the tendrils.

Without thought, we collide in a forceful kiss: lips mashing together, teeth nipping, tongues dueling, fingertips bruising by gripping and pulling. We punish each other. We punish Ez, even if he doesn't give two-shits and will never find out. With a gasp, I push Cort off of me, but only after I've fiercely returned his kiss.

Was it wrong to kiss Cort? Yes.

Was it thrilling to do it? Yes.

Do I want to do it again? Abso-fucking-lutely.

Will I do it again? God, I hope not.

I'm not ready to admit to myself how I'd be perfectly happy fucking all three of them. My subconscious is calling me a whore, but I don't give a shit. I have a lot of living to make up for, and a lot of rites of passages to experience, all because I allowed fear to rule over me.

It's freeing.

I feel independent in my whoredom.

"I'll call Aaron." Cortez reaches for his cell phone.

"No!" I shout, grabbing Cort's cell from his hand. "Aaron loves Ezra too much. He'll spoil our plans. Don't worry. He'll be in on the action. We all will," I say ominously. A wicked, devious smile stretches across my face as I think of all of us doling out the ultimate of punishments.

Restraint 374

Chapter Thirty-Eight

"Thank you for coming. Ladies and gentlemen. Mistresses and Masters of Restraint. Dominants and submissives. Restraint members and their guests. We have a fun and exciting show planned for you this evening." I announce grandly, exhibiting the bravado of a circus ringmaster. My tone demonstrates the excitement flowing through me into the gathering crowd.

This part of the punishment is twofold: Ezra isn't an exhibitionist, nor has he ever been topped. He will be humbled by something we all have to deal with on a daily basis, swallowing one's pride while taking directions we wish not to heed. Ezra will hate the lack of control, the powerlessness, and the inability to be the master of his own destiny.

Basically, Dr. Ezra Zeitler is getting a taste of his own bitter medicine, and as a man of his dominant level, he'll have a harder time swallowing it than the rest of us.

In anticipation of Ezra's punishment, Cortez had rounded up Restraint's membership, and each are accompanied by a guest or two. The dungeon is packed wall-to-wall with hungry voyeurs, impatiently waiting for their resident antagonizer to be knocked back down to Earth from his god-complex pedestal.

"Aaron," I call to my reluctant lover, if one can call a one-night-stand a lover. By the nasty bitch-glare Aaron is throwing my way, he is now my *ex*-lover.

Aaron doesn't tolerate anyone being mean to his hero, and that was why I couldn't allow Cort to call Aaron beforehand. Aaron would have done everything in his considerable power to stop me, meaning I'd be locked in my apartment right now, with no hope of escape. He wouldn't be mean to me. He'd just thwart me at every turn.

"Please bring in our misbehaving, multiple pseudonym-using master," I order Aaron, and he shoots me another death-glare.

If I was a lesser woman, I'd be shaking in my boots as Aaron stalks off to get Ez, snapping the last thread on our tentative friendship as he goes. Wistfulness and sadness threaten to descend, but I have more important matters at hand than Aaron's emotional immaturity at the moment.

Ezra strides across the floor, head held high, shoulders back, a perfect, unfaltering gait, with his eyes peering at me through the cutouts in the hood he uses for anonymity purposes. I hate how he must cover his face. I'd do anything in this moment to read his expression.

My belly stirs, lust and need awakening, and another powerful emotion I cannot name joins the mix. My God, this is what I want. I am about to top my own master, and it feels fan-fucking-tastic.

Ezra, seeing my visible excitement, smirks at me, eyes dancing with mirth.

Oh, Master Ez, you won't be smiling in a few seconds.

"Boss, stand directly in the center of the dungeon, beneath the suspended hook hanging from the ceiling," I command.

I'm taken aback when Ezra actually obeys me by standing exactly where I ordered him to do so. He flashes me a look, as if asking, '*What now?*'

"Our gracious master gifted me with a pair of cuffs, ones I had no way of removing. I think I should return the favor, don't you? What do you think? Should I leash our boss?"

I jingle the cuffs in front of Ezra's slowly widening eyes, as the crowd whoops and catcalls their agreement. The excitement in the room is palpable, almost beating against my skin.

"Master Ez, don't move, or else you will leave me with no recourse but to educate you. It would hurt me more than you. You don't want that, now do you?" I mock the tone he used on me when he spoke those very words.

Ezra's lips part as he drags more air into his lungs, clearly torn between worry and amusement. His unexpected reaction makes me grin wider. I'd feared Ezra would be furious with me, and I'd see the threat of payback dwelling in his eyes.

As I'm lifting Ezra's arm to give me better access to his wrist, he gives me a gentle squeeze to my fingertips, silently telling me he's not angry with me. We hold a conversation without saying a single word as I latch a leather cuff to each of his wrists. I give the latch a good yank to make sure they are secure.

"Feel good?" I give another tug.

"Yes, it's not too bad." Ez say loudly, voice tripping into arrogant territory. His lips upturn at the corners into a sly grin.

I whip out two pink wristbands, and slide them over the leather cuffs while snickering at the abrupt change that overcame the cocky man. Ezra looks positively humbled by the wristbands adorned with tiny, furry mice.

I smile sweetly as I snap each into place. "Still not too bad?" I say in return, using Ez's cocky swagger against him.

Oh, Master Ez no like. His pupils dilate, his nostrils flare, and he bares his teeth in a silent snarl. He doesn't yank away from me, but I can feel the tension filling his muscles, and the desperate struggle to submit versus beat me into submission with his mind games.

I flash my fangs at Ezra in retaliation. "Maybe I'll gift you with a set of caps. That snarl of yours isn't nearly as intimidating as mine." I flash my fangs again.

"You did always like to bite," he says defensively, but it's as if his words have multiple meanings. "Allow my flesh to be your canvas as an apology."

I trail a laugh as I lower the chain, bringing the hook within my grasp. Accessing the metal rings on the leather cuffs hidden beneath the mouse wristbands, I use a carabiner to attach them to the hook. Once all is secure, I yank the chain until Ez's arms string tight overhead. I pull a bit more, until he has to find purchase with the tips of his shoes.

During the whole process, I can only see Ezra's eyes and mouth through the cutouts in the hood, noting both are taut from strain. Strain to surrender to my orders, not from any true physical discomfort.

"Hmm, we have to do something with these feet of yours. I wouldn't want you to accidentally kick me."

The crowd releases laughs, guffaws, and chuckles when Ez pretends to kick me, only to lose his proper footing to begin swinging like a pendulum from his hook.

I reach to the side, and produce a spreader bar. I wave it in front of Ezra's face, antagonizing him, watching for his reaction, and he doesn't disappoint.

"Katya, that won't be necessary. You know I won't hurt you." His voice is pleading, dry and thick with fear. Apparently Ezra doesn't like being restrained, suffering from the ultimate loss of power and control.

"It's a very humbling experience to be at the mercy of others," I school Ez. "Things do happen in the heat of the moment. Sometimes you can't control your visceral reaction to fear. I trust you not to harm me on purpose, but I don't trust you not to harm me by accident. Isn't that why we're here in the first place?"

Ezra's eyes cloud over with guilt, his lips form a hard line, and his knuckles turn white, acknowledging his defeat.

"Would you all like to know why the almighty, always-in-control Boss is being punished?" I rotate in a circle as I address the crowd. They create a perfect arc around the four of us: Ezra, Aaron, Cortez, and myself.

"Master Ez told me I should trust him, and then he betrayed the trust he stole. All because he didn't cherish that in which he never earned. He just took my trust, thinking it absolute, and then he abused it as if it was infinite. We all know he'd never put up with the likes of that from us. His punishment, or as I'd rather call it– *education* –was his own idea. Now, should I trust Master Ez not to lash out with a foot in the middle of his education, when there is no trust established between us anymore?"

BOOOO... erupts from the crowd.
NO!
Kick his ass!
Show 'em who's boss!
Knock that arrogant ass down a few pegs.
Cum-dumpster cunt!

The last expletive mysteriously sounded as if it was directed at me, distinctly sounding feminine. I ignore it, knowing Master Ez has his devoted followers who will act just like Aaron when push comes to shove.

"The masses have decided your fate, Master. Perhaps you should have been nicer to them," I chastise.

Ezra growls at me, baring his teeth again. But, thankfully, he doesn't move a muscle.

I squat down to remove Ezra's shoes and socks, giving the arch of his foot a little tickle and the heel of his foot a bit of a relaxing squeeze. I place the spreader bar between his feet, and secure his ankles with leather straps. The chain strings him so tautly that his big toes are the only things touching the concrete. I push my palm on his bulging crotch and shove. He grunts, sounding simultaneously pleasured and pained as his body rocks back and forth until he comes to a rest.

I link my toes on a footstool to drag it in front of Ezra. With a hop on top, I'm standing face-to-face with him.

"I really don't like that hood of yours. It doesn't suit you. You have such a lovely face. I miss your sharp nose and your chiseled jawline. It's a shame to cover it up."

"Don't," Master Ez commands in a deep voice filled with the promise of violence, even if his eyes are bulging from fright.

"I should punish you for your insolence. Worse is your lack of faith in me." We lock eyes as my expression flashes bitter disappointment. "Trust is a two-way street. If it's one-sided, it will never work. This is something you are in desperate need of learning. Your actions scream that you don't trust anyone."

"Not entirely true," Ezra whispers.

"Not me, though," I murmur with sadness creeping into my voice. "And I've never given you reason to doubt me, unlike you for me."

"I will acknowledge that," Ez concedes.

"Baby Boy," I call to our reluctant Aaron, who quickly places a mask in my palm. "This–" I shove the mask in between us. "–is for your face. Proof in how little you trust me. We are all to trust in you. I think it's time you returned the gesture. After all, this is what put you in your current predicament." I whisper the last in Ez's ear.

I'm sure the majority of the people in this dungeon have

met Ezra personally or professionally, or they wouldn't be allowed in here in the first place, especially with his penchant of distrust.

I slide the hideous sack-like hood up to Ezra's nose and place the new mask underneath it, being extra careful to hide his true identity. I fit the elastic over his perfectly-shared ears, securing the mask over his eyes. I yank that god-awful sack from his head and toss it to Cortez.

"Burn that damn thing," I order, loving the feeling of control that overcomes me. "I don't want to see it ever again. And get a new one for your gorgeous face while you're at. The pair of you look like deranged executioners at a hanging."

I try not to smile in the face of Ezra's seriousness. I stroke his newly revealed sculpted cheeks and rounded chin, feeling the power of being able to touch him any way I want, and he can't do a damned thing about it. I nuzzle his flawless skin with the tip of my nose, and he relaxes for me and nuzzles back. A purr-like noise falls from his parted lips.

"I hate the hood, because it hinders all access to your mouth. I happen to love that sensuous mouth of yours." I lean forward and lick Ezra's lower lip, he groans in response and loses his footing as he tries to get closer to me.

For a moment, I watch as Ezra sways in his binds, making sure he doesn't harm himself. When he comes to a full stop, I hop down from my perch. I release a thrilled laugh as I kick the stool out of my way.

"What do ya think, members? Doesn't the Boss look adorable?" The crowd erupts into a fit of raucous laughter at the sight of their master. His new mask is a mousy: big puffy cheeks, whiskers, and a set of pink-lined ears.

"What? What's so funny?" Ezra sounds frantic, head turning left and right, as the crowd laughs at his new mask.

"Payback's a bitch, Boss." I flick his gift to me as a hint—the kitty cat ears that sit atop my head. My Kat to Ezra's mouse. "I think he's overdressed. Who, here, has always wanted to know what's underneath all these designer, Italian rags?"

Take it off!

Woo!
Strip! Strip! Strip!
Let's see that cock!
Wagers! I bet ten grand he's hard!
I'll take that wager. I bet two grand he's not.
You better pay me that twelve grand to look.
I'd give anything to see that cock! I'd even pay a hundred grand to see it hard.

"You have a fan," I snicker, blushing at whoever that over-enthusiastic dude is. "It seems the crowd agrees with me. I really want to see you naked," purrs salaciously from my throat. I grab Ezra's package while I nip his chin with my front teeth. He rocks in his binds, grunting, trying to grind his bulge into my palm without avail.

"I don't see what the big deal is. He's not *that* impressive," Cort deadpans. "I'd know," he mouths to me, grinning like a villain.

Bullshitter.

"I deserve this, I guess." Ezra sighs like we're actually executing him. "I should have placed restrictions and boundaries on my punishment. My fault. *Again*." He reaches new heights of martyrdom and passive-aggressiveness.

I shake my head in utter disbelief as Aaron and Cortez chuckle in unison.

"Boundaries? You think you have the right to set boundaries on what happens to you, when you offer us none," incredulity is thick in my tone as my eyebrows reach my hairline in astonishment. "That's fucking rich."

"I won't apologize for that," Ezra murmurs petulantly, like a small child who is incapable of taking responsibility for his own actions.

"No apologies necessary, because you'll be punished for it, and you'll learn your lesson well," I issue as a warning. "Skull-fuck, bring me the instrument of clothing removal, please." I hold my hand out for the shears I gave Cortez earlier.

"N-i-c-e," Cort drawls, impressed how I've managed to incorporate his punishment into Ezra's as well. He places the shears into my outstretched palm, and my fingers immediately curl around the cold metal.

Cort leans in to whisper to me. "Kitten, the members will think it's for an entirely different reason. So you better explain, or I'll kick your tiny behind."

"Let it be known that from this moment forward. He–" I point to a naughty and grinning Cortez, "–shall only be known only as Skull-fuck."

The crowd erupts, cackling and throwing insults.

No shit.

His mouth is like a bottomless cavern.

Skull-fuck has seen more action than a gay porn star!

Any porn star!

Such a sweet, tender mouth.

Who here hasn't fucked him?

Not me! He punched me!

My only regret was screwing that cocksucker, and I've had a hard life.

I volunteer!

It seems Hundred-Grand-Man is partial to both of the Ezes in his enthusiasm.

"Fix this," Cort seethes into my ear, growling, "Before Ez thinks I've been doing shit I haven't been. You think I'm jealous and territorial, you ain't seen shit until you've seen Ezra in full-out psycho-mode."

I have to wait for the crowd to settle down before I can explain, as they lob very pointed insults, which means the majority of the members knows exactly who is whom underneath those stupid hoods. Kristal's husky voice flows to my ears, evidently on the Pro-Cort side, going on and on about his pussy licking prowess.

"Dude, we're going to need some negative test results before I ever let you kiss me again. *If* I ever let you kiss me again," I murmur out the side of my mouth, amusing the hell out of Aaron, but simultaneously pissing Cortez and Ezra off at the same time.

"It's Skull-fuck's punishment for fucking my throat raw without permission. While the Boss punished that beautiful mouth of his," I murmur affectionately as my fingertips outline

Cortez's pouty lips, and he eagerly presses into my touch. "I haven't had the pleasure of educating him right from wrong. I have a strap-on with his name on it. So, until I get to use it, let us call him Skull-fuck."

Skull-fuck sounds in unison from dozens of voices.

"Fuck, girl. You're a brutal bitch," calls Queen from the crowd. "We all thought you'd let him walk all over you."

I look into Queen's awed green eyes, and I show her that I'm strong enough to equal them. They will not turn me into a submissive groveling at their feel. I am their equal, and I will only submit when the need strikes. I'm a switch, and no amount of manipulation and mind games will change my core personality.

I show Ezra the shears, and revel in the sight of his fear. Hmm, that's some heady shit. It's beyond intoxicating to hold all the power– to offer them either pleasure or pain.

I start at Ezra's wrists, running the blade up his sleeves as I cut them away. He shivers as if cold with fear, but his bulge is doing its damnedest to nudge my hip, begging for attention. I grip each side of the front of Ez's shirt, and give a quick yank. The buttons pop off and fling around the dungeon. Several of the watchers scatter after the disks, whooping when they catch their souvenirs.

I take care removing Ezra's cuff links, and then hand them to an ever-helpful Aaron for safekeeping.

"Hmm… hope that wasn't your favorite shirt, sir," I say sarcastically, knowing full and well how one of Ezra's shirts costs almost as much as the entirety of my wardrobe.

I watch emotions war on Ezra's beautiful face. He's embarrassed and humiliated, lowered to a humbling position, and he doesn't want to admit it's arousing him. He's failing on all accounts, and it's obvious when I cut away his pants.

"Oh, master," I whistle out when I take in the sight of him, seeing him in the flesh for the first time. "That's mighty impressive. It's no wonder Skull-fuck didn't think I'd notice the difference." I gaze unabashedly at his hard, thick cock as it throbs, trying to bob closer to my face.

Nudging to the side to offer them a quick view, "Ladies

and Gentlemen, our master has nothing to be ashamed of at all. What do you all think?"

Holy shit!

Horse cock!

Doesn't that rip you in two?

Lord, have mercy.

Mine's bigger.

So's mine.

Wager: cock measuring contest. Who's willing?

NO! Not if Dexter's third leg counts.

It's not a leg. It's my dick, and you'd all lose.

Aaron looks pissed, and he's scowling in my direction. But Cortez is laughing hysterically and watching little Ezra with unveiled interest. I laugh right back at Cort when he licks his lips as if he's hungry for a taste of something he's gone a decade without, when he just had a taste last week. The way Cort's eyeing Ezra's cock like it's the fountain of life, makes me wonder if he still has a taste for male flesh.

Yet again, I know I've gotten in way over my head.

Ezra's face and chest are bright red from embarrassment, yet little Ezra is bobbing up and down, begging for attention. At least a part of Ezra is enjoying itself.

"I hope you all appreciated the view. But this Kitty Kat doesn't wanna share, so I have a special outfit for our misbehaving master."

Ah!

No!

Don't cover him up!

Yes, cover that up. I don't want to see it!

I pick up a piece of gray fabric, and tie the top around his neck and the middle around his stomach. I wiggle the fabric until his cock pokes out the tiny slit up the front. He bobs his head in approval. Ezra's cock likes eyes on him. I step back as I try not to laugh hysterically.

"What do we think of the Boss's apron?" I bite my tongue against the rising giggles.

Make me a sandwich, bitch!

What's cooking, good looking?

Kat, use his whisk!

Does he need some cheese? I have some nut-cheese he can lick off my taint.

Asshole! I thought you smelled like fromunda cheese.

Behave, children. I'm not going to break you guys up, nor am I going to clean up spilt blood. Just because tattoos hide bruises...

"Your membership seems a bit hostile," I mutter to Cort as the same 'cum-dumpster' shouting woman tears into a new voice, with Queen running interference.

"I'm just glad it's Dalton and not me. Syn's a cruel bitch, but so is Dalton," Cort snarls, evidently his hate-list is rather long.

When the crowd continues to cackle overtop of the fighting Dalton and Syn, Ezra demands, "What's so funny? What's on the apron?" He sounds more confused than angry. The struggles begin as he tries to look down at himself but the mask is impeding his view. "Dammit!"

I prance around Ezra, swaying my hips and shaking my ass. I'm dressed up as Master Ez's Kitty Kat: black latex catsuit and kitty cat ears. I rub my ass on little Ezra, twitching my tail. I hear a satisfying groan as I stand back up. I sashay around him again, scratching my nails down his back and ass. I stand before him and crouch. I wait until his eyes meet mine, and then I pounce, baring my fangs with a playful hiss.

"What the fuck?" Ezra laughs out, looking at me like I've lost my mind, and it's so unexpected that he can't possibly wrap his mind around it.

I scent mark Ezra's chest as I make purr noises. "Meee-oooowww," I whisper in his ear, and then I nip the lobe with my fangs. He laughs that intoxicating sound in response: smoky, deep, and highly addictive.

"I think for the rest of the night the Boss should be called Mousy, don't you?" I ask the crowd.

Mousy! Mousy! Mousy!

Ezra stormy eyes narrow, eyebrows turning into angry slashes on his forehead. His lips flatten taut with fury. "You didn't dress me up as a fucking mouse, did you?" he spits out.

"You better not have, Katya. Tell me you didn't."

"You don't want me to lie to you, do you?" I ask innocently, eyes downcast while rocking back and forth on my heels with my hands tucked behind my back like a good girl. "What happens in the dungeon stays in the dungeon, especially for the Kitty Kat's Mousy." I smile menacingly, revealing my kitty cat teeth.

"This isn't fucking Vegas or Fight Club, and this isn't fucking funny, Katya," Ez spits.

"You can't punish me for what happens during your own punishment, Master. After all, it's your own fault for not setting clear boundaries," I say patronizingly, with a wicked edge to my tone.

In answer, Ezra releases a string of obscenities that would make a drunken sailor proud.

"Now shut the fuck up, or I will gag you," I threaten in a syrupy sweet voice. "Skull-fuck, punish him for being disrespectful," I order with a smile.

I step aside so Cortez can stand before Ezra. He lifts a camera and takes a series of shots from different angles. Ezra is so incensed that he is swaying, arms straining to hold his weight. He looks like an enraged fish dangling on a hook.

I grab Ezra's hips to steady him, and he feels so good under my hands that I sigh. I glance up at him from beneath the lace of my eyelashes with intense heat glowing from my eyes. I show Ezra, rather than tell him, how I feel about him. Ezra's lips part on a sharp intake of breath. Even though I know I shouldn't, I can't help myself from comforting him in the only way I can provide right now.

I start kissing a path up Ezra's lanky chest, luxuriating in his musky, manly scent and the sensation of his velvety skin beneath my lips. I notice a small ridge of scar tissue, and tongue it, lapping around the edges. As my tongue makes contact with the crescent-shaped mark, Ezra groans gutturally deep from his chest, and his cock throbs against my belly, spurting its scorching hot release.

We both freeze, shocked with Ezra's reaction, neither sure of what just took place.

"What's so special about this scar?" Confusion strongly laces my voice.

I place a soft kiss on the indentions. A bite mark? I fit my teeth over the marks, testing their size. They're small– a female marked him. I roll my eyes up to meet Ezra's, and his penetrating gaze pierces me like a dagger to the heart.

"She must have been very special for you," I whisper.

"She is," he whispers back, voice husky with want. "She left her eternal mark at the climax of our first time together." His voice is soft and full of affection. Something about his tone and words makes my heart ache– an ache I cannot handle.

Emotionally distancing myself, I reach my arm out. Anticipating my needs, Aaron places the torn shirt in my palm. I clean up my catsuit, and then gently wipe little Ezra dry. Master Ez sputters when my fingers make contact with his bare flesh. I whimper, hungering to explore his body with more than a passing, accidental touch.

I could have humiliated Ezra by allowing the crowd to see his release. But Ezra was so good at hiding his reaction that I want to respect him by keeping it a secret.

I hook my foot on the stool again, tugging it closer, and then mount it. I need to be face-to-face with Ezra.

"Say you're sorry. Apologize," I demand. "And mean it."

The crowd eggs Ezra on. *Apologize! Apologize! Sorry! Apologize! Sorry!* They chant for several long minutes, until I hold my forearm up to halt them, and they shush immediately.

"I am so sorry, Katya Evangeline Waters. I would kneel before you if I could." Ezra's voice is so sincere that I almost stop everything, but I can't, though. He has to learn, or he'll do it again, never understanding the consequences of his actions or the pain he's placed on others. Ezra needs to repent, and we, his victims, need the closure. Our relationship needs to be about trust and mutual respect, or it needs to not be at all.

"Why are you sorry?" I murmur softly, needing to hear the words said out loud, to make sure Ezra isn't just going through the motions and telling me what I want to hear.

"I'm sorry I impersonated both Jeannine and Kimber. I thought I was doing the right thing at the time. I understand your grief at their loss. I didn't anticipate that when I formulated the plan. I'm sorry I played this as a game. I should have just come to you three years ago when I found you, and told you everything. I just didn't know how to say the words." Ezra closes his eyes, cutting off all access to his emotions.

"Holy fuck, this is hard," Ez hisses, sounding agonized. "They don't make a Hallmark card for what I need to say to you. I still believe you must uncover the truth for yourself, and I will not ruin your progress by doing it for you. I deeply apologize for any harm and pain I have unintentionally wrought upon you." He leans towards me to rest his forehead against mine. "I do trust you," Ezra breathes against my face. "I will earn yours again. I promise you this."

Overcome with intense, unexpected, forbidden emotions, I grab Ezra's face and kiss him fiercely. I inhale him into me: his intoxicating scent and taste, the silkiness of his lips against mine, the feel of his hard body against my softer one. I can't get close enough to him. I climb his body and wrap my legs around his waist. Ezra's cock readily rises against my tummy and privates, and I rock salaciously against him, reveling in the friction between us. I moan so loudly that it echoes around the dungeon.

Hands, multiple sets, are on my calves, softly caressing me, lulling me to continue.

The deafening silence of the crowd and my own tortured sounds of pleasure draw me out of the little, fictitious world I had created. A world where it was okay to touch Ezra, to feel emotions for Ezra, to take pleasure from Ezra. But this isn't a world of my creation. We live in reality, and what I just did was wrong on so many levels.

Ezra's arms are straining under my additional weight. Worried, feeling remorse for so many reasons, I climb off of him and onto my stool. I rub Ezra's arms, making sure they are all right. The expression on his face is pained, pure agony, but it's not because of his restrained arms.

"I want to be with you again. Watching you and Aaron almost killed me. I would have done anything to make love to you." The look on Ezra's face is full of ache and wonder, and I would do anything to take the ache away.

I'm unsure why Ezra pushed Aaron and me together if he didn't want us to have sex. Ez has always been in control. Even when I was lying in bed with Aaron, Ez was still warping and manipulating our emotions, forcing us to do and feel what he wanted us to do and feel. The entire thing confuses me.

"You could have joined us," I whimper, frustrated.

I don't regret being with Aaron. It was pleasant to be with someone I trusted, cared for, and felt a real connection of friendship, but I would have chosen Ezra first over everyone on this planet. I have no idea if I would have regretted being with Ezra or not, even with the insurmountable roadblock known as Adelaide Whittenhower. Regardless, Ezra would have been my first choice– always.

"I wasn't sure if you would freak out or not. I… I can't be with you until you remember everything," Ezra cries.

"Okay, let's just say I remember!" I shout as I throw my hands up in the air while staring at Ezra with great incredulity.

"No." His expression is truly pained. "It doesn't work that way, Katya. I can't remember for you. You have to work this out for yourself."

I feel an uncomfortable sensation crawling up the back of my neck. I turn slightly, and notice the forty-some people surrounding us. The crowd is silent in their shock. Our private moment is very much on display. Yes, a dungeon isn't the place to discuss making love, therapy sessions, or the fact that what I just did, and what I was contemplating, was tantamount to adultery.

I said I wouldn't go there with Ezra because he is in a committed relationship, and when the lust is riding me, I don't seem to give a shit. I can't allow this to happen again. I have to avoid being in this type of situation with Ezra, at all costs.

I draw in a deep breath, and make myself a promise on the exhale. No sex with unavailable men, especially those who have been stalking me for three years.

During our exchange, Cortez and Aaron had moved closer. The pair is shoulder-to-shoulder against Ezra, holding him stationary. Each has an arm around Ezra's back. They must have held us up when I played horny monkey. Their hands were the ones fondling my legs.

I mouth '*Thank You*' to the both of them, and then give them each a light kiss to the cheek. The crowd expresses a collective sigh at the affection.

"Are we enjoying the show?" I ask to distract everyone from my mortifying display of faithless whore.

Loud cheers and *Whoop, Whoop, Whoop* course through the crowd.

I blush bright red, and notice the trio joins me in mutual embarrassment. I remember Queen saying how they always played in their private room. This is probably extremely uncomfortable for them. I know it is for me. I've never done anything in public.

"Properly humbled, I think since we've gotten the humiliation segment out of the way…" I pause to laugh, and the crowd joins me. "It's time for the punishment to begin." I expected the crowd to go crazy with that, but I'm met with silence.

I look up at them, not able to see a single face in the sea of bodies. The trio and I are illuminated by a single light bulb in the center of the dungeon, casting a dark shadow over the rest of the room. No need for anonymity when you are blinded to everything but the object of your desires.

The crowd is waiting in anticipation, saying absolutely nothing. The air charges with excitement, with trepidation. A throat clearing brings my focus back to Ezra.

"What do you mean, punishment? Isn't that what I've already endured?" Ezra's voice breaks with fear.

"Not so fast," I rapidly murmur. "We have several heinous crimes for which you must atone." I look to Aaron, "Baby Boy, bring us the toys." He glares at me, but otherwise, does as he's told.

"This is a members-only punishment. Please create a line in an orderly fashion," I politely order Restraint's dungeon residents. "You may select one toy from the cart, and then inflict your punishment on our deceiving master. Don't leave any permanent damage, or else I will damage you."

My eyes rove over the crowd at the last part of my statement. I want them to know I am dead serious. Whereas I couldn't see them before, I can now as they line up by the toy cart. I'm surprised by some of the faces gazing up at me with a myriad of expression. Most definitely they all know Dr. Ezra Zeitler in either a professional or personal relationship, and I doubt the need for anonymity at this point. They all know the man beneath the mask, as they know who the man is beneath the hood covering Cort's face.

"Okay, good," I mutter in relief, glad they aren't turning on me. "I will take the last turn. Skull-fuck, you may begin, and then please supervise the other members during their turn, as we discussed earlier. Wouldn't want this perfect specimen of a man to be harmed in any way."

I hop on my stool again, bringing me face-to-face with Ezra. He offers me a wan smile, as if understanding he brought this upon himself.

Ever the martyr.

I grip Ezra's hips, fingers biting into his firm flesh, to keep him from swaying too much and injuring himself.

"Have you ever been struck before?" Ezra flinches as I ask, answering my question with reaction instead of words.

"No. I haven't. I've never been in the submissive position." He may have never submitted, but I can tell from his demeanor that he has been struck. I wish I could remove that experience from him. To submit and accept your fate is not the same as being victimized.

"Well, Master, if you can dish out a punishment, I believe you better be able to take it. You should know what those who follow you are feeling. Now it's your turn."

"You sound too much like my father right now," Ezra mutters, lips quirking up into a funny little smile. "Creepy."

I watch as Cortez selects a riding crop from the cart, and then tests its weight in his hand. One strong flick back, the leather bounces off his palm. Clearly Cort has been trained with impact toys, and he enjoys wielding the power.

Cortez and I, we lock eyes while he strikes out, as we share our mutual pain this man has caused us. Ezra sways in his binds from the solid hit. I grip tighter to immobilize him. He doesn't flinch from the pain or make any noise. The only change is in his breathing– sharp intakes of breath through his parted lips.

"Aaron, don't pussy out on me," I warn. "Do as requested. You will not like the consequences for pulling your hit. This is for *his* benefit, not our own. In order to learn, he has to suffer the consequences of his actions. The rules of this lifestyle are no different than those a mother employs against her children: boundaries, trust, and every act of defiance has a cost. A cost which usually someone else has to pay while you hide like a coward. If you believe yourself dominant enough to hold dominion over others, then you must own up to your own mistakes."

Young face taut with fury, Aaron takes the crop from Cortez. All the while he's glaring at me as if he's dreaming of beating me into submission with the riding crop.

"You shouldn't have chosen this punishment. It's wrong. It's too much for so little." Aaron looks at me with outward hostility, trying to provoke me.

"It's too much for so little? Really, Aaron? Pretending to be two separate people to stalk me for the past three years is so little? Is it so little to lose two people you came to rely on? One in a therapeutic capacity and the other as one of my only friends? They are dead to me, Aaron. Gone. I was played and deceived. They were real for me– alive –and now I grieve. What don't you get about that?"

"You didn't lose anything, Katya," Aaron hisses. "They're right there!" he shouts while pointing at Ezra. "They aren't dead. You're hitting *them*!"

We stare each other down– a true faceoff. Aaron's pissed at me for teaching his precious Ezra how there are consequences to every action made, and I am angry with Aaron for not getting it. Judging by the look of sympathy on Cortez's face, this has been an ongoing issue between the three of them, with Ezra never being held accountable for anything.

"The feeling's mutual right now, Aaron," I mutter in a voice laced with deep sadness, knowing I'm losing a friend I just made, when it's a short list to begin with. "I know you would protect him with your life, always making excuses for him, always cleaning up his messes. But you need to do this for him. He needs it to repent." I try to sound reassuring, but I can tell by the angry set of Aaron's eyes that he isn't hearing me.

"Aaron, Katya is correct. I need this in order to heal from what I've done. Please do it for me." Ezra's voice is gentle, coaxing.

Before my eyes can track the hit, it has already came to a stop, barely tapping Ezra's back. Tossing the crop to the floor like an angry child, Aaron stomps off, shoulder-bumping me on his way by, nearly knocking me off the footstool. As I watch him leave the dungeon, I come to the realization that not only did I just lose a friend, I just made an enemy.

This is why I didn't want Aaron's help earlier. This is why Cortez and I make a better demonic duo. Aaron makes love to me one night, yet hates me the next.

I sigh deeply and blink the tears away. I guess this answers the question that's been plaguing me: where do I fit in? I'm at the bottom of the list when it comes to the trio.

Katya, no shit! It's a trio, not a quartet!

Several members take their turns as I'm lost in my own little miseries. Dexter's approach catches my eye. Hmm… this could go really badly. He selects a flat paddle from the cart, and smiles to himself, as if he loves the feel of a weapon in his palm. I wince as he takes his swing, but Ezra doesn't sway in my hands at all. I'm surprised, of all the people who would pull their hit, it was Dexter.

Picking up the riding crop from the floor, Queen's short strawberry locks glow in the light. Her lips split into a grin as she barely flicks her wrist on her swing. Ezra doesn't move an inch because the six foot tall woman didn't put any force behind her strike.

In fact, Ezra smirks at me, silently screaming an '*I told you so.*' I'm learning a valuable lesson during Ezra's punishment: I'm the outsider, and I always will be. Ezra is safe in that knowledge, never fearing the members of Restraint would harm him. It's a fact that just adds fuel to my resolve. I don't belong here. I don't fit in here. No one will ever accept me. Ever.

Queen whispers in my ear for only me to hear. "I should be up here, too, for my part in Kimber. Don't fret, you're doing this for the right reasons, and most of us recognize that. I'd love to tell you pretty lies on how Aaron will get over this, but he won't. Ever. I'm sorry."

The last member strides up and holds my stare. I gasp in shock as Monica's brown eyes shoot pure, unadulterated fury my way. In life, the woman is a powerhouse bitch, putting off the air of dominance. But her appearance here tonight suggests she's a submissive, which makes sense since she used to play with Cortez.

Pure hatred emanates from Monica as she swings a paddle lightly at Ezra's bum. His reaction, or lack thereof, suggests he didn't even feel the hit. Monica flashes a wicked smile my way as she departs– promises of my own punishments to come.

"Well, folks. It seems we only have one hit left." I hop down from my perch and stalk to the cart. I select the cat o' nine tails. "A cat for the mousy? How apropos." I prance around as a Kitty Kat with the cat in my hands, even though I feel no thrill or enjoyment. Aaron's revelation ruined the experience for me.

I run the soft leather over Ezra's reddened skin. I lean forward and kiss a few of the welts. His back and rear are red, but not how I figured it would look. The members respect and love their master, and they took mercy on him. I doubt I would receive the same reprieve.

With a flick of my wrist, the cat connects with Ezra's ass and thighs. However, I do not pull my hit. He receives the full brunt of the force. Cortez is playing spotter, holding Ezra in place. Ezra bites back a scream, but just barely. He's panting wildly, chest expanding with every breath.

I'm not sure why I hit Ezra so hard. Something inside of me forced my hand. My subconscious said I would only ever get one chance to expel my anger and frustration, so I took the opportunity when it presented itself.

I refuse to apologize.

This man has fucked with my head in the name of healing. He has manipulated me. He has warped my sense of self. He has made me go back on my code of ethics. He has made me care about him to the point that I would ruin everything just to get his approval. I think I hold a well of resentment in a small spot inside me, and it lashed out eagerly.

Of all the hits, only two people gave Ezra a respectable lashing: Cortez and myself. The rest pulled their hits, barely caressing him with instruments meant to impact flesh, not comfort and tickle. I'm angry. I'm jealous. I feel lost. I feel set apart.

I am alone.

"Please go about your normal business," I release the crowd. "Master Ez and I thank you for your participation." I glance at Ezra, "Say thank you."

"Thanks, guys." Ezra lets out a relieved, hearty laugh because his punishment is finally over. I notice he didn't thank me for his education.

Restraint 396

Chapter Thirty-Nine

I learned the power of being a dominant at Restraint. With one word, Cortez had all the submissives cleaning up the dungeon, washing and putting away the toys, and then we were off in a matter of minutes.

Aaron insisted that we take Ezra back to his place, and tend to him there. I wasn't surprised when we entered The Edge Building. However, I gasped in shock when Aaron unlocked the apartment adjacent to mine, and ushered us in.

For the past few minutes, the realization has been pinging inside my head, how Ezra, Aaron, and Cortez have lived next door to me this entire time.

I feel like such a fool.

A stupid girl.

Ezra is lying naked in the center of his bed, on his belly with his head propped up in his palm. He's watching us with avid interest, like rats in an experiment. Cortez and I just stand in the center of the room, unsure what to do next, as Aaron sits in a chair in the corner– pouting, refusing to acknowledge my existence.

Feeling guilty and confused, the mother in me erupts. "I have some ointment in my bathroom. We can use it to soothe Ezra's skin. I'll be right back," I tell the trio, and it just so happens to be the same ointment Ezra used on my gnarled wrist.

"Here," Cortez offers as he opens a door-sized panel on the bedroom wall, like a wall becoming a doorway is a normal, everyday occurrence. "Your living room is right though here."

"You've got to be fucking kidding me!" I stomp my foot, throwing a girl tantrum. "Seriously?"

No wonder they were always in my apartment and I couldn't ever figure out how. I was baffled by how they got past four deadbolts and the chain lock. Sometimes they entered my living room with me sitting in it, and I assumed I was seeing shit since I never heard the locks engage. When Aaron was babysitting me, he kept bringing out different things to occupy himself, things not found inside the confines of my apartment. Now I know how and why.

I rush to my bathroom for the ointment, trying not to think about how disgusted I feel. Every swear word in existence flows through my mind.

I don't feel badly over punishing Ezra. I feel vindicated.

Holy shit!

The stalker has a portal to my living room... from his bedroom. He has surveillance on me at all times. He plays imaginary people on the internet, for Christ's sake. I don't think I punished my stalker enough. Aaron can just take a big, fat suck of my ass!

I toss the tube on the bed. "Who has the honors?" My tone is downright bitchy.

"I would think since it was your brilliant idea, you should be the one to fix what you've fucked up," Aaron says snottily back to me, still refusing to look at me, as if I disgust him.

Lovely.

Aaron reminds me of a mother who gets angry when you yell at their child for beating your defenseless puppy with a broom. The puppy accidentally jumped into the broom the kid was wielding, while managing to wrap its leash around the little darling's fist so it couldn't escape. It's always someone else's fault, so we have a world of budding sociopaths thanks to mothers just like that, who were raised by mothers just like them. Thanks to people like Aaron.

Ezra did the wrong thing, so he was punished to learn a lesson.

The end!

I straddle a naked Ezra's thighs, and sit on the backs of his knees. Ignoring his perfect male form for sanity's sake, I stare down at everyone's handwork. I notice Ez's back is only a little bit red, and the welts are mild, and were caused by Cortez and myself. In a few hours, Ez won't even be feeling a sting.

I squeeze a bit of the ointment onto my palms, not warming it up first, knowing the coolness will be soothing. I work the ointment into the skin of his back, thighs, and ass. He doesn't flinch or scream in pain. It's quite the opposite, actually. He squirms underneath me, moaning as if he's getting off on the sensation.

Curiosity: Ezra doesn't like to be struck, but loves the after-effects.

"Call her," Ezra moans to Aaron, sounding in agony. Finally hearing Ezra's voice after an hour of silence breaks into my movements. Hands stilled, my fingertips hover over Ez's pink ass cheeks.

Call who?

Sounding stunned, Aaron mumbles, "Are you sure?"

"Yes, I can't be around Kat or Cort right now. They have to leave. Call her."

"Call who?" Cortez whispers, looking devastated all of the sudden. "Why?"

"Cortez, please take Katya," Ezra begs while shoving me off his legs– thoroughly rejecting me. "Stay with Kat. I can't be around either of you right now."

I flinch at that, stumbling to my feet. Aaron hates me, and now so does Ezra. Well, I know a dismissal when I hear one. I'm above bitching and pleading and begging for attention. I know my position in this hierarchy. I leave without saying a word of goodbye to anyone, and Cortez dutifully follows.

"Nah. Thanks. I'm pretty sure I won't get lost on the way to my apartment. Even a dipshit like me can make it the two inches through the wall," I say sarcastically as I enter my living room.

"Katya, even the dominant shouldn't be alone after a scene," Ezra's voice calls after me. It takes all of my self-control not to charge back into his bedroom and give him a piece of my mind– a violent, not-so pleasant, piece of my mind.

Power courses over me because I was able to keep my mouth shut long enough to make it to my living room. I would have regretted none of the words, but I know how to pick my own battles. It's not my choice if Ezra doesn't wish to be around me. I can't make someone like me if they don't. It would be wrong of me to lash out and be angry because Ezra feels as he does. But the rejection hurts just the same.

I drop onto my sofa and issue a nasty glare at Cortez, who is standing a few feet from the open portal to my apartment. "We've already established that I don't do cuddling and coddling. Leave," I point to the offending hole in my living room wall. "And don't let the wall hit your fine ass on the way out."

Cort looks at me with endless patience and pain, and I've learned that he isn't known for patience. Which makes it seem that much more annoying.

"Stop looking at me like that," I hiss. I pick up a decorative pillow with an owl embroidered on it, and then hug it to my chest like a comfort object. If Cort doesn't stop staring at me, I'm liable to cover my face with it.

"Like what?" He arches a brow at me.

"Like you want to fuck me," I mumble underneath my breath, hating how I couldn't speak any louder because my voice was threatening to break. "Like you want to fuck me as a distraction because we're both about to cry."

"I'm angry at Aaron for how he's treating you, but I'm furious at Ezra right now. Hurt. Betrayed. But I'm not about to cry. I'm about to go postal," Cort warns. "But what I want from you isn't a distraction, because I do want to fuck you," he admits without shame. "How else am I to look at you?" The bastard smirks at me.

"Just don't. All right?" I speak softer than I wanted. "It's not going to happen."

"Don't get all soft on me. Aaron will get over it... eventually," he teases, flashing me a wicked smirk.

"It's not that. I'm not screwing any of you– like ever." I say with conviction.

The last part of my comment takes Cortez by surprise, and he drops into the nearest chair. He slumps forward, with his elbows on his knees. His face is tan and manly, yet soft, as if he's quick to laugh. It almost hurts to look at him, knowing he's something I can never have, even if I long for a taste.

"Why? Don't you want me?" An expression of hurt etches across Cort's face, showing insecurities I never would have guessed in a million years he possessed.

"Yeah, that's why," I laugh out. "You know damned well that isn't it. You're hotter than fuck, and you know it, stud. So quit the hurt pride shit. You're married, or did you suddenly forget all about your wife, Divina?"

"So," Cort says with a shrug, and has the audacity to sound confusion.

"I'm not a whore," I growl. "Even I have standards." Cort just blankly looks at me, still confused. "I want to be someone's number one. I know I'll never be someone's wife, or even their girlfriend, but I draw the line at screwing attached men. I know Aaron wasn't a good idea. I feel bad about it now, because I was using him as much as he was using me. I just wanted to feel good for a few minutes." I brush a few stray tears from my cheeks. "Aaron wasn't married like you are, or engaged like Ezra. But, the thing is, Aaron's more emotionally attached to the two of you, than you both are to your women. I'm sure the same is in reverse. I can't compete with that– I won't."

"It's not like that," Cort tries so badly to deny my claims. Seeing my expression, he adds on, "With *you*."

I snort a snide laugh. "Yeah, I'm just a joke. Someone who gets a pity fuck. I'm here because Ezra wants to heal me– that's it."

"I don't understand how you jump to these ridiculous conclusions," Cort mutters, incredulity thick in his voice. He flashes me a look, as if I physically exhaust him.

I just bug out my eyes and part my arms to the side. "How can I see it any differently? Damn, do I need a sign? Ezra and you touch me, but you're still very much attached to your women, with no desire to leave them, effectively treating me like a goddamned whore. Yet neither of you will allow me to touch you back. I have sex with Aaron, and it was supposed to mean something, and a few days later he hates my fucking guts. I might be daft, but not *that* fucking daft."

"We care a great deal for you, Kat." Cort's voice is filled with soft affection as he leans forward, trying to get closer to me. "You are a part of us."

"Yeah, is that so? Aaron would find great pleasure in

hurting me right now, and Ezra wanted me out of his sight, and all you want from me is a revenge fuck to hurt Ezra's feelings for shoving you out of his bedroom. The revenge isn't because I'm some prize to Ez; it's because *you* are. Your version of care is different than mine." I shake my head in disgust. "I'm sick of being toyed with and used."

"None of that is true, Katya. Not a fucking thing you just said is reality," Cort vehemently bites out.

"Well, it's not open for discussion. Aaron won't voluntarily touch me again. I've punished Ezra, so now I'm the Anti-Christ. Ezra has never wanted to have sex with me in the first place. So I guess that only leaves you."

In need of a distraction. In need of a win. I stalk over to Cortez, swaying my hips as I walk the few feet. Cort's hungry gaze empowers me, numbs the pain I feel on the inside. I need to release the pent-up frustrations that are strangling me before I lash out and hurt those who do matter. I'm hurt, confused, and I can feel the memories creeping in from around the edges.

I offer Cortez an impossible task as the distraction we both need. One I am guaranteed to win. One I need to use in order to feel in control of my own life again.

"I have a proposition for you. You have two minutes to take me. But you have to catch me first," I purr from deep within my throat, getting into Cort's face. "If the timer ends, or if I get out of this apartment– game over."

"You mean if I catch you, I can fuck you?" Cort's voice is awed, shocked. I nod yes, and he swallows audibly, Adam's apple bobbing.

"Two minutes to catch me *and* fuck me to completion. It all has to happen within that time frame. But if you don't catch me, we don't revisit this ever again. We leave it as friends. No sex. Friends," I reiterate. "That's all."

"Unless you change your mind," Cort adds, sounding hopeful. A wicked smirk twisted his lips, as if he's confident in his abilities to charm me into his bed.

"Yeah... sure... unless I change my mind." I shake my head, knowing full and well that is never going to happen. "Are you giving up already?" I taunt.

"Oh, as I said before: I've been called many, very bad things, but a coward ain't one of 'em. I never give up," Cort says with a cocky grin.

I lean over Cortez, with my hands on the arms of the chair he's sitting in, and purr slyly into his face. "Listen, Cort. I really do like you. You're a fucking sick and twisted bastard, to my fucking sick and twisted bitch."

That intoxicating, thick and fattening laugh spills from Cortez's parted lips, causing me to shudder violently. He pulls his phone from his pocket, setting a two-minute timer countdown.

"Ready.... Set.... Kitten." I look up at Cort, grinning like crazy. His eyes are dilated with excitement, the gray irises completely eclipsed by his pupils. We aren't predator versus prey as he thinks. It's predator versus predator. "R U N!"

In an instant, I scale the sofa, trailing a giddy giggle of excitement. I love playing, and Cortez Abernathy bleeds playfulness. Sometimes you just have to let go and be the kid you never got to be. We need to bottle these simple moments of delight for when we are feeling down on ourselves, and take them out to remember how it's the small, free things in life that truly matter.

I feign run to the bedroom. I'm not dumb enough to get cornered in a room without exits. Cort tries to cut me off, except I'm not going that way. I hop from the sofa to the coffee table. I have the advantage of being small. Cort may be taller with a greater stride, but I am lighter and can walk on furniture.

I count silently in my head as I race Cortez around my apartment. We're almost to the halfway mark. Seconds are a lot longer when you're racing the clock. Imagine waiting at the microwave for your popcorn. Now pretend that timer is counting down to an attack.

As I jump to the kitchen island, Cort's hand just grazes my ankle, fingertips finding no purchase as they slide off my skin. He starts swearing, and I cackle in response as I run along my countertops, jumping over small appliances and my dish drainer. I slide to my knees and crawl on my hands and knees to avoid hitting my head on the upper cabinets. I vault to the floor, and then scuttle underneath the kitchen table.

Cortez, anticipating my maneuver, is waiting for me, his Italian leather shoes taunting me, mere inches from my face. As I jerk away, his hands come into view, latching onto my wrists to pull me out from beneath the table.

I don't struggle. I allow Cort to take me. I become boneless, limp in his arms. I have twenty seconds left until *game over*. Hell, if I manage to lose, then I guess Cortez earned the right to a good, hard fuck.

Cort tosses me against the table, forcing a grunt out of me when my chest hits the edge. With forceful precision, his fingertips grip my latex catsuit, and with a sharp tug, he tears it down the back, exposing my bare ass. I grip the edge of the table, fingernails biting into the wood, panting laboriously as I try to formulate a plan.

"I'll buy you another one," Cort purrs huskily. "I'm quite partial to you dressed as a Sex Kitten."

Cort chuckles that addictive sound, firing lust in my veins. The grind of a zipper lowering has my thighs drenched in anticipation.

I play to win. But in this case, it's win-win either way.

I groan deeply from my chest when Cort rubs the velvety thick head of his exquisiteness along my wet pussy. My eyes roll up, and I allow myself half a second to enjoy the sensation of Cort glided through my slickness. I bite my lip on a moan when he moves into position.

Five seconds…

Cortez is completely distracted by the feel of our bodies beginning to connect. I wait until he pushes an inch inside of me. I almost don't go through with it. Sex with Cortez Abernathy would be an epic experience.

I yank as hard as I can with my hands on the table edge, pulling myself up and over. I scale the table, hopping to the floor on a lunge, and then run through my living room towards the open panel to Ezra's bedroom.

Three seconds…

Two strides. I just need two strides and I will be outside this apartment, and then the timer will strike zero!

Two seconds…

Angry curses growl out of Cortez's throat as his prize flees his grasp. His hand skims my shoulder, fingers gliding off my sweat-slickened skin.

One second…

My feet hit Ezra's apartment as the tone sounds from Cortez's phone.

"I! W I N!" I laugh from the exhilaration that flows through my veins. I turn to Cortez, about to tell him I want to fuck him as my prize, when what I see instead, tears a gasp of shock and heartbreak from my chest.

Before me, Ezra is fiercely rutting on Adelaide, yet to notice us even with the noise of our scrimmage. He is completely enthralled with the woman beneath him.

Call her, Aaron.

Who?

Adelaide.

The blood drains from my face, along with all of my enjoyment. This is why I wanted to bottle the playful nature, because it is always so short-lived. We need to remember that sensation in order to deal with life's bitter, little miseries. Even with the playful nature just seconds ago, I forget its taste in the face of agony.

Cortez's face changes to unadulterated betrayal as he notices my expression of pain. I watch as he turns from a man on the hunt, trilling with energy, to someone who loses the fight. His golden face is pale. His gray eyes turn black. He looks like he just met death face-to-face, and instead of fighting, he surrendered to the loss.

"I've wanted you so much that I've ached," Ezra moans, his voice dreamy.

Ezra hypnotically rolls into the rail-thin blonde. Adelaide's face is hidden in the crook of his neck, but I've no doubt it's filled with ecstasy. Her moans mingle with his, creating a symphony that curdles my stomach. Her red talons grip his ass, leaving half-moon imprints. I can't look anymore.

"I won't leave you this time. I promise," Ezra vows reverently.

My breath hitches as I hear Ezra's utter devotion to his fiancée. Somewhere in the back of my mind, I'd held out hope that it was an engagement of convenience, some type of a business arrangement between two high-profile families. But what I see before me is no arrangement. Everyone tried to warn me, and I never listened, and now it's too late.

I leave before Ezra regains his composure and notices us. He is so in love with his fiancée that he appears to be in a trance. My breath keeps hitching on sobs. I will not break down. I won't... or at least not until I am alone.

I can feel Cortez keeping pace with me as I walk slowly to my bathroom. "Just go," I hiccup.

"You were going to fuck me, weren't you?" Cort says with confidence.

His question is so off base that I bark a sharp, bitter laugh. It's not a real laugh, and it's laced with an edge of madness, but it's a laugh nonetheless. Leave it to Cortez's highly inappropriate nature to lighten the situation.

"Thanks, I needed that," I genuinely say. "And yes, I was going to reward us both with a good, rough fuck." I laugh again. "Um... yeah. We didn't see what we just saw, okay? No telling on us. It would be too embarrassingly painful for all of us involved."

"I'm not Aaron," Cort spits angrily. "I'm not Ezra's bitch. He doesn't always come first with me," He says in all seriousness. "Because contrary to how Ezra behaves, his interests are the only ones that matter, even if he makes you think he's doing it for you. It's always all about *him*."

"Well, apparently I'm not Ezra's number one bitch, either." I laugh, not feeling funny in the least. "Yeah, you and I know exactly who our number one is." The *'ourselves'* goes without saying.

"That bullshit we just saw back there, is exactly why Ezra and I have been disconnected for the past decade. I could never trust him not to hurt me. Everyone always blames me, blames me for being straight, and blames me for refusing to touch Ezra. It was the point you tried to make in the dungeon. Ezra never takes responsibility for his own actions."

"Well, Adelaide is Ezra's fiancée. He's not wrong for touching her, no matter how we feel. We're wrong for allowing him to touch us. It makes me feel weak."

"I get that. Ezra is my weakness, too. We'll help each other avoid him," Cortez promises.

"Thank you," I breathe as a sigh of relief. "Thank you for understanding."

Cortez squeezes my chin with his thumb and index finger, tilting it back so he can look into my downcast eyes. "You'll change your mind about me. I know it," Cort says with absolute certainty. His eyes blaze into mine with confidence.

I falter. Cort is right. He'll wear me down eventually. Being around him is like being around myself. One day I'll get too comfortable and give in to my needs, and it scares me to death how low I will sink.

"Did you suddenly get a divorce in the last thirty seconds?" I draw Divina into the conversation to thaw it, to bring back my resolve. The fact that I can hear the lovers reaching their mutual crescendo isn't helping matters. I think I'm going to throw up if I don't shut the door to my bathroom and close out the sounds.

"That's irrelevant. Divina has nothing to do with us," Cort professes, still showing signs of the confusion I don't understand.

"You're an ass–" Cort cuts off my insult with a heated kiss– the exclamation point to the fact that he is an asshole. He kisses me as a dying man draws his last breath. Before I can return the kiss, he ends it.

"I'll buy you some alone time. You have a lot to process. I am so damned sorry about what you just saw." Cort shakes his head, trying to clear the confusion. "Ezra will regret what he just did. It makes me sick. I don't even know what the fuck that was," he hisses.

I'm about to explain the birds and the bees when Cort turns on his heel and leaves. I hear a sickening crunch, and I know a fist just connected with a doorframe.

Chapter Forty

"Hold her down, boys," a sinister voice commands.

Warm hands, that aren't much bigger than mine, wrap tightly around my wrists. A heavy weight settles on my legs. Bigger hands grip my thighs, fingers denting into my already wounded flesh.

I panic, and try to buck them off. I wiggle and writhe. I yank my hands and feet. None of it does any good. The only thing I manage to do is hurt myself as their fingers bruise me and the rocks beneath me draw blood.

I bite back a primal scream over a loss so deep I doubt I will ever recover. The loss of my dignity. My power. My innocence. The loss of self.

The more I fight, the louder I breathe, the louder they breathe— three sets of lungs inhale and exhale in time with mine.

Their leader cackles down at me, sickness flowing from him in a wave of pure evil. I still my struggles because I don't want to please him. He wants me to fight. Some instinctive part, which is buried deeply inside of me, recognizes that this man wants me to struggle, to scream. It will add to his sick thrill.

I give one final try to escape. I arch my back as leverage to pull at my hands and feet. As I struggle to get free, my eyes connect with the one holding my wrists. I gasp. Huge, blue eyes gaze down at me with pity and fear.

He's a child— a boy no more than fourteen or fifteen. Bile rises in my throat. I know why I'm being held down, and I won't allow a child to do that to me. I renew my efforts to escape. I fight like a wild animal caught in a trap. I manage to pull one hand free, using it to claw at the fingers gripping my wrist, scratching my own flesh in the process.

"Aaron, she'll hurt herself," the third boy says calmly. He quickly clutches my hand and gives it back to the boy. I whimper as my wrist is shackled between his boyish fingers.

"Shh... Please calm yourself," a smooth voice murmurs to

comfort me.

I cry out as reality hits me. The three boys holding me down are children. I'm at least two years older than the oldest. I turn my face to the side and vomit.

Wave after wave of dry heaves wrack my body. The acid burns my throat, but it's nowhere near as painful as my thoughts.

"I'm not doing this," the boy holding my legs cries. His tan cheeks are wet from tears. "This isn't like the whores Ray brought us. They were far from innocent, but even they didn't deserve their fate. I can't do this to a girl, Ezra. I'll die first. So help me God, I'll kill myself."

"Cort, I know. I won't let him do this to you and Aaron. You won't have to, I promise. Just follow my lead. Trust me," the one named Ezra breathes.

"What are you going on about down there?" the leader shouts.

"Nothing, Ray. She's ready." The boy at my side, Ezra, and the one holding my legs, Cort, communicate with their eyes– identical gray eyes.

"Well, which of you wants to go first? She's definitely ready now." Ray speaks of me as if I'm truly an animal. Meaningless. I no longer have a purpose, other than to be defiled for their entertainment. Once broken, I will be utterly worthless, even to them– especially to them.

"No," Ezra says. "You aren't going to subject her to all of us," he growls with authority.

Ezra turns my face to the side so I can no longer see their leader. My view is of the lake. Its crystalline water, which once promised safety, now taunts me from feet away. I try to reach out to the water for help. A whimper escapes my lips when it doesn't envelope me in its watery embrace.

"Well, son, this is your first hunt. I thought we'd share in the spoils, and then dispose of the body in the lake after we've broken her." A sinister laugh bubbles up from his chest, pure evil anticipation.

My body tries to shudder, but it's immobilized by the two boys known as Aaron and Cort, but nowhere near as immobilized as I am by my fear. Terror rolls over me and takes me under, rendering me incapable of rational thought. Panic wraps me in its darkness. It leads me to a place that can only be described as Hell. The dark recesses of my mind are far scarier than my violent reality.

"This way we can do anything we want and no one will hear us." Madness leaks from Ray's voice. "We can take our time. And look at that lake... no one would find her for days. I planned this perfectly."

"No," Ezra repeats. "It's my first time and my first hunt. I will not share." His voice sounds strong, but his body betrays itself. His hands shake against my face. Ezra's eyes meet Cort's gaze and hold for a moment as they communicate silently.

"No, I wouldn't want to share on my first time, either. It's Ezra's birthday, he should get to pick," Cort says, stationed at my feet.

"Son, what exactly do you propose? My patience is wearing thin with your petulance." Ray's voice is softer when he speaks to his son.

"Just me. Cort and Aaron can go into the woods a distance. I don't want an audience. No harming her, either. She's just a girl." Ezra strokes my face like I'm his pet. I try to ignore the calming, affectionate gesture, but it overpowers everything else.

"Fine, you have a choice. We all get a turn, and then I end her life when we're through, or we go with your plan, but I get to have a go. I promise that she will live, but I doubt she will wish she had when I'm finished," he gloats threateningly.

"No, it's just me," Ezra hisses into his father's face.

"Take it or leave it, son. This is not a negotiation. I didn't go to all the trouble of making you, getting you back, and bringing you your friends, only for you to disrespect me like this in front of our catch." Ray's voice is cold and detached.

With a swift kick, a boot connects sharply with my ribs, eliciting a crack to wrack my body. I bite my bottom lip to keep the building scream from erupting. The pain is excruciating, sharp and burning agony– fire races across my ribs and flows *down my spine. It's difficult to breathe. Every breath shoots painful stabs up my side. I bloody my lip to keep the wounded sounds at bay.*

I count slowly and breathe shallowly. Eventually I am able to concentrate on the feel of the moss beneath my cheek, the damp scent of the ground, the lapping of the water on the shore, anything except my circumstances.

Hands disappear from my body, signaling that the negotiations have ended. A pair of young men slip into the woods just out of sight. Detachably, I realize that this means I get to live. They chose the option where I get to live when this is over, but I may wish I hadn't.

I release a heavy sigh, and then draw in a lungful of clean, fresh air. My lungs fill to capacity, and my rib protests the pressure. My body eases with the realization that I may get to see another day. I know the leader thinks I will regret his son's choice, but as long as I have a tomorrow, I can endure today.

Self-preservation wins out over the fight-or-flight response. Instinctively I know that if I try to fight back, if I try to run, they will catch me within seconds, and then the leader will have no issue crushing the life out of me as if I were an insect.

I lay numbly on the ground, not moving, barely breathing, heart pounding so loudly it deafens me. I don't fight as Ezra unbuttons my shorts, draws the zipper down, and then slides them off my hips along with my panties.

My heart rate goes into hyper-drive as Ezra spreads my thighs and kneels between them. With gentle hands, his fingertips dig into my hips as he lifts me, anchoring my thighs with his own, and then places my bunched up shorts underneath my bottom as a cushion.

"Look away," Ezra orders his father in a scratchy rough voice.

"Now, son, where would the enjoyment be in that?" You can hear the wry, evil amusement bleeding through Ray's tone.

I close my eyes and tell myself to let nature take its course. It will be less violent if I submit— surrender. Ezra is being surprisingly gentle, reluctant, as he rubs my tummy, trying to calm me.

"Son, do I need to show you what to do? I know this is your first time with a girl, as this incarnation. I've had much fun with you and your friends, but it's time the gay side of you enjoyed a woman. Come on, you have a minute to do it, or I will," Ray threatens menacingly.

"I'm doing this. Don't do anything rash," Ezra says to his father.

"You aren't making love to the girl. Just fuck her and get it over with. I know you know how to fuck," Ray spews in disgust.

The metal-on-metal sound of a zipper lowering has my eyes squeezing shut tightly. If I can't see it, it's not really happening. Betraying tears leak down the sides of my face to wet the hair near my ears. A warm, heavy weight lies on top of me, covering my body. His hand reaches forward, cupping the back of my head, to pull my face against his chest.

"There… there… Shh… He can't see any part of you with my body hiding yours. I promise," Ezra murmurs softly, but his voice breaks in fear. I know it's not a promise he can keep.

I start to shake uncontrollably. I'm too smart to think the thoughts most people would dwell on. 'This isn't supposed to happen to me.' 'I can't believe this is happening to me.' 'What did I do wrong to deserve this?'

I know there are no guarantees in life, and I find no comfort from the thought. My life or death is in the hands of Ray and Ezra. There is no escape, no rescue, no reasoning or pleading my way out of this. My only option is to endure and pray that I live through it.

I try to distance myself as I had during the negotiation, but I can't find the switch in my brain. I start to panic. I bite my lip against the terrorized scream that is threatening to spill from between my lips. I'm frozen in fear. I can't even move my fingertips.

"Can I at least enter her without you hovering?" Ezra whispers.

"Fine. I'll be back in two minutes. I have to make sure the boys didn't run off. If they run again, I'll kill them this time,"

Ray threatens.

"I know. They know." Ezra speaks as if he's heard the threat a thousand times before, and he's bored with it.

"I'm so sorry. I don't want to do this to you. None of us do. Well, I'm positive he does," Ezra says snidely about his father. "He kidnapped us. First he took me from my home, from my bed, and then he went back and took the others. I know he's capable of exactly as he said... we've seen him in action over the past few days. I'm so sorry," Ezra repeats like it changes a damned thing.

Ezra shifts his body until I feel the hot, firm press of him against my sensitive flesh. I whimper in fear as I try to press my back into the unyielding ground beneath me to get away.

"I'm sorry. It has to be this way. It's the only way I can protect the others. He's already taken so much from my friends; they'll never heal from this. This way you'll have two less people inside you, and they can keep what little innocence they have left. I am so sorry," Ezra cries in shame.

With the flex of his hips, Ezra enters me with searing pain, tearing through my innocence. Penetrating. Impaling. He pushes deep where nothing has gone before. My eyes pop wide open and my mouth forms a silent scream. My fingernails claw into the compacted earth and dig– breaking my nails until I feel the wetness of their blood spill.

The switch flips over in my mind as Ezra slowly rocks into me. I process very little with the exception of his control. He holds so much back in an effort not to harm me.

My eyes hold wide with fright as I concentrate on the wisps of clouds peeking through the voids in the treetops. I stare at the canopy instead of feeling the sensations rocking my body. I zone out and watch the magnificent beauty of nature instead of experiencing the brutal nature of man.

A sinister cackle draws my focus to Ray holding my wrists above my head. His nails bite into the thin skin, leaving crimson crescents filling with blood. His pale, clammy skin is revolting, but not as vile as the lewd, evil expression on his face.

The sensations rush into my system as Ray leers down at

me. The pain throws the switch wide open. I see more clearly than I had before. I finally register what Ezra looks like, his musky, masculine scent filling my nose, his touch on my flesh, his taste on the back of my tongue, and our bodies connected at our sexes. Pain and terror mix, racing my heart and creating a chemical reaction in my blood. Adrenaline rushes through my body as I try to fight. Every movement causes the nails to dig deeper, to draw more blood.

"Look at me– not him." My eyes flash to the husky, smoky voice. "That's right... look at me," Ezra coaxes.

Gunmetal-gray eyes captivate me. Ezra is rocking into me from above. He's barely eighteen years old, if a day over. He is tall and slight, as if he hasn't filled out into the man he will become.

"No son of mine stops before he's finished," Ray hisses at Ezra when he slows his thrusting.

"It's just you and me. Don't look at him." Ezra's voice holds sympathy, and I remember how badly he fought his father. How he was forced to take me, sacrificing us both to save his friends.

"Stay with me," Ezra murmurs. His pace increases, and I whimper from the ensuing pain, and for another sensation I don't want to admit.

"Let go of her hands," Ezra seethes. "She's not going anywhere. You'll get your turn. This is mine. Step back." His anger terrifies me, reminding me of animals fighting over a fresh carcass.

I freak out, struggling in earnest, no matter how badly my wrists are bloodied.

"Shh... I've got you. Just look at me," he croons, trying to soothe me.

My hands are released, and I flex my fingers, but Ezra instantly recaptures them. I startle and cry out.

"I just want to hold your hands. I won't hurt you or hold you down. It's okay. Stay with me," he begs. He draws our clasped hands between our bodies and settles them at our chests.

"It's just you and me. We're all alone. I saw a pretty girl

walking the trail, and asked her to join me at the lake. We walked and talked. When we got to the water, we kissed, and then it turned into something more. Now, it's just you and me, making love next to the sparkling water. Imagine it with me," Ezra coaxes me into his fantasy world. "It's just you and me..." he moans. "Stay with me," he draws me deeper into his fantasy.

I no longer feel the agony and terror. I fall into Ezra's eyes and I'm swallowed by his imagination. He whispers words of comfort to keep me with him. We lock eyes and block out the rest of the world.

The pain turns to unfamiliar ache. My legs part and my hips angle up, completing a deeper connection. Shame slams into my soul as I feel pressure build and heat spread throughout my body. Ezra's face echoes back his own displeasure with our bodies' reactions.

Green and gray eyes fuse together, dual victims and victimizers as our bodies betray us.

I try to restrain myself as little whimpers sneak past my lips. The boy bends down. His lips feather against mine as he speaks, "What's your name?"

"Kat," wheezes out.

"Kat, call me Ezra," he pants, an almost pleading sound. "Say my name."

"Ezra," falls from my lips as my body releases the ultimate betrayal.

Ezra pours inside me as I tighten all of my muscles against the need to writhe. I bite into the chest above me, teeth sinking deep into his flesh, drawing blood to fill my mouth, as I repress the sounds trying to escape my throat. My fingers squeeze his, and his squeeze mine in return.

Moments pass as we freeze in our shame. A throat clearing brings us back to the present. Ray's expression is awed. For once he is speechless. Even with my body broken and violated, the thought of unnerving him brings me vindication.

"Good job, son. She was a virgin, wasn't she?" Ray's pleasant, not at all like the rapist he is.

"Yes," Ezra replies, tone filled with shame.

Ezra slowly eases out of my body. The movement causes me to wince and dig my fingernails into the backs of his hands– and it's not from pain. He looks down at me with a similar expression: a mix of shame, guilt, and pleasure.

Ezra brushes my hair from my ear and whispers, "I'm sorry for what I'm about to do. If you survive, I promise I will find you and always protect you. Kat, we will be together again," he swears.

…My body thrusts off the bed in a silent scream. The death moan pours from my throat until my lungs are deflated of air.

My mind no longer feels the need to protect me from my memories. Nothing is blurred or fuzzy; it screams with absolute clarity.

Restraint 418

Chapter Forty-One

"Hi, baby girl." I smile in relief when my mom answers the phone instead of Ava. Ava is too perceptive; she will hound me until I break down sobbing, spilling my guts.

I haven't cried since the truth of my past returned with a vengeance. I spent a good hour in the shower, screaming into a towel to muffle the sounds of my torment. It's been four days, and I haven't heard a word from the trio, nor have I spotted them lurking in the shadows.

It's obvious that I've been banished for punishing Ezra, with neither Ezra nor Aaron wanting to have a thing to do with me, while Cort is off licking his wounds somewhere private.

Apparently if you piss off the Boss, the repercussions are losing Kayla. I've come to realize how much I depended on my assistant. It's been interesting, trying to keep a staff, clients, and edits flowing while taking my own phone calls and making my own appointments.

One thing about the extra workload, is that I haven't had much time to think– that is until I try to sleep. The memories return in the dark morning hours before sunrise. They have helped me come to terms with my decision.

"I'm surprised you answered, since you guys have been dodging my phone calls for the past week. I was scared something happened to you."

"We had a visitor last week, one who told us to give you some space." My mom sounds sheepish, and fury boils in my blood.

I erupt. "Jesus Christ! You have got to be fucking kidding me!"

"Kat, really?" Mom drawls out, and I can almost hear her rolling her eyes.

"Are you chastising me for swearing? You're the one who expanded my vocabulary in the first place."

"I taught you to be more creative than that. There is a huge difference between expletives and blasphemy."

"Never mind. About this '*visitor*', was he a walking Greek

marble statue? Tall, white, and stoic? What's the matter with you? Didn't Grandma tell you never to speak with strangers?"

Mom's laughter flows from the other end of the line, reveling in my obvious discomfort. "When a man rings your doorbell and he's the spirit and image of your only grandchild, you tend to open the door and let him in."

"Spill it all. Spill every goddamned, high-handed detail. Now," I order.

"Katya," Mom begins, sounding brokenhearted. "We know more than you think. We've always known what you kept as a secret. The District Attorney told us every detail, even if it was expunged from the record because the boys were juveniles who were victims themselves. Even Ezra, since he was taken when he was a minor."

Renewed humiliation descends upon me. "I... never knew... I never knew there was a record of everything that took place. I never imagined Ray would tell the truth," I muse. "Anyway, what happened when Ezra showed up at the house?"

"So, when I opened the door to find the same young man I met three years ago at the parole hearing, I let him in. But I didn't let Ezra speak to Ava until he and I sat down with your father."

"Ezra has the manipulative powers of God," I warn Mom, voice breaking in fear.

"Your father and I became well-aware of that fact after about a minute into the conversation. Where we only allowed him to answer with yes and no or straight facts. We weren't born yesterday, Kat."

"What did you do?" I squeak out.

"It's what your father did," Mom stresses. "He allowed Ezra to meet with Ava, supervised, of course."

"Why?" I breathe out, suddenly feeling like my father betrayed me.

"As a man with two daughters and a granddaughter, the thought of not knowing you girls killed your father. He couldn't with good conscience do that to Ezra, or to Ava. A father needs his daughter, just as much as she needs her father."

"Fuck," I rasp.

"I gather from this conversation that your repressed memories aren't repressed anymore," Mom treads lightly. "That is why I haven't allowed Ava to answer the phone. All eleven-year-olds have a propensity to spew whatever thought comes to mind. Ezra stressed you had to remember on your own, otherwise it would harm you psychologically."

"I'm fine. I'm coming home on the next flight. I'll be there in about four hours. That's why I was calling. Boy, am I glad I am. I have a shit-storm to clean up now."

"I'm glad you're visiting. We've missed you. We've all been terribly worried about you. I hate that powerless feeling of having your hands tied behind your back, unable to help your child through the worst times in their lives. It's a mother's job to be there, Katya, and I'm sorry I couldn't."

"Mom," I cry out, desperately trying to keep my tumultuous emotions in check. "Don't worry. You can mother the fuck right out of me in a few hours, and for years to come. I'm not visiting. I'm moving back."

"What?" Mom gasps.

"I know. It fucking sucks. I… this entire life I've built is a façade. I can't live here, work here, and try to start a life here, just because Ezra feels guilty for something neither of us had any control over. I won't leach off the man. I want to make my own way through life. I want to be a woman you and Dad can be proud of, a woman Ava can look up to and strive to become."

"MA!" Ava shouts, causing my mother to release a squeak of surprise. "Is that Ma on the phone? Give her to me, now!" Ava demands, and suddenly the repressed memories make sense.

I didn't repress the memory of Ezra to save myself. I repressed it in order to save my daughter, so I could fall in love with her as a mother should, so I would hold no resentment over the fact that she looks, behaves, and sounds exactly like her tyrannical father.

For almost twelve years, Ava was an extension of myself, the reason I fought to survive. I never once saw her as an extension of my rapists, because I couldn't remember who they were, what they looked like, or what truly happened. Now I can look at my daughter and see the man I respect, care about, and genuinely like, no matter how badly he pisses me off.

Now I understand nature versus nurture better, as well. No amount of nurturing could ever make my daughter behave. None. It is in Ava's nature to be domineering, bull-headed, and demanding. For years, I've blamed myself, thinking myself too lax when respect and rules were the very foundation of my mothering. I love my daughter just as much as any mother does, more so because of the circumstances of her birth, but Ava doesn't make it easy to love her.

The sound of a struggle vibrates my ear, as my daughter wrenches the phone away from my mother.

"Ava Evangeline Waters," I scold. "Never treat your grandmother with that level of disrespect. Do you hear me?"

"Sorry, Ma," Ava sounds oh-so pitiful, managing to pull off a sniffle. "I just missed you so much. I wanted to hear your voice."

I try to sound light and airy, when I feel anything but. "I've missed you, too. Anything new, buttercup?"

"No, I'm bored. There's never anything to do here." My daughter is a goddamned pathological liar, just like her father. So much for Mom's fear of Ava spilling the truth. "You sound sad. Are you sad, Mommy?"

"I am very sad, Ava. I just miss you so much, that's all. Listen, I'm coming home. I don't think this living apart is good for either of us."

"We won't be living apart. I thought you were sending for me when you saved up for the school we picked out," Ava sounds upset, and it breaks my heart.

Every night, when we spoke on the phone, she'd ask if we were any closer to our goal. I have the money saved. I was waiting until summer vacation to enroll Ava in Hillbrook, not wanting her to make the move at the end of the school year's final semester. I wanted it to be a surprise. I'm glad I hadn't told her yet, or she'd be even more heartbroken.

"Don't worry. This is what we need. I need to see your

face and hear your voice every day. I can't live apart from you because you are a part of me. A mother and daughter should be together. I even miss arguing with you," I say wryly.

"Don't give up on your dream for me, Mommy," Ava murmurs into the phone, and I can hear her disappointment. "We'll be okay."

"You're too grown up for your age, Ava. You really need to be a kid. I'm not giving up anything to be with you. You are my greatest joy, best accomplishment– you *are* my dream."

"I don't see why we can't just live in Dominion with…" Ava coughs loudly, trying to cover up her fuck-up. "I really, really want to go to Hillbrook. You promised. I don't care if we have to be apart for a couple more weeks. Don't come home. I want to go to school where I belong. Get me out of Vacuum Valley."

"We'll enroll you in the new private school for those gifted in math and science. It's only twenty minutes from the house. I'll pick you up and drop you off myself."

"NO!" Ava shouts, readying for a temper tantrum. "I was told I'd be a legacy at Hillbrook!"

"Nothing new, eh? Just bored." I snort, shaking my head at Ava's blatant lies. "I have to go, someone's knocking at my door. I'll be home in a few hours. I love you."

"I love you, too, Mom." I'm back to Mom or Ma, instead of Mommy, because Ava is furious with me. "I'd love you more if you'd stay in Dominion and not mess with our plans."

Ava hangs up on me just as Aaron enters my apartment.

Restraint 424

Chapter Forty-Two

"Wow, you actually used the door this time. I'm impressed. Is the wall-hatch stuck?" I mutter sarcastically. "What can I do for you, Aaron?"

The last time I saw Aaron, he was angry with me– violently so. I highly doubt his stance has changed over the past few days. Aaron is a big, burly guy with a huge teddy bear heart, but I have a feeling he's a wicked grudge-holder.

Looking beyond sheepish, refusing to look me in the eye, "I was just checking on you," Aaron says as he sits opposite me on the love seat.

"Couldn't you figure out how to tap into the security feeds broadcasting into my living room?" I mutter snidely. "Did your master send you looking for me, or were you actually curious?"

I try to keep the hurt and anger out of my voice. It's not about the wounds of the past; it's about the present. It's about how Aaron treated me after I was with him, how he froze me out like I was dog shit he stepped in and couldn't wait to scrape off. All because I made Ezra own his bad decisions. I understand Aaron choosing Ezra over me; I would expect nothing else. But it doesn't take the bad taste out of my mouth.

"Both," Aaron reluctantly admits.

I snort at his reply. There was no way in hell Aaron wanted to see me. No doubt he was ordered to check on my progress because Ezra is through with me.

"How's it been the past few days with Cortez? He hasn't been too rough with you, has he?" Actual concern infuses Aaron's voice. The concern defuses some of the pent-up anger I feel toward Aaron. I still feel used, just not as angry over it.

"Huh?" I grunt. "What are you talking about?"

Baby face blushing, Aaron grumbles, "Ezra can't be around you right now, so Cortez said he was going to take care of you for a while."

Ah! This was Cortez's way of buying me some alone time– smart man! I think I just fell in love with the charming bastard a little bit.

I pretend that my broken heart doesn't throb at the '*Ezra can't be around you right now.*' What am I, diseased?

"Uh... yeah. Cortez knew I needed a few days to myself. So... ah... I didn't know he would lie to you guys. Actually, that surprises me." But in a way, it doesn't. I have a feeling that Aaron freezes Cort out, too, and that Aaron and Ezra gang up on him.

"When was the last time you saw Piggy?" Aaron asks, calling Cortez a derogatory nickname with a voice dripping with anger.

I debate lying, but we've had enough lies between us to last a lifetime. "The night of Ezra's punishment." I think for a moment, calculating time. "About twenty minutes after Cortez was told to walk me those two inches to my apartment."

"What!" Aaron jumps from his seat as he yelps.

"Sit your ass down," I grumble, sick to death of the theatrics. I just want to move on with my life. "What's the big fucking deal?"

"What if you... what if you remembered and we weren't around?" Aaron asks in a panic.

"Since I haven't remembered, it makes no sense to me why that's an issue," I lie smoothly, because self-preservation is ruling me at the moment.

I remembered four nights ago, and every night thereafter, and every morning since, and every waking moment. I'm dealing with it just fine. All alone. Being alone has left little distraction. The past and the present have been throbbing in my mind like a sore tooth.

"Ezra is going to be pissed," Aaron promises.

"Run along and go tattle, then." I wriggle my fingers at him. "Be off with you." Aaron narrows his eyes at me.

"What did I do to you that pissed you off so much?" Aaron gazes at me with huge, confused, blue eyes.

"Seriously? You have to ask me that?" I ask, incredulity thick in my voice.

Aaron just looks confused, and lost, and very, very young. I forget how emotionally stunted Aaron is when I'm looking at his very masculine body, but when I'm talking to him...

"You chose Ezra over the punishment he *earned*. Even if I tickled Ezra with a feather as punishment, you would've been pissed at me. You think the Earth revolves around Dr. Ezra Zeitler. The sun and moon set for him. The stars shine because of his greatness," I say dramatically.

"What the fuck, Katya? Since when do you have a hate-on for Ezra?" Aaron spits out at me.

"I don't hate Ezra at all. The entirety of that statement was about *you*," I stress.

"I… I… I don't get it," Aaron stammers out.

"If someone pulled a gun on us, what would you do?" I quickly blurt out.

"I'd save Ezra. You know that," Aaron admits in all honesty, and all I can do is shake my head.

"Exactly." I say no more. Aaron proved my point.

"Why, what do you think everyone else would do?" he asks in confusion.

"Ezra would try to talk them out of it, saving everyone even if it meant sacrificing himself. Cortez and I would do the same thing, except we'd go after the gunman. A moving target is harder to shoot. Plus, we may save someone else in the process. You'd save Ezra while sacrificing the rest of us."

"I don't get it," Aaron mumbles again.

"I know, Baby Boy. That's the point. I care about you. I just can't hand you my heart and trust, because you already have a number one in your life. You said Ezra can't be around me right now. Well, I can't be around him, either."

"Why?" Aaron breathes, sounding like a lost child.

"Ezra has too many number ones in his life, making the position meaningless. I'm worth more than being at the bottom of Ezra's list of importance, even if he doesn't think so. Someday, someone will realize this, and that special man and I will share our place as number one in each other's lives. Until then, I won't settle for last place."

I move to stand before Aaron. As I stroke my fingertips down his cheek, it's hard to look at him and not feel the pleasure he gave me. I lean down to kiss his forehead in goodbye. Ever-so softly, just a feather-light brush of a touch.

"Goodbye, Aaron," I whisper against his soft skin. His eyes sheen with unshed tears, letting me know he reads my underlying message.

"Ezra's away on business. Please, don't do this," Aaron pleads. "I don't know how to stop you, other than physically. But I don't ever want to harm you." Aaron's voice holds barely leashed panic.

"It's all right, Aaron. I promise." I crawl into his lap, and allow him to hold me while I finally open the tide of pain I've warded off for the past four days. "I already know," I whisper in his ear. "I already know. You held my wrists. I remember."

"I'm so terribly sorry," Aaron sobs out, body quaking from the force of his guilt and shame. "I hate myself every day for the things that monster made us do. But we all regretted you the most. You were the only victim who lived. We left you as bait, forcing you to save us by letting that monster rape you. We could have teamed up and stopped it, but we were selfish and used you instead. I will *never* forgive myself for as long as I live."

We hold each other and sob, releasing our mutual pain and guilt– our humiliation. A vital part of me heals as Aaron cries with me, as he holds me, as he shares his past with me until it fuses with mine.

"I know," I whisper. "I forgave you all a long time ago, because there was never anything to forgive. I have never blamed anyone except for Raymond Hunter. None of us wanted it, but we survived it nonetheless. Subconsciously, I believe I knew who you all were all along."

"Why are you going?" Aaron's tone is childlike– lost.

"I don't belong here. I didn't earn this job. Everything was out of guilt or pity. You all need to heal, and how can you do that with me in your face as a constant reminder? Ezra has Adelaide, and I really do wish them the best. Cortez? Well, Cortez is just Cortez." I chuckle instead of bawl like my heart is screaming to do.

"I hope you open up your heart and allow someone special into your life, someone who will finally make you their number one. Aaron, you deserve nothing less."

I kiss Aaron one last time. This kiss is longer, full of desperation as much as it's full of agony and acceptance. Forgiveness. Forgiveness of oneself.

Chapter Forty-Three

I close my eyes on the forty-minute flight home, and remember my last moments in the life I had for what felt like a blink of an eye. It was only a dream. A deliciously torturous, healing figment of my imagination.

Small-town girls like me do not deserve high-profile jobs at publishing houses, working for egomaniacal billionaires. Yes, I deserve a better life than the one I was born into, just as my parents bettered themselves from the lifestyle they were born into, and my daughter will do the same. Every generation better than the next, making our family name worth more than a few letters on a page, making it a title, making it an identity worthy of pride.

It must be *earned* in order to truly feel pride, to feel a sense of accomplishment. I didn't earn my life in Dominion, and that leaves a bitter tang in my mouth.

Edge Publishing was better with me at the helm. I acknowledge this as fact, not as a warped sense of self. But I cannot in good conscience hold a position I didn't earn, even if I proved my mettle. It will always be tainted with guilt, with shame, with pity. The only reason I was at Edge, was because I was a rape victim.

I am *not* a victim.

I understand Monica better– her anger towards me. Whether I was better at the job than she would've been, remains to be seen. But what is solid fact, is that Monica earned her rightful place, whereas I never did. It was handed to me by a martyr.

After Aaron left me, I walked to Ezra's office and moved the chess pieces to end the game. I checkmated his Black King with my White Queen. I couldn't bring myself to remove his king from the board, though. I placed the king and queen side-by-side on his end of the board.

I made Monica's day when I told her I was leaving. She said if I hadn't, she would have told Zeitler that I was playing with Cortez and Aaron at Restraint. She threatened that there had to be some sort of violation of Edge's rules of conduct for messing around with one of our authors– the owner's right-hand man, no less.

I laughed in Monica's face and wished her well. Damn, I would have loved to witness the expression on Ezra's face when Monica brought that information to light. Hell, Monica was at Restraint, spanking her own boss.

I placed the key to my apartment on the counter, and then left with only a few bags to my name. Everything in the place was Ezra's. Actually, everything I thought I had in Dominion was Ezra's: job, friends, home, and furnishings. Ezra placed his victim in a gilded cage for observation.

I'm no one's victim.

I will always make my own journey, never the one provided for me.

This morning as I sat at my desk staring at my daughter's photo, I was struck with a memory. Ava has an expression that is like no other. Except for one other.

Three years ago, I had just finished my testimony at Ray Hunter's parole hearing.

I was walking down the hallway at the courthouse, and I heard a man's smoky laugh. It hit me deep– soul deep. My head turned, homing in on the sound, and I found a pair of stormy gray eyes instead. They widened as they took me in. The man captivated me: tall, lanky, gray eyes, and fair of hair and skin.

"Is that her?" a deep voice asked, breaking my daze.

I gazed at the speaker, who looked similar to the first man: not looks, their demeanor. He was darker of skin and hair, but with the same eyes and build as the fair man.

"It's her," a young man said with a husky voice. He was huge, built like a brick house. His bright blue eyes shined with innocence and curiosity.

I was confused. I'd never drawn attention, yet all three were solely focused on me. I was tempted to turn and look over my shoulder to see if someone was behind me, and they were talking of her instead.

As I walked closer to the trio, I waited to hear what the

first man's voice sounded like. If I judged it by his laugh, it was probably spectacular.

"What's your name?" His voice was so smooth, I wanted to bathe in it. I shuddered at the intoxicating sound. My eyes flicked back up to his, and I was captured.

"Katya Waters. I... I... I mean Kat. Everyone calls me Kat," I stuttered out. I'd never really spoken with the opposite sex. They unnerve me. He didn't, though. Something about him was calming– familiar.

He spoke as I walked past, "Ezra. Call me Ezra."

I tried to be angry. It should have been the appropriate emotion to feel when you realize the three people who you've come to trust, were leading you down a horrific path to a repressed memory. But I wasn't angry with any of them.

I finally understood them.

We all do things we need to do in order to survive. We all do strange things in the name of healing. We all live the only way we can to make our way through this life. Call me selfish or selfless. I understand their needs better than anyone, except for each other.

I now understand why I am an integral part of the group. Not because they chased me as prey, held me down while my life was in the balance, and then ultimately watched my rape or participated in it. It wasn't because I saved them by taking one for the team while they ran, leaving me to be violently violated by Raymond Hunter.

No, we share a bond on a baser level: victims of the same monster. We share the experience, the sense of powerlessness, the degradation, the guilt, the shame, the pain.

The four of us, we aren't one of Raymond Hunter's countless victims. We are his only survivors.

Restraint 434

Epilogue

Ava and I are enjoying an afternoon in the sun, chatting and singing out on the back patio while painting our nails. It feels good to be home after so long, back in my own bed, roaming around my own home, hearing the sounds of my family, smelling the scent of my mother's home-cooking. It feels good, but it's lessened somehow by the ache of missing three assholes.

They say home is where the heart is. My daughter is my heart. As long as she is with me, I am home.

"Have you thought any more about my suggestion of the gifted math and science program?" This has been a point of contention between us over the past few days, with many a violent tantrum to be had.

I understand why Ava feels as she does, needing a sense of power over her life. She's growing into a beautiful, poised, young woman, who thinks she knows everything and needs absolutely no guidance from her mother or grandparents, when she's still a child, who knows absolutely nothing.

Ava's childlike playfulness has been slowly diminishing over the past year, and it saddens me to realize she may not have the childhood I longed to give her.

I've worked so hard to provide a better future for her, one where she didn't have to do manual labor instead of playing with toys and experimenting to find her hidden talents. I was working on jobsites from the time I was a toddler, following my father around as a little helper, gradually learning more and more, contributing more and more. While it was a great experience, I lost out on my childhood. I wanted more for Ava, but she's stubbornly refusing to act like an eleven-year-old child.

"What's my dad like? Grandpa wouldn't let us talk." Ava scrunches her eyes in the bright sunlight.

My father allowed Ezra and Ava to meet, and it was very awkward with the pair of them staring at each other, scrutinizing their similarities. But Dad refused to allow Ezra to say anything aside from pleasantries, fearing Ezra's obvious manipulations.

"Ezra is commanding. Not in a mean way. It's more like a moth drawn to a flame. At least that's how it is for me." I laugh without humor, feeling that damned ache for the billionth time today.

I made the right decision in coming home. If I would've stayed, I wouldn't have respected my actions or myself, and that means no one else would have respected me, either. The thought of Ezra not respecting me makes me feel sick inside.

Ava gives me the look, the one so similar to her father's: she tilts her face to the side and squints, reading me. It's unnerving. She's scrutinizing me, seeing right through my act. She's eleven years old in body, but ancient in spirit.

"I think you guys will get along famously," I say brightly. "What would you like to know?"

"I've been writing a list of question to ask him since I met him," Ava admits. "Stuff like, do I call him Dad? What does he watch on TV? Does he like sports? Does he have any pets? What are my grandparents like?"

"All very valid questions," I mutter, feeling like the world's worst mother. "I'm sorry. Ezra keeps things so close to the vest that I can't answer any of those questions, and the ones I can answer are not for young ears."

"I just want to know him as much as I know you," Ava mutters, looking crestfallen.

As a distraction, I paint polka-dots on Ava's pinkie, completing her manicure. "Look good to ya, does it?" I pick on her, trying to cheer her up.

Ava's like her mom in this regard. We aren't very girly, but naked nails are a no-no. It's also one of our inexpensive, guilty pleasures. We don't go to the salon for manicures and pedicures. Doing each other's nails, even if we are piss-poor at it, is good mother-daughter quality time, usually with some Grandma-time thrown into the mix.

I hear a sharp intake of breath, and my eyes dart up. I gaze wide-eyed with a gaping mouth at our visitor. I quickly snap my mouth shut and blink a few time to see if the ghostly man is an apparition.

"Welcome, Ezra." I just stare. I never thought I'd see him walking across my patio towards me. This is a surreal moment, one I never thought would happen in a million years. Ezra's eyes flick over me, and then settle on our daughter.

"Hello, little one," he says softly, as if fearing he'll spook her. But our daughter is also like her father. You do not spook Ava.

"I have questions for you. A lot of 'em," Ava drawls as she sizes him up, seeing if he's worthy to be her dad. My father has set very high standards in his girls' lives, one all men will have to live up to.

Ezra stares back at Ava, doing an inventory as well. "So I've just heard," Ezra whispers, sounding awed. "You may call me Dad, if you'd like. I watch a lot of book adaptations. I used to play soccer as a child, but now I just play tennis several times a week. I don't have any pets as of yet. My adoptive father is going to shit his pants when he gets a look at you, because you are a miniature version of my mother."

My daughter, at eleven years old, is already several inches taller than me. She has Ezra's fair hair and gray eyes instead of my fiery red and green eyes. Ava's face is all me, with her skin tone more pink than the paleness of Ezra's ghostly appearance. Ava's personality is split right down the middle between Ezra and me– scary, that.

"All right… Dad," Ava tests the word out on her tongue and deems it pleasing. "Dad." She smiles at us both. "I know you've upset Mom, and that's why she's back home. You need to fix it. I don't want to live here forever. I wanted to move to Dominion and go to Hillbrook. Whatever you did screwed up my plans of going to a good school. Vacuum Valley doesn't produce kids who go to Ivy League Universities. Fix it," she demands as she stands up.

"Oh, there's no doubt on your parentage, now is there? I'm not sure if that was me or your mom coming out your mouth, right there. But I'll let it slide… for now." Ezra laughs to soften the threat.

"Normally Ava isn't so rude. But she's been in a tizzy

since I ruined her future." I roll my eyes at Ava. "Go greet the rest of our guests. I guarantee Aaron and Cortez are waiting in the car for an engraved invitation."

"Why'd you leave?" Ezra asks as soon as Ava's out of earshot. He stands a few feet from me, but it feels like an unbridgeable chasm. I so badly want to run into Ezra's arms, to press my cheek to his chest, to inhale his natural scent, to gain comfort from him. The urge is so strong that I don't dare feed the need. It's utterly terrifying.

"I wanted a fresh start. No games played between us, no repressed memories, no secrets and lies. I don't want pity jobs or pity friends or pity sex. I don't want you housing me out of remorse. I want to earn what I get by my abilities, not by your misguided guilt. I want to create my own future, and make of it what I may."

"That isn't at all accurate, Katya," Ezra chastises me.

"I'm not your daughter, Ezra. I'm a grown woman who needs to feel productive. I'm one of you, so I want to stand shoulder-to-shoulder, not kneel at your feet like a pampered pet. I want to be respected," I say calmly and quietly, trying to impart the truth to Ezra.

I cannot live the life Ezra had me living these past few months. I would slowly die inside.

My daughter's excited giggles reach me before our guests do. I smile at both of the guys. Of course Cortez is outrageously flirting with my minor child. I would anger over it, except Cortez flirts like I breathe oxygen. Aaron's baby blues flick towards Ava and his dimples appear.

"Hey, guys," I call out, never standing from the picnic table.

"That's no way to greet us, Kitten." Cortez makes a tsk-tsk noise as he approaches me. When I'm in arm's reach, he kisses me fully on the mouth, much too long for platonic. My skin flashes red at the contact.

Shit!

Ezra glares at Cortez, I assume for doing that in front of our daughter.

I give Aaron a light kiss on the cheek. "I'd prefer the kiss

Cortez got," he chuckles into my hair. "But that might confuse Ava." He leans away from me. "It's amazing to see your daughter. I'm speechless," Aaron addresses Ezra and me. "Wow, anyone who meets Ava would immediately know who she belongs to. It's uncanny."

"I'm going to record Diane and Ava's first meeting. It will be like meeting your clone for the first time. Marcus is going to shit a brick." Cort's voice takes on an evil note, making me beyond curious to decipher the true meaning behind his words.

"Ava, Diane is my mother, and Marcus is my adoptive father. Just in case Cort was confusing you."

"Oh." My daughter turns bright red from the attention, looking uncomfortable.

"Ava, go tell Grandma that we will be having guests for dinner," I say to ease Ava some. This is a lot to deal with all at once, and she is only but a child.

"Also inform your grandmother how your mother and you will be coming home with me in the morning," Ezra tacks on.

Ava squeals in delight, and to both our shocks, kisses her father on the cheek.

Ezra stands in stunned silence, hand hovering over his freshly kissed cheek, until I burst his bubble. "I believe you should have asked me first. It's not right, getting Ava's hopes up only to have me say no. It makes me look like the bad guy."

"Are you saying no?" Ezra raises a quizzical brow. "Because if you are, then it will only force me to resort to means you will not enjoy. I'll tie you down and ship your ass back to Edge. Aaron won't bat an eyelash if I ask him to stow you in the trunk."

I ignore Ezra. "Who wants to go for a walk with me while Ava and my mom make dinner?"

Ezra immediately walks to my side. When Aaron and Cort say they're joining us, he orders, "No, stay here."

"Jeez, you're full of yourself today. They aren't dogs." I groan, annoyed.

"I want some alone time with you, Katya." Ezra looks like he's about to implode if I don't give him five minutes without any outside interference so he can manipulate me.

"Okay," I drawl out. "But it will have to be later." As in never. "This walk is important for the four of us."

I don't bother to explain. I just start walking to the edge of the lawn and enter the woods. I don't look over my shoulder to see if they follow. I can feel that they are. I just know somehow. When I hit the hiking trail, I chance a glance at the trio. All are staring at me with expressions of horror.

"Don't be such pussies. I'd think Dr. Zeitler would approve." I smirk at the man in question.

"Katya, this isn't a good idea for you," Ez replies stiffly, but it doesn't hide the quiver in his voice, either from fear or excitement.

"It is. Don't you see? This time I'm not running from you. We'll run together, towards the future while letting go of the past."

I don't wait for an answer. I break into a jog. When I hit the spot on the trail where they first began chasing me so very long ago, my heart starts beating into overdrive. I can almost feel the tension riding the air. My heartbeat reacts to theirs, all equalizing.

I follow the same path as before. The direction is burned into my memory. As I reach the point where I veered off the trail, adrenaline floods my veins. I start panting as fear and excitement flow through me.

"This is a horrible idea on so many levels. It may help you heal, but it's just amping up our needs." Ezra's speech is raspy.

Yeah, I could see that. I loved chasing Kayla around my office. I loved running from Cortez during our two minutes of deviant fun. My eyes light on each one of them. They all seem to be excited– thrilled by the hunt. Eyes glazed from the high, breath sawing in and out, arousal bulged in their pants.

When we arrive at the spot where my attack occurred, it's like being reborn. I haven't been back here since my rescue. It feels anti-climactic after how all of my thoughts have centered on it for nearly twelve years.

This was one of my favorite spots on Earth. I would walk along this path to think, to sort out my life. That one day ruined it all for me. I haven't been back, fearing the memories would inundate me, bringing the nightmares to life.

This place no longer holds power over me, not in peace or in fear. I hop in place, chuckling manically, ecstatic that I've overcome this insurmountable obstacle.

Suddenly, the guys surround me, trapping me. I look to their eyes as fear stabs through me. All three look feral: their eyes glazed, panting, and aroused, with barely leashed control.

"Rein it in. You're stronger than your needs. Show some restraint," I warn.

I walk off, acting as if they aren't scaring the shit out of me. I know on a baser level, they would never harm me. I know that if they did attack, eventually I would enjoy it. But I'd rather have a say in the matter from the get-go, saving us all a lot of shame and guilt to be compounded on the layers that already exist. Plus, I'm not sure how they would behave in a pack situation. Maybe this wasn't such a good idea.

I sit on the shore, looking out over the lapping water, waving at a fisherman as his boat floats by. I tug my shoes off, placing my feet on the small pebbles, allowing the water to cover my legs up to my shins. I watch as the water clouds my pearly toenails for a few moments, and then they finally join me after getting their emotions in check.

"Sorry about that. I wish you would have told me what you were up to first." Ezra settles beside me with one of his patented, heavy sighs.

"You would have said no," I mutter out the side of my mouth in his direction.

"So you did it anyway?" Ezra doesn't sound surprised at all by my antics. "Ah, Katya."

"That's how we have to do it, or else we'd have to ask your permission for every little thing. We're adults, Ez. You're not the Master of the Universe." Cortez says as he sits on my other side, trapping me between him and Ezra.

I turn my face, smiling conspiratorially at Cortez. Yeah, he and I are too much alike. Don't ask for permission. Ask for forgiveness. I burst out laughing.

"What?" Aaron asks from beside Ezra.

"I have a motto for our little gang– Hunter's pack. Don't

ask for permission. Ask for forgiveness." We all share a laugh directed at Ezra.

I rest my head on Ezra's shoulder and take Cortez's hand in mine. I glance over to see Aaron and Ezra's hands are linked as well.

"I like that– Hunter's pack," Ezra whispers as we watch over the peaceful lake. "It brings honor to my true surname."

Katya Waters' Continuation: **Unleashed**

The long-standing Mistress & Master of Restraint series is dark and mysterious, with a warped sense of morality. Erotic romance fans, would you prefer something just as twisted, but not as dark? Try the Blended Series, beginning with Good Girl.

Good Girl

There aren't many options for a girl who falls in the middle. I wasn't an athlete or a geek. I wasn't an artist or a musician. I didn't shake my pom-poms along with my ass. I was just a good girl, who got good grades, and kept her mouth shut. I didn't date my high school sweetheart and promptly get married the second I was handed my diploma. I'm not shiny enough to attract notice, nor dark enough to be a problem.

I don't have a tragic sob story. My daddy didn't leave us destitute, and I'm not a victim of a bad neighborhood. I am a middle-America, middle of the road, middle class girl with both parents fussing over their youngest daughter, who has no aspirations or goals. I've had every opportunity to succeed– supportive parents, stability, and a strong upbringing. I'm wayward and everyone looks at me like I'm an alien.

My philosophy: how should I know what I want to do with the rest of my life the day I graduate? How am I supposed to know the second I turn eighteen what I am destined to become? One moment you are a disillusioned seventeen-year-old with the world at your fingertips, and the next, congratulations, you're eighteen and you're on your own.

To purchase Good Girl, or any of Erica Chilson's other titles, please visit her website (ericachilson.com) for details.

Acknowledgements

A lot of work goes into writing a novel, and it isn't just by the writer herself. **My parents:** for their unconditional support. **My sister:** for her patience with the cover art. **My readers**: thank you for reading my twisted words and spreading my books to the masses. For without you, no one would have ever heard of my stories. My readers are my lifeblood. A shout out to the members of the **M&M of Restraint Group on Facebook**: thanks for the endless entertainment and inspiration. Thank you to my street team: **Erica Chilson's Deviants!** You guys ROCK! **Wicked Reads**: (in all its incarnations) **Amber D & Angela G**. Thank you for taking over and making Wicked Reads better than I could have done by myself. **Angela**: thank you for helping me promote my work, and the work of other authors. A huge thank you to the **Wicked Writer's Betas:** for keeping me grounded and encouraging me to keep trudging along when I get frustrated. Your thoughts and observations are invaluable. ((Hugs)) **Kris D. Suz A. Darcy V. Sandy D. Diana C. Billie Jo H. Diane P. Lisa J. Jacki G. Shelby H. Linsey T. Alexis W. Tassie M. Alicia P. Jonelle M. & Liz S.** Someday, I'd love to meet you all in real life– it would be the experience of a lifetime.

About the Author

Erica Chilson does not write in the 3rd person, wanting her readers to *be* her characters. Therefore, writing a bio about herself, is uncomfortable in the extreme.

Born, raised, and here to stay, the Wicked Writer is a stump-jumper, a ridge-runner. Hailing from North Central Pennsylvania, directly on the New York State border; she loves the changes in seasons, the humid air, all the mountainous forest, and the gloomy atmosphere.

Introverted, but not socially awkward, Erica prides herself on thinking first and filtering her speech. There are days she doesn't speak at all. If it wasn't for the fact that she lives with her parents, giving her a sense of reality, she would be a hermit, where the delivery man finds her months after expiration.

Reading was an escape, a way to leave a not-so pleasant reality behind. Reading lent Erica the courage she gathered from the characters between the pages to long for a different life. Writing was an instrument of change, evolving Erica into the woman she is today– a better, more mature, more at peace thinker.

Erica has a wicked mind, one she pours out into her creations. Her filter doesn't allow all of it to erupt, much to her relief. Sarcastic, with a very dark, perverse sense of humor, Erica puts a bit of herself into every character she writes.

Erica Chilson loves hearing from readers. If you would like more information on release dates, works in progress, teaser chapters, and random bits of madness...

FB Fan Page: https://www.facebook.com/thewickedwriter
Website: ericachilson.com
Via email: wickedwriter.ericachilson@gmail.com
DEVIANTS ONLY, if you'd like to join Erica Chilson's closed Facebook group, M&M of Restraint:
https://www.facebook.com/groups/MistressandMaster/

Made in the USA
Middletown, DE
05 May 2015